DATE DUE

Jan 18, 2016	

THE NEPTUNE STRATEGY

This Large Print Book carries the
Seal of Approval of N.A.V.H.

THE NEPTUNE STRATEGY

John J. Gobbell

Thorndike Press • Waterville, Maine

Maps by Mark Stein Studios

Published in 2004 by arrangement with
St. Martin's Press, LLC.

Thorndike Press® Large Print Adventure.

The tree indicium is a trademark of Thorndike Press.

The text of this Large Print edition is unabridged.
Other aspects of the book may vary from the original edition.

Set in 16 pt. Plantin by Al Chase.

Printed in the United States on permanent paper.

Library of Congress Cataloging-in-Publication Data

Gobbell, John J.
The Neptune strategy / John J. Gobbell.
p. cm.
ISBN 0-7862-6723-2 (lg. print : hc : alk. paper)
1. Ingram, Todd (Fictitious character) — Fiction.
2. World War, 1939–1945 — Naval operations,
American — Fiction. 3. World War, 1939–1945 —
Naval operations, Japanese — Fiction. 4. Submarines
(Ships) — Fiction. 5. Large type books. I. Title.
PS3557.O16N47 2004b
813′.54—dc22 2004042196

To the brave men and women of our
Armed Forces
who so well carry the proud tradition and spirit of those who have gone before.

. . . Hail, Liberty! Hail!

National Association for Visually Handicapped
serving the partially seeing

As the Founder/CEO of NAVH, the only national health agency solely devoted to those who, although not totally blind, have an eye disease which could lead to serious visual impairment, I am pleased to recognize Thorndike Press★ as one of the leading publishers in the large print field.

Founded in 1954 in San Francisco to prepare large print textbooks for partially seeing children, NAVH became the pioneer and standard setting agency in the preparation of large type.

Today, those publishers who meet our standards carry the prestigious "Seal of Approval" indicating high quality large print. We are delighted that Thorndike Press is one of the publishers whose titles meet these standards. We are also pleased to recognize the significant contribution Thorndike Press is making in this important and growing field.

Lorraine H. Marchi, L.H.D.
Founder/CEO
NAVH

★ Thorndike Press encompasses the following imprints: Thorndike, Wheeler, Walker and Large Print Press.

ACKNOWLEDGMENTS

One's essence is a direct product of God, family, and friends. And this writer has been richly blessed in all three categories. My thanks go to Commander George A. Wallace, USN (retired), now a novelist in his own right, Dr. Frederick J. Milford, Dr. Russell J. Striff, Keiko Halop, and James D. Bailey. Special tribute goes to Hugo Fruehauf and the late Gordon Curtis, naval fighter pilot of World War II, who patiently explained to this surface squid the characteristics of naval aircraft of the time. Any mistakes herein are mine.

Thanks also to Marc Resnick, my editor at St. Martin's Press, and to my agent, Jane Dystel, of Dystel & Goderich Literary Management, for their tireless help and encouragement. And always, never-ending thanks to my wife, Janine, who not only does a great job editing my manuscripts but has stuck through the hard times with love, encouragement, and understanding.

A wonderful surprise comes from my readers who contact me via e-mail at jgobbell@johnjgobbell.com. Many have gotten into it and some of us have had marvelous exchanges. Thank you all for your kind thoughts and please visit my Web site at www.johnjgobbell.com for charts and images.

JJG
Newport Beach, California
September 2003

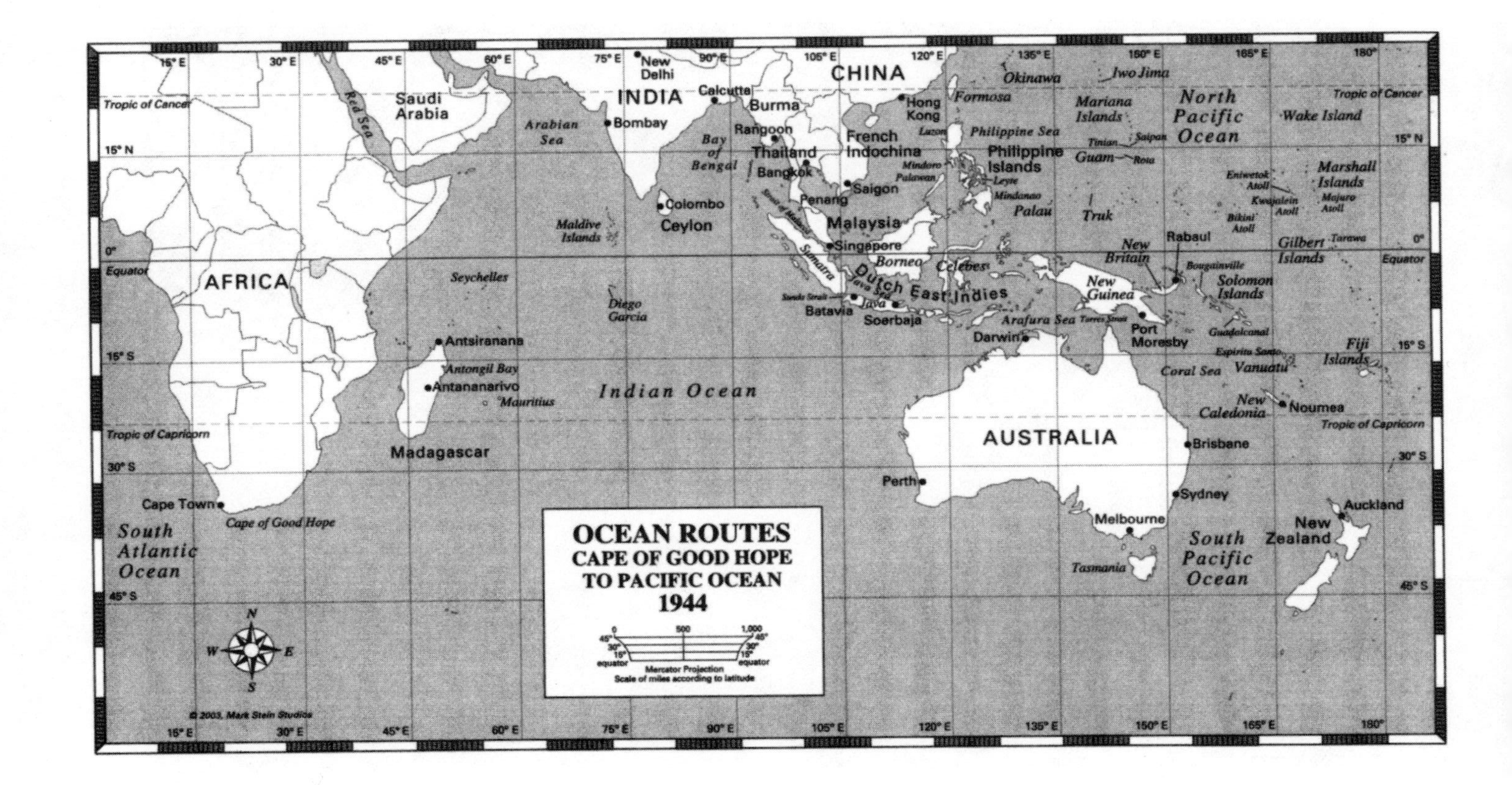
OCEAN ROUTES
CAPE OF GOOD HOPE
TO PACIFIC OCEAN
1944
Mercator Projection
Scale of miles according to latitude
0
500
1,000
45°
30°
15°
equator
N
S
E
W
© 2003, Mark Stein Studios
15° E
30° E
45° E
60° E
75° E
90° E
105° E
120° E
135° E
150° E
165° E
180°
15° N
0°
15° S
30° S
45° S
Tropic of Cancer
Equator
Tropic of Capricorn
AFRICA
Saudi Arabia
Red Sea
Arabian Sea
INDIA
New Delhi
Bombay
Calcutta
Bay of Bengal
Colombo
Ceylon
Maldive Islands
Seychelles
Diego Garcia
Antsiranana
Antongil Bay
Antananarivo
Mauritius
Madagascar
Indian Ocean
Cape Town
Cape of Good Hope
South Atlantic Ocean
CHINA
Burma
Rangoon
Thailand
Bangkok
French Indochina
Saigon
Hong Kong
Penang
Malaysia
Singapore
Sumatra
Borneo
Celebes
Dutch East Indies
Java Sea
Java
Batavia
Soerbaja
Formosa
Okinawa
Philippine Sea
Luzon
Mindoro
Palawan
Philippine Islands
Leyte
Mindanao
Palau
Iwo Jima
Mariana Islands
Tinian
Saipan
Guam
Rota
Truk
North Pacific Ocean
Wake Island
Eniwetok Atoll
Kwajalein Atoll
Bikini Atoll
Marshall Islands
Majuro Atoll
Gilbert Islands
Tarawa
Rabaul
New Britain
Bougainville
Solomon Islands
Guadalcanal
New Guinea
Port Moresby
Arafura Sea
Torres Strait
Darwin
Espiritu Santo
Vanuatu
Coral Sea
Fiji Islands
New Caledonia
Noumea
AUSTRALIA
Brisbane
Perth
Sydney
Melbourne
Tasmania
South Pacific Ocean
New Zealand
Auckland

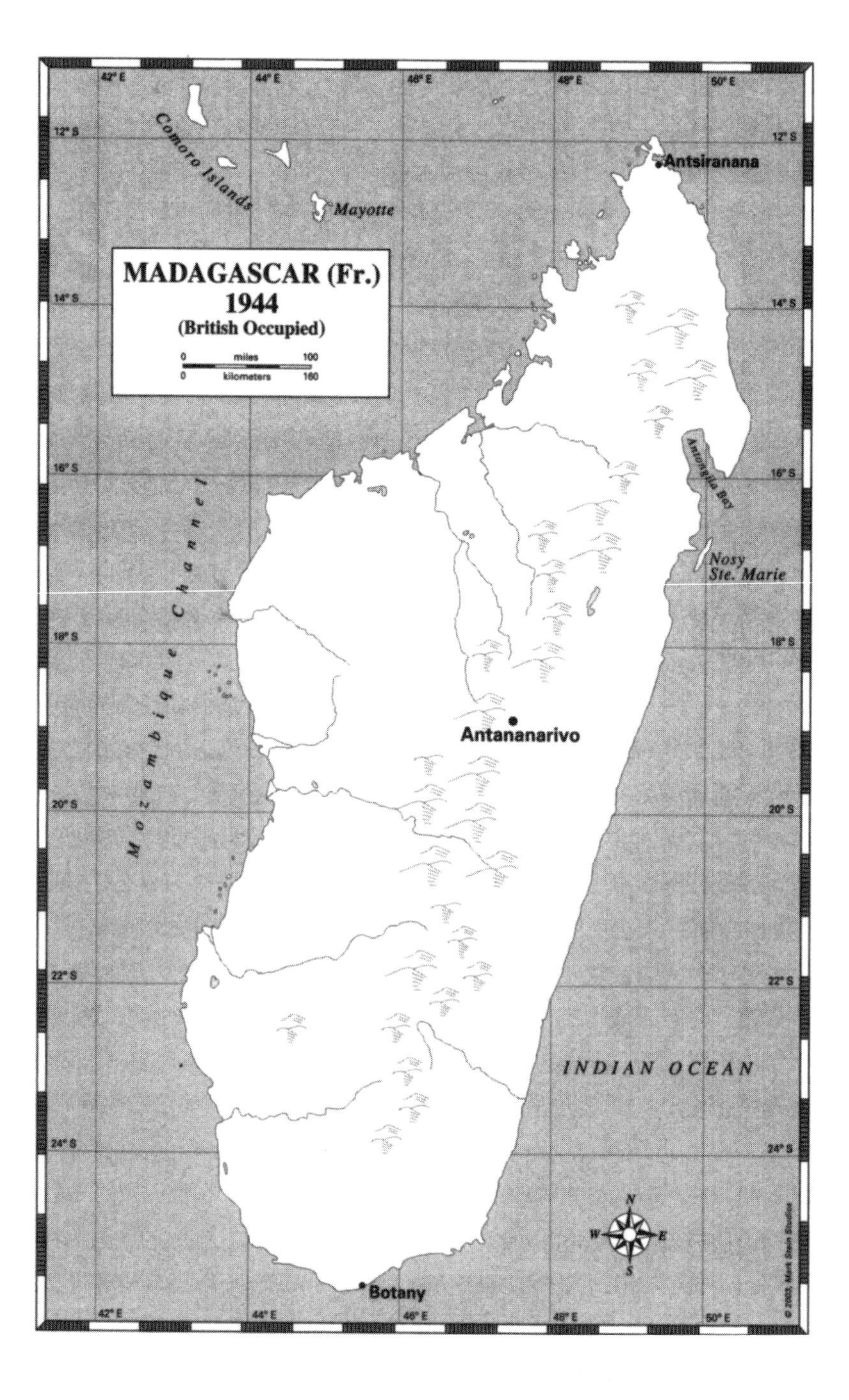

MADAGASCAR (Fr.)
1944
(British Occupied)
0 miles 100
0 kilometers 160
Comoro Islands
Mayotte
Antsiranana
Antongila Bay
Nosy Ste. Marie
Mozambique Channel
Antananarivo
INDIAN OCEAN
Botany
N
W
E
S
42° E
44° E
46° E
48° E
50° E
12° S
14° S
16° S
18° S
20° S
22° S
24° S
© 2003, Mark Stein Studios

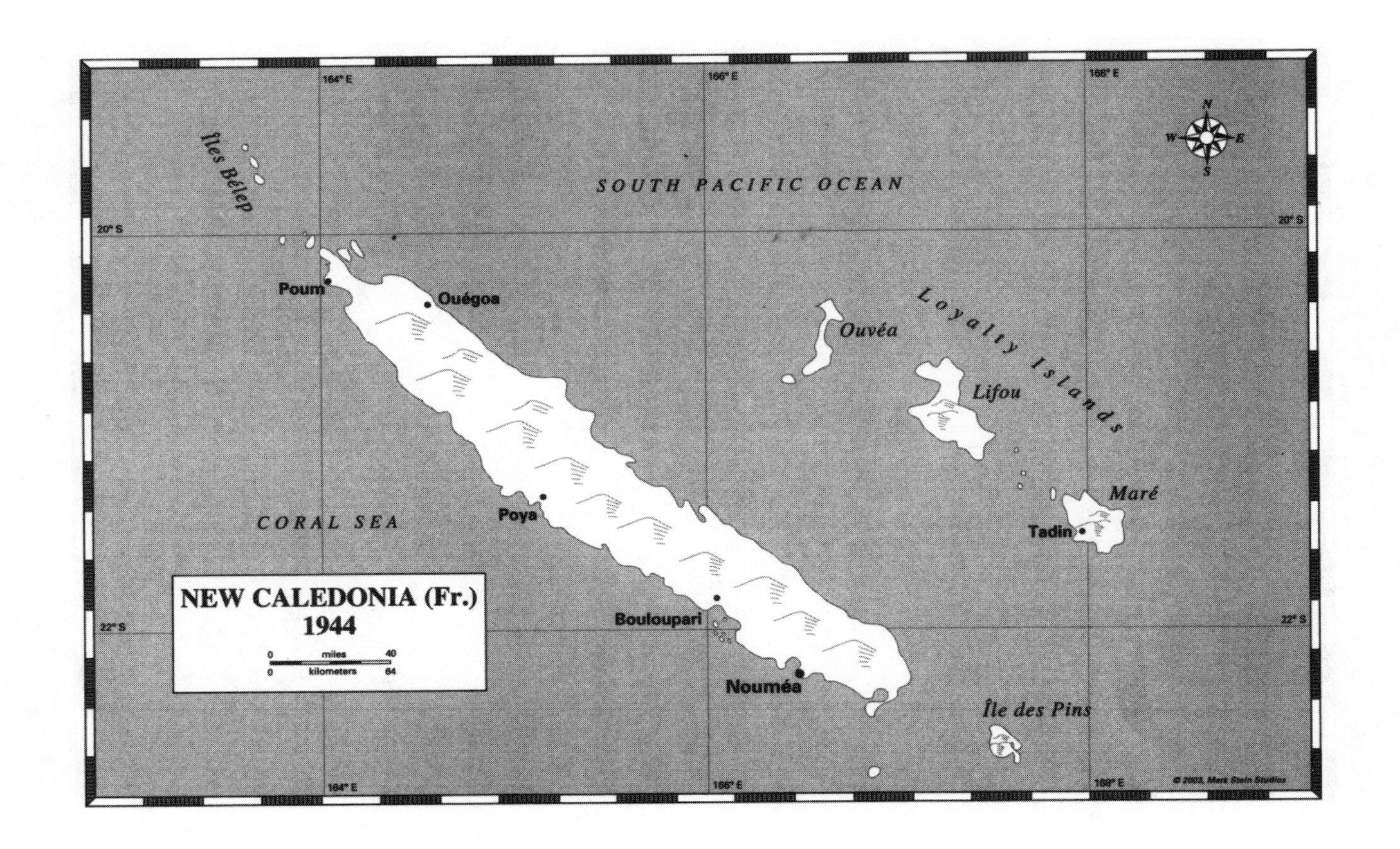
NEW CALEDONIA (Fr.)
1944
0 miles 40
0 kilometers 64
SOUTH PACIFIC OCEAN
CORAL SEA
Loyalty Islands
Îles Bélep
Poum
Ouégoa
Poya
Bouloupari
Nouméa
Ouvéa
Lifou
Maré
Tadin
Île des Pins
N
S
E
W
164° E
166° E
168° E
20° S
22° S
© 2003, Mark Stein Studios

ENGLAND
North Sea
London
NETHERLANDS
English Channel
Calais
Cherbourg
GERMANY
Brest
Le Havre
BELGIUM
NORMANDY
SAARLAND
Lorient
Paris
LUXEMBOURG
St.-Nazaire
Bar-le-Duc
Strasbourg
Tours
Dijon
Basel
La Rochelle
Bay of Biscay
Bern
FRANCE
SWITZERLAND
St.-Cergue
Geneva
Lake Geneva
Bordeaux
Lyon
ITALY
Turin
Toulouse
Marseille
SPAIN
Mediterranean Sea
FRANCE, 1944
0 miles 100
0 kilometers 160
Corsica
N
W
E
S

CAST OF CHARACTERS

U.S. NAVY
U.S.S. *MAXWELL* (DD 525)
(CRACKERJACK)

Alton C. ("Todd") Ingram, Commander, USN	Commanding Officer
Henry E. ("Hank") Kelly, Lieutenant Commander, USN	Executive Officer
Jack W. Wilson, Lieutenant, USN	Gunnery Officer
Eric L. Gunderson, Lieutenant, USN	Operations Officer
Anthony M. ("Tony") Duquette, Lieutenant (j.g.), USN	Communications Officer
Dexter	

U.S.S. *MORGAN J. THOMAS* (DD 543) (FIRST EDITION) (FLAG DESDIV 11)

Jeremiah T. ("Boom Boom") Landa, Captain, USN	Commodore of Destroyer Division Eleven (DESDIV 11)
Ralph R. Sorenson, Captain, USN	Interim Commodore, DESDIV 11
Howard Endicott, Commander, USN	Commanding Officer

U.S.S. *LEXINGTON* (CV 16) (FLAG TF 58)

Arleigh A. ("Thirty-one Knot") Burke, Captain, USN	Chief of Staff for Admiral Marc A. Mitscher
Marc A. Mitscher, Vice Admiral, USN	Commander, Task Force 58

U.S.S. *DIXIE* (AD 14)

Theodore R. ("Rocko") Myszynski, Rear Admiral, USN	Commander, Destroyer Forces, South Pacific

TWELFTH NAVAL DISTRICT, SAN FRANCISCO, CALIFORNIA

Oliver P. Toliver III, Lieutenant Commander, USN	Deputy Intelligence Officer
Jonathan H. Sorrell, Vice Admiral, USN	Commander, Twelfth Naval District
Henry T. ("Hank") Wellman, Chief Warrant Officer, USN	Code Specialist

SAN PEDRO, CALIFORNIA

Helen Ingram, Captain, U.S. Army	Todd Ingram's wife
Emma Peabody	Helen's next-door neighbor

HOLLYWOOD, CALIFORNIA

Laura West, pianist, West Coast Division, NBC Symphony Orchestra	Landa's betrothed

Arturo Toscanini, NBC Symphony Orchestra	Conductor
Roberta Thatcher	Business Manager, West Coast Division, NBC Symphony Orchestra

IMPERIAL JAPANESE NAVY
I-57

Hajime Shimada, Commander, IJN	Commanding Officer
Shigeru Kato, Lieutenant Commander, IJN	Executive Officer
Koki Matsumoto, Lieutenant, IJN	Engineering and Diving Officer
Fumimaro Ishibashi, Lieutenant (j.g.), IJN	Communications Officer
Kenyro Shimazaki, Superior Petty Officer, IJN	Chief enlisted electrician

Takano Masako, Seaman Second Class, IJN	

I-49

Norito Yukota, Commander, IJN	Commanding Officer

KRIEGSMARINE

Martin Taubman, Korvettenkapitän (Lieutenant Commander)	Kriegsmarine attaché, Tokyo
Conrad Blücher, Kapitänleutnant (Lieutenant)	Commanding Officer, *U-497*
Rudolph Krüger, Fregattenkapitän (Commander)	Commander, Seventh U-Boat Flotilla, Lorient

OTHER GERMANS

Wolfgang Schroeder, Standartenführer, SS (Colonel)	TAD, Seventh U-Boat Flotilla, Lorient

Dieter Hauser, Stabsfeldwebel, Luftwaffe (Warrant Officer)	Storch pilot

GENEVA, SWITZERLAND

Walter Taubman, Managing Director, Montreux Bank des Switzerland	Martin Taubman's half brother

FOREWORD

June 6, 1944, was a day marked by the largest movement of arms and fighting men the world has ever known. In Europe, nearly 7,000 ships sailed the English Channel. This force consisted of two battleships, two monitors, twenty-three light and heavy cruisers, 105 destroyers, 1,076 support ships, 2,700 merchant vessels, and 2,500 landing craft. Under General Dwight D. Eisenhower, this armada delivered 162,715 Allied troops and their equipment to the beaches of Normandy on that one day.

On the same day, halfway around the world, seven fleet carriers, eight light carriers, seven fast battleships, eight heavy cruisers, thirteen light cruisers, and sixty-nine destroyers of the United States Navy got under way in the Marshall Island's Majuro Lagoon. Designated Task Force 58 under the command of Vice Admiral Marc A. Mitscher, this armada, albeit smaller than the D-Day invasion fleet, was a decidedly more powerful naval force. The heavy cruiser *Indianapolis*, part of Task Force 58, was the flagship for Admiral Raymond A. Spruance, commander of the entire Fifth

Fleet. It was the largest group of capital ships ever accumulated under a single flag.

It took five hours for Task Force 58 to weigh anchor, clear the reef, and stand out to sea, where they formed into groups, spanning the Pacific from horizon to horizon. From Majuro, they headed northwest, shaping course for the Marianas and the Philippine Sea.

About the same time, Vice Admiral Jisaburo Ozawa's Mobil Fleet of five fleet carriers, four light carriers, five battleships, eleven heavy cruisers, two light cruisers, and twenty-eight destroyers weighed anchor at Tawi Tawi in the Sulu Archipelago and headed east.

From one standpoint the developing Battle of the Philippine Sea, as it came to be known, was similar to the 1942 Battle of Midway. Except now the balance of power was reversed in terms of ships and aircraft. Spruance (who commanded the U.S. naval forces at the Battle of Midway) and Mitscher had the upper hand in absolute numbers of ships: Spruance had 112, Ozawa only 55. And at Midway Spruance had parity with Japanese aircraft. Now he had far more of every type than Ozawa: 956 versus 473. But as the offensive force, the American strategy was far different. At Midway, the Japanese were bent on drawing out the American fleet and annihilating it; Midway was secondary. With the Marianas invasion, capturing and securing Saipan, Tinian, and Guam was the primary objective; wiping out the Japanese fleet was secondary.

Behind Task Force 58 was the V Amphibious force of Rear Admiral Richmond Kelly Turner. This was composed of 535 ships of all sizes, carrying and supporting 128,000 combat troops, two-thirds of them Marines.

Spruance's orders from Chester W. Nimitz, Commander in Chief of the Pacific Fleet, were succinctly stated in CincPacFlt Operation Plan 3-44: *Capture, occupy, and defend Saipan, Tinian, and Guam and develop bases in those islands.* It was up to Spruance, the strategic thinker and Fifth Fleet commander, to figure out how to do it. It was up to Mitscher's Task Force 58 to carry out his plan.

The 112 ships of Task Force 58 would have been an unwieldy armada had it not been divided into five task groups. Three groups, labeled Task Group 58.1, 58.2, and 58.3 constituted Mitscher's striking power. Twelve fleet and light aircraft carriers were divided among them, and each group was separated by twelve miles on a north-south axis. These three groups each had a screening force equally distributed on a four-thousand-yard circle around the carriers consisting of about fifteen destroyers and another three to six cruisers.

Another group, TG 58.7, was set up as a surface striking force and was composed of seven fast battleships screened by four cruisers and fourteen destroyers. A fifth task group, 58.4, consisting of three carriers, three cruisers, and seventeen destroyers, was responsible for aerial defense of the striking group TG 58.7. The five task groups were arranged in a reverse *F* pattern. At the two prongs were TG 58.7 and TG 58.4, positioned fifteen miles ahead of TG 58.1, 58.2, and 58.3.

One hundred twelve ships: a mighty seagoing fortress, nearly impregnable. By sunset that day, Task Force 58 settled on a formation course of 342 headed for Kwajalein and Eniwetok Island, the outermost of the Marshall Islands. One thousand miles ahead lay their objective: the Marianas and her four main islands, Guam, Rota, Tinian, and Saipan. With the destroyers pinging for submarines and the combat air patrols orbiting overhead, all was secure as the sun sank toward the horizon.

Japanese submarines really did have long legs. Some were built for carrying cargo over long distances. In spite of this, the Allied antisubmarine network, ranging across three major oceans, seriously nullified Japan and Germany's exchange program via submarine. Each new perturbation of the Freedom of Information Act provides further clues on how this was done through Allied code-breaking and how the Allies tracked German and Japanese shipping. Also amazing was the American development of the Mark 24 passive acoustic homing torpedo. Spearheaded by Bell Telephone Laboratories and the (then) Harvard Underwater Sound Lab, the Mark 24 was code-named FIDO and was first conceived in November 1941. Just eighteen months later, in May 1943, the Mark 24 FIDO sank its first U-boat. Thus, the Mark 24 helped break the back of the Axis submarine effort, sinking thirty-seven submarines and damaging eighteen. The incident described herein is from an actual occurrence. The IJN submarine *I-52*, en route to U-boat pens in France, was sunk in the South Atlantic on June 24, 1944. A FIDO dropped from a Grumman TBF off the escort carrier U.S.S. *Bogue* (CVE 9) did the job.

www.johnjgobbell.com

PROLOGUE

We knew thee of old,
O divinely restored,
By the light of thine eyes
And the light of thy sword.
From the graves of our slain
Shall thy valor prevail
As we greet thee again —
Hail, Liberty! Hail!
— *HAIL TO LIBERTY*,
DIONYSIOS SOLOMOS (1798–1857)

PROLOGUE

11 FEBRUARY 1944
IJN *I-49*
ARAFURA SEA

It was a hell Yukota could never have imagined. Truly, it sounded as if a fifty-foot giant were outside his submarine pounding the hull with a five-ton sledgehammer. Nonstop, the depth charges thundered all around, lifting him and his men off the deck, casting them about. Glass shattered. The entire submarine vibrated like a huge tuning fork.

Yukota hadn't counted on this. He thought he'd taken the *I-49* deep enough. One hundred meters should have done it. And yet the damn things hammered his boat, unleashing ten thousand agonies at once. His mind flashed with another image: this one a dragon ripping at them, trying to open a seam with sharp teeth. How did the Americans know how to set those charges so deep?

"Coming in for another run, Captain." It was Kosuga, the sonarman, seated at the aft end of the conning tower.

It wasn't long before they heard the

American's sonar. Soon, their eyes grew wide and they fixed on the overhead, beseeching the destroyer to go away. Louder, louder, the pinging becoming more rapid. Then it stopped, as the destroyer charged overhead. Soon —

WHAM! WHAM! WHAM! WHAM! WHAM!

The 2,500-ton, 358-foot submarine shook violently. More gauges ruptured; lightbulbs shattered, plunging the conning tower into total darkness. Yukota turned to the bulkhead and screamed. Instantly, he covered his mouth. *What have I done?* He was glad he was up here; not as many people. The men in the control room below surely would have noticed.

Then the death above them was gone. They were alone. They were alive.

Yukota shouted down the hatch into the control room, "Emergency lights, quickly!"

It became quiet. A man sobbed down in the control room and the odor of vomit ripped at Yukota's nostrils. There was something else: someone had lost control of his bowels. Yukota reflected that at least he hadn't done that. Something clanked; a sailor trod on broken glass; water gushed from a ruptured valve. "Sasaki, dammit! I said 'emergency lights.' "

"Yes, Captain." As diving officer, Lieutenant Ryozo Sasaki was closest to the emergency panel. It was a standard drill practiced many times.

After a moment, the lights mercifully flicked on.

"Sasaki, take her down to one hundred twenty meters."

Sasaki stepped under the hatch and looked up, the question obvious on his face. Test depth on the type C-2 attack submarine was one hundred meters.

Yukota said hoarsely, "Do it, Lieutenant. Do you want to keep living?"

Sasaki gulped, "Yes, Captain." Turning to the bow planesman, he ordered, "Make your depth one hundred twenty meters."

"He's coming back, Captain," said Kosuga.

Yukota shouted down the hatch, "Sasaki. Destroyer's coming back. Get ready."

Sasaki's eyebrows went up. "What?"

"Sasaki, dammit! Get ready. That's why we're here, you fool."

A light seemed to go on in Sasaki's eyes. He turned to his talker and said, "Engine room, torpedo room, stand by, on my mark."

Once again, the destroyer rumbled overhead.

Grabbing a stanchion, Yukota ordered, "Right full rudder. Steady on three-two-five."

They had just taken up the new course

when the first depth charge exploded, throwing the *I-49* almost onto her beam ends. Yukota had to shout as more charges went off. “Now, Sasaki, now!”

Sasaki concentrated, trying his mightiest to think through the destruction going on about him. Finally, he yelled at his talker, while Yukota prayed that the word had been passed quickly enough so their pumping noises would be suppressed by explosions.

The destroyer was gone. Yukota couldn’t see the gauges — they were shattered anyway — and he hadn’t heard the hiss of high-pressure air, so he didn’t know if they had brought it off.

Their eyes snapped to the talker.

The man clamped a hand to his earphones, listened, then leaned toward Sasaki, mouthing his report.

With a nod, Sasaki relayed it up the conning tower hatch. “Engine room reports 200 gallons of fuel oil pumped to sea. Torpedo room reports tubes one, two, three, and four fired successfully.”

“Excellent. Now to get out of here. Sasaki, one hundred forty meters.”

“Sir,” Sasaki began, “we —”

“One hundred forty, dammit! We’re not done yet.”

Sasaki gave the order; the *I-49* took on a five degree down-bubble, then groaned and rattled her way to the new depth.

Kosuga raised a hand, then turned to Yukota.

"What?"

"I think . . ."

"Say something, damn you." Yukota's temper was short, not because of their current predicament, but because he was embarrassed at his earlier loss of control. Desperately, he hoped no one had heard him. Fortunately, there had been so much noise.

Clamping his hands to his headphones, Kosuga said, "Rain squall. Two-six-five."

Salvation! Yukota ordered, "Come left to two-six-five. How far, Kosuga?"

Kosuga shrugged, "Five hundred, a thousand meters. I can't tell." Then he sat up. "We're making noise, sir."

Wrenches clanked forward and a sailor cursed as he slogged in bilgewater, trying to fix something. Yukota said quietly, "Mr. Sasaki. Remind the crew we are rigged for silent running — that it's important to minimize noise."

Sasaki's voice echoed up, "Yes, sir."

Yukota turned to Kosuga. "What noise?"

"Something aft. A rumbling of some sort."

The telephone buzzed. Yukota yanked it from its bracket. "Conn."

It was Lieutenant Inichi, the chief engineer. "Starboard shaft bent, sir. It's a yard job. Also, the main condensate pump is —"

"How much speed can you make on the port shaft?"

"Three knots, sir. And I wouldn't go any faster. Too much loose stuff flapping and clanking around outside."

"Hold on." Yukota turned to the helmsman. "Starboard motor stop. Port ahead one-third. Maintain course."

The helmsman spoke the order into the sound-powered phone. Then he nodded. "Engine room reports port motor ahead one-third."

Yukota asked, "Kosuga?"

Kosuga slowly shook his head. No more noise.

Yukota turned back to the phone. "That's it, all right, Inichi. Starboard shaft's making too much noise. Is it still operative?"

"Can't tell until we surface and run it up."

"Anything else I should know about?"

"Well, the bilge pump strainers for the engine room are clogged, and we're having trouble keeping pace with the —"

Wham. Wham. Wham. Wham.

Kosuga looked up. "Those were much farther away. And I think we're under the rain squall. It sounds like it's right overhead."

"All stop," Yukota ordered. He turned back to his phone. "We're going to try to hold her here, Chief. How much flooding do you have back there? Inichi? Inichi?" The line was dead. Beset with problems, the chief engineer had hung up. Yukota sat on a padded bench and wiped his brow.

Wham. Wham.

Farther away. Maybe they were below the layer. An interminable, dripping silence passed. At length, Kosuga sat up straight. "No screw noise, sir."

"What? How can that be?"

"Maybe he stopped?" Kosuga's eyebrows went up.

Stopped. It was too much to ask. For a brief moment, Yukota considered going to periscope depth and snapping off a shot at what could be a sitting duck. But then maybe it was a ruse. Maybe —

"Small screw noise. Barely hear it. Maybe a motorboat." Kosuga turned to Yukota. "Captain, if they've put a boat in the water, that means —"

Yukota waved a hand. "I know what that means." He looked to Sasaki and nodded. Possibly, it had worked. All that crap they'd pumped through the torpedo tubes: instruction manuals, newspapers, old codebooks, rice cakes, chicken bones, plenty of *I-49* stationery, and clothes. And two corpses stolen from a Tokyo morgue.

For a bit of irony, a May 3, 1943, issue of *Collier's* magazine was sent along.

And now the Americans had lowered a whaleboat to go out and examine the wreckage. Unusual, Yukota thought. They had taken the bait so easily. The Americans were supposed to be more cautious than that. Or were they just plain impatient? Maybe it was a new crew, or maybe they were in a hurry to see their movie tonight: it was seven in the evening topside. Yukota visualized a beautiful Australian sunset on golden seas.

Two humidity-laden hours later, it was dead quiet. Yukota slapped his knees and stood. "Anything, Kosuga?"

The sonarman listened intently, then slowly shook his head. "No, sir."

"Very well. Port motor ahead slow. Come to course two-six-five. Sasaki, take us to periscope depth."

"Sir!"

With a meter of water in the engine room, the *I-49* took eighteen minutes to labor her way up to periscope depth.

"Sonar?"

"All clear," reported Kosuga.

Yukota trusted Kosuga. He was a good sonarman. If he said all clear, then nothing was there. The enemy destroyer must be gone.

"Very well. Up periscope."

The periscope hissed up the well; Yukota squatted to grab the handles, then rode it to full height. Doing a tedious 360-degree scan, he found the sea calm. Stars glittered on an oily surface. No squall. No destroyer. "All clear. Lookouts to the conning tower. Stand by to surface." Yukota peered down the hatch into the control room. "Sasaki?"

"Ready, Captain."

"Very well. Surface!"

High-pressure air hissed, and the *I-49* rose from the depths of the Arafura Sea. With her conning tower hatch clanging open, Yukota scrambled to the bridge and made a quick binocular scan. No moon. Brilliant stars. Sharp horizon. No contacts. "Lookouts up."

Inichi got the *I-49*'s two great 5,503-horsepower diesels going, their exhausts tearing at the night. Inside, new air was sucked into the boat, the crew gratefully heaving their lungs with pure, rich oxygen. Yukota looked down the hatch into the conning tower, where instantly, it seemed as if the bulkheads changed from a dripping, putrid green to their original stark white.

"All engines ahead two-thirds. Make turns for twelve knots. Steer course two-six-five." Water frothed under the *I-49*'s stern as her screws spun.

Sasaki joined Yukota on the bridge and

handed over a mug of tea. "Just spoke with Inichi. Starboard shaft holding up. Vibration not too bad. But noisy."

"Did he say how much speed we can get out of her?"

"Fifteen to eighteen knots."

The rest of the damage reports were passed up. Nothing terribly bad. Everything could be put right within a few hours except that damned starboard shaft. Yukota whipped off his cap and let the wind whip at his hair. Soon, he would have to go below and draft a radio message for Shimada.

To the world, the *I-49* was dead. The Americans topside had fished the evidence from the Arafura Sea, and in the next two or three weeks naval headquarters in Tokyo would list them as overdue and write them off.

They had planned this so well. Luck was with them. But he didn't want to admit the depth charges had been far worse then he'd ever imagined.

Reading his thoughts, Sasaki asked. "This still going to work, Captain?"

Yukota allowed a smile. "We've done our job, Ryozo. Now it's up to Shimada and that German riding with him." He swept a hand across a star-glazed sky. "Beautiful, isn't it? How does it feel to be dead, Ryozo?"

Sasaki stood straight. "I'll let you know after I have a beer."

PART ONE

Stay with me God. The night is
dark
The night is cold; my little spark
Of courage dies. The night is long;
Be with me, God, and make me
strong.

— ANONYMOUS BRITISH SOLDIER
IN NORTH AFRICA, 1942

ONE

6 JUNE 1944
U.S.S. *MAXWELL* (DD 525)
NORTH PACIFIC OCEAN
11°56.3'N, 147°32.1'E

She rolled easily in the swells, her mast sweeping a thirty-degree arc across a red-streaked sky, as she emerged from a rain squall. Indigo wavelets slapped her hull and steam rose off her glistening decks, compressing a setting sun to an orange-red oblong sphere. She was the U.S.S. *Maxwell* (DD 525), a *Fletcher*-class destroyer of 2,100 tons heading east at twenty-two knots for a rendezvous with Task Force 58.

Her crew consisted of 332 men, twenty-three officers, and one illegal monkey named Dexter. Dining on scraps in the chief's quarters, Dexter was given the run of the ship. He often slept in the flag bag on the signal bridge, just aft of the pilothouse. Many times, a signalman would reach in the bag for a pennant, only to be surprised and terror-stricken as the screeching animal leaped out, spitting and baring razor-sharp teeth. The legend went that a second-class torpedoman, long since transferred off the *Maxwell*, had won Dexter in a poker game while the ship was nested with the three other destroyers of Destroyer Division Eleven (DESDIV 11) in Nouméa. That was supposedly eighteen months ago, but now, with rapid crew turnover, nobody was certain how or when the monkey had boarded the ship. Instead of attributing Dexter's origin to an inglorious poker game in Nouméa, the ship's company now preferred to convey the honorific of "plank owner" to Dexter. In essence, they claimed he was part of the original crew when the *Maxwell* was commissioned. But the *Maxwell* had been built and commissioned by Bethlehem Steel in San Francisco, California. Nobody tried to justify how Dexter, an obvious non-California native, had embarked in San Francisco.

Dexter played cards, smoked cigars, pitched a pretty good softball, and was often timed hand-over-handing up the starboard shroud to the top of the mast and down the port side. Best time: twenty seconds. Once, he was allowed to squeeze off a few rounds of twenty-millimeter cannon fire when the officers weren't looking. With this, Dexter was presented a regulation blue jumper, complete with gunner's mate third-class rating sewn in the appropriate place on the left arm.

Dexter's sublime moments were interrupted when the *Maxwell* steamed in a seaway producing rolls of more then twenty-five degrees. In those conditions, the ship would pitch and pound, corkscrew, and generally bob like a tin can in a rough bathtub. Dexter would stagger down to the chief's quarters and lie on the mess deck, groaning and turning a virulent shade of green. Sometimes the little creature would vomit and could barely move. So the task fell on Bucky Monaghan, the chief hospital corpsman, to bring Dexter out of it. Most of the time, Monaghan took the monkey to sick bay but refused to say what he did, claiming protection under the Hippocratic oath and patient confidentiality. Voodoo science, some grumbled. Others chided Monaghan for creating Frankenstein, the Monkey. The rumor was that he gave Dexter a shot of some heavy-duty drug, maybe ether, to put him out of his misery.

But this evening Dexter was asleep, presumably in the flag bag, when the 1MC sound system clicked and screeched. Denver Falco, boatswain mate of the watch, cleared his throat and stood close to the bridge microphone. He bleeped his pipe and announced, "Now man your battle stations, condition three. Now set material condition Zebra throughout the ship. Duty damage-control petty officer make reports to the chief engineer's stateroom." After a five-second wait, Falco bleeped his pipe again and gave the message everyone really wanted to hear. "Movie call will be on the messdecks tonight at twenty hundred. Tonight's movie is *The Bride Came C.O.D.*, starring James Cagney and Bette Davis."

In the Captain's sea cabin just behind the bridge, Commander Todd Ingram heard a collective howl from the bridge. They'd seen the movie several times. And Falco had made the announcement rather sarcastically, not caring about the crew's reaction. He was new to the ship and was having a hard time adjusting.

Ingram stretched, feeling better with the quick snooze he'd taken after chow. He sat up on his bunk and bent to tie his shoes.

Nouméa.

They'd done everything Mitscher asked for. They'd run 1,000 miles ahead of Task Force 58 on picket duty. They'd sent weather data and, last night, Ingram had volunteered to plunge another 350 miles ahead to look for a downed PBY crew. Miraculously, they found all eight in good shape. Now, they were heading back to rendezvous with Task Force 58 and transfer them to the *Lexington*. While alongside, they were to refuel, pick up Captain Jerry Landa, commodore of Destroyer Division Eleven, Todd's friend and superior officer, and scram. From there, the *Maxwell* was scheduled for an overhaul and much-needed bottom job in Nouméa. As sorry as Ingram was to be missing the show with Task Force 58, he knew that the *Maxwell* would be hard pressed to keep up. Even though she was just a year old, she'd been operating continuously; her boilers needed retubing and her bottom was coated with a disgusting six-inch-thick growth.

The best part was that upon reaching Nouméa, Ingram and Landa were due to fly home for thirty days of leave. He smiled at the thought. His wife, Helen, was eight months pregnant, and he was counting on being there for the child's birth. At the same time, Landa was due to be formally engaged to Laura West, the well-known pianist with the NBC Symphony Orchestra. Ingram hoped he and Helen could make Landa's engagement party before she delivered.

Once again, the 1MC squawked: Falco blew his pipe and announced, "Now hear this. There are men working aloft. Do not rotate, radiate, or energize any electronic equipment while men are working aloft."

"Damn." Ingram stood. The phone

buzzed. He yanked it from its bracket. "Captain."

The line crackled with, "XO, Captain. The SC-1 radar antenna motor crapped out again. Mr. Duquette is right on it." It was Hank Kelly, the executive officer. Ingram had met Hank Kelly aboard the U.S.S. *Howell* two and a half years ago. Kelly, a Purdue graduate, had been the ship's engineering officer and a damn good one. After the *Howell* was lost and Ingram given his new command, he'd been lucky to dig Kelly up and fold him into the *Maxwell*'s crew along with other *Howell* survivors.

Ingram moaned, "Not again." Kelly was telling him the air search radar was on the fritz, the third time in as many days.

"Sorry, Captain. We expect it up in ten minutes," said Kelly.

A sickly feeling swept over Ingram. They were steaming blind. Instinctively, he glanced out the porthole, his eyes darting about, looking for squalls in which to hide. It was a weird equipment casualty. For no plausible reason, the motor that rotated the antenna just stopped working. It took two men to climb the mast, unscrew the access plate, and fiddle with it. "Who's aloft?"

"Mouselle and Hogan." Mouselle was a second-class radarman, Hogan, a first-class electronics technician, both top-notch.

Ingram rubbed his chin. "Very well, Hank. Sound general quarters, Condition I AA. I'm coming out. And tell combat to inform the screen commander." Ingram had no choice but to put the ship at her peak of vigilance when a key piece of equipment failed. Especially now, at sunset, when they were vulnerable to an air attack from out of the sun.

The general quarters gong sounded. Men dashed about the ship. Ingram grabbed his windbreaker and stepped through the gun director barbette room onto the open bridge.

Falco announced, "Captain on the bridge."

Ingram looked in the pilothouse and nodded. All hands were donning sound-powered phones and helmets with professional sangfroid. He stuffed his pant legs in his socks, donned a life jacket and helmet, and stepped to the starboard bridge wing. He was met by Howard Clock, a rail-thin yeoman, who looked like a sixth-grade reject. With a longish face, Clock had clear blue eyes, rimless glasses, and acne. But he was a good yeoman and a good talker as well. "All stations report manned and ready, Captain," he said.

"Very well." Looking up the mast, Ingram saw two men up high wearing safety slings, much like telephone linemen:

except these two couldn't dig their feet into the mast. It was made of aluminum, not wood, and oftentimes, it was difficult to hang on up there. Ingram's position on the bridge was thirty-five feet above the water. Here the ship's motion seemed slow, easy; one could wedge himself against a chart table or bulwark and hardly notice a thing. But aloft, Ingram shuddered to think, those men were one hundred twenty feet up in the air, swinging though an arc of at least two hundred feet, with nothing but the mast to hold on to.

Lieutenant (j.g.) Anthony Duquette climbed up the inner companionway and walked up to Ingram. Like other officers, Duquette wore khakis. But there the resemblance ended. He'd been a lightweight boxing champion, and, although he was only five-six or -seven, he had a well-defined muscular body, which was enhanced by tailor-made clothes. His dark, shiny hair was always perfectly combed, and the other officers chided him for often glancing in the mirror. Duquette was an electrical engineer from the University of Michigan. He knew radars and things that went zap. The problem was, he lacked maturity. Too much of a pretty boy, too much looking in mirrors and thinking about girls. Ingram wondered if Duquette was running the communications division or his men were.

Sort of like the monkeys running the zoo, he figured. Or, in this case, Dexter running the zoo. Fortunately, this Dexter was good and highly motivated. Aside from Duquette's distractions, Ingram could have asked for no better man to be in charge of the finicky surface search and air search radars.

As usual, Duquette was bareheaded. Still, he tipped a finger to his brow and said, "Evening, Captain. Sorry about all this." He snorted, checked his watch, and squinted aft into the sunset. "Bad timing."

Ingram drew a thin smile. "Yes, bad timing, Mr. Duquette." He wasn't going to let the young man off the hook. With the air search radar down, they were vulnerable.

Duquette made an elaborate show of pulling a face. "We'll have it back up, chop-chop, Captain."

Lieutenant Eric Gunderson, the GQ officer of the deck, stepped onto the bridge wing and said, "Excuse me captain, XO asks for you to please pick up the phone."

"Very well. And Eric, make sure your lookouts are vigilant. We're blind as hell."

"Yes, sir." Gunderson walked away and began talking to lookouts.

Ingram eyed Duquette. "Better get back to CIC, Tony."

"Yes, sir."

Ingram walked into the pilothouse, grabbed the phone, and said, "Captain."

It was Hank Kelly, muffling his mouthpiece with his hand. "Message from the Commodore, sir."

"Read it."

"Yes, sir." Kelly cleared his throat and paper rattled. " 'Interrogative status.' "

"That's it?"

"Yes, sir."

It was a classic Landa gibe. He knew about the *Maxwell*'s radar troubles and couldn't resist sending Ingram a blast. Ingram sighed. "Okay, Hank. Send 'ETR ten minutes.' That's all we can say for now."

"How about 'Get off my ass'?" Kelly, the consummate engineering officer, could be so crude at times and he didn't hesitate to speak his mind. That's why Ingram had sought him out. Not a yes-man, Kelly was loaded with talent. Unfortunately, Landa liked to pick on Kelly, making life miserable for him. Ingram told him over and over to just roll with it, that Landa's style was to pull strings and watch people dance. All Kelly had to do was to keep his mouth shut and say, "Yes, sir." But Kelly's pride often got in his way, making Landa turn the screws tighter.

"Just send it, Hank. I'll talk to Jerry when we rendezvous."

"Aye, aye, sir." Kelly hung up.

Ingram turned, finding Duquette still on the bridge, a smile stretched across his face. Ingram followed his gaze, seeing the two men scaling down, the radar antenna turning. "Can we radiate?"

"Looks like it, but we have to wait for them to get down," said Duquette.

"Very well," Ingram said. "Clock. Tell CIC the SC-1 antenna motor is repaired. We'll start radiating momentarily. Ask Mr. Kelly to so inform DESDIV 11."

There was a loud screech, and Ingram felt something zip against his leg.

"Dammit!" It was dark-faced Falco chasing the animal.

"Falco," called Ingram.

The boatswain's mate drew up, sharply. "Sir."

"What happened?"

"Damn thing tried to bite me." Falco jabbed his thumb in his mouth.

"May I go, sir?" Duquette interrupted.

"Sure enough, Tony. But I want to see you and the exec in my day cabin as soon as we secure from GQ."

Duquette's Adam's apple bounced. He almost saluted but thought better of it. "Yes, sir."

He seemed rooted to the spot, so Ingram said, "Go, Tony. Get back to combat and make your radars sing." He slapped

Duquette on the butt. The young officer's leather soles clacked on the companionway as he dashed two decks down to CIC.

Something squealed, and Ingram looked aloft. Dexter was climbing up the mast via the starboard shroud.

Falco gave a thin smile and drew his bosun's knife, a converted bayonet at least eight inches long. "Sort of trapped, ain't he, sir?"

"Leave him alone, Falco. We've got more important —"

Gunderson thrust his head out of the pilothouse. "Captain, jeez, you better take a look at this."

Ingram walked into the pilothouse and bent his head to the hooded radar repeater. "Working okay?"

Gunderson nodded.

What Ingram saw made him suck in his breath. Eight dots were headed for the *Maxwell* directly from the west, range — he quickly twirled the knob — ten miles. "Damn! What are they doing way out here?" But then he realized they had snatched that PBY crew out from under the Japaneses' noses. A snooper must have spotted them and called in a strike. They were still within range of Guam airfields.

Ingram dashed out onto the open bridge, spotted a rain squall, and called over his shoulder, "Mr. Gunderson, come left to zero-zero-zero. Head for that squall." With Clock in tow, Ingram walked through the pilothouse to the port bridge wing.

"Clock," Ingram shouted. "Ask CIC if there's any IFF on those contacts."

Clock pressed his talk button and spoke. Five seconds later he received his answer. "Negative, Captain."

"Very well. Tell Mr. Kelly to inform DESDIV 11. Tell him we need air cover, chop-chop."

The *Maxwell* heeled into a left turn, swinging to the north. Ingram called up to Jack Wilson, the gunnery officer. "Jack, you've eight bogies coming out of the sun, range about six miles. Get on it."

Wilson swung his binoculars to the west. "Sir."

Was there time to unmask batteries? Ingram guessed so. One more thing. He ordered, "Eric, increase speed to twenty knots!"

"Aye, aye, Captain."

"And Eric, double-check your lookouts. See if they can pick up the targets before the fire control radar." Ingram squinted into the sunset, willing his eyes to find the enemy. For some reason, he looked up, seeing Dexter in the shrouds doing the same thing, wind blowing at his fur. *Where are they, Dexter?*

Clock reported, "Captain, bogies have

split into two groups, four to the south, four to the north. Looks like a coordinated attack."

Dammit! "Mr. Gunderson, shift your rudder and come back to course two-seven-zero."

"Yes, sir."

Looking aft, Ingram shaded his eyes against the still brilliant sunset. Before, it hadn't seemed so bright. Now he couldn't see a thing. What he could see was that damned monkey, halfway up the starboard forward shroud, peering into the sunset.

"A hell of a lookout you are," Ingram muttered.

TWO

7 JUNE 1944
U.S.S. *MAXWELL* (DD 525)
NORTH PACIFIC OCEAN

"Jack, split the battery. Forward five inch and forties, take the bogies to the north; the aft battery, take the south."

As gunnery officer and coordinator of the ship's battery, Jack Wilson was key to the ship's defense. That's why he was atop the pilothouse with an unobstructed view in all directions. "Got it!" Wilson punched his microphone, designating the ship's two forward five-inch and forty-millimeter cannons under the control of the main battery director; the after five-inch mounts and forties to be controlled by the secondary director aft. That way they could engage targets attacking from different directions.

While Wilson was setting up his split battery, Ingram grabbed the pilothouse telephone handset and punched COMBAT.

"CIC." It was Hank Kelly in the combat information center.

"Hank, anything more on our air cover?"

"Four F6Fs just took off. ETA fifteen minutes."

"Not soon enough."

"No."

"And no IFF?"

"Zero."

"Okay, keep me informed." Ingram hung up and walked back to the starboard bridge wing.

A lookout atop the pilothouse screeched and pointed. "Bogies!"

This had happened so many times before, and yet Ingram never grew used to it. Always, he felt as if twenty pounds of lead lay in his stomach. And lead was not only poisonous, but it slowed you down, didn't it? Lethargic. Like the way he felt right now. This time was no different, as he forced his binoculars to his eyes, almost afraid of what he would find. Immediately, he picked out the four dots heading directly for them from the north. In a V-formation, they were at about five thousand feet.

Wilson shouted, "On target and tracking, both groups. Look like Kates."

Ingram tightened his focus, seeing they were indeed Nakajima B5N2 single-engine carrier attack bombers. Originally used for torpedo attacks, these Kates carried an 800-kilogram bomb under their bellies.

With Clock trailing, Ingram dashed

through the pilothouse and spotted the other four Kates approaching from the south. Much farther away, he decided. Dashing back to the starboard bridge wing, he yelled, "Range?"

"Ten thousand to starboard, fourteen to port," replied Wilson.

Time to get on with it. "Commence fire, both batteries!"

All five of the *Maxwell*'s five-inch guns erupted, spewing cordite-laden smoke over the weather decks. Ingram's world became thundering cannon fire and choking fumes that momentarily obscured the dive bombers headed for them. His eyes watered, and when he could finally see, two of the attacking planes had broken off and were circling back, while the remaining pair droned closer. In fact, now he heard their engines.

A blotch of smoke blossomed beside the Kate on the right. Flame burst from its cowling and oily black smoke trailed, but somehow the plane plodded on.

Ingram asked, "Jack. How 'bout the group to the south?"

Wilson shaded his eyes. "Dispersed, Captain. I don't —"

"Down!" Clock jerked Ingram to the deck. A roaring and crashing caromed through the pilothouse. Someone screamed. Metal ripped, glass shattered as enormous fist-sized holes punched into the bulkhead above Ingram. Seconds later, a Japanese Zero fighter roared overhead.

"Where did he come from?" Ingram sat up, not believing the transformation on the bridge. What had been an orderly navigation and watch-standing area had been recast into hell's operating room, the devil's own surgeons using twenty-millimeter cannon. *Good God, I'm still alive.* He bent to his talker. "Thanks, Clock."

Lying supine, Clock raised his head. His helmet was tipped onto his nose, but Ingram could see his lips wiggle. "Ahhhh . . ."

"You okay?"

Clock nodded, pushed his helmet back, and gave a lopsided grin.

Ingram patted Clock on his shoulder, then rose, seeing a crazed tangle of bodies on the open bridge. Some moaned and tried to stand. In the pilothouse, Billy Overton, a second-class quartermaster, gritted his teeth and wobbled to his feet. With a grunt, he stood clutching the ship's helm, shaking his head and blinking his eyes.

Ingram leaned into the hatchway. "Okay, Billy?"

"Think so, Cap'n." Overton's gaze traveled to his right. His eyes widened and he drew a quick breath seeing Collins, the lee helmsman, lying in a crumpled heap, his midsection a glistening dark red. "Jeez!"

Gunderson staggered out, holding his head. Blood ran down from a deep cut on his forehead. "Where the . . . what was that?"

Ingram grabbed Gunderson by the shoulders. "Eric? Eric?"

"Gimme a minute . . ."

Another Zero zipped overhead, this time from the port side, raking the ship with its twenties. These shells were directed aft of the bridge, spewing into the men on the forward torpedo mount. But the Zero's luck ran out as Mount 41 walked a stream of forty-millimeter rounds into the plane as it screamed for safety. A shell hit the gas tank, and the plane exploded with a soft puff. Parts twirled in all directions, eventually smacking the ocean, leaving a grimy, flaming oil slick.

Ingram yelled, "Falco, Falco?"

"Uh, sir?" Glass crunched under the boatswain mate's feet as he rose among a tangle of bodies.

Ingram leaned into the pilothouse and said, "I have the conn. Take over the lee helm! Get those phones on and tell main control I want full power. Then ring up all engines ahead flank and make turns for thirty-two knots."

"Aye, aye, Captain." Falco eased the

sound-powered phones off the dead lee helmsman and then stepped over his body to work the engine order telegraph. The bells clanged as he rang up FLANK. The ship vibrated momentarily as she dug in her stern and leapt forward.

"You with me, Overton?"

The helmsman's gaze was still a bit distant.

"Overton!"

He straightened his helmet. "Yes, sir."

"What's your course?"

"Two-seven-zero, sir."

"Very well." Ingram turned to his talker. "Clock! Tell combat that a couple of Zeros came in on us from the deck, undetected. Tell them to tune that damned radar."

"Yes, sir."

"And dammit, ask them about our air cover."

"Yes, sir."

Another Zero zipped toward them, pouring its cannon fire into the bridge. Once again, they dropped to the deck as white-hot chunks of metal flew about. Simultaneously a bomb smacked the ocean a hundred feet to port, sending up a tall column of grayish-white water. Then another, further aft.

Ingram struggled to his feet. *Dammit. Get busy.* He looked up, seeing two more Kates at about their release points. Soon black specs detached from under their bellies and began their deadly journey down.

"Overton, left ten degrees rudder. Steady on two-six-zero."

Overton repeated the order and eased his rudder over. The *Maxwell* lunged into her turn, leaning to starboard. Soon two bombs crashed into the ocean, straddling the track where the ship would have been.

"Shift your rudder. Steady on three-zero-zero." Whipping his head around, Ingram said, "Clock, what's combat doing? We need target info. Clock? Clock? What the — ?"

Rupert, a corpsman, bent over a sailor wearing sound-powered phones. It was Clock. The corpsman turned to Ingram and slowly shook his head.

"Wait a minute — he just saved my life."

The ocean roared as another pair of bombs hit, nearly obliterating Ingram's words.

"Sorry, Captain." Rupert rose and walked over to Gunderson, who had collapsed to the deck.

"My God." Ingram looked at Clock's limp body. "Rupert!" He choked.

The hospital corpsman looked up. "Sir?"

He was ready to say, *You can't be* that *sure, can you?* "Sorry, take care of Gunderson."

Then Ingram shook his head and yelled

to Wilson, "Jack, tell combat to send up a talker for me. Clock is dead."

"Yes, sir."

More bombs exploded to starboard as the *Maxwell*'s guns raked the sky. Ingram kicked himself mentally. He'd lost the picture. Too many distractions. Frantically, he scanned with his binoculars, trying to find the closest planes. Another burst of cannon fire tore into number-one stack, rupturing a steam line to the whistle. A roaring white cloud leaped into the air. Ingram yelled up to Wilson, "Get that sonofabitch. They're chopping my ship to pieces. Jack? Jack?" Ingram stood on his tiptoes.

Wilson sat on the fly-bridge deck, his feet splayed, his back braced against the director barbette.

"Jack!"

"Sir?" Wilson's eyes blinked.

"Get up!"

Wilson looked at Ingram, his gaze unfixed. Then he grimaced and clamped a hand over his right shoulder, blood oozing between his fingers. Above Wilson, the main battery director was riddled with large holes. On top of the director, the Mark 22 fire-control radar antenna was crumpled as if a giant hand had smacked it. Inside the tanklike structure, seven men were dead or injured, he figured. Shutting his mind to the carnage in there, he marveled that the ship's guns had shifted to local control and still fired. But that's what the crew had practiced time and time again.

"Rupert! Can you get up there and help Mr. Wilson?" Ingram stepped up on a pedestal to get a better view of his gunnery officer.

Rupert whipped a field dressing around Gunderson's head. "Almost done here, sir."

"Good." Then Ingram shouted into the pilothouse, "Falco, call CIC and tell Mr. Kelly to get up here."

Just then, Mount 52 roared, its muzzle no further than fifteen feet from Ingram's face. He'd been standing high on a pedestal, and the muzzle blast knocked him against the bulwark. He was grabbing for the bulwark when another explosion went off, this one with an incredible white-hot heat. An enormous compression instantly followed. He thought he'd never draw another breath. He was spinning and tumbling through a slow-motion kaleidoscopic journey. Then, nothing . . .

The shock of the water brought him to consciousness. Coughing and gasping, he struggled to keep his head above water. *Take a breath. Easy now.* Something detonated close by. He tried to open his eyes, but they seemed welded shut. An airplane roared overhead. Another explosion.

With great effort, Ingram opened an eye — his left, he thought. Through a miasma of vaporous clouds, he saw a yellow-orange sky, the remnant of a virulent sunset. To his left, the *Maxwell*'s fantail swooped past, her guns firing port and starboard. Suddenly, the white-foamy quarter wake lifted Ingram, then dropped him into an enormous trough where he tumbled and rolled and choked, fighting for air. It seemed to go on forever. And beyond forever, as he twirled and spun. Desperate for breath, Ingram wondered if he could last. *Maybe I should just pack it in and suck in a lungful of ocean water.*

Instinct took over. He clawed at the water. *Which way is up?*

After a torturous sixty seconds, the water became smoother. But it was dark.

Eyes open, dammit!

Salt stung his eye as he cranked it open. It was still dark.

Which way is up?

He raised a hand and kicked. Bursting to the surface, he filled his lungs just before a wave lapped over him. He was under for another swirling, tumbling ten seconds before he came up again. Gasping desperately, he fought to keep his head above the foamy surface, kicking against the *Maxwell*'s churning, boiling, thirty-two-knot wake. Panting for air, he again opened his eye.

"Where the hell's my ship?" he gurgled, spitting water. Spinning, he finally spotted the *Maxwell*'s upper works, ghosting into a rain squall, her guns still blazing. Overhead, the attackers buzzed about like vultures after carrion. His last glimpse of the *Maxwell* was of steam belching from the riddled number-one stack and smoke pouring from her superstructure. And she carried a list to starboard. Then she disappeared.

It hit him. The *Maxwell* was no longer his. "My God."

THREE

7 JUNE 1944
NORTH PACIFIC OCEAN

This is some sort of ludicrous joke. Ha, ha, ha. They'll be back for me soon.

But as the sky grew more red, it struck home that the *Maxwell* was gone. Really gone. *They can't do this to me. Come back!* "Get back here!" he shouted.

Darkness rushed in. Waves rose and fell, lifting him, then dumping him into troughs. With each wave, the thought grew more final. *They aren't coming back.* The ship was heavily damaged, her crew desperately fighting to survive the bomb hit or whatever it was. Many would have been killed or injured. The dead, wounded, and missing wouldn't be sorted out until the damage was contained. That could take a long time.

A wave washed over Ingram, punctuating the possibility that maybe the *Maxwell* had gone down. When Ingram had last seen her, she'd been listing to starboard and smoke was pouring from either the forward fireroom or the deckhouse itself, he couldn't tell which. A hit in the fireroom could have been fatal. Forward of that was CIC and the officer's living quarters. Less fatal, but a chance of more men killed and wounded. With so many dead or missing, Ingram would be assumed lost among them, and that would be that. It could take hours, maybe days, to sort it all out. One thing he did know was that they wouldn't deploy a serious search and rescue effort tonight. No searchlights. Too many enemy planes and submarines about.

Ingram began to wonder if he would last the night. *Maybe not. Maybe this is my last night on earth. Will I ever feel land beneath my feet or see God's golden daylight again?*

Shut up and stop sniveling. Take stock.

He listened, hearing nothing. No gunfire, no airplane engines. The Japs must have withdrawn. Water lapped in his mouth and he kicked hard to keep his head up. The kicking made Ingram realize his water-logged shoes were still on. *Off!* He bent to untie them, but remembered something in the survival manual. *Leave your shoes on or tie them together and hang them around your neck. You'll need them when you go ashore. I am going ashore, aren't I?*

What else?

He patted himself, checking for bruises and broken bones. All he came up with was a cut somewhere on his face. His right eye was swollen shut. But there was no major pain and everything seemed to work. But as he turned his head he found his neck painful, and there was an abrasion of some sort under his chin. Then he realized his helmet was gone. *Damned strap must have caught my head when it came off.*

What else?

His life jacket seemed to be supporting him all right. He shuddered with the thought that a chamber could go dead and he'd have to swim again. But then another survival session flicked through his mind. *Take off your pants, tie knots at the bottoms of the legs, scoop in air, and use that to stay afloat.*

A wave lifted Ingram, tossing him atop a bigger wave. It crested and broke; throwing him into a trough and forcing him under. Even with an eye open, it was completely black. *Am I dead?*

NO!

Out of breath, Ingram panicked and fought against the water. Harder. He felt that his head would burst. Kicking his feet together, he shot to the surface, drawing in a great lungful of air. Once he stopped wheezing, he realized it was almost dark. It had been hazy at sunset and clouds were moving in, meaning it would be overcast tonight: no moon or stars.

Tonight? Here tonight? All alone? *Oh, God help me.*

Ingram became acutely aware of his feet.

And between his feet and the bottom were about a thousand fathoms of water, give or take a few hundred, since he'd last looked at the chart. Six thousand feet straight down: That's over a mile. *I don't want to go down there. Oh, God . . . I don't want to go there. I've a wife and a baby yet unborn whom I desperately want to see. There's a life before me with a wonderful woman. Helen, I love you. I'll come back.*

There was a low roar off to his left. *What? Which way is off to my left? No idea. North?*

He bobbed and whipped about for a few minutes as the roaring grew louder. *What the hell is it?* Louder. Then he figured it out. Rain. Sweet rain. The water roared as the rain pounded about him, making little glistening craters, the pattern enticing. As he studied the water, a rivulet of rain ran down his face onto his lips.

Wonderful. It tasted sweet and pure.

Raising his head to the sky, he opened his mouth wide, trying to catch as much rainwater as possible. Drop by drop, the water invigorated him. A wave lapped over his head, and he gagged and coughed and sputtered. But the rain tasted so good that he raised his head once more, risking another dunking.

The rain ceased abruptly, and the clouds parted to reveal a sliver-sized moon rising in the east. Unaccountably, that made Ingram smile and he raised his wrist to check his watch. With the pale light, he could barely discern the radium dial: eight twenty. Another ten hours to morning. *Dammit! How do I last ten hours? What the hell do I do for ten hours? And then what do I do after that?*

Helen, I love you. Stay with me, honey; stay in my heart. We'll be together. Looking up in the sky, he could almost see Helen. Her dark, near-black hair, her eyes full of mirth, compassion, and love. Simple and yet complex. He never tired of looking into Helen's eyes. Each time he did, he found something new. The joy about Helen was that she was an unending mystery; something always unfolded to delight him each day. He'd never get over her.

A wave slapped him in the face, making him choke and sputter. It made him realize that he hadn't been dunked for a while and . . . yes . . . the sky was almost completely clear overhead. The wind was calm, the waves not quite so steep. In fact, they were rolling now, the period between crests longer.

Thank you, God.

His teeth began to chatter and his hands shivered. Suddenly, his mind was seized with the thought of hypothermia. *What do I do about that?*

Think. The last time Ingram checked,

the *Maxwell*'s water injection temperature was seventy-six degrees. Not bad. Surviv-able, but still miserable. His hands curled up and became like claws. *No! Please!*

With chattering teeth, Ingram rubbed his arms and legs. But the more he did so, the more his teeth chattered.

Pain shot into his right calf, the muscles wadding up into a ball. Ingram dunked his head under, his fingers furiously kneading his calf.

Then he raised his head, drew a breath. With a gasp, he sucked in another breath, ducked under, and went back to work.

The charley horse wouldn't go away and he grew frustrated as he gasped and choked and wheezed, knowing he couldn't do this much longer.

"Chee . . . chee . . ."

Ingram ducked again. In a rage, he thumped at his calf, his lungs feeling as if they would burst. Again, he raised his head, gasping and woozy from lack of breath. Cool air washed his face and he opened his eye, seeing the moon a bit higher.

"Chee . . . chee . . ."

Ingram whipped his head around. "What is that?"

"Screeech!"

"No!"

He rose on a wave. Silhouetted atop the next wave was a small furry creature. It waved. "Chee . . . chee."

"Dexter! For crying out loud." Twenty feet away, the monkey was perched on something, all the way out of the water. A piece of dunnage of some sort. "Hold on, Dexter." With long, powerful strokes, Ingram swam. But the life jacket slowed his progress. A minute later, he stopped to catch his breath. But he'd only halved the distance. Dexter waved with both arms, screeching and growling as Ingram put his head down and dug in.

Ingram finally pulled to within three feet of Dexter, who jumped and screeched. "Hold on. It's okay."

He put out his hand, finding a long, smooth section of painted wood perhaps ten feet in length. At one end were weatherbeaten metal letters, DD 525. It was a wrecked section of the whaleboat's hull. Ingram reached and found the gunnel. Kicking and wiggling, he pulled himself aboard.

The section sank a bit; waves lapped over, but except for Ingram's feet and calves, he was out of the water.

Instantly, Dexter jumped on his back screeching and pawing at Ingram's face. At length, Ingram flipped onto his back and looked up to the moon. Dexter calmed a bit and settled in the crook of his arm, laying his head against Ingram's chest.

FOUR

8 JUNE 1944
NORTH PACIFIC OCEAN

Sleep was impossible. Waves lapped over the whaleboat wreckage constantly, jolting Ingram and the monkey awake. Twice they were swept off, with Dexter clinging and screeching as Ingram kicked and sputtered and cursed his way back aboard. But in the open air he quickly grew cold and his teeth chattered. The water seemed warm when he was dunked, and he considered staying there, but kicking and holding on to the wreckage was too much of an effort.

After midnight the ocean calmed, and he fell asleep. But once again, a wave slapped him, abruptly yanking him back to consciousness. Wiping water off his brow, he glanced at his watch: 0236. *It's darkest before dawn, isn't it? Tomorrow, they'll pick me up for sure, eight o'clock at the latest. I'll bet Jerry Landa has lots of planes lined up right this minute, just waiting to launch at first light.*

The sea calmed even more, and he worked himself into a precarious spread eagle, with Dexter shivering in his armpit. Looking up, he marveled at the stars and planets that glittered across a deep velvet backdrop, framing the three-quarter moon overhead. This view always made Ingram feel small and insignificant. It was especially so here, tonight, when he was so vulnerable and far removed from Helen and their little house on Alma Street.

It brought to mind his escape from Corregidor just over two years ago. He'd been skipper of the minesweeper *Pelican*, stuck in Manila Bay. The Japanese had captured Manila and Cavite, leaving them without access to fuel. With no chance of escape, they were relegated to an air defense role around Corregidor. A bomber raid finally sank the old bird, leaving Ingram and his crew stranded on "The Rock." Two nights later, the Japanese mounted an amphibious attack, seizing Corregidor and the three other islands guarding the entrance to Manila Bay. Contrary to Major General Jonathan M. Wainwright's orders to surrender, Ingram and his men decided not to give up. They'd seen too much Japanese brutality, the Bataan Death March was a horrible example. In desperation, Ingram and nine of his men jumped into a thirty-six-foot launch and made it all the way to Darwin, Australia, a miraculous voyage of over

1,900 miles. Without the help of navigational aids, they lived off the land by day and were under way at night.

Ingram snorted at the irony. They'd made their way through the inner islands of the Philippine archipelago, known as the Central Visayan, exited the Surigao Straits, and sailed down the east coast of Mindanao toward the Australian continent. *Surigao Straits, here I am again.* Ingram looked west; the Straits were about 1,300 miles away. He was in a desperate fix now and he was in a desperate fix the night they transited the Straits. He'd met Helen Durand, an army nurse, on Corregidor, and they'd fallen in love. She, too, escaped and made it to Nasipit, a coastal logging town in Mindanao. She and Ingram were set up to escape when a Japanese raiding party surprised them. Under a hail of enemy gunfire, Ingram was forced to push off with his men, leaving Helen behind.

But later, he'd parachuted in and rescued her. In the process, he was wounded, but the resistance grabbed them and they escaped to the verdant, rain-drenched mountains above Nasipit. Under the noses of Japanese search parties, they married, and Helen nursed him back to health. A month later, they were extracted by submarine. Ingram took comfort that Helen had been in far greater danger compared to now. She'd waited months for rescue. He had only to wait another — he checked his watch, 0346 — another four to five hours before someone plucked him from the water.

He lay back, dreaming of the island not too far away where he'd married Helen. Ingram looked down at the shivering little creature curled in his armpit, brown fur matted to his body. "Not too far, huh, Dexter?"

Dexter groaned, curled his hands under his chin, and tried to squeeze closer.

What if they don't come tomorrow? he thought. Impossible. They have to. That's all there was to it. But maybe not. *What then?* He smacked his lips and it made him realize he was thirsty.

What if no one shows up and I'm out here for days, weeks? With nothing to eat?

He looked down at the unsuspecting Dexter and shivered with the realization that he'd really have to be desperate to eat monkey meat. *How hungry must one be to do something like that? No, can't happen.* Besides, Bucky Monaghan had taken an interest in Dexter and drew a few books on natural primates. Dexter, an adult male macaque, weighed about forty pounds. Monkey meat, Monaghan explained to Kelly and Ingram, was extremely tough, which helped nullify a groundswell among the chiefs who considered barbecuing

Dexter after a particularly bad rampage. But Monaghan also discovered Dexter was most likely from the Philippines. Monkeys didn't exist in the Solomons. Ingram looked down again. "You from Mindanao, Dexter? You know the place where Helen and I were married?"

He'd be in great shape if they drifted to Mindanao. The east coast was sprinkled with villages; the natives were some of the finest people Ingram had ever met. There was one village in particular he remembered, an idyllic little hamlet in Langa Bay, just north of Port Lamont. The water was very clear that day. Ingram closed his eyes, seeing the bay's white sand glitter through a turquoise brilliance. The 51 Boat, a thirty-six-foot launch, had easily sidestepped dazzling coral heads and worked through the reef. Inside, they cruised over a long, boomerang-shaped lagoon. Hundreds of brightly colored fish, each seeming a different size, shape, and variety, darted beneath the launch as the boat headed for a rickety dock. Once moored, they found the dock empty, the locals hiding in their *nipa* huts. After Ingram and his men convinced them they weren't Japanese, Filipinos emerged in large numbers, pouring from their huts and the jungle, laughing, jumping up and down, and talking all at once. Most of the men had worked at the

Port Lamont lumber mill until it was devastated by the Japanese. Three months previously, the enemy loaded the mill equipment on a barge and hauled it off to their homeland.

The locals guided Ingram and his men though thick overgrowth to a pristine pond, a pearl-white beach at one end. About four feet deep, it was fed by a waterfall carrying fresh water down from the mountains. Ingram and his men luxuriated in the fresh water, scrubbing themselves clean and washing their clothes. Then they filled their water cans while their hosts piled wild papaya, comote, jackfruit cooked in coconut milk, and roast chicken in their launch. They even added a half bottle of Fundatore brandy. Then they convinced Ingram that the launch needed work to survive the voyage in the open ocean. Using local mahogany they worked furiously, decking over two-thirds of the 51 Boat so she would shed the waters of the Philippine Sea, particularly when digging her nose into a trough. They finished in two days. Fearing Japanese reprisals, Ingram shoved off for the Pacific and Morotai, their first landfall in the Indies.

The Filipinos were great people. He hoped to return after the war and thank them properly.

"Huh?" Ingram's head snapped up. He'd

been sleeping, for how long he didn't know. His watch read 0420. Daylight soon. As was his morning practice, he wound the watch. He looked up to see the moon had journeyed to the western horizon. The sky seemed a bit lighter, and he could distinguish more of the wreckage upon which he was adrift.

There was no wind, and except for long, undulating rollers, the water was almost flat, glassy, the stars reflecting clearly. *God, Helen, I miss you. Please let them find me today. I can still make that plane in Nouméa. It leaves in five — no — four days, now. Three days of flying and I'll be with Helen. Please, God. Let it happen. Let it happen.*

A wavelet lapped at the side of the wreckage, once again drenching his trousers. He rose quickly and looked around. Definitely getting lighter.

Dexter fell onto the cold wood and growled a couple of times, giving Ingram a dirty look.

"Good morning."

Dexter's eyes darted up to him, then looked out to sea. He gave a long screech.

"What do you want? Breakfast in bed?"

Dexter screeched again, jumped up and down, and spun in circles, looking out to sea then back at Ingram.

"Eggs Benedict? Yes, sir. I'll put a man right on it."

Dexter was staring.

"What is it?" Ingram followed his gaze.

A periscope.

"Oh, my God!"

It was unmistakable. A long, black, glistening shape cut a soft wake toward him. Perhaps a hundred yards distant, it headed right for them. The periscope's black lens was fixed on him, he knew.

Ingram stood and waved his arms. "Come on, you guys. Pull the plug or blow the toilet or whatever you do and put that wonderful, glorious tub on the surface." The wreckage wobbled, and he slipped, fell on his rump, and tumbled into the water, taking Dexter with him.

"Damn!" Sputtering and coughing, Ingram scampered back aboard the wreckage and blinked water from his eyes. Fifty yards away, the periscope arrowed past the wreckage at no more than two knots, its lens still fixed on Ingram. Just as it passed, another periscope rose, stubbier, its lens training around the compass. Meanwhile, the first periscope kept its lens fixed on Ingram.

He exaggerated his lips as he said, "It's okay, guys. No honorable sons of Nippon around here." Sweeping his arms across the sky, he yelled, "NO JAPS. ALL CLEAR."

The first periscope went down, then the

other disappeared. The Philippine Sea became calm and flat and very quiet. Dexter moaned, sat on his haunches, and put a hand over his eyes.

"Maybe you scared them, Dexter. You know it's against Navy regs to have a monkey aboard. On the *Maxwell*, we were lenient. Maybe this guy is an admiral's son or something and is striking for CNO. You know, a by-the-book type."

Minutes passed with Ingram searching the horizon, his attitude turning sour. The stars were gone and it had grown light, the ocean an iron, flat gray. And no submarine.

Dexter spun and screeched, looking directly behind.

The periscope came from the same direction where they'd originally seen it, but it was much farther away, perhaps five hundred yards this time. The other periscope rose, and both grew taller and taller. Patting Dexter's back, Ingram said, "She's coming up."

Air broke the surface in great bubbles as the submarine's bow and conning tower pierced the surface, heading right for them.

Ingram stood and waved his arms, yelling, "All right, you beautiful sewer pipe. I take back everything I said about submariners." Dexter stood beside him, jumping up and down, squealing. He did a perfect backflip and landed on his feet but skidded off the wreckage and into the water. Ingram laughed and bent to help him aboard. When he looked up again, the submarine was fully surfaced. Her diesels coughed to life, exhaust pouring from both sides in a light blue plume.

Dexter slipped again, and once again Ingram bent to pull him from the water. "Don't make a habit of this. There's hot chow and fresh water aboard that pigboat. So we can't wear out our welcome."

The submarine drew closer and was perhaps a hundred yards away now. Men were on her foredeck, one poised with a life ring. The others, he saw, had weapons. Someone leaned out of the bridge, perhaps her skipper, as he conned his ship for the pickup.

Fifty yards.

He could see their faces now. "My God."

The monkey looked up to him, a question on his face.

"Japs."

Indeed, the submarine's lines were not of the U.S. Navy's fleet type. Long and narrow, her faired conning tower had deadlights that made the submarine looked like Lucifer personified. Her configuration was one he recognized as a Japanese I-class submarine. Water lapped from her black and rust-streaked bow as she eased closer. Smoke poured from her exhaust as she backed down, stopping just ten yards away.

This guy is good, I'll give him that.

Ingram looked up to see a group of ten or so Japanese sailors leaning casually against the deck gun, looking curiously at him. A heavyset man stepped forward with a life ring and tossed. The ring sailed perfectly over Ingram's head, the line slapping the wood to his right. All he had to do was reach out and grab.

I don't have to take the line, do I? No, I don't. Someone else will find me. Americans. He folded his arms and shook his head. *So solly.*

The man who tossed the life ring called to the bridge. Quickly, a reply was barked in return.

Two men stepped to the deck's edge and raised their rifles.

"No." Ingram raised his hands. "You can't —"

They opened fire, shooting holes in the boat wreckage. Dexter squealed and jumped in the water just as rifle bullets stitched the spot where he'd been standing.

"God! Stop! No! Stop!"

The two lowered their rifles and the heavyset ring-throwing man gestured and yelled at him in Japanese. No translation was necessary. *Get up here, now!*

Ingram grabbed the line and the Japanese sailors hauled. He was soon pulled over the ballast tank, where a pair of sailors climbed down, reached under his armpits, and yanked. The men were strong, and Ingram found himself flopping on a wood-grated deck like a slippery fish trying to wiggle out of a tuna net.

Someone shouted again. The engine's tempo increased and the submarine vibrated, wake surging down her narrow hull. The skipper was losing no time getting under way. Coughing and sputtering, Ingram rose to his hands and knees to see the whaleboat wreckage, stitched with dark, ugly holes, bobbing in the submarine's wake.

He looked up to one of the sailors. "Dexter. What'd he ever do to you?"

Another guttural shout. Shadows converged overhead as men lifted him to his feet and shoved him forward toward a hatch.

"Get your damn paws off."

Someone cuffed him in the head.

"Oww!"

Another man kicked him in the butt while another pointed down the hatch. Just as he started to descend, he looked up to see a man standing high in the conning tower, his hands splayed on the bulwark, studying him. Then he tipped a hand to his forehead in a casual salute.

"Bullshit."

The man stiffened, raised his binoculars, and scanned the horizon.

FIVE

8 JUNE 1944
IJN SUBMARINE *I-57*
TWO HUNDRED MILES
SOUTHEAST OF GUAM
NORTH PACIFIC OCEAN

The temptation to go below for food, water, and sleep was overwhelming. But then it hit Ingram that the enemy lived down there. Lifting his chin to the sky, he realized freedom was fleeting, and, although alive and physically safe, he would soon be forced to enter a dark and ominous world.

Someone shoved at his back, making him stumble toward a hatch. There, a pair of hands gripped each elbow and pushed him to the lip.

"*Yare!*" one shouted.

Ingram peered down a good fifteen feet into the faces of two sailors who looked up curiously. *I'm not going down.* "Ahh!" He wrenched himself free and lunged for the submarine's starboard side. Another step and over the side — except — he tripped on a pad eye.

Japanese sailors were on him instantly.

Pain shot through his head, neck, and back as they screamed and punched and kicked him. To Ingram the beating seemed to go on for hours, but it lasted only five agonizing seconds. Then they held him down while one muttered *"Baka"* and tied a blindfold over his eyes. Ingram was yanked to his feet and pushed back toward the hatch.

Oh, God. They're going to throw me down headfirst.

Someone grabbed his belt, another his armpits, and they guided his feet onto a ladder. They shoved, with Ingram groping for a handhold. Finding a rung, he hand-over-handed his way down until he was caught by the sailors below.

Place smells like hydraulic fluid.

The blindfold had loosened on his way down the hatch and he saw a grated deck at his feet. Below deck level to his left was the gleaming bronze door of a torpedo tube. Around the tube was a myriad of pipes, valves, and gauges. On all sides, he sensed the presence of men, some of them laughing. Someone grabbed Ingram and spun him around.

"Hey, hey," he protested.

"Hai hai," they shouted back. Other hands spun him again while they laughed. Someone kicked him in the rump and their laughter grew to a full-throated roar. He

was shoved from man to man, the sailors in the compartment bellowing with glee.

Above, the hatch slammed shut. A klaxon sounded and compressed air hissed loudly. In moments, the submarine's easy rolling dampened. Then she took a slight down angle.

We're diving. Probably for the day. Too many Americans topside to run on the surface. It struck him that the U.S. Navy had an effective antisubmarine capability. In fact, he'd been part of it aboard *Maxwell.* His stomach churned as he realized he was at the other end of it now. He could end up getting depth-charged by his own countrymen. *I'll be squashed like a watermelon with my body decomposing six thousand feet down, lying next to my enemy, Japanese sailors I don't even know. Oh, God, please let me out of here.*

An order was barked. They stopped spinning Ingram and the compartment became silent. Ingram tried to stand erect but felt woozy and stumbled, his arms fluttering in space. He toppled, but a pair of hands caught him and held him straight until he regained his balance.

A voice said, "Hokay, Joe, follow me."

Ingram's hand was pushed onto a man's belt and he started walking. In moments, they were at a hatchway. He reached out, feeling the opening, surprised it was circular, unlike the oval hatchways of American submarines. And more difficult to crawl though. He heard voices ahead, but someone spoke harshly and they stopped talking. He was led through a narrow passage with curtain-covered doorways.

Berthing space.

One doorway was open, and through the bottom of his blindfold, Ingram saw a pair of bare legs bent beside what appeared to be a washbowl. The man gargled and spat. *Yes, a washbowl.*

They passed through the next hatchway and he stumbled down another narrow passageway: more berthing. Then he passed through an open area tiled in small black and white squares. Water ran in a deep sink, steam hissed, and his nostrils were tinged with the odor of garlic and fish and tea.

As before, the men were silent in the next compartment. Ominously quiet. Through the blindfold he saw many feet. Some were seated facing banks of valves and gauges. *Control room.* He felt their eyes cutting into him. *That's the enemy,* they were thinking. *An American bastard. Let's kill him and be done with it.* He was glad to go through the next hatchway where once again men lapsed into silence. In this compartment, he was surrounded by a great warmth. He knew what it was before he saw the diesel's foundations. *These damn things are big.* They weren't running, of course, but they still radiated a beckoning heat as he passed. There were just two of them, unlike the four smaller diesels found on American submarines.

He stepped into the next compartment, where he was greeted by the whirring of electric motors. *Maneuvering room.*

The man before him drew up and said, "Hokay, Joe." Placing his hands on Ingram's shoulders, he eased him onto a bench and tied his hands with a thin leather strap.

A minute or so passed with the whirring of the submarine's electric motors. People were in here, close by; how many, Ingram couldn't tell. But he cheated a bit and saw, beyond his own feet, a pair of boots opposite.

A voice came from the booted man, "We're taking off your blindfold now, Commander."

The blindfold came off. Sitting before Ingram was a European: thin, no more than 170 pounds; blond, with an unkempt beard. He wore a dark tunic bearing the Kriegsmarine emblem.

Ingram said, "You're German."

He nodded.

"You speak good English."

"And French. And Japanese. And

Spanish. My Italian is a bit rusty, though. But I do have a gift." He tilted his head. "Korvettenkapitän Martin Taubman, at your service. Do you perhaps speak German?"

"Sorry, none of the above. Are you a commander in submarines?"

Taubman gave a thin smile. "In your navy, a korvettenkapitän is a lieutenant commander. Therefore you outrank me. Yes, I am qualified in U-boats. But for now I'm just a lowly naval attaché returning to my homeland."

"How do you expect to get there?"

"My friend, you are aboard the *I-57*, a submarine of extraordinary capabilities. With her range, we could sail twice to Lorient and back."

"Lorient? France?"

"You will not make the whole trip, unfortunately. You will be dropped in Penang, where we top off with fuel. But don't worry. For you the war is over."

The submarine's bulkheads seemed to close in on Ingram, and it suddenly grew cold and clammy. His heart sank. Penang, an island off the Malay peninsula, was a major Japanese naval base. From there he would most likely go to a POW camp to work the roads in French Indochina. His heart raced as he recalled hearing the survival rate there was no higher than forty percent. Smacking his lips, he asked, "You wouldn't have a drink of water, would you?"

Taubman leaned forward and raised his eyebrows. "Are you all right, Commander?"

"Look, I'm thirsty and hungry and wet and haven't slept for at least twenty-four hours."

"In due time. What is your name, Commander?"

"Ingram."

"So. Ingram? Ingram who?"

"Ahh, jeez." Realizing he wasn't handling this well, Ingram straightened up. As he did, he noticed a man sitting to his right. It was the man who had stood in the conning tower, most likely the submarine's captain. To Ingram's left was a thickset sailor dressed in whites, a rifle with fixed bayonet in his hands, his guide. Behind the sailor was another hatchway leading to, he guessed, another berthing compartment.

Taubman said, "Go ahead, please, Commander."

Time to dance. "Ingram, Alton C., Commander, United States Navy, 638217."

"Alton?"

"That's it."

The man to Ingram's right cleared his throat.

Taubman waved a hand and said, "May

I present the captain of this ship, Commander Hajime Shimada of the Imperial Japanese Navy?"

Shimada stood and bowed with a grunt. He was taller than most Japanese, powerfully built, with a wide face and intense, glistening eyes. He wore dark green trousers and a short-sleeved white shirt with twin silver leaves pinned on the collar. Curiously, a red-checkered scarf was gathered around his neck. He leaned close to Ingram, examining him, then sat, jamming his fists on wide-spread knees.

Taubman said, "And to your left is Seaman Second Class Takano Masako, your escort for the voyage."

The man with the rifle, realizing he was being introduced, stiffened slightly and nodded, his face curious.

"Takano's responsibility is to tuck you into bed every night and make sure you are comfortable." Taubman raised thick bushy eyebrows. "Tell me, what have you heard about the invasion?"

Ingram almost jumped. Hoping they hadn't noticed, his mind flashed with what he knew of the upcoming operation in the Marianas: Guam and Saipan were to be invaded, he knew for sure, but not exactly when. Even so, they could torture what he knew out of him. He'd be forced to talk after they pulled all of his teeth or whatever they would do. Once more he felt clammy, and his forehead broke out into a sweat. "What invasion?"

"You know. The big one."

"Mr. Taubman, I have no idea what you're talking about."

"It's been on the radio. Don't you listen to it out here?"

"We don't get commercial radio if that's what you mean." That wasn't exactly true, but they'd been so busy they hadn't listened for the past few days.

"You don't know?"

Ingram gave a blank stare.

"*Festung Europa,* Mr. Ingram. American, British, and Free French forces invaded France yesterday. They landed at Normandy. And we expected it at Calais. Can you believe that?"

"Oh." Ingram hadn't heard. But France was so far away, and he was so cold and tired and hungry, he couldn't imagine the invasion's enormous ramifications.

Taubman turned to Shimada and explained something to him, using the word *Normandy.* Shimada nodded slowly. Taubman turned back to Ingram and said, "You're lucky it was calm topside. We might have missed you."

"I'm not so sure."

With a nod, Taubman continued, "Also, it was your rank that intrigued us. We were surprised to see a full commander bobbing about all by himself."

"And a defenseless monkey, which you killed. Did that make you feel good?"

Taubman shrugged. "What is your ship?" Taubman and Shimada leaned forward.

"I don't have a ship."

"No?"

"Not me. I'm a supply officer."

"A what?"

"A supply officer. You know. Food and typewriters. I keep the fleet stocked in toilet paper and rubber bands. There's a shortage back home, you know."

Shimada grunted.

Taubman interpreted. Then he asked, "Well, then. What is a supply officer doing out here, so close to Guam?"

Good question. "My plane went down. Nobody made it out except me. You see, we were blown off course in the storm yesterday and —"

The blow hit Ingram above the right kidney. The next thing he knew, he was on the deck, blinking, seeing two of everything as pain raced through his body. "God —"

Taubman leaned over and said, "Commander Shimada would like to know the name of your ship."

"Ahh, supply officer. They don't let me on ships. I —"

It was Masako, Ingram noticed, who kicked him in the side. Luckily, Ingram squirmed a bit and the blow went off course, the sole grazing his hip. Still, it hurt. And Ingram made sure he screamed loud enough to make it sound good.

"If you are a supply officer, Commander, then why were you bobbing on a piece of wreckage marked DD 525?"

Another good question. "I ran into it in the middle of the night. I — ouch!"

Masako grabbed Ingram's bindings, yanking him to his feet. Quickly, Masako patted Ingram down, finding only a pocketknife and a fountain pen in his shirt pocket. He handed the items to Shimada, who turned them over in his hands, then stuffed them in his pocket. Looking up at Ingram, he grunted at Masako. The stout sailor leaned down, yanked Ingram's watch off his wrist, and handed it to Shimada, who examined it as well.

Ingram said, "Enjoying yourself, Captain?"

Shimada must have caught the insolence in Ingram's voice because he barked at Masako. The sailor backhanded Ingram across the face. And then again.

Ingram felt a warm trickle as Masako once again was at him, this time grabbing his left hand and twisting his Naval Academy ring off. He handed it to

Shimada, who examined it for a moment. Then he passed it over to Taubman.

Taubman held the ring close to his eye and asked, "There is an inscription — "ACI — 1937." What does it mean?"

"Alton C. Ingram. I graduated from the Naval Academy in 1937."

Taubman said softly, "Beautiful. Simply beautiful." He tossed it in the air and caught it. "Good weight. Good setting; yellow gold. And a special stone, no?"

"My parents had it made especially for me as a graduation gift."

"Some gift. Semiprecious stone. A star sapphire, hmmm, cornflower blue. Two carats, I'd say."

"You know your stuff."

"Where did they get this?"

"My uncle. He's a jeweler." That was a lie. Miriam, his first wife, had given it to him. She could afford it. Rather, her father could. And that's what led to their breakup.

Taubman pursed his lips and turned the ring over while holding it close to his eye. "The cabochon. You've scratched it. You should be more careful."

"Life is rough."

Taubman shrugged, then let it go. He leaned over and spoke softly to Shimada. Shimada nodded and Taubman said, "I have been ordered to keep this safe for you. I hope you don't mind. Otherwise, there may be more dents in the setting." He smiled. "We can't have that, can we?"

"Like the dents in my watch?"

Taubman said, "Our captain will look after that. And you should know that he doesn't tolerate insolence. Commander Shimada is esteemed among submariners. He holds Japan's highest honor, the Order of the Golden Kite. Like you, he graduated from Japan's Naval Academy at Etajima. But in 1935."

Shimada spoke at length.

Taubman nodded, then said to Ingram, "Here are the captain's instructions, Commander. He will tolerate no insolence or slacking off." He held the ring up to the light and slid it onto his fourth finger. His eyebrows knit as he worked it on his finger. It was too loose. He tried every finger, finding it would fit only on his thumb. "In return for your life, you will scrub toilets and bilges, no questions asked. Your wages will be the ship's garbage. After arrival in Penang, you'll be interned with other POWs in the area. Above all, you are to keep your eyes to yourself and ask no questions. Do you agree?" Taubman took the ring off his thumb and dropped it in his pocket.

Ingram straightened and glared at Shimada.

Five dark seconds passed, the whirr of the main motors echoing through the compartment.

Suddenly, Ingram was floored by a blow to his head. It happened so fast he didn't see it coming. When his eyes opened, he saw Masako's split-toed sandals right before his eyes. It was hard to draw a breath and he realized this man was an expert in delivering pain.

Taubman said softly, "As I said, the war, for you, is over, Commander. Why wreck your body? You're going to need it."

Ingram gasped, "Okay."

Taubman reported to Shimada, who grunted. Adjusting his scarf, he stood and walked out. When he was gone, Taubman leaned over and said quietly, "You are fortunate, Commander. Don't fight it. You'll be treated well. From time to time I'll be able to sneak something to you. All right?"

Ingram still lay on his stomach, the pain barely subsiding. "Okay."

"Do you play chess?"

"What?"

"Chess. These people only play mahjongg. I want to know if you play chess."

"A little."

"Excellent."

SIX

11 JUNE 1944
U.S.S. *MORGAN J. THOMAS* (DD 543)
FOUR HUNDRED MILES EAST OF SAIPAN

Task Force 58 ran through a slate-blue sea, an eighteen-knot wind whipping foam off the wave tops. Formation course was into the wind at zero-seven-two; formation speed, fifteen knots. Task Group 58.3 steamed among the other four task groups, each a massive assembly clustered in a protective circle around carriers and battleships. Stationed at the center of Task Group 58.3 was the fleet carrier U.S.S. *Lexington* (CV 16), acting as formation guide. Surrounding the *Lexington* in a two-thousand-yard circle were the heavy carriers *Princeton* (CV 23), *Enterprise* (CV 6), and *San Jacinto* (CVL 30), the latter a light carrier built on a cruiser hull. Also in the circle were four light cruisers and Raymond Spruance's flagship, the heavy cruiser *Indianapolis* (CA 35). Screening this formation in the four-thousand-yard circle were thirteen destroyers providing antiaircraft and antisubmarine defense. Above were two four-plane groups of F6F Hellcats keeping watch beneath a 2,300-foot ceiling of swirling dirty-gray clouds.

At the head of the screen of TG 58.3, the destroyer U.S.S. *Morgan J. Thomas* (DD 543) pulled out of station number one, swinging into a one-hundred-eighty-degree turn to starboard. Long, rolling waves were not kind to the *Thomas* as she bucked, pitched, and corkscrewed through deep, narrow troughs, her helmsman fighting her all the way through the turn. Finally, she steadied on the opposite course and zipped through the fleet at a relative speed of thirty knots, the other ships seeming to slip by in an eyeblink. Quickly, she penetrated the two-thousand-yard circle, and, when nearly abreast of the *Lexington*, her officer of the deck ordered right standard rudder. This time, the *Thomas*'s helmsman patiently coaxed the ship back to formation course, and she took station a thousand yards astern of the *Lexington*.

Time after time, the *Thomas*'s bow rose high in the air only to crash into a wave, spraying a watery lather over a group of boatswain's mates on the 02 level. The boatswain's mates were setting up a high-line station on top of Mount 52 forward of the bridge superstructure. It was humid and the air temperature was seventy-two;

nobody minded getting soaked, and they kept working.

Behind the bridge superstructure, where the weather decks were dry and relatively pleasant, an officer in khaki work trousers and a short-sleeve shirt climbed the aft ladder to the *Thomas*'s signal bridge. The eagles of a full captain glinted off his garrison cap and collar points. Jammed under his left arm was a light foul-weather jacket, and he carried a worn leather briefcase in his right hand.

Eight or so sailors were gathered at the top of the ladder, smoking cigarettes and laughing. Suddenly, a chunky sailor wearing a T-shirt, khaki trousers, and a chief's hat shouted, "Make a hole, er, gangway. Good morning, Commodore." He snapped to attention and saluted. The others pressed their backs to the bulkhead and did likewise.

"Morning, Wesley." Captain Jerry Landa flashed his signature thousand-watt smile and returned the salute. "Stand easy." He eyed the men as they relaxed. The older ones had leathery faces, but two or three were young strikers, seventeen and eighteen years old, fidgeting in the proximity of a full captain.

It took a certain type to ride tin cans. Landa saw it in their faces: young, confident, strong, self-reliant, cocky. And intelligent, sometimes to the point of arrogance. They lived and worked in close quarters; tempers flared and fights occasionally broke out. But ashore, the same sailors fighting each other aboard ship would stand back-to-back defending the *Thomas*'s honor against the world, be it against other sailors, Marines, soldiers, or the enemy. Especially the enemy. Every chance they had they fought the Japanese bravely and viciously. And Landa was proud of every last one of them, these and the men in the other ships in his division.

Landa said, "Take care of things while I'm gone, Wesley."

Wesley waved a tattooed arm across the ocean. "Out here, ain't no problem, sir."

"I'm not following you."

Wesley continued, "It's ashore I can't guarantee, sir. That damned R&R on Majuro. Just ain't cutting it. Baseball, three-point-two beer, a shitty windup phonograph record player, and no broads. Lotsa gooney birds and clean white beaches, I'll grant you, but, ah, you get my drift, sir."

Landa flashed another Pepsodent smile, "Nouméa, soon, Chief, maybe even Sydney."

Wesley's eyebrows went up. "No sh— on the level, sir?"

"You bet, Chief." Landa lowered his voice and nodded to the group around him. "But do me a favor. Take care of the kids, 'cause for sure you'll see some Japs while I'm gone."

Wesley drew himself up. "No worries there, Commodore. You send us some Japs and my kids will give 'em the old one, two, three."

"Promise?"

"Short rhumba, long cuba libre." Wesley winked. "Have a good trip, sir."

A signalman on the port bridge wing yelled, "Romeo, close up." He'd been watching the *Lexington*'s signal bridge through powerful pedestal-mounted binoculars. The carrier had raised an R flag, a yellow cross on a red field, to the top of her hoist, meaning, "I'm ready to receive you alongside." By day flag hoists and by night flashing light signals were the preferred method of communicating, lest the enemy eavesdrop on radio transmissions.

Landa edged around the pilothouse bulkhead and spotted Commander Howard Endicott, the *Thomas*'s commanding officer, standing high on a pedestal at the port bridge-wing conning station. Redheaded, with a crew cut, Endicott weighed just 155 pounds and was dressed in working khakis, a garrison cap, and dark-brown aviator's glasses. He acknowledged Landa with a nod, then leaned toward the pilothouse and said, "This is the captain. I have the conn." With a look at Wesley, he jabbed a thumb in the air.

Wesley bellowed to a young signalman striker, "Two-block Romeo!" Furiously, the sailor hauled the flag from the dip, or midpoint position, all the way to the top of the hoist. It signaled to the carrier, "I am commencing my approach alongside."

Sometimes Wesley really laid it on. One could have heard him from the midst of a Rocky Mountain thunderstorm fifteen miles away.

Endicott called into the pilothouse, "Steady on course zero-seven-two. All engines ahead full. Indicate two-five-zero turns for twenty-five knots." The *Thomas*'s uptakes whined, feeding air to her four Babcock & Wilcox boilers. Her screws dug in and soon she was up to speed, making a rapid approach to the *Lex*. The increasing wind rippled Endicott's shirt. He whipped off his garrison cap and stuffed it into his back pocket as Landa stepped quietly next to him.

The sheer power of the *Thomas*'s 60,000 shaft horsepower vibrated beneath Landa's feet. These destroyers were the ultimate racing machine. Given the right talent, one could do anything with them. And Landa knew Endicott was doing what hotshot destroyer skippers loved to do: stand tall, let his boys know he was captain of the U.S.S.

Morgan J. Thomas, and have fun with his ship.

Right now he was attempting a one-bell landing, which meant maneuvering the ship exactly alongside the carrier at a formation speed of fifteen knots with just one engine order, that is, one bell. If Endicott reduced the *Thomas*'s speed to the carrier's speed at the exact moment, no other engine orders would be necessary. The *Thomas* would settle to a position 150 feet alongside the *Lexington* and remain there as if parked. With the wind, waves, carrier wake, it was a tricky call. The reward for winning was nothing more than a hero's welcome and bragging rights at the officers club. For a botched approach, maybe a career. Many skippers were more careful and elected to do the maneuver in precise increments. That took time. And they became nervous thinking about the brass on the carrier's flying bridge looking down at the greenhorn tin can driver, maybe shaking their heads.

As she worked up to speed, the *Thomas*'s bow heaved up, only to crash down into a wave. Wind whistled stridently as she peaked the waves, her bow once more digging deep into troughs, throwing a foamy mist over the bridge. Landa glanced at Endicott, remembering his own hot-rod approaches. Landa had an uncanny seaman's eye. One-bell landings became his signature. Even though he appreciated the eagles on his collar, he missed like hell not having his own tin can to play with.

Endicott looked down at Landa, "Going to miss you, Jerry."

"I'll bet." Landa was going to miss them, too. Months ago, he'd filled out a leave chit and it had been approved. That turned out to be a mistake. Now he would miss the *big* show. They had ordered someone to take his place while he was gone. Captain Ralph Sorenson needed screen commanding experience, and this would do nicely, they said. Landa had protested several times, but they wouldn't let him out of it. The die was cast.

Landa squinted. The *Lexington*'s 33,000 tons grew large, and his seaman's eye told him the range was down to about five-hundred yards. She was painted a smudgy dark gray, and from this angle she reminded Landa of a seagoing tenement house. A rendering from his Brooklyn beginnings, he supposed. And if the wind caught you just right, the damn thing could smell like a tenement house as she spewed stack gas in her wake.

Nonchalantly, Endicott glanced at the compass card, assuring himself the helmsman was on the right course. "I can't believe it," he said.

"Believe what?"

Four hundred yards.

"Boom Boom Landa getting engaged."

Landa looked up and grinned. "I'm not married yet."

"Yeah, but she's way too classy for you, Jerry. I mean, my God, Laura West, star of stage, screen, and radio, tying the knot with Boom Boom Landa." Endicott returned the smile.

Two hundred yards.

Many times, Landa had had the same thought. In one sense, he'd been halfway expecting a Dear John letter from Laura, calling the whole thing off. "Animal magnetism," he replied.

Endicott snorted at that and began concentrating. The carrier loomed massively along their port side. Men peered down from her gun tubs. On the flight deck above, sun glinted off canopies of tightly packed Helldivers, Avengers, and Hellcats. Above that, bareheaded khaki-clad figures braced a foot on the rail, looking down from the flag fly-bridge. "You giving her a diamond ring?"

"Well, I have this deal on —"

Endicott barked, "All engines ahead standard. Make 150 revolutions for fifteen knots." He stooped to look in the pilothouse, making sure the lee helmsman executed the order promptly.

Landa watched the *Lexington*. Endicott

had reduced speed just as the *Thomas*'s bow crossed an imaginary perpendicular extending from the carrier's fantail. Next came an anxious twenty seconds to see if it worked. Soon it was evident that she would glide smoothly into place. Course zero-seven-two, speed fifteen knots, and just 150 feet on the starboard side of the U.S.S. *Lexington*.

Good call.

Behind aviator's glasses, Endicott's eyes crinkled for just a moment.

Landa smiled to himself. *Endicott, you lucky bastard.* And what an actor. Talking casually to his boss while conning his ship to a hero approach alongside the flagship of Task Force 58, carrying Vice Admiral Marc A. Mitscher. Landa, who thought he had cornered the flamboyance market, had to give it to Endicott. His ship rated well, his men loved him, and he was one of the squadron darlings. And a good team player, too. That's why Landa had chosen the *Thomas* as his division flagship.

The *Lexington*'s flight deck towered over them, aircraft wings and tail empennages protruding over the side. An engine revved up, and an F6F Hellcat right above them unfolded its wings and locked them into place. They couldn't see the canopy, but they heard the engine thundering for a full ten seconds. Then it rolled forward and lunged off the carrier's bow.

"Jeez." Landa whipped off his hat as he watched the Hellcat claw for altitude. Carrying a drop tank, she sank to within twenty feet of the water, flying in surface effect. But the Grumman fighter soon sucked in her landing gear, gained speed, and rose higher, curving up to the left and out of sight.

Endicott stepped off his perch shaking his head. "There are times when zoomies earn their flight pay."

A loudspeaker on the carrier clicked and a deep voice resonated, "On the *Thomas*, stand by for shot line."

A moment later, a bosun's mate on the carrier slowly swung a weighted ball, called a monkey fist, around his head. After about five complete circles, he let it go with a graceful heave. The monkey fist sailed across the chasm between the ships, landing on the *Thomas*'s 02 deck just forward of the bridge. One of the *Thomas*'s sailors scrambled to grab it. Soon they were pulling in the messenger lines attached to larger lines that would haul over the high-line gear.

Something drew Landa's and Endicott's attention to the carrier's flag bridge towering above them. Thin, and wearing a long-billed ball cap, Vice Admiral Marc Mitscher looked down at them and waved.

Landa and Endicott saluted. Landa whispered from the corner of his mouth, "You made points, Howard."

"Anything for the Old Man."

Mitscher returned the salute and clasped both hands over his head, a broad smile on his face. On Mitscher's left stood his chief of staff, Captain Arleigh "Thirty-one Knot" Burke, hero of Destroyer Squadron 23 and the Battle of Cape St. George. But today Burke didn't look like a hero; his countenance was hard and cold.

Endicott said, "Jeez, I'd forgotten Burke was aboard." He waved up to him, but Burke remained motionless.

Landa said, "You're uncovered, Mister."

Endicott whipped his garrison cap from his back pocket and adjusted it in place. "Aw, come on, Jerry. You don't think he'd ding me just 'cause I didn't have a cap on."

Landa looked over the side to see if the high line was ready. An empty bosun's chair rose off the carrier's deck and bounced and jinked its way to the *Thomas*. "I'd say you'll only get ten years in Leavenworth." Landa held out a hand. "Time for me to head down there. Thanks for the ride, Howard. You run a good squadron flag. Please take care of Ralph Sorenson. He's a good man."

Endicott took Landa's hand. "You can

bet on it, Jerry. And when you come back, we'll have rigged a bar in your cabin. Ladies, too. All you want."

Landa gave a dazzling white smile. "Thanks, but I've got to be a good boy from now on in. I'm destined to be a married man." He turned to head for the 02 level.

"Jerry?"

"Yep."

"You think they have any dope on Todd over there?"

A shadow crossed Landa's face. He'd had a hard time talking about Ingram. "Don't know. You'd think they would have told us if they found something."

Endicott's shoulders slumped a bit.

"The *Maxwell* is due in Nouméa tomorrow. I plan to stop by and look her over before I head for home."

"Say hello to everyone."

Landa drew up and saluted. "Permission to leave the ship, sir?"

"Granted."

An ensign escorted Landa to the 02 level forward, where they'd landed the bosun's chair. It was painted white and was tasseled with fancywork: a flagship's bosun's chair. His gear bag waited alongside, and the bosun's mates said they'd ship it over on the next run.

The *Thomas* nosed into a wave,

drenching Landa while he donned a life preserver. Water ran down his face and dripped off his nose as he sat in the cagelike contraption. A sailor cinched a series of buckles, which reminded Landa of a condemned man strapped in the electric chair. Someone patted him on the shoulder. "Have a good trip, sir. Stay dry."

"I'll try." He looked to see who spoke, but a bosun bellowed an unintelligible order. Suddenly, the chair was jerked up and rode high in the air, bouncing and swaying its way back to the *Lexington*. Landa had done this many times, and against the caution of others, he looked down, fascinated with the waters racing between the ships. It was a classic example of the Bernoulli effect: a fluid compressed into a tight area, water flowed at a dizzying pace between the ships. It generated a green-white turbulence that looked like the gates of hell without the fire. If one were dunked in there, his chances of survival would not be good. It made Landa wonder why he wore the damned life preserver. Down in that maelstrom, he'd be chopped to pieces by one of the ship's churning screws.

It hit Landa that this was the area where the *Maxwell* had been attacked. He imagined he could see through the creamy vortices and into the ocean depths. *Hi, Todd.*

This is as close as I can get. Thanks for everything. I'll always remember you.

Something made him look up. Most of the flag officers had left their fly-bridge, the show being over for the time being. But Arleigh Burke remained, hands widely braced on the bulwark, his cold blue eyes staring down at him.

Landa smiled.

Burke stared.

"Jeez, what have I done now?"

SEVEN

11 JUNE 1944
U.S.S. *LEXINGTON* CV 16
FOUR HUNDRED MILES EAST OF SAIPAN

There were stories of prankish bosuns who allowed the high line to droop just a bit, with hopes of giving the brass in the chair a butt wash. But the bosuns aboard the *Thomas* worked the high line with care, giving Landa a dry ride. Outhaul and inhaul were smoothly coordinated, and Landa soon looked down on a group of burly sailors on the *Lexington*'s hangar deck. The high line was eased, and Landa boarded the carrier as if he were stepping off an elevator.

A bosun helped him unbuckle, and he rose from the chair and saluted the flag. A dark, curly-haired lieutenant (j.g.) walked up, a long, shiny brass telescope tucked under his arm. His name tag said SYMMONS.

Landa saluted. "Permission to come aboard, sir?"

Returning the salute, the jaygee said, "Permission granted, Commodore. Welcome to the *Lexington.*"

A chunky man wearing garrison cap, life vest, and captain's eagles walked up and extended his hand. "How goes it, Jerry? We all set over there?" He nodded to the *Thomas*, riding smoothly alongside.

Landa shook hands with Captain Ralph Sorenson, his relief. He followed Sorenson to the bosun's chair and said as they began strapping him in, "As best as it can be, Ralph. Full mutiny in progress, half the crew down with the clap, and the ship has only ten percent fuel oil remaining. The rest of your tin cans out there only have five percent."

Sorenson grinned, as two sailors tightened buckles. "Situation normal." He whipped off his cap and stuffed it in his shirt. "How about Endicott?"

"Cut into little pieces and pitched over the side days ago."

"I get the picture." Someone handed Sorenson a briefcase and a large box. Clutching them to his chest, he saluted Symmons. "Permission to leave the ship, sir?"

"Granted," said Symmons.

Landa leaned close. "They're good boys, Ralph. All of 'em."

Sorenson knocked Landa's arm with a fist. "I'll take care of 'em for you, Jerry. And thanks for giving me the chance to do this. I know you could have made a lot more noise."

Landa sighed. "I tried, but those guys are cold as a whore's heart. 'No dice,' they said."

"I'm sorry." Sorenson extended a hand.

They shook. "You'll do fine. Have fun. In the meantime, stay dry."

"They better not."

Landa turned and nodded to the bosun's mates. In a moment, the chair rose in the air, and Sorenson was on his way to the *Thomas*.

Symmons stepped up and said, "I'm supposed to tell you that Captain Burke requests your presence when convenient."

"When convenient." That means get your butt up to flag plot now, Landa. "How do I get up there, Mr. Symmons?"

The jaygee nodded to a Marine corporal wearing a class B uniform. He had a lot of ribbons, Landa noticed. Many with battle stars. Symmons said, "He'll take you up."

"Very well." Landa watched Sorenson land on the 02 level of the *Thomas*. It looked as if he'd had a good ride also. They quickly had him out of the chair, packed in Landa's duffle bag, and sent it to the *Lexington*. Soon the chair was landed and detached. Hooked in its place was a small cargo net filled with boxes carrying ice cream and 16-millimeter movie reel cases.

"Nice of the admiral to do that," said Landa.

Symmons nodded, "You bet, Commodore. The admiral likes to take care of his boys." He nodded to the duffle. "We'll send it up."

"Thanks." Landa took a few steps inboard, finding himself in the midst of a vast hangar deck. He gazed for three hundred feet in either direction on an impossible jumble of Plexiglas, fuselages, and propellers belonging to Hellcats, Avengers, and Helldivers. Like model airplanes, two obsolete SBD Dauntlesses hung from the overheard in a far corner, looking forlorn and abandoned, their landing gear tucked in.

Blue-gray folded wings jutted everywhere. Engine cowlings and .50-caliber machine guns were scattered on the deck. Men scrambled about the airplanes cursing and shouting at one another. The whine of vent and exhaust blowers competed with the sounds of tools clanking and pneumatic wrenches knocking off nuts, while expediters pushed parts-laden carts about, occasionally tossing a box or sack to waiting hands. Landa took a deep breath, feeling the power and energy of the men around him. He always enjoyed the smell of hydraulic oil. And here it mixed with a sharper odor of paint as an airman sprayed non-spec blue on a TBF wing panel just ten feet away.

Beneath his feet surged the engineering plant of this 33,000-ton ship, where eight Babcock & Wilcox boilers generated 850-degree superheated steam that delivered 150,000 horsepower to four screws, giving the *Lexington* a speed of thirty-three knots. But it was the 872-foot-long *Essex*-class aircraft load-out that amazed Landa: thirty-six F6F Hellcat fighters, thirty-seven SB2C Helldiver dive-bombers, and eighteen TBF torpedo bombers. That, plus 230,000 gallons of 100-octane aviation fuel, parts, ammunition, food, accommodations, and 2,500 men, made it all work.

Landa shook his head. There were thirteen *Essex*-class carriers just like this already commissioned; another eleven *Essex*-class carriers were on the building ways. Added to them were nine more light carriers built on cruiser hulls, eighty-nine escort carriers, many of which had joined the fleet, and the veteran fleet carriers *Enterprise* and *Saratoga*. Then there were the three new *Midway*-class ships now on the ways at 55,000 tons each, almost twice the size of this ship.

Landa shook his head slowly. *How could the Japs be so stupid?*

The Marine stepped alongside and coughed politely.

Landa waved a hand at the airplanes. "I don't get to see this very often. Amazing."

"Yes, suh."

"Where you from, Corporal?"

"Alabama, suh."

"That's great. Lead the way, Corporal."

"Suh." The Marine nimbly led Landa up five companionways before he slowed. Instead of dull, bare metal bulkheads and hatches, this passageway was painted a brilliant white. Brass gleamed everywhere; green curtains and burled walnut decorated the doorways, and the decks were covered with shiny green linoleum.

Flag country. Landa's father had been a stevedore, his own upbringing humble. For years, he'd felt out of place around senior officers, especially admirals. Even now, a momentary flash of nervousness coursed though him.

The Marine walked to a hatch that gave onto a platform and nodded. "Captain Burke's out there, Commodore. I'll go pick up your gear." He walked off.

"Thanks." Landa stepped to the hatch, seeing just one man: Captain Arleigh Burke. He was of average height, weighed about 180 pounds, wore no hat, and stood at the railing, his hands still braced far apart.

Hasn't moved. Landa stepped onto the platform and walked up to him. "Afternoon, Arleigh."

Through and through, Burke was one hundred percent Swedish stock, and his blond curly hair and pale blue eyes stood in evidence.

"Landa." Burke gave him a quick glance, then went back to watching the *Thomas*. They'd met once before at a Seventh Fleet conference in Nouméa. At the time Captain Arleigh Burke was in his heyday as commodore of Destroyer Squadron 23, infamously known as the "Little Beavers." Admiral William F. Halsey Jr. had hung the Navy Cross on him after his amazing victory at the Battle of Cape St. George. Even more amazing was Burke's surprise appointment as chief of staff to Mitscher, commander of Task Force 58, the main aircraft carrier striking force in the Pacific. Burke's loud protests that he was just a surface officer, not an Airedale, went unanswered. Glumly, he'd reported to an equally astonished Mitscher, who was barely civil to Burke. But both were street fighters. They developed a mutual admiration and eventually formed an unbeatable team. The frail Mitscher did all the thinking, then went back to reading seedy detective novels (Landa admired Mitscher for that) while Burke rounded up the staff and put his plans into action.

So I'm "Landa" to him. Both held the

same rank, but here, it seemed, Burke held all the cards.

"I miss tin cans," Burke said, studying the *Thomas*. She had just about completed her breakaway.

"Yep."

The bosuns on the *Thomas*'s 02 level were paying back line to the *Lexington*. Landa smiled inwardly. He looked down and saw Sorenson had joined Endicott on the bridge. Both looked up and waved.

Landa waved back. Burke's hands remained on the railing.

"Endicott's a good man," Landa said.

"One of the best. So's Sorenson."

"Mmmmmm."

The *Thomas*'s uptakes squealed like a banshee as air was rammed into her boilers. Ever the showman, Endicott had cranked up a flank bell for her sprint to the number-one position at the head of the screen.

Lucky bastard. He really wants to make this look good.

Water churned under the destroyer's screw guards as her propellers revved up. Her pitching became more pronounced and she eased forward, beginning a shallow turn to starboard. The bosuns had cleared the gear off the forward weather decks. And not too soon, for her bow began to dig deep. White water cascaded over the

Thomas's forward five-inch gun mounts and she gained speed, water boiling in her wake. Soon, her fantail drew ahead of the *Lexington*'s bow, waves smacking at the destroyer amidships, white water tumbling over her bulwarks and onto the main decks, where it sluiced aft to spill from the gunnels and back into the sea.

Burke sighed. Waving a palm at a hatch, he said, "Shall we?"

Landa followed Burke into a compartment having a long table perhaps twenty feet in length. It was covered in green baize, with ashtrays and half-empty coffee cups scattered about. *Flag wardroom.*

Burke waved a palm at a chair. "Coffee?"

Landa sat. "Please."

Burke poured and was returning with two cups when something clicked off to Landa's right. He turned and saw a door with a plaque bearing three stars. Mitscher walked through and was headed for the port side when he saw Landa and drew up. "Welcome aboard, Jerry."

"Afternoon, Admiral." Landa shot to his feet.

Mitscher couldn't have weighed more than 125 pounds. With a craggy, weather-beaten face, thin lips, receding hair, and a sharp nose, he looked more like an undertaker than the commander of Task Force

58. The only adornment on his crumpled uniform was the three stars of a vice admiral at his collar points and aviator's wings pinned over the left breast pocket. Mitscher nodded to Burke. "I'd like to watch the CAP go, and then we're scheduled to get together in . . ." He looked at his watch.

"Five minutes," said Burke.

"Okay. Elliott, Duke, and Tom notified?"

"Yes, sir. Should be on their way up."

Mitscher's eyes quickly shifted to Landa. "I think we're in for a lot of Japs."

"That's what I hear, too, Admiral. I just wish I could be in on it," said Landa.

Mitscher grimaced. Burke slapped his hands over his eyes, exhaling loudly.

Shit, what have I done?

Mitscher's lips twisted into a grin. "Aren't you the one they call Boom Boom?"

Landa, who hated the name, tried to paste on a benign grimace. "In my younger days, sir."

Mitscher's expression matched Landa's. "I see. And it looks like nobody told you what's going on around here." Mitscher drew a deep breath. "I promised Ralph Sorenson some screen commanding time, which will qualify him for next billet as a type-commander. There's no doubt you're more qualified, but he needs the experience."

"But . . . I . . ." sputtered Landa.

Mitscher held up a hand. "But then I have good old Arleigh Burke to back up Sorenson, in case he screws up. So everything's going to be all right." He slapped Burke on the back. "Sit, please, Jerry."

Burke groaned.

Landa sat.

Mitscher reached for Landa's hand and shook it. "Don't worry, Jerry. You'll see plenty of Japs before this is all over." He checked his watch and threw a glance at Burke. "You told him yet?"

"Just about to."

"Very well. Good seeing you, Jerry. Come back to us rested and fit. We need you." Mitscher slapped on a long-billed ball cap and walked toward the door. Then he turned. "Sorry to hear about the *Fredericks*. How many survivors did she have?" The *Fredericks* was one of two destroyers sent out to look for Ingram. "A hundred five, Admiral," replied Landa.

Mitscher's mouth opened and closed. Finally, he managed, "Is that all?"

"Took a shot down the throat doing eighteen knots. Bow blew off, the forward magazine went, and her screws literally drove her under."

"My God. Those poor boys."

"Yes, sir."

Five seconds passed. "Well, then, goodbye." Mitscher walked out.

The only sound was an occasional aircraft engine and the whine of the wardroom exhaust blowers. Burke took a long sip of coffee and exhaled.

"What are you supposed to tell me, Arleigh?"

Burke fixed Landa with a stare. "Always the impatient one, aren't you."

Now it was Landa's time to stare.

Burke said, "You and I come from different molds, Jerry."

"If that means I didn't go to the trade school, I suppose you're right." Burke was a Naval Academy graduate; Landa was not.

Burke's nostrils flared for just moment, then he sighed. "I'm sorry. Guess I had that coming."

"It's okay. I thought I was here to jump on a TBF and go home. What's up?"

"You are going to jump on a TBF that leaves in about" — he checked his watch — "twenty minutes. But we would like to give you a little job while you're home."

Aw, come on. I'm getting engaged. "What job?"

"You ever heard of Magic?" Burke folded his hands.

Landa had vaguely heard of Magic, but this sounded like he'd better play dumb. "Don't think so."

"In a nutshell, it's a code-breaking effort from our cryptology guys in Hawaii and Washington. Magic is top secret, Jerry. What it does is let us read the Japs' mail. I mean everything. Their fleet codes, dispositions, op-orders, everything."

"Jesus."

"Access to Magic is granted only on a need-to-know basis. And the admiral had you cleared."

Landa felt a rush of blood to his head. Having stepped away from destroyers, he was out of his element. "What the hell for?"

"Drink." Burke nodded to Landa's coffee, untouched.

Landa raised the cup and took a sip. "Ahh, that's good stuff."

"Now sign." Burke produced a folder of War Department documents. "Four places, there, there, and two more, here." He handed over a Parker 51 pen.

Landa turned the pen over in his hand. "Nice."

"Gold plated. Cost me thirty bucks."

Landa began signing. "Do I get copies?"

"Absolutely not. And if you do any blabbing, we get to tie you to a stake and shoot you."

Landa looked up to see Burke smile for the first time. They stared at each other for five long seconds. Finally, Landa signed the last document and shoved papers and pen back.

"Okay." Burke jogged the papers and put them into a folder. Then he looked up and nailed Landa with a stare. "Todd Ingram is alive."

Landa jumped in his chair, spilling his coffee. "Shit. What? Arleigh, don't do that to me."

"Serious. Our boys in OP-20-G — that's the code-breaking unit in Hawaii — intercepted a message from a Jap sub. The *I-57* has him. Sounds like Ingram was in the water all night and they picked him up the next morning."

"Good God."

"What do you think about that, Boom Boom?"

Now it was Landa's turn to shoot a glance. He thought he'd made the point with Mitscher. "It's really great news. Does his crew know?"

"Absolutely not."

"What about —"

A door opened. Mitscher walked through, gave Burke a look, and then walked into his room, the door clicking softly.

"That means I gotta go." Burke waved a palm at Landa. "Listen up, will you?"

"Right."

"Apparently, the *I-57* is en route to

France. Lorient, I believe. It's a technical exchange mission with the Krauts. They do those things from time to time."

"Okay."

"We've decided we want Ingram to live. Hell, he's one of our best destroyer skippers."

"You bet."

"By the time the *I-57* gets to France, Lorient should be pretty well surrounded by our forces. So I'd say Ingram has a reasonable chance of repatriation after the sub reaches those U-boat pens."

"Where do I come in?"

Two commanders and a lieutenant (j.g.) filed in. Wordlessly, they poured coffee then headed for Mitscher's quarters. One of them looked at Burke.

"Two minutes," said Burke.

They disappeared into the compartment and Burke continued. "There's a carrier group, headed up by the U.S.S. *Purvis Bay*, stationed in the South Atlantic. They've been apprised of the *I-57*'s itinerary. The *Purvis Bay* is on station and is ready to jump anybody that crosses her path, including the *I-57*. And let me tell you, Jerry, the *Purvis Bay* has a good record."

Landa rasped, "And there goes Todd."

"There goes Todd, the *I-57*, and the German milch cow that's going out there to refuel her." A milch cow was a German submarine fitted with large fuel tanks to refuel other U-boats at sea.

"What can we do?"

Burke stroked his chin. "We'd like to finesse it. Save the *I-57* and sink the milch cow."

"How?"

"With your destroyer and ASW experience we figure you're the one to coordinate it."

Landa's fists balled. "You're sending me to the Atlantic?"

Burke waved him off. "Keep your pants on, Jerry. You do all this from San Francisco."

"Do what?"

"You know Lieutenant Commander Oliver Toliver?"

"Sure, he was Todd's best man at his wedding. Last I heard, Ollie was gunnery liaison to the Twelfth Naval District there."

"Toliver has been transferred to the San Francisco office of OP-20-G. He's now the crypto expert; you're the destroyer-submarine killer group expert."

Mitscher's door opened. A voice drifted out: "Captain?"

Burke's eyes jumped to the doorway. "Gotta go, Jerry." He shoved over another file folder. "Here're your orders. You get to take your leave, but you'll be TAD to OP-20-G in San Francisco to coordinate. We want you to save the *I-57* but sink the milch cow. Understand?"

"I think so."

"Yes or no?" Burke fixed him with a stare.

"Yes. Of course."

"Then, please sign."

Landa held out his hand. Burke produced his Parker 51.

"Captain?" Mitscher's voice resonated from the next room.

Burke turned pale. "Keep those. Those are your travel orders."

Landa quickly signed and pushed the papers back.

Burke held our his hand. "Okay. The TBF will fly you to Majuro. Then it's a PBM for Espiritu and priority-travel home. And congratulations on your engagement. You'll have plenty of time to fly back and forth."

"Thanks."

Burke extended a hand. "Sorry I'm in such a damned hurry. No hard feelings?"

Hell, yes, you dope. "Not at all."

"Have a good trip." They shook. Burke gathered his papers and strode quickly into the next room.

The door clicked shut and Landa was alone. He looked around for a moment.

Todd alive. My God, oh God. And I can't tell anyone. Well, maybe Helen. But she'll have to sweat it that he'll be in a POW camp for the rest of the war.

Dammit! How the hell am I going to bring this off?

He realized he still had Burke's pen. He leaned over and scribbled a note: *Dear Arleigh, thanks for the pen. Jerry*

Outside, he was met by the Marine. "Your plane is ready, sir. I put your gear aboard myself."

"Thanks. Lead the way."

It was noisy, and the wind blew on the flight deck. When they reached the TBF, Landa had to shout at the Marine to be heard. "When you going off duty?"

The corporal glanced at his watch. "Right now, sir. I'm done until the midwatch."

"Do me a favor?"

"Yes, sir."

Landa pulled out the Parker 51 and handed it over. "Please give this to Captain Burke next time you go on watch. Okay?"

The corporal pocketed the pen. "Yes, sir. Will do. Have a good trip." He backed away.

The deck officer introduced Landa to a freckle-faced pilot who showed Landa a hatch beneath the TBF's rear gun turret.

"Beer hop?" Landa asked, scrambling in.

"I wish, Captain. Right now, it's just guard mail and movies." He slammed the hatch. But from the look on the pilot's face, it was obvious he couldn't tell why Landa grinned from ear to ear.

EIGHT

12 JUNE 1944
IJN SUBMARINE *I-57*
PHILIPPINE SEA

Ingram had to admit Masako had devised a beautiful solution to keep him guarded during the night. It enabled Masako to stay in his own bunk in the after berthing compartment for a full night's sleep. He'd parked Ingram in the maneuvering room, the next compartment forward, his leg cuffed to a pipe under the workbench. Lying or sitting on an old blanket, he could either sleep or watch the motormen spin rheostats and throw enormous levers that fed electricity to the submarine's main motors.

Most of the time he slept, unless the submarine dived or surfaced. That's when things became intense in the maneuvering room.

One night the diving klaxon went off at around 0100, an unusual time. He later heard a destroyer had caught them on the surface, a cold, brilliant searchlight stabbing at the *I-57*'s conning tower. Soon after that, five-inch guns opened up, trying to catch her in a deadly bracket, shells pummeling the water to port and starboard. Shimada jabbed the alarm and, with his lookouts, scrambled down the conning tower hatch as the *I-57* clawed for the safety of the depths. With her ballast tanks belching great clouds of vapor, it took an agonizing 102 seconds to get the ponderous I-boat beneath the surface.

But all Ingram saw was the motormen. And that was enough. They prattled at one another in high-pitched, strident tones. Worse, their eyes darted wildly, and Ingram knew they were scared. And the fear was contagious, especially when he heard the destroyers moving closer. There were at least two.

One began its run in. *Thrum, thrum, thrum, thrum.* Right over the top it went and he thought he heard a splash —

Wham! Wham! Wham! Wham! Wham! The first explosion was close aboard, and, like an animal, Ingram curled into the fetal position under the workbench, his hands over his ears. Gritting his teeth, he yelped involuntarily each time a depth charge went off.

The destroyers supported each other. One held contact while the other made a run-in, dropping depth charges.

Again they dropped, and again Ingram was thrust into a world of screeching, compressing sound. The bulkhead next to him flexed inward, throwing him into the midship passageway as if he'd been kicked by an elephant. Valves burst; the motormen shrieked as a thick stream of water shot into the maneuvering room. The shrill sound of the water made it impossible to think, let alone speak.

While the motormen frantically worked on whatever had burst, Ingram cried out loud, "Oh God, I pray thee, please protect my wife and child."

The forward hatch flew open and Masako rushed in. Bending down, he unlocked Ingram's leg cuff and gestured frantically.

"You want me forward?"

"Ike, ike." Masako waved a hand at the forward hatch.

Ingram rose slowly. "Okay, but I don't —"

Masako whipped off his cap and rapped it across Ingram's butt. *"Ike!"*

"Right." Ingram quickly walked for the hatch, ducked through, and headed forward at Masako's urging. Soon they were in the control room and Ingram saw why. It was ankle deep in water. Water cascaded from a broken line overhead, where three men were gathered on a stepladder frantically wielding wrenches. A bucket brigade was formed below them to transfer the water forward to where, Ingram supposed, the pumping was more efficient. All this, while officers and men of the control room watch sat or stood at their stations, nervously looking around, waiting for the next order. At the periscope was Shimada, on his haunches, ready to raise it from its well. Opposite him was Lieutenant Commander Shigeru Kato, the *I-57*'s executive officer, notepad in hand, watching Shimada's every move.

Across the control room was Martin Taubman, wearing just trousers and a T-shirt. Sweat ran down his face in rivulets and his eyes darted as men around him spun valves and flipped switches. He lurched into a corner as a valve failed. A quarter-inch jet of water shrieked past his head. Men shoved him aside, shouting, demanding tools. The lighting system blinked on and off as men at the main fuse panel threw enormous knife switches. Two feet from Ingram, Taubman looked up from the deck, his eyes wide, jumping in their sockets.

Masako grabbed Ingram by the collar and dragged him to the forward part of the control room to join a bucket brigade. Soon, a full bucket was in Ingram's hand and he passed it along, water slopping over the edges.

"Ready to meet your maker?" Taubman

now stood next to Ingram, bucket in hand.

"Trying to save your skin, huh, Martin? Don't work too hard. I'd hate to see you get calluses."

"I'm afraid we're all working for the same cause at the moment," said Taubman. He passed another bucket and asked, "Don't you find it ironic that you're about to be killed by one of your own ships? You probably know some of the men up there."

"Probably do. And it's fine with me if it makes you guys rot in hell."

Taubman's nostrils flared. "You don't really mean that."

"I'm as scared of dying as you are, Fritz. But I guess this is as good a time as any."

The sonar officer held a hand in the air and whipped off his earphones. Officers and men dropped to the deck as a destroyer approached: *thrum, thrum, thrum, thrum, thrum.*

Shimada dropped to his haunches and wrapped his hands around a stanchion, his knuckles white. Ingram did the same.

Wham, wham, wham, wham, wham. Lights flashed; men screamed; circuit breakers arced; the odor of vomit drifted . . . the screws fading in the distance.

Taubman's eyes were a picture of abject terror. For sure, Ingram knew he looked the same. But miraculously the control room quieted, and somehow order was restored. Incredibly, Shimada again stood at his periscope. Ingram didn't realize they had risen to periscope depth.

Speaking rapidly, Shimada barked out a series of commands.

"What is he doing?" asked Ingram.

"Shhh," said Taubman, kneeling. Ingram kneeled beside him. "It's called 'down the throat,' something we learned from your submarine colleagues, now guests of the government of Japan."

A shudder ran through Ingram. What Taubman was telling him was that captured American submariners had talked under torture. "Bullshit."

"You're too naive, Mr. Ingram," said Taubman. "You're about to witness a truly amazing feat, one in which Captain Shimada is extraordinarily experienced. One which earned him the Golden Kite."

Ingram snorted, "This, I gotta see." Then it hit him that he could well be dead in the next minute or so. "Why don't we just, you know, amscray. Go deep or something?"

"Watch. He's reversing course, backing on the starboard engine, going full ahead on the port," whispered Taubman.

Ingram looked up to find a magnetic course repeater. It was true. The heading was changing rapidly, the helmsman calling out course changes. In turn, Shimada carefully worked his periscope handles while Kato cranked a handle on a bulkhead-mounted console.

In the distance, Ingram heard the *thrum, thrum, thrum* of another destroyer. "This doesn't look too good," said Ingram, his stomach churning.

Kato turned to Ingram with an iron stare.

"Sorry," he whispered.

The submarine's course had reversed. The *I-57* was actually heading for the destroyer. He'd heard of the down-the-throat technique in the American submarine fleet. Incredibly, he now watched it play out. He would have shouted if he thought it would do any good. Fellow sailors, destroyermen up there, were about to die. Frantically, he looked about for a lever to pull, something to disrupt the firing solution.

Too late. Shimada barked, *"Dai ikki hassha! Dai niki hassha!"*

Twice, Kato hit the fire control panel with the palm of his hand, the submarine shuddering each time a torpedo left the tube. He repeated the command, *"Dai ikki hassha! Dai niki hassha!"*

A rating knelt close to Shimada, stopwatch raised in the air, calling the times. Suddenly, he and Shimada looked up.

WHUMP!

Shimada raised his periscope and jammed his face to the eyepiece. He shot a fist in the air. Men cheered and hooted and pounded each other on the back.

Ingram rose from his knees, an empty bucket dangling from his hand. The water was gone. He looked around, finding the other men of the bucket brigade had walked off. It was then that he saw Shimada's eyes on him, a long, thin-lipped grin drawn across his face, the red-checked scarf tied around his neck. He took off the scarf, retied it, and then looked at Ingram again. It was the first time Ingram had seen the man smile. And then Ingram realized that he hadn't been called forward for the bucket brigade. There were plenty of men for that. He'd been called forward to watch Shimada sink a U.S. Navy destroyer.

"You bastard." Ingram started after him.

Taubman stepped in front. "I wouldn't, Commander. He'll have you cut down in seconds."

Shimada was at the periscope again, his back to Ingram. Air roared in the ballast tanks as the *I-57* surfaced.

Ingram doubled his fists. "Out of my way, Fritz."

Taubman nodded. Masako hit him in the kidneys. It took three men to drag him off. He didn't awake until the next morning.

NINE

16 JUNE 1944
ALAMEDA NAVAL AIR STATION
OAKLAND, CALIFORNIA

The PBM eased into a blustery San Francisco Bay, her engines backfiring softly. White spray swirled under the amphibian's high gull wings as she bounced on whitecaps, the water capturing her hull, arresting her speed. The pilot gunned the port engine to swing the PBM off the fairway and toward the taxi ramp at the Alameda Naval Air Station. Close to shore, six sailors waded into the forty-eight-degree water, fixing beaching gear — a series of dollies — to the PBM's belly. Once done, the sailors slogged clear of the hull while the pilot goosed the twin R-2800 engines. With a roar, she taxied up a ramp and onto a concrete revetment, where she eased to a stop. Chocks were thrown against the wheels as the propellers quit whirling.

A metal stairway rolled up to the fuselage and the hatch popped open. A two-star admiral clad in dress khakis descended; in tow was his harried flag lieutenant, carrying two heavy black briefcases. Jerry Landa was next, followed closely by three other captains, while a group of four commanders stood at the hatch impatiently waiting their turn. A gust whipped at Landa and he plopped his hand on his hat, holding it in place, as he trudged toward the flight operations center.

"Captain?"

"What?" Landa turned, seeing a thin lieutenant commander hobbling toward him on a cane. "That you, Ollie?"

Oliver Toliver's grin was wide as he limped up to Landa, his right hand raised in a salute. "One and the same. Welcome home, sir."

Landa returned the salute. "Thanks."

"How was your trip?"

They shook hands and Landa ran a hand over a stubbled chin. "Man oh man. My butt is tired." He checked his watch. "Damn flight took half my life. Lemme tell you: five hours from Espiritu Santo to Funafuti. Then another five to Canton Island. We barely had time to shave and wash our faces, then it's four hours to Palmyra. And then we bounce around in a damned storm for another eight hours, grinding our way to Hawaii. And I got stuck on hard seats all the way." Landa made a show of rubbing his rear end, oblivious to other officers walking past.

"How about the ride from Hawaii?"

"Another eleven and a half hours bouncing on a hard seat."

"What a grind."

"Yeah, but it sure beats shipping home." Landa nodded to a cart full of luggage being towed toward the operations center. "There's my stuff."

They started walking, Toliver puffing to keep up. Landa couldn't help asking, "Leg giving you problems, Ollie?"

Toliver's lips pressed white. "Hip's getting stiff. Could be the weather. I don't know. Arthritis, maybe. They may have to operate again." Toliver had been seriously wounded with a broken hip as gunnery officer aboard the destroyer U.S.S. *Riley* (DD 542) at the Battle of Cape Esperance in October 1942. The *Riley* had been blown out from under him, and he'd been shipped back to San Francisco, where a specialist at the Stanford Lane Hospital nailed his hip back together. The doctors recommended that Toliver be placed on limited duty and not be ordered back to combat. *You've done your share, Ollie,* Landa thought as he took in the decorations on Toliver's blouse: the Distinguished Service Medal, a Purple Heart, a combat service commemorative medal with three stars, and a Navy unit commendation. "Hope it doesn't come to that."

"Right now, they have me on exercises and mild painkillers. We'll find out." They rounded the building and he waved to a gray Plymouth sedan with black Navy lettering on the doors. "Here's our ride."

"Where's the Packard?"

"Sold it. Got an Oldsmobile, Hydramatic drive."

"Snazzy." Landa stopped. "I don't need wheels. I have a flight set up for Long Beach in two hours."

Toliver gave a lopsided grin. "That was canceled. Plane didn't show up."

"Figures. Say, look. Can I get to a phone? I'd like to call Laura and let her know I'm back."

"My office. As soon as we get there."

"Thanks."

"Tell her I've set up a hop for you on a bug-smasher. I sort of chartered it, so don't worry about a specific departure time." With a blunt nose and an oversized windshield, the bug-smasher was a twin-engined SNB-1 seven-passenger utility plane built by Beech Aircraft. "So you'll have plenty of time to shower and get something to eat, leaving time for us to —"

Landa nodded, "Talk. Okay, let me grab my B-4."

The San Francisco-Oakland Bay Bridge tunnels though Yerba Buena Island, a three-hundred-foot peak rising in the middle of San Francisco Bay. The official residence of the commandant of the Twelfth Naval District was located high among pine trees on the eastern side. A road led to a short causeway giving access to Treasure Island. In 1939 both islands were the site of the Golden Gate International Exposition. But the U.S. Navy took over Treasure Island, turning it into a ship repair and staging area. Situated at the bottom of Yerba Buena, the Expo's two-story art deco headquarters building was a convenient location for the Twelfth Naval District. The building nestled against the mountain, which made it convenient to tunnel a cryptography and intelligence center directly inside. Most tunnels and rooms were finished in utilitarian cold concrete and spartan metal furniture.

Once inside his office, Toliver quietly dialed a security code, dialed Laura's number, then handed Landa the phone and walked out.

She picked up on the second ring.

"Hi, honey. I'm in Frisco."

"God. Jerry."

The line was free of static. Her voice was sweet and clear and lifted him from the wartime miasma he'd been living in for the past few months. He grinned. "No, it's just Jerry."

"Ahhh, you're two days early. I was just out the door for Helen's. I made a lasagna."

"Sounds good. Except why don't you stay there? We'll have the lasagna there, just you and me."

She laughed. "There's plenty for the four of us. Garlic bread, salad, even a bottle of dago red."

Landa rubbed his eyes, fighting off exhaustion. "Uh, honey, can't we just stay there? Just you and me?"

"Sure, honey. You bet. I was being selfish. And Todd, I know, will want to be with Helen, as well."

Landa felt as if he'd been kicked in the stomach. *What the hell do I say?* He snapped his fingers, making a decision. "Uh, on second thought, take the lasagna to Helen's. I'll fly into Terminal Island, catch a car and meet you there." *May as well get this over. Be good to have Laura there to help.*

"Well, if it means —"

"It's quicker, honey."

"Okay," she paused. "I love you, Jerry. Call when you land?"

"Sure will."

"How soon?"

"Four, maybe five hours."

"Hurry."

"I love you, too." He hung up, feeling as

if a thousand demons were crawling through his veins. *What the hell do I do?*

The conference room was across the hall from Toliver's office. Finished in wood paneling, it had wall-to-wall carpeting. Photographs of President Roosevelt and Admirals King and Nimitz hung on the wall at the head of the table. Paintings of eighteenth- and nineteenth-century naval battles adorned the other walls. Incongruously, a wet bar surrounded by mirrors was situated at the opposite end, where Toliver fiddled with glassware.

Landa sat near the head of the table, his blouse open, tie undone, and hat pitched to the back of his head. He ran a hand across thick chin-stubble as a thin, cigar-chomping Army major stood before them. The major jabbed a wooden pointer at an easel bearing a map of northern France, a Top Secret legend posted in the upper left- and lower right-hand corners. The major was a thin man, weighing no more than 140 pounds, a long jagged scar running from the corner of his left eye down to his ear. His Bakelite name tag read CURTIS and his Eisenhower-style short-cut blouse bore parachute wings and three rows of ribbons with battle stars. The major had seen a lot of war before moving into the intelligence business.

Curtis slapped his pointer to the map and said, "So it looks like we've secured the Normandy beachhead. Montgomery has consolidated his position in the east as far as Lion-sur-mer. In the west, Major General Lawton Collins is driving up the Cotentin Peninsula to Cherbourg with his VII Corps."

Toliver asked, "So Operation Neptune is basically complete?"

Curtis's eyebrows went up. "Yes, that and Overlord."

Landa waved a hand. "What's this Neptune and Overlord stuff?"

Curtis replied, "Neptune is the plan for the Allied invasion of Northern Europe. France, if you will. Overlord is the amphibious phase of it."

"I see." Landa scooted forward. "I had no idea we were moving so quickly. Any idea when Collins will take Cherbourg?"

Curtis shrugged. "July 15 is our best estimate, Captain. But anything can happen. We do know the Krauts will defend strongly. They already have a solid ring around it."

Ice clinked into highball glasses as Toliver poured Coke. "And then?"

Curtis smiled, making his scar turn dark red. "After we consolidate Cherbourg, we drive south for the U-boat pens on the Atlantic Coast, here, here, here, and here."

Like an M-1 Garand, the pointer cracked each time Curtis slapped the map at Brest, Lorient, Saint-Nazaire, and La Rochelle.

"How long to take them?" asked Landa.

Curtis waved off a Coke offered by Toliver and said, "Two, three months."

"Why so damn long?" demanded Landa.

The major began stuffing papers in a briefcase. "Heavily defended, Captain. Intelligence tells us that the U-boat pens are the last things the Krauts will surrender. For obvious reasons."

"Any word on what's happening out there?" Landa pitched his head toward the Pacific.

With a look at Toliver, Curtis said, "That's your bailiwick, Commander."

Toliver offered, "Nothing yet, Captain. So far, Mitscher and Spruance are maintaining radio silence."

Landa turned back to Curtis. "What do you think will happen when the *I-57* —"

"I think that's all, Major," interrupted Toliver. "Thank you very much." He cast a glance that Landa quickly understood: Curtis was not cleared for that part of the meeting. He was there simply to brief them on the advances of Allied forces in northern France.

With a nod, Curtis grabbed his easel and briefcase and said, "Glad to be of service." He walked out.

When the door clicked shut, Landa said, "Does that mean the Jap sub might not get into Lorient?"

"My guess is that he will. The Germans have a solid barrier around their U-boat pens and they'll fight ferociously. It could take months. So the *I-57* will be able to discharge her cargo, whatever that is, and head back."

"That leaves Todd in a very unstable situation."

"Very. But we can't do anything about that. What we can do is assure the *I-57* is not attacked en route to Lorient."

"Can't we do something after he lands? I'd hate to see him shot up by a bunch of Army Air Corps throttle jockeys."

Toliver, holding Cokes in both hands, limped over to Landa, handed one over, and sat. "Maybe."

Landa accepted the Coke, held the glass to his cheek, and said, "You don't have a beer in there, do you?"

Toliver spread his hands. "Why, Captain, this is a United States Naval Station."

"Yeah, yeah." Landa took a long sip and then smacked his lips. "Ahhh. Not bad. It's been months." A cloud ran over his face. "I don't know what you mean by 'maybe.' "

Toliver drummed his fingers for a moment, then said, "There are things I can tell you and things I can't. So please don't press me on issues that —"

"Knock off the bullshit and tell me what we're going to do about Todd."

". . . will compromise Magic." Toliver sat back and steepled his fingers. "For example, that major wasn't cleared for Magic. That's why I had to excuse him."

"That was obvious."

"We're on a need-to-know basis, so there are things I can't explain. You have to know that up front, so that when I say no, you'll realize that's as far as I can go. Please remember that Captain Burke gave you only a limited clearance, and he gave me discretion in these matters. And it gives me great pleasure to tell you in here, Captain, that rank doesn't mean a damn thing."

Landa's nostrils flared. "Dammit, Mister, I don't have time to . . ." He paused and drummed his fingers. "Okay. I'm sorry. Guess I'm tired. And my ass still aches. What kind of clearance do I have?"

"Didn't Captain Burke give you anything?"

"Not a damn thing."

A corner of Toliver's mouth raised. "Good. That means there's no paper trail."

"No paperwork? Jesus. What's this Navy coming to?"

Toliver leaned forward, his voice dropping

a notch. "So now we come to the *I-57.*"

"Please."

Toliver nodded toward the door where Curtis had just exited. "We're borrowing a term from Eisenhower and code-naming this Operation Neptune."

Landa pursed his lips and said, "Ike's okay in my book. So what's the Neptune strategy?"

"We've been copying the *I-57*'s radio traffic. She's regular. Noon reports. Fuel status. Ship sightings. The works. On June 8, we intercepted a report that she'd picked up an American Navy commander by the name of Todd Ingram. They even tossed in his serial number. And their position report matches the area where he was lost."

"So, it's for sure." In spite of his exhaustion, Landa's heart beat faster. "Any mention about how he is?"

"None beyond the original report."

"What does Jap headquarters say to do with him?"

"We're not decrypting headquarters traffic. Too much of it. What we did discover from a different source is that the *I-57* was originally headed for Lorient, France, on an exchange mission with the Krauts. But now it looks as if she's TAD to act as a picket line against Task Force 58."

Landa's eyebrows went up.

"After that, we believe she refuels in Penang and *then* heads for France."

"What if they leave Todd in Penang?"

"Don't think so. They have clearance to take him all the way."

"Wow."

"So, now we come to a hunter-killer group that is situated across her path in the South Atlantic. And I can tell you with pretty good certainty that they would intercept her and put her down — if left to our current operating procedure."

"Which is what?"

Toliver sat back, smiled, and spread his hands.

Landa said, "Excuse me, sir. I'm just a lowly captain. I forgot there are things I'm not supposed to ask."

"Mmmm."

"What can you tell me about the HUK group?" HUK stood for hunter-killer.

"The *Purvis Bay* is a jeep carrier. There are eight DEs escorting her."

"Specifically, I am to do what?"

"This is where we're counting on your ASW-screen-commanding experience. You are to act as liaison between OP-20-G and the *Purvis Bay* HUK group, transmitting orders and giving them updates relative to the *I-57*'s route. It's your job to make sure the *I-57* passes through safely."

"Is that it?"

"More or less. Except to try and sink the milch cow — *after* she refuels the *I-57*."

"And you'll be giving me updates on the *I-57*?"

"As best I can. We'll need you up here when she nears the *Purvis Bay* HUK group, to make sure it's all coordinated properly."

"You mean I can stay in Long Beach?"

"Yes. There's lots of time. We ran a track. It's a sixteen-thousand-mile voyage, more or less — eighty days."

"Sounds simple enough. Save the *I-57*; put down the milch cow, right?"

"That's it."

"Okay." Landa heaved to his feet. "Now I've got to figure a way to break this to Helen." He started walking to the door.

"Captain?"

"What?"

"You can't tell her, sir."

Landa spun. "Whaaat?"

"This is top secret. Magic. I mean, I thought you knew. Didn't Captain Burke tell you that?"

"Yeah, but —"

"And you signed a nondisclosure agreement, didn't you?"

Landa smashed a fist on the table and roared, "I did. But Arleigh didn't let me read it. Further, he didn't say I couldn't tell her. In fact, he was in such a big, damned hurry he didn't tell me anything!"

"Jerry . . . Captain . . . I'm sorry."

Landa bared his even white teeth. "Listen, you little bastard. There's no way in hell I'm not going to tell her."

Toliver rose to his feet and yelled back. "You think I'm enjoying this? I was best man at Todd's wedding. I knew Helen when she was a nurse in the Corregidor tunnels. The three of us escaped from under the Japs' noses. All that time." He grabbed the table for support. "All that time." His voice grew soft. "He'll get through this. So will she." He sat.

"What a damned curveball." Landa rubbed his face and eyes. "How the hell am I going to do this? Hell, she'll get a telegram. Is that what you want?"

"Not for a few weeks. In the meantime, just fake it."

"How do I explain his absence? He's supposed to be with me."

Toliver shrugged. "TAD of some sort?"

"Bullshit. She'll see through that."

"Play it by ear. Besides, if everything works out from our end, she may be getting letters from Todd in prison camp before the telegram arrives. Except . . ." Toliver pressed a fist to his forehead.

"Except what?"

"I forgot. She's Kate Durand's daughter."

"Meaning?"

"Meaning . . . I don't know." Toliver sighed. "They have an inner resolve in situations like this. It's uncanny, almost clairvoyant. She may know what's happening before you show up."

"Sonofabitch. This isn't working. And damn it, she's pregnant, almost ready to deliver."

Toliver spread his hands. "I wish I could say something. You want me to call? I know her better."

"That won't make it any easier. No, damn it. I'll take care of it." Looking around the room, Landa said, "Where's the rain locker?"

Toliver jabbed a thumb over his shoulder. "To your right and down the hall. Full shower and dressing room."

"Any chow around here?"

"How 'bout an early dinner at Wong Lee's?" Wong Lee's was a restaurant in San Francisco's Chinatown District.

Landa headed for the door. "I'd love to. But I'm kind of anxious to see . . . well . . . you know, Laura."

Toliver pushed himself to his feet. "Okay, when you're ready, I'll drive you back to the bug-smasher."

Landa headed for the door. "You still dating that girl? Who was it? Wong's daughter?"

"Suzy."

"Yeah, Suzy. She was going to school. Cal or something."

"Stanford. She graduates next June."

"You're too old to be running around with college chicks. Hell, you're robbing the cradle."

"Go take your shower, Captain. Towels are in the cupboard."

TEN

16 JUNE 1944
SAN PEDRO, CALIFORNIA

It was just after sunset when the twin-engine SNB eased into its downwind approach over Palos Verdes, swung over the Long Beach Pike, and lined up on final for the Terminal Island Naval Air Station. There were no other passengers, and the pilot, a forty-six-year-old lieutenant commander with service in World War I, had given Landa the copilot's seat to keep him company. But Landa fell asleep after takeoff and woke up only when the wheels bleeped at touch-down.

"Welcome to TI, Captain," said the pilot, whose name Landa had forgotten. "Have a good snooze?" He braked to a halt before an operations Quonset, revved the engines, then killed them.

Landa blinked for a moment. "Ummmm, comfortable seat." He yawned and stretched. *Wow. Happy homecoming.*

"Sir?"

"Thanks for a nice ride, Commander." Landa shook his hand, then made his way aft, picking up his B-4 and exiting the small hatch. It was a warm, balmy Southern California evening, with Landa feeling homecoming pangs for the first time. In retrospect, Alameda and the Twelfth Naval District headquarters were just Navy bases. Here, he was really home, and he felt lightheaded as he made his way into the ops hut, with thoughts of Laura swimming through his head.

Suddenly it hit him. *My God. I've forgotten what she looks like.* He reached for his wallet to retrieve a photo but then felt foolish as a young Marine second lieutenant strode past throwing a crisp salute. As he returned it, Laura's image sprang to his mind, as if someone had pulled his wallet photo and laid it before him. She had sandy hair that was pulled back when in concert — very professional looking, especially when she wore rimless gold glasses. Her wide-apart green eyes were accentuated by a small nose and a full mouth that dazzled Landa and her audiences when she smiled. And, of course, her show-piece exquisite hands never ceased to fascinate him. With long, slender, and powerful fingers, it was as if each were carved from ivory by a master. It was all the more entertaining when she spoke, for she waved them a lot, punctuating her language.

Laura.

Inside, a second-class aviation boatswain's mate in undress blues sat behind a desk labeled OFFICER OF THE DAY, making notes on a clipboard. He looked up. "Help you, Cap'n?"

Landa dropped his B-4. "Can I use your phone for about seventeen seconds?"

The petty officer grew wide eyed.

"Relax, sailor. I just want to call over to San Pedro."

"No, sir. I mean . . . are you Captain Landa?"

"That's right."

"Well, we got a call from COMTWELVE two hours ago. We have a car waiting outside, sir. And please, use the phone. Here." The sailor stood.

Good on you, Ollie. "Thanks, sailor. I'll be out of here chop-chop." He dialed.

Laura picked up on the first ring. "Hello?"

God, her voice sounds good. "I'm here."

"Where?" Her voice was muffled, as if she were holding her hand over the mouthpiece.

"Terminal Island. Everything okay?" Something began to gnaw at him.

"I'm fine, honey. I'm glad you're here. But I got to thinking on the way down. You said from San Francisco, 'I'm here.' And you just said it again. First person. What about Todd?"

Oh shit. Bull it through. "That's right. Todd got delayed." *Come on, Jerry, think of something, you dumb sonofabitch.*

The line crackled.

"Laura?"

"What do I tell Helen?"

"Like I said. He got delayed, honey. Sorry. I'll explain it all when I get there. Okay? You don't have to say a thing."

"Can't wait, hon. Please hurry." She blew a kiss and hung up.

Landa hung up slowly. It was then that he made the decision he'd put off for so long.

"You okay, sir?" asked the petty officer.

I think I need a drink. "Fine, sailor. Now, where's that car?"

They rode in a Plymouth sedan painted in Navy gray. A third-class signalman drove while Landa drummed his fingers as they headed to San Pedro. The ferry ride seemed to take forever, and by the time they headed up Seventeenth Street past San Pedro High School, it had turned pitch-dark.

"Turn left here, sailor."

"Sir."

Landa pointed to a little two-bedroom white stucco house on Alma Street. It gave him a warm feeling to see Laura's light green Cadillac convertible parked out front. "Right there." The Plymouth drew up and Landa pitched his duffle out the door. "Thanks, sailor. I'm done for the evening. So go on back."

"Yes, sir."

The car drove away, and when Landa turned, Laura ran up to him, wrapping her arms tightly around his neck. He held her high, kissing deeply.

"Uh. You're really back," she gasped. "I feel as if it's been years."

He kissed her again, then said, "A couple of decades at least." Her scent was marvelous, like that of fresh soap. "Lilacs." He buried his nose in the nape of her neck.

"I think so." She raised her mouth to him again. "God, Jerry, I missed you so."

Again they kissed. Then something rubbed against Landa's ankle. "Huh?" He looked down to see a gray tabby.

"Fred." Landa reached down to pet the cat. He was rewarded when the cat purred instantly. "Wow, good old Fred." He looked back to Laura. "Especially you, hon. You look marvelous."

She wrinkled her nose. "You want to go in, or should we stay out here all night?"

"Would Fred approve?"

"I don't think so." Then her face darkened. "What's with Todd?"

"Helen inside?"

"She's probably watching."

Once more he kissed her, knowing that would have to tide him over for a while. Worse, they'd been necking in the street with all the world looking on, and he felt sick with guilt. Most likely, Helen was desperately wondering where Todd was. *God, give me strength.*

"We better get going." He gathered her under an arm, picked up his duffle, and headed for the door. He walked in, finding Helen standing before the Gulbrandsen upright piano, her hands clasped before her. She wore a white sleeveless maternity smock over a black skirt, all eight and a half months of her condition in full array. In spite of it, she looked radiant, perhaps enhanced by the mask of pregnancy. Dropping his duffle, he walked up and took her in his arms. "Helen."

Helen clutched his biceps tightly, her intense, dark eyes raking his face. Perfume wafted around his head, Chanel No. 5, he thought. Helen had made up for her husband's homecoming and now her world was falling apart. *Todd, I hope you know what's waiting for you.* "Helen . . . I —"

She stepped back and fixed him with a look. "Tell me he's okay, Jerry."

The question devastated Landa, and he bit his lower lip. He hadn't cried since he was a child, but now he felt as if he were going to. The hell with Mitscher and

Arleigh "Thirty-One Knot" Burke and superspy Oliver Toliver. The hell with nondisclosure agreements and . . . firing squads. Helen deserved to know. His mind raged. *Tell her the truth! Damn it!*

Her eyes darted about his face until he said, "He . . . he's not going to make it, hon."

Laura caught her breath.

"I'm sorry."

"Jerry." Helen reached up and pulled him to her.

"Jeepers." He stepped back. "Something jumped." He felt her belly and it moved again. "I'm sorry, kid." He looked up to her. "And to you, too, Helen, I'm sorry." Laura stepped close, dabbing a handkerchief to her eyes. His arm went around her, all three loosely collected in the same embrace. "I'm not handling this well," he said.

"It comes with practice," said Laura, staring at the floor.

"No. What I meant was —" The baby jumped again. "Holy cow."

"He's been doing that a lot. Ahh . . ." Helen patted her belly. She reached back and steadied herself on the piano. "Are you sure?" Her eyes glistened and her voice was up a notch.

"I'm sorry."

"His ship, too?"

"The ship got sort of mauled and they lost twelve guys. But repairs are under way and the Mighty *Max* will be back in action in two to three months."

"Something's not right. I don't believe it." She bit her fist and stumbled.

Laura and Landa each grabbed an elbow to steady her, but she shrugged them off and asked, "What happened? Were you there?"

"No, I was back with —"

"Why weren't you there?"

"Hon, I was back on the *Thomas*, quite a distance away."

"You should have been there," Helen nearly shouted.

"I would have given my left arm to have been there."

Helen yelled, "If you had been there, maybe he would have . . ." She raised her fists to beat Landa's chest.

He caught them, "Honey, I'm sorry."

Laura ran an arm around her. "It's okay, hon."

Helen looked up at Landa and screamed, "Damn it! Don't you see? You let him down. He shouldn't have been out there. Don't you think he's done enough already? You're all alike, you bunch of . . . oh." She slumped.

Landa caught her. "God, I'm so sorry. He was . . . I mean Todd was like . . . my best friend." A lump grew in his throat. "Like a brother . . . he was . . . aw, damn it." He pulled her close.

The three hugged and swayed for a moment.

"I'm sorry, Jerry." Helen's voice was muffled against his chest.

"Shhhh," said Landa.

Helen raised her chin. "What happened?"

"Later."

"I'd like it now, please." She wiped tears from her eyes.

Landa handed over a handkerchief. "You sure?"

She nodded, dabbing her eyes with the handkerchief. "I'm sure."

With a sigh, Landa pitched his hat on top of the piano and shrugged out of his coat. "The *Max* was on picket duty far ahead of the formation. A bunch of Jap planes jumped them and did their best to sink her. But the *Max* shot down three, at least, before she took two bomb hits. They figure one bomb sent Todd over the side. Same thing happened to Dexter. They found him the next day. They looked all over the place for Todd, but they . . . never . . ."

Helen asked, "Hank Kelly?"

"He's fine. Rallied the crew and saved the ship."

"I'm glad."

"Who's Dexter?" asked Laura.

"Ship's monkey." *What a hell of a homecoming.*

"Oh."

Squeezing his eyes closed, he said, "This is bullshit." *Tell her, you dope! Just Helen, not Laura. That's it!*

He turned to Laura and cupped her chin in his hand. "Can you excuse us for a moment, hon? Classified stuff, and Captain Helen Durand Ingram here is cleared."

Laura drew away. "Of course." She turned and walked into the kitchen.

When the door closed, Landa said, "Helen, I want you to know that . . ." An image of the *Lexington* swam into his mind, her wake roiling as the destroyer *Thomas* zipped into station, Endicott standing high and proud. "Awww, damn it."

"What, Jerry?"

Arleigh Burke and Mitscher, too.

Landa rubbed his eyes and finally ran his sleeve across his face. "He's . . . he was the best man I've ever known." He slapped both hands over his face and gave a long, anguished sob.

Throwing her arms around him, Helen said, "It's okay, Jerry."

"I'm so sorry. I wish it was me."

"It's okay." She pushed back. "Look. You have a fiancée in there. It's time you two spent some time together."

Landa drew a deep breath. "All I'm trying to say is —"

She placed a hand over his mouth. "I know what you're trying to say. Now go. Go to your fiancée. She needs you right now. I'll be all right." She actually smiled.

"Helen, damn it."

Helen stood on her tiptoes and kissed him on the forehead. "I'm going to bed." She patted her belly. "Take care of you-know-who." With another smile, she reached down, picked up Fred, and cradled him in her arms.

"Honey, I'm so sorry," said Landa.

"Go to your fiancée, Jerry." Helen walked into the bedroom, the door clicking softly behind her.

A hell of a homecoming.

Landa stepped toward her door and listened for a moment. Had Helen cried out, he would have been there beside her in an instant. But she didn't, and at length he turned and walked into the kitchen.

Laura leaned against the sink, a half-full glass of dark amber liquid in her hand. "I imagine you're ready for a shot." A statement.

With a quick glance, he took in the scotch bottle on the sink, the half-full glass held loosely in her hand. She reached in the cupboard and brought out a glass.

He took it. "Think I'd better. Ice?"

"If you must." She nodded over her shoulder to the refrigerator.

She tossed off the rest of her drink while Landa fixed his. He took a sip, the scotch burning its way down. "Ahhh."

"Is there any hope at all, hon?" She handed over her glass, wiggling it. Landa reached for the refrigerator door.

"Skip the ice, hon."

Unaccountably, Landa shivered. He recalled the first time he met Laura. She'd been drunk. Her husband, Luther Dutton, had been Landa's gunnery officer aboard the *Howell*. He'd died when temporarily assigned to another destroyer that suffered a direct Japanese bomb hit to her boiler, vaporizing the ship. Landa helped straighten her out, and they'd fallen in love.

He took a deep breath and poured two fingers in the glass. "Water?"

"Uh-uh." She took a sip then leveled a gaze on him. "You hungry?"

He pointed to a bowl of wax fruit on the small kitchen table. "Like I could eat the whole damned thing."

"Sit. I'm gonna fix you the meal of the century." He took a chair and she tossed off the drink and reached for the bottle.

"God. Please don't," he blurted.

"Why not? We live in a temporal world. Why not temporize just a little bit?"

"Because I feel like crap, and I just had

to do one of the toughest things of my life, damn it!"

Her face softened. "You're right." She put the glass aside. "I'm not doing this well. You know, it sort of takes me back to . . . to . . ."

"Luther."

"Yes. Good old Luther," she said absently. Then she smiled. "Guess what we have for you?"

"I'm all ears."

"Lasagna, salad, garlic bread, even a bottle of" — she turned and fiddled at the cupboard, pulling open the door — "dago red, San Pedro's finest." She pulled out a large glass dish, the lasagna done to perfection. "Plenty for four — I mean, plenty to go around."

In spite of his plight, it smelled wonderful. It had been days since he'd had solid food. "Ummmm."

"You bet. Now just relax. Won't take a second."

Landa sat back, watching Laura move swiftly about the kitchen, setting their places, pouring wine. At length she set out green salads and plates of lasagna. "Dig in."

Raising a fork, he asked, "How 'bout you?"

"Cheers." She held up her glass. Landa lifted his and they clinked, with Laura tossing off the dago red in one gulp. Nodding toward his food, she said, "Go on. I'm dying to see if you like it." She screwed a candle into an old wax-laden Chianti bottle.

"Aren't you hungry?"

"I had tons before you showed up. Had to test it, you know." She lit the candle and said, "Be right back. Must freshen up." Flicking off the light, she walked out.

It was the first time in months Landa had been left alone without an exhaust blower howling, the wind shrieking at his face, steam turbines whining, or an aircraft engine rumbling close by. Gone were the voices of men laughing or shouting or snoring. It seemed even more pronounced because of the near darkness. He was alone with just a candle, its solitary glow golden and compelling, making the lasagna glisten and beckon. Captain Jeremiah T. Landa had always known where he was going in life. He'd grown up by himself and had raised a little brother to boot. He'd had no trouble leading men and asking them to do the impossible. And much of the time, they got away with doing the impossible. But now he felt so alone and so incompetent. And this little house, where they'd all known so much happiness, was now so silent. All on a beautiful June evening.

The lasagna was wonderful. He thought

he should feel guilty eating it, especially alone. But he didn't. It had been too long since he'd eaten so well and he ate it all — including seconds — all washed down with dago red.

Silence. Blessed silence. By candlelight, he drank another glass of dago red. After tossing it off, he rose, scraped his plate, then kicked off his shoes. Padding softly toward the guest room, he found Laura waiting there. Softly he muttered, "A hell of a homecoming."

"Never mind." She raised her arms. He pulled her close and kissed her deeply.

ELEVEN

17 JUNE 1944
SAN PEDRO, CALIFORNIA

"Oooff!" Landa's eyes blinked open, finding the living room flooded with sunshine. Sitting on his chest was Fred, looking down at him, blinking. He petted the cat, which started purring.

"Mmmmm." The smell of coffee filled the air, and there was something else. Bacon. He heard it sizzling and lay back, luxuriating; he hadn't slept in for months. Checking his watch, he saw it was — "Good God!" — ten after ten in the morning.

"Hello?" Laura peeked around the corner, a wide smile across her face. "Good morning." Dressed in a pink chenille bathrobe, she looked delicious.

"Come here." Landa sat up, unseating Fred. He searched her face as she ran to him but saw no remnants from the night before. She kneeled at the couch and he pulled her in. *Forget it.* They kissed long and intently, until Landa said, "Uh, where's Helen?"

Her hair tumbled as she laid her head on his chest. It smelled wonderful. "Off for a walk with Mrs. Peabody. She'll be back soon." Emma Peabody, a widow in her late sixties, was Helen's next-door neighbor.

"How soon?" He held her tighter.

"Take it easy."

"You don't expect me to give up just like that."

"They'll be back any minute, you dope."

Landa forced himself to relax. "How is Helen doing this morning?"

"Looks like she's been pulled through a knothole, but I think she's holding up."

"I'd say she needs someone to be with her for a while."

"Well, there's Mrs. Peabody."

He ran his hands over her back. "How is Mrs. Peabody?"

"The same. Gained a little weight, maybe."

"She still brew her own beer?"

"You can smell it a mile away."

Landa sighed and said, "You know, we need time together. Last night was not one of my better homecomings." He kissed the top of her head.

She turned up her face and gave him a long lingering kiss. "I'm sorry about last night. I don't take things like that well. It's like when Luther —"

"Shhh, don't." He put a finger on her lips.

"And I'm afraid I didn't help you, either. I know you have to do things like this a lot."

"It's not easy." He breathed deep, running his fingers through her hair. She felt wonderful, and he began to pull her closer.

She melted in his arms. "Jerry, I —"

Papers rattled to the floor, and they jumped. Fred, who had found a perch on top of the piano, stretched and blinked down at them as more sheet music spilled over.

Landa chuckled. "You'd think someone fired a cannon."

Laura laid her head back on his chest. "I don't see how you do it, writing letters and visiting war widows. It has to be rough. I remember with Luther that —"

"I said stow it, beautiful." He sniffed at the air. "What is that?"

"Coffee. Oh, breakfast. It's burning." She rose quickly and dashed into the kitchen.

Stepping into the bathroom, Landa did quick ablutions and pulled on a set of working khakis. After shaving, he walked into the kitchen and circled his arms around Laura, pulling her close.

"Jerry, don't."

"I don't give a damn."

She turned to kiss him just as the front door opened. Helen walked in with Mrs. Peabody behind, closing the door.

"Er, excuse us," said Helen, taking off a light windbreaker. Her eyes were moist and red, with dark splotches beneath.

Landa walked over and gave her a hug. "How you doing?"

Helen tried a smile. "I've done better."

"Cold out there?" asked Laura, who was now flipping eggs on the griddle.

"Not bad out there, but hot enough in here," said Mrs. Peabody, her hands jammed on her hips.

Landa opened his arms. "Emma, how the hell are you?"

Mrs. Peabody walked up and they hugged. With a peck on his cheek, she said, "Welcome home, Boom Boom."

"Dammit, don't start that again."

Mrs. Peabody stepped back and said, "Will you look at that? A captain's eagles on your collar. Nobody asked me for references."

Landa sighed. "That's why I didn't recommend you."

Laura said, "Okay. It's ready. Everybody please sit."

Mrs. Peabody looked at the frying pan and sniffed. "Bacon looks kind of overdone, hon. What's been going on?"

"Sit!" Laura flushed, Landa noticed,

something rare for her.

Chairs scraped and they sat, with Landa at the head of the table. Reluctant to speak, they concentrated on their food, all aware that the loudest sound was Ingram's screaming absence.

It didn't take long for Landa to wolf down three eggs and four slices of toast. Then he sat back and asked Helen, "How far along are you?"

"Two more weeks. Then he should be ready," said Helen.

"He?"

Mrs. Peabody offered, "She's football shaped."

Landa's eyebrows went up.

"That means a boy."

Landa sipped coffee. "What means a girl?"

"Basketball."

He leaned around the table to look at Helen's belly. "Can't tell the difference."

Crunching a piece of bacon, Mrs. Peabody, said, "Well, you wouldn't, you fool, unless you could see her in a more, ahhh, natural condition."

"Ooops. Sorry."

The corners of Helen's mouth turned up for a moment.

Just then the phone rang. Helen rose. "I'll get it."

Landa waited until Helen went into the other room to answer the phone. Then he said to Laura, "Maybe we should get her out to her folks. Especially for the delivery."

Mrs. Peabody said, "Actually, Kate said she would come up here. Plus, Helen's OB is here in Pedro and she really doesn't want to leave."

Helen walked in. "Roberta Thatcher for you, Laura." Roberta Thatcher was the business manager of the West Coast Division of the NBC Symphony Orchestra.

Laura finished off her coffee and stood. "Duty calls." She walked into the other room.

Helen laid a hand on Landa's arm and said, "Jerry, I don't want you to worry about me. I'll be fine."

Landa said, "I had no doubt that you wouldn't. But I was just wondering if you shouldn't be with your folks. You know, go out to the ranch and let your folks dote on you at delivery time."

Helen shook her head. "Don't think so. I'm on call for the Fort MacArthur Infirmary and —"

"You still working there?" Fort MacArthur was a U.S. Army artillery installation, featuring two fourteen-inch, long-range guns for the defense of Los Angeles Harbor.

"On an as-needed basis. They're shorthanded."

"Hell, you're ready to pop. Who do

those guys think they are?"

"I know what I'm doing. Besides, my doctor is here."

"Well, I want to make sure that —"

She raised a hand. "There's another problem."

"What?"

Helen tilted her head toward the cupboard. "There was a half bottle of scotch in there last night."

Landa's shoulders slumped. "Yeah, I know. She went after it when I came up with the bad news."

Helen drew a deep breath, then let it out. "Well, we're going to have to do something."

"Why?"

"Now it's empty."

Landa's mouth dropped. "You're kidding."

Mrs. Peabody shook her head slowly, "Saw it in the trash can out back this morning when I came over. Floored me, I'll tell you."

"Jeez. She must have swallowed it in one gulp." His eyes searched Helen's, then Mrs. Peabody's.

His voice had risen a notch and Helen went, "Shhhh."

"God." Landa toyed with a fork. "I thought she licked the habit. Has she done this before?"

Helen shook her head just as Laura walked in, her brow knit.

Landa asked, "Bad news?"

Laura sat and poured more coffee. "I . . . I don't know what to say. The orchestra just received a contract to do a feature-length training film for the U.S. Navy. Gene Kelly will be narrating, and they want us to start rehearsing immediately."

Landa sat back. "What's that do to us?"

"Nothing and everything." Laura rubbed her hands over her face. "I've been through this. The work schedules are brutal. Up at five. Home at eight. On and on until we wrap."

"For how long?"

"Three, four weeks." She looked at him, tears welling. "Including next Saturday night."

Landa looked at her face and said, "But isn't that the night of our engagement party?"

Laura nodded and looked down.

Landa said, "Aren't we supposed to have this enormous party with Bob Hope and Bing Crosby on stage singing to us while all of Hollywood stands around drinking champagne?"

"Well, I was planning a blowout. Maybe not Hope and Crosby. But now —"

"We can't do it?" asked Landa. "We can't get engaged?"

Laura's voice was low. "I'm not sure. I think we're committed for Saturday and for several weekends after. I have to wait for the schedule. Jerry, I'm sorry. This wouldn't have happened but for —"

"This is getting out of control," said Landa.

"I'll know more Monday morning. Maybe we can schedule for next Sunday."

"Hold on a moment." Landa rose.

"What?"

Landa walked into the living room, rustled in his duffle bag, then came back and kneeled before Laura. "Honey, I deeply regret to inform you that the schedules of the Fifth Fleet and the Imperial Japanese Navy do not coincide with that of the NBC Symphony Orchestra. When Uncle Sam snaps his fingers, I must jump. So all I can say is that I love you, Laura West. And I want to get this done somehow, the engagement party be damned. Therefore, I ask you, Laura, in the presence of these two wonderful ladies, will you marry me?" He held out a small box. "Please?"

"Oh." Laura took the box and opened it, finding a gleaming marquise-cut, near colorless, one-carat diamond in a silver setting. "God, Jerry."

"No, it's just me. You're getting the raw end of that deal."

She looked at the box. "From Shreve

and Company, San Francisco. Jerry, when did you find time to do this?"

"Yes or no, damn it."

"Yes, of course."

"Here we go, then." Landa took the ring from the box and, with a flourish, placed it on her fourth finger.

"Oh, yes, yes." Laura ran her arms around his neck and they kissed.

Emma Peabody smiled from across the table. "Hope and Crosby. Would have been a great party. Sure you can't schedule them in later, Laura?"

TWELVE

17 JUNE 1944
IJN SUBMARINE *I-57*
STRAIT OF MALACCA

Time passed peacefully with no more contact with the U.S. Navy. For Ingram that meant a steady regimen of beatings, starvation, and humiliation. As a diversion, he focused on the passage of time and their current position. This evening he reckoned they'd been under way for ten or so days. That would make this the seventeenth or eighteenth of June. They'd been on the surface most of the time, and Ingram figured their speed at about twelve knots, which meant they had traveled nearly three thousand miles. But to where, exactly?

He eventually figured it out during the trash-dumping detail. During the day, Ingram was given a basket of rags and assigned to clean machinery in the pump, main engine, and maneuvering rooms, where the motor-generators were housed. Oddly, he was not told to clean bilges, which was the first place any petty officer would send cheap labor. But protesting under the Geneva Convention was useless, Ingram knew. The Japanese hadn't ratified it, and he knew enough about Japan's brutality from his days on Corregidor to realize he was lucky to be alive.

From the beginning, his routine each evening was to walk from the forward torpedo room to the after berthing compartment in the stern, gathering trash in a gunny sack. En route, he usually accumulated three to four gunny sacks, along with special sacks from the ship's galley containing remnants of the day's meal. Accompanying him, of course, was his guard, Seaman Second Class Masako. After the pickup in the torpedo room, they headed down the narrow passage through the officer's berthing spaces, where Masako would halt before a little shrine. It was mounted on a bulkhead in a dogleg in the passageway between a bulkhead and a tool locker. It was a ten-by-sixteen-inch wooden box containing a few pieces of wood and rock. Taubman later told him the box was from the Ise Grand Shrine, built in a dense forest along the Isuzu River, in southern Honshu's Mie Prefecture. And the box was made from white paulownia wood, a variety considered sacred in Shintoism.

Masako would bow and meditate for a full sixty seconds, while Ingram stood behind, hands clasped before him, as others shoved their way through the narrow passageway. Sometimes sailors and even officers would step beside them to bow and meditate, some praying in low tones.

Once through the boat, Ingram would stack the trash bags around the after hatch, where he was required to toss in weights not unlike thick pancake-sized plates of pig iron. Then he hauled the trash bags up the aft hatch out onto the afterdeck and threw them over the side. When he ventured on deck, Masako would draw a pistol and tightly secure a tether around Ingram's neck, lest he try to jump.

Most of the nights were overcast or hazy and he couldn't see the moon or stars. Often, the massive two-cycle, ten-cylinder, double-acting diesels put out so much smoke that it was hard to see anything, and, coughing and sputtering, Ingram couldn't wait to get below. But one night he ascended the ladder to find the seas calm under a spectacular jewel-studded sky, a gentle breeze sweeping the *I-57*'s smoke to starboard.

Ingram looked at Masako and bowed.

Masako grunted and took up what little slack there was on the tether.

Ingram smiled, spread his arms wide, and took deep breaths, his face raised to the sky. He was taking a chance. Normally, Masako would boot him for being slow.

But this time he didn't, and Ingram's eyes frantically darted about the sky as he groaned and stretched with exaggerated purpose. *Where is it?* He bent to touch his toes.

Masako grunted, *"Iko!" Let's go.*

"Okay, okay." There! Off the starboard quarter. Polaris, the North Star, low on the horizon. They were traveling southwest. Quickly, Ingram did the arithmetic. They must be headed for the Dutch East Indies! Ingram felt lightheaded and his spirit soared. For eleven days, he hadn't known where he was, and he'd felt like a man adrift in a galaxy. Now his life had regained purpose, although he had no idea what he could do about it.

"Hieeeyiii," screeched Masako.

Ingram quickly kicked the bags over the side and jumped down the ladder.

Masako followed, pulling the hatch shut, and then descended the ladder to the maneuvering room. Giving Ingram a dirtier-than-usual look, Masako handcuffed Ingram to a pad eye beneath a workbench that supported a lathe, drill press, and grinder. It was a three-by-five-foot space and they'd given him a blanket. Once he learned to position his legs behind a generator mount, he slept quite comfortably. With that, Masako stepped aft for the berthing compartment and turned in, his duties for the day complete.

The *I-57* had decent food, as far as Ingram could tell, and everyone seemed reasonably fit. But, of course, they fed him scraps, a type of rice gruel called *kaya*. Once in a while the cook would ladle up an indistinguishable meat paste that tasted like cardboard. But after choking it down, he felt much better. Ablutions consisted of a quick hose-down with salt water in the after torpedo room head. Predictably, his khakis quickly became splotched with grease.

What Ingram hated most was the bowing. He couldn't get used to it. Every time an order was given, or even when someone spoke to him, he was expected to bow. In a show of zeal to get to the task, Ingram would often forget to bow. Howling triumphantly, his captors would set upon him, Lieutenant (j.g.) Fumimaro Ishibashi leading the pack.

Ishibashi, the communications officer, was five-seven, was slight of build, weighed close to 160 pounds, and was all uncompromising sinew. With the slightest excuse, Ishibashi would punch Ingram in the stomach or box his ears, oftentimes kicking him in the butt to round things out. Others followed to satiate their frustrations of the day, because on this submarine everything ran downhill. Compared to the American

Navy, where Navy Regulations prohibited officers from touching enlisted men, the IJN *I-57* conducted business otherwise. Senior lieutenants and, on occasion, Commander Shimada himself would boot a subordinate, an enlisted man in most cases, and it would cascade down from there; the lower the rank, the heavier the blows.

Masako was at the bottom of the chain and received kicks and shouts from a number of petty officers during any given day. That done, Masako would turn to Ingram, exacting his revenge. His gestures and grunts ascended the octaves as he ordered Ingram to a task. Stooping to the job, Ingram grew to expect the blows, shouts, and curses that Masako rained upon him. But Masako's beatings were not as bad as Ishibashi's. Because of his anger, Masako's blows were ill-timed and indiscriminate, often missing their mark. But Ishibashi's blows were calculated. Once he hit Ingram full in the face, loosening a tooth.

Some of the crew sat back and watched with a stoic curiosity. It was almost an indifference, a complete uncaring. It mattered not that Ingram was a fellow human being, a prisoner of war. To them, Ingram was less than that, an animal perhaps, or an insect, eventually to be squashed or discarded.

Martin Taubman would politely stand

aside when Ingram was being beaten. When it was over, Taubman's expression would say, *You damn fool, can't you remember something as simple as bowing?*

And yet, there was another side to Taubman — a grace, a charm, that became more evident as time went on. No doubt there was a cultural yearning as well, both seeking a convoluted form of European companionship. Oddly, they became friends of sorts, and Shimada gave permission for Ingram to play chess with Taubman. Thus, they played almost every night after the *I-57* surfaced to recharge batteries, and, of course, after Ingram had emptied trash.

One night, Taubman waited in shadows for Masako to disappear aft. Then he walked over to where Ingram was shackled and held out a chessboard and a box of pieces. "Hmmmm?" He flipped over a bucket, pulled it up to Ingram, and sat. "White or black?" He thrust out two fists.

Ingram sat up, making sure his head didn't hit the drill press. He tapped Taubman's left.

With a flourish, Taubman flipped open his left fist and produced a black pawn. "Too bad."

Ingram let it go. He knew Taubman offered black pawns in both fists. The man usually wanted to play white.

They set up the board and Ingram eyed the overhead, saying, "Ship's hardly rolling. Smooth out there tonight."

Taubman opened with his king's pawn. "Too bad you couldn't have been up earlier. We passed Singapore at sunset. Quite beautiful."

Ingram sat up, bumping his head on the drill press. Singapore. He hadn't realized they had gone that far west. But the idea they were near land made his heart beat quickly. He raised his eyebrows.

Taubman said, "Move, please."

Ingram matched Taubman's move with his own king's pawn.

Nodding in approval, Taubman said, "We've turned into the Malacca Straits, heading for Penang. Remember I told you?" He attacked with his queen's knight.

Ingram mulled that one over. As much as he wanted off the *I-57*, Penang gave him an uneasy feeling.

"Georgetown docks tomorrow at eight o'clock. You'll be on your way by nine." Taubman looked up and steepled his fingers. "Of course, you don't have anything to pack so there should be no worries from that quarter." He gave a short, strange laugh.

"What?"

"Something wrong?"

"I . . . I thought I was going to Europe

. . . to France, you said."

"Yes, well, apparently Captain Shimada has changed his mind."

Ingram felt as if he were falling down a well. "But . . . I . . ."

"Yes, I'm sorry. We won't be able to continue our little chess games. Which reminds me. Are you going to move, Commander?"

Ingram moved his king's bishop's pawn one square. *Penang. Shit. That's the road to the Burma death camps.*

"Ahhh." Taubman clapped his hands. "King's Indian defense. You amaze me, Commander. Where did you learn that?"

"Move, please," said Ingram, looking at Taubman. The man cared not one whit about how he felt.

Taubman cast an eye, his expression saying, *We're supposed to be having a friendly game.* He shoved out his queen's pawn.

Just then, Lieutenant Ishibashi stepped through the hatch. Following him was Captain Shimada.

Taubman looked up as Shimada grunted something.

"Hai!" Taubman shot to his feet and bowed.

Shimada said something to Ishibashi. With a glance at Ingram, Ishibashi strode aft and through the hatch into the berthing compartment.

Taubman and Shimada conversed for a

moment, and it seemed as if they were discussing the chess game, with Taubman picking up pieces and handing them to a nodding Shimada.

There was a sharp *crack!* A long painful cry drifted from the aft berthing compartment. Ishibashi yelled, *"Baka!"* Another blow was delivered.

Ishibashi reemerged through the berthing compartment hatch, followed by Masako, clad only in a loose T-shirt and loincloth. Tears ran down his face, and blood trickled from a corner of his mouth.

With a nod from Shimada, Ishibashi began talking to Masako. Soon, the lieutenant's questions flowed more rapidly, more staccato, with Masako darting glances at Ingram. At length he leaned over and uncuffed Ingram.

After a sharp command from Shimada, Taubman said, "Game's over, Commander." He quickly reached down and gathered his chess set. "Looks like you did something very stupid."

Masako jerked Ingram to his feet.

"Hey, hey," protested Ingram.

With an open hand, Masako slapped him twice across the face.

Ingram rolled his eyes wildly. "What is this, Martin?"

Taubman stepped back. "It is a pity. We trusted you."

"Trusted me — oooff!" Ishibashi drove a fist into Ingram's stomach, doubling him up.

"What have I done," Ingram cried. "What —"

With Masako holding him up, Ishibashi hit him in the eye. Ingram tried to duck the next one, and the blow glanced off. Blood ran freely from a cut on his lip and on his nose. Ishibashi hit him twice more; once in the chest, the other in the throat.

Pain radiated inside Ingram's head, making it feel as if it were going to explode. He choked on his blood, tried to swallow, then gagged. Darkness drifted in and he reached for the merciful corners of unconsciousness.

"Baka!" Ingram barely recognized Shimada's voice.

Masako released Ingram and he tumbled to the deck.

"Commander?" It was Taubman.

"Uhh . . ."

Water splashed in Ingram's face. Some ran into his mouth and he spit it out with blood. He tried to open his eyes, but only one obeyed the command. Standing above him, not clearly distinguishable, were three figures.

"Not an intelligent thing to do, Commander," said Taubman.

Ingram managed to make his mouth

work. "I don't understand," he mumbled.

"The trash bags."

Ingram's heart raced. *How the hell did they know?*

"You haven't been putting the weights into the trash bags."

"Yes, I have. How can you —"

Someone stomped on Ingram's stomach. He doubled up and lost his wind in one large *whoosh.* It took several minutes to catch his breath. He still choked blood, and after a while, he ran his tongue over his teeth, finding miraculously they were still there.

Taubman said, "No more chess for a while, you fool. Now I have no one to play with. Come to think of it, it doesn't matter, since you'll be leaving us tomorrow."

"I don't —"

Taubman's voice was like a pistol shot. "One of Lieutenant Ishibashi's collateral duties is to take inventory of the galley equipment. That includes trash-bag weights. Why is it, Commander, that there are only two weights less then when we handed you the job over two weeks ago?"

Something clicked in Ingram's chest. He ran a hand over his collarbone, but it seemed all right.

"No wonder those destroyers found us.

They were tracking your damned trash bags."

"No. I —"

Ishibashi hit him in the face. For the second time, Ingram thought his head would burst. But he opened an eye to see Ishibashi standing over him, his hand gnarled as he rubbed his knuckles.

Taubman looked down. "We could have been such good friends."

Masako recuffed Ingram to the workbench, bowed, and backed toward the after berthing compartment, managing to slither through the hatch backward. The other three officers walked forward, Ishibashi massaging his knuckles.

Ingram lay back after they were gone, wondering if he could pull that stunt again. He had had no idea a depth charging could be so horrifying. But the thought of Ishibashi and Masako beating him up as Shimada and Taubman looked on dispassionately enraged him. That, and the U.S. destroyer taking a torpedo right before his eyes.

Painfully, he rolled to his side. Just before darkness set in, he muttered, "Screw you, Fritz."

THIRTEEN

18 JUNE 1944
IJN SUBMARINE *I-57*
STRAIT OF MALACCA, EN ROUTE PENANG ISLAND

The sea was a solid sheet of smoked glass as the *I-57* ran on the surface, a long undulating wake curving off her black hull. Time after time, she picked her way through minefields on her way to Georgetown, Penang's main harbor. The Malay coast was ten kilometers to starboard. One hundred and thirty kilometers to port, Sumatra's great verdant landmass lay below a horizon, obscured by a gray haze. The day hung heavy with humidity and no wind; the odor of guano and decaying sea life from drying reefs filled the air. Shoals reached out to them, constricting their passage. Lobster pots and timeless fishing junks bobbed in the *I-57*'s wake, their sails hanging limp.

Ingram was below in the moisture-laden maneuvering room, the air so thick he could barely see across the compartment. Everything was wet as condensation ran down the bulkheads; it was only ten in the morning, the temperature soaring to well over a hundred degrees. The humidity, he was sure, was just as high. Blue-white bolts of electricity occasionally arced from a large bulkhead-mounted electrical cabinet standing about ten feet from Ingram. Ever since they had surfaced, the place smelled heavily of ozone, the cabinet discharging temperamental blue arcs. A white sign was posted on the cabinet with red Japanese characters and a lightning bolt at the bottom.

With his watchdog, Masako, posted topside as a lookout, a shirtless Ingram was handcuffed to his "bunk" under the workbench. Bracing his arms on a slippery deck, sweat trickled down his chest, and a makeshift bandanna was tied around his forehead, his scraggly uncut hair sticking out in all directions.

Three hours later the sea detail was set, the bridge annunciator ringing stridently as the *I-57* wove her way through tight quarters. Three sailors had taken positions at the electrical switchboard in the after part of the maneuvering room, about twenty feet aft of Ingram's perch. Two of the sailors, Third-Class Petty Officer Samara and Leading Seaman Takada, were motormen who threw enormous levers, controlling power to the two main motors that turned the *I-57*'s twin screws. Hovering behind them was Superior Petty Officer Shimazaki, who watched a bank of electrical gauges, occasionally giving orders. Like Ingram, the three were shirtless; sweat cascaded down their torsos. In fact, Samara and Takada wore only shorts, while Shimazaki maintained the decorum of his office by wearing oil-splattered trousers, white combination cap, and sound-powered phones. An annunciator bell would ring an order on the maneuvering board console, one of the two motormen would reach up and twirl a repeater to acknowledge receipt of the bell, then throw one of the large levers to execute the command. Shimazaki would follow up with a verbal reply on his sound-powered phones. Their procedure was not unlike in the U.S. Navy, Ingram thought. And these men were good, he noticed. Every move was calculated, exact, thoughtfully executed. There was no extemporaneous talk as they awaited the next command. Occasionally, one would glance at Ingram, his face expressionless, then return his attention to the controls.

Only once did Shimazaki raise his voice. Leading Seaman Takada, the shorter of the two, threw a lever the wrong way.

"Ahhhh!" went Shimazaki, whipping off his hat and slapping it across Takada's back.

Quickly, Takada reset the lever and things settled down, the motors steadily feeding power to the *I-57*'s propellers as they crept around Penang Island's northern approach to the Georgetown docks.

An hour later, the motors whirred at a low hum, the shafts turning slowly. Backing bells were ordered on one shaft or the other, sometimes on both, telling Ingram they were approaching an anchorage or a dock. It was immediately noticeable that the slower they went, the less air there was to funnel down the maneuvering room hatch, making the compartment more oppressive. Ingram's tongue seemed thick, and he sweated from head to toe. Compared to this, the Philippines were a cakewalk. Of course, Penang was about three or four degrees north of the equator, he recalled, much closer to it than the Philippines.

At length, the annunciator bells chimed three times. The motormen placed their levers in neutral, stepped back, and sat on stools, talking animatedly. Shimazaki walked forward and soon returned with a pot of tea. Ingram watched him pour and, as hot as it was, found himself licking his lips. It made him terribly hungry. He forced himself to look away.

Something brushed his shoulder. Ingram whipped his head around, finding

Shimazaki, the superior petty officer, holding out a chipped mug. *"Hai,"* the man said softly. He nudged Ingram's shoulder, his face barren of expression.

Ingram nodded and accepted the mug. "Thanks."

Shimazaki walked away without a word.

Ingram sipped and, in spite of the heat, it tasted wonderful. Beside plain water, he hadn't had anything decent to eat or drink since the evening before he was plucked from the Pacific Ocean.

He took another sip. Then another, letting his mind wander back eighteen months to a night in San Francisco. They sat in Wong Lee's café. Newly married, he and Helen were celebrating their escape from the Japanese-held Philippines. Wong Lee, an old friend, had given them his best private booth and they were enjoying tea. Then the waiter padded in with two steaming bowls of hors d'oeuvres and —

His mug was knocked from his hand and went flying across the compartment, hot tea spraying over his arm. "Oww." He looked up.

Wearing fatigue whites, Lieutenant (j.g.) Fumimaro Ishibashi stood over him, his lips compressed, his hands on his hips. Masako stood directly behind, clad also in fatigues.

"You sonofabitch!" Ingram yelled.

Ishibashi jerked his thumb up. *Rise.* At the same time, Masako bent and uncuffed his leg.

As soon as the manacle was off, Ingram sprang onto Ishibashi, wrapping his arms around his waist in an open-field tackle.

"Ooof!" went Ishibashi.

They fell onto a large tool cabinet, Ingram punching at the man's face with his fists. But they were too close and his blows weren't landing. With a loud growl, Ishibashi wiggled mightily and heaved, throwing Ingram to the side. Ingram tried to hold him down, but the man was wiry and began to slip out from under.

A pair of hands yanked on Ingram's shoulder, pulling him away. But not until he landed a fist on Ishibashi's nose, making cartilage crunch. Another pair of hands fumbled an iron grip around Ingram's throat, and he was jerked to his feet. He could hardly breathe and he flailed his arms, wiggled around to find it was the tea-serving superior petty officer motorman who held him. Someone pinned his arms behind his back. A quick glance told him Masako was backed against an electrical cabinet, his eyes wide open. Everyone yelled as Ingram kicked at his captors.

A fist drove into his stomach. But he'd tensed his muscles and turned a bit sideways to parry the blow.

It was Ishibashi relishing the moment. Blood ran freely from his nose as he stood back. His right arm was cocked, and he rubbed his right hand with his left, preparing to deliver another blow.

The men shouted as Ingram kicked out.

"Stop, all of you!" someone yelled.

Another man bellowed something in Japanese.

Suddenly, it became quiet. Ingram was released, and he stumbled, nearly falling to his knees. Grabbing a stanchion, he looked up, seeing Commander Shimada and Martin Taubman, both in dress uniform, elbowing their way through what had become a considerable crowd.

With a sharp command from Lieutenant Commander Shigeru Kato, the ship's executive officer, all drew to attention.

Ishibashi glared at Ingram and wiped blood off his chin with the back of his hand. Some of it had splattered his dress-white shirt.

Kato barked another command and they lined up in a file, Ishibashi the most senior to the left, Masako the most junior to the far right.

With his hands behind his back, Shimada walked down the line of sailors and finally drew up before Ishibashi. The man's head dipped as Shimada quietly talked. Ishibashi sniffed and raised a hand to wipe blood, but Shimada batted the hand away, speaking rapidly.

With a final glance at Ingram, Shimada walked out, followed by Kato and Ishibashi. Then the rest of the men walked out, leaving only Taubman, Masako, and the three motormen, who had returned to their console to write in logbooks. *Why am I still alive?* Ingram thought in amazement. Due to be disembarked in Penang, it was his last day on this ship, and now he wondered if it was the last day of his life.

Masako walked up and pointed toward the hatch leading topside. *"Ike!"* he grunted. *Let's go.*

"What the hell?" Relief poured through Ingram. He had felt certain that he'd be executed.

Taubman said, "This whole incident was so unnecessary, Commander. All they wanted was to escort you topside to join your friends." Taubman folded his arms and leaned casually against the recalcitrant electrical cabinet. The place still smelled of ozone, and Ingram hoped Taubman was about to get zapped with ten thousand volts.

"Shocking." Ingram walked past Taubman.

"What?"

He climbed the ladder and muttered under his breath, "Screw you, Fritz."

* * *

Masako waited topside as Ingram crawled through the hatch. Even though it was gloomy, it was the first time he'd had seen the full light of day since he'd been captured. Moored forward of the *I-57* was a large seagoing tug, while aft, a rust-streaked cargo ship that looked as if she'd been salvaged from the ocean's bottom brooded in her berth, her decks swarming with workers and swinging cargo booms. Outboard of her was a fuel barge with two black hoses snaking over the cargo ship's bulwarks. Ingram was amazed at how Shimada had squeezed the *I-57* in here. Ships and workboats were crowded around, the docks piled high with crates, pallets, and barrels. An ancient steam locomotive chuffed down the pier and lumbered past, its heat reaching out to stifle him. The engine pushed three greasy-black tank cars with a flatcar tacked on the front carrying an ack-ack battery, its cannon raised to the sky, soldiers winding the training and elevation wheels. The air carried an odor universal to harbors worldwide: a mixture of creosote, decaying fish, and human refuse.

A *Mutuki*-class destroyer was moored to another dock a hundred meters off to the right. In front of the *Mutuki* was a gracefully raked *Takao*-class heavy cruiser. Except this *Takao* didn't look too good. She listed heavily to port, and her after turret was blackened, one gun barrel raised to the sky at an obscene angle.

With all its intensity, Penang looked quite commercial except for the ack-ack battery on the train and, of course, the cruiser and destroyer across the way.

A warm drop or two fell on Ingram's face and he looked up, seeing a roiling sky overcast, threatening rain. As if in confirmation, thunder rumbled in the distance as dockyard workers walked among puddles, waiting for a gangway to be lifted into place by an overhead crane.

With a grunt, Masako shoved Ingram's back.

"Okay, okay." Ingram walked forward and edged past the conning tower, as Commander Shimada and Lieutenant Commander Kato looked down on him. Lieutenant Ishibashi was nowhere to be seen.

A dozen sailors were gathered around the torpedo hatch. Working a block and tackle, they drew out a massive Type 93 torpedo. Another lay on the deck, its main body a gleaming black, the warhead an iridescent copper. Just then, the fuel barge that had been alongside the cargo ship slid alongside the *I-57*, her crew tossing up messenger lines for fuel hoses. With its diesel engine growling, a crane lowered an anchor on the *I-57*'s foredeck next to a considerable amount of chain. Ingram ran that through his mind. American submarines didn't carry anchors in wartime. Too much of a chance of the anchor or the chain breaking loose and rattling during a depth charge attack: easily detected by sonar.

Masako pushed Ingram over the gangway and onto the pier toward a stack of crates, cartons, and burlap sacks piled ten feet high. Seated around the piles in shadows were men he hadn't seen before. Their clothes were far worse than rags. Some wore crude straw hats. Some were without shirts, while others had no shoes. By comparison, Ingram's oil-soaked working khakis looked like he'd just stepped from Brooks Brothers. Their skin was a dark brown, but there was something familiar about them as Ingram stepped closer. *Damn. These are POWs. Americans.*

A soldier stepped before the men and blew a whistle. Universally grumbling, the men rose. One was on a cane, Ingram noticed, and grimaced as he got up. A Japanese soldier walked up to him and hit him with a rifle butt, knocking off a crude straw hat.

The man yelled in agony but stayed up as the soldier, now satisfied, walked away. With a stick-thin arm, the POW bent to pick up his hat, but he couldn't reach it as Japanese soldiers screamed orders for the men to form ranks.

"Donnie?" Ingram said softly. Ignoring Masako, he walked over to the man on the cane. "Donnie?" Ingram called. The man was towheaded and thin, his collar bones bulging through his skin. He looked up as Ingram called, "Donnie. For cryin' out loud." Now Ingram was sure. It was Donnie Alberts, a classmate from the Naval Academy, a year senior to him. A track star from Hollywood High School, Donnie's nickname was "Easy Don."

Recognition flashed over Alberts's face as Ingram approached. But he turned away.

Ingram picked up Alberts's hat. "Donnie, you sap. It's me, Todd." He reached around and handed the hat to Alberts.

"Fer crissake, Ingram, shut up. You never could do things right. Trying to get me killed?" Alberts jammed on the hat and hobbled over to the group of men, now lined up before fifteen or so army guards.

Ingram called after Alberts. "Donnie, all I wanted to do was to —"

Something exploded in Ingram's back. The next thing he knew he was lying on his side, pain cascading up and down his spine. He looked up to see a Japanese soldier leaning over and yelling down at him.

"Huh?"

The man bent closer and yelled louder, jerking his thumb over to the group of POWs. He also caught Masako in his vision about ten feet away, looking entirely helpless. "Give me a minute." Ingram settled back to see if he could move properly.

The guard muttered something and drew his bayonet and mounted it on his rifle.

"Ahhhh." Ingram rose, pain shooting up into his neck, and stumbled over to the group of POWs and fell in beside Alberts.

Two soldiers dragged a pair of crates before the POWs. A Japanese army officer waited until the soldiers jammed the crates together then finally stepped up. He wore a sword, and with his hands on his hips, slowly turned from side to side, looking over his prisoners. The guards withdrew to stand at attention with the others. Looking entirely out of place in his whites, Masako fell in beside them.

The officer rubbed his hands together. "I see someone new has joined us from the Imperial submarine *I-57*." The man looked at Ingram. "Welcome to Camp 642. Your presence is most honored here. I am Captain Abe." The man paused.

Alberts said in a bare whisper, "Ingram, bow, you stupid bastard."

Stunned that the man's English was so good, Ingram gave a deep bow.

"Very good." Abe turned to the POWs.

"And now, it is time to load the submarine. It must be done quickly and efficiently. Any pilferage or damage to goods will be quickly dealt with. We must finish in" — he raised a wrist to check his watch — "exactly two hours. So line up over there and get moving." Captain Abe stepped down.

The guards began shouting and shoving the prisoners into a line that extended across the pier, over the gangway, and onto the *I-57*'s foredeck at the hatch. The men alternately faced each other, and crates soon came down the line. Ingram didn't recognize anyone else, and their uniforms were so bedraggled he couldn't tell what branch of the service they were in.

Five minutes passed with Ingram settling into a routine, passing food crates and boxes. Apples, bananas, tangerines, oranges came down the line along with canned goods. After a while, Alberts muttered in a low voice, "Welcome aboard, Todd. What brings you to us?"

Ingram gave a quick account of being blown off the bridge of his ship, noting more than a few ears cocked his way. Then he asked, "How 'bout you, Donnie? Last I heard, you were on the *Houston*." The cruiser U.S.S. *Houston* (CA 30) stumbled on a major Japanese amphibious force invading Java on the night of February 28,

1942, and, after having sunk at least four transports, was sunk by the Japanese covering force.

Alberts's eyes momentarily fixed on Ingram. "With her to the end. After she went down, we swam ashore and tried to hook up with the natives. Found some, but they started hacking us up. Remember Jerry Jenks?"

Ingram brightened at the thought. Jenks was another Naval Academy classmate in Ingram's class. "Yeah."

"Damned native split his head open with a machete."

"Sonofabitch."

"Shhhh!" They passed crates for a moment. Then Alberts continued, "Those Java bastards don't like us. Four hundred years of Dutch rule and they hate white people. They're glad to have Japs."

"Shaddup, you guys," hissed the prisoner on Ingram's right. Just then a guard strolled by, his eyes darting among them.

After the guard walked off, Ingram asked, "Is this as bad as it looks, Donnie?"

"Afraid so. Some guys have it worse, though, working on the railroads in Burma. I've been with these guys for about six months. Before that, I was working the docks in Batavia." He paused for a moment. "What's it like back home?"

"Beautiful as ever. Except the Japs

bombed Hollywood."

Alberts looked up, his mouth open.

Ingram flashed a grin. "Just kidding. It's wonderful back home. We have a place in San Pedro."

"We?"

"Yeah, I married this army nurse I met on Corregidor who —"

A guard shouted and one of the prisoners, a short redheaded man, broke from the line and ran for the edge of the pier.

"Baumgartner. What's he up to this time?" muttered Alberts.

Captain Abe drew his Nambu pistol and took aim on Baumgartner. The pistol cracked and Baumgartner dropped, squirming and groaning. With blood trailing from his thigh, he clawed to within three feet of the pier's edge until a guard ran up and kicked him in the head. Baumgartner lay quietly from a moment then groaned while the guard nonchalantly fixed a bayonet to his rifle.

"No!" shouted the POW to Ingram's right. He started to break ranks, but others grabbed his elbows.

"He's not going to do it," said Ingram.

"Shut up, Todd," said Alberts.

Baumgartner rolled onto his back and extended his hands. "I didn't do anything, honest."

"No!" Ingram screamed as the guard raised his rifle.

The guard plunged the bayonet deep into Baumgartner's chest. Baumgartner gave a long, ululating scream, his hands spasming in space. Then he went limp. But his body twitched and convulsed, so the guard bayoneted him three more times.

Baumgartner finally lay still and the guard yanked out his bayonet. Then he reached down and pulled an apple from Baumgartner's pocket. Walking back, he smiled at his fellow guards and took a big, crunching bite.

"Bastard." Ingram had never known such rage. He turned toward the guard.

"Todd. Shit! Don't," Alberts whispered loudly. "If you do anything, it's not just your skin. They take it out on all of us."

"Back to work," yelled Captain Abe.

Morosely, the POWs returned to the task, the crates going to the *I-57* while the overhead crane lifted torpedoes off. Ninety minutes later, a stack of torpedoes lay ashore where the crates had been. Two other piles of boxes and barrels had gone aboard as well.

Now, high in the sky, the sun had burned through, and with a shout, the POWs were herded to a large wooden water barrel, its sides glistening with condensation. Ingram had never known such exhaustion. Sweat ran from every pore as he crowded among the POWs, grappling for one of the crude wooden ladles. Fortunately, the barrel was full and there was plenty of water. Finally, he grappled a ladle and greedily drank in long, dripping gulps, even taking time to pour water over his head.

Someone shouted on the *I-57*'s foredeck and her two diesels rumbled into life. Ingram looked over to her, thinking of the dangerous voyage ahead. In a way, he still wished he were going to France, to Europe, and an existence less harsh than here at the hands of the Japanese. But then he looked over at the POWs. Americans. Friends. Donnie Alberts. Others he would know, for sure. They would pull for one another, and he knew he owed it to them to help out as much as he could with his relative freshness.

Two large stake trucks bumped and rattled down the pier, stopping before the prisoners. The soldiers ran around behind, dropped the tailgates, and began herding them aboard. A guard spun in behind Ingram and shoved him so hard he stumbled into another prisoner who was waiting to climb aboard. "Damn you!" Ingram said.

"Hai." The guard stepped back and drew his bayonet.

Captain Abe walked up. "Something wrong?"

"Nothing." Ingram bowed and stared at the ground. It was his *I-57* training, and he felt sheepish that it came so automatically to him.

A corner of the man's mouth turned up. And his left eye twitched. Drawing his pistol, he said, "You are the new one, Ingram."

"Yes."

"You wish to join your friend over there?" Abe's head jerked to Baumgartner's body, now covered with a dingy tarp. "Perhaps you need some special training."

Ingram bowed again. "I'm sorry, sir." He wanted to gargle with a gallon of mouthwash. He seethed that he'd called this enemy, who was the equivalent of a naval lieutenant, this totally demented junior officer, "sir."

Someone shouted from the *I-57*'s bridge. Moments later, Lieutenant Commander Kato and Masako walked across the gangway and up to Captain Abe. The discussion went on for two or three minutes. Finally, Captain Abe threw his hands up and walked away without looking back.

The POWs were loaded into the trucks, the guards slamming the tailgates shut and climbing aboard. "What?" said Ingram. Masako materialized with his rifle, and nodded to the *I-57*.

"What's going on?" he asked.

Sailors aboard the *I-57* singled up lines as Kato dashed back across the gangway to the submarine. Grunting and muttering, Masako pushed Ingram toward the *I-57* with his rifle. "What are you doing?" he demanded.

Masako pushed harder, and Ingram knew the answer.

"Todd." It was Donnie Alberts calling from the truck.

Ingram looked up seeing hollow-eyed prisoners crowded around him. "Yes?"

"My wife, Laurie, tell her I love her."

"How do I find her?"

"In Ho—"

A guard rifle-butted Alberts from behind, and he fell.

Masako pushed, and Ingram walked across the gangway, just as riggers fixed lines to the crane hook dangling just above. As soon as Masako crossed, the crane took a strain and the gangway was lifted clear. The tug was made up on the *I-57*'s starboard side and she tooted twice. Taubman walked up as sailors pulled in the stern lines. "You were lucky you weren't stuck with those poor fellows."

Blood oozed from under the tarp covering Baumgartner's body. Ingram tore his eyes away to watch the POW-laden trucks rattling up the pier. "I'm not so sure." He looked up. "Why are you doing this?"

"Captain Shimada is curious."

"What?"

"He wants to see if you really are a warrior."

FOURTEEN

20 JUNE 1944
IJN SUBMARINE *I-57*
STRAIT OF MALACCA

The afternoon was thick with haze as the *I-57* ran on the surface at eighteen knots. Georgetown lay in her wake and her course was due west, with Shimada intending to cross the Strait of Malacca and leave Rondo Island, the northernmost island off Sumatra's northwestern tip, thirty kilometers to port. The *I-57* cleared Rondo on schedule, but once out of the protection of Sumatra's landmass she was greeted by twenty- to thirty-foot waves and forty-knot winds, where she plunged into the great channel of the Andaman Sea. The *I-57* crested wave after wave, only to corkscrew her way down into stygian troughs, the submarine completely immersed. The conning tower hatch had to be closed, with the submarine's sole source of air through the main induction, a large pipe giving air to the engines. The main induction rose in the after conning tower a few feet above the bridge.

In these conditions, Shimada insisted on

a bridge crew of two officers and four lookouts. But the waves were steep, and green water often swept over the bridge, requiring the men to strap themselves to the ship lest they be swept overboard. Holding one's breath was a survival trick, and after an hour topside, they were completely exhausted and had to be relieved after desperately holding their breath and wrapping their arms and legs around the periscope shears. On the other hand, the sailors below became seasick, the odor of vomit penetrating every corner of the boat, triggering more seasickness. Officers and men not on watch lay sprawled in their bunks, moaning, hollow eyes staring at the overhead. Their arms grasped stanchions or bunk hoists, unable to sleep due to the *I-57*'s insane pitching and rolling.

The next day they left the Andaman Archipelago to starboard and surged into the Indian Ocean, where the waves grew to fifty feet, the winds screeching to sixty knots. The crew became worse, and Shimada apparently gave up; for at first light on the twenty-second, the *I-57* dived into the Indian Ocean. Blessed peace and quiet descended as they settled to a depth of thirty meters, everyone except the watchstanders falling into a drugged sleep.

Strangely, Ingram wasn't as sick as the others. He put it down to his time in destroyers, which did a lot of bouncing around. So his reward was to clean vomit off the decks. Today, he was in the control room. Water from the bridge cascaded through the conning tower hatch as the watch scrambled down and secured the hatch. With the *I-57* safely under, Shimada set the underway watch, then ambled forward to his stateroom and drew his curtain. With that, conversation in the control room settled to a bored minimum, some watchstanders shaking their heads to stay awake.

With mop and bucket, Ingram was on hands and knees near the air manifold, while a soaking Masako, who had just been on watch topside, kept an eye. But it was obvious the man fought sleep as he stifled a yawn and sat heavily beside the stern planesman.

Ingram figured this was as good a time as any to figure where they were. With the bad weather, he reckoned the *I-57*'s speed was ten knots, which justified staying on the surface if Shimada was sticking to a schedule. Otherwise, why not just dive and get below this mess? They'd off-loaded all but two of the torpedoes, so it was obvious the *I-57* wasn't on an offensive patrol, meaning they weren't looking for targets; in fact, Shimada was most likely avoiding them.

Ingram looked up, seeing the nav station and Masako in one furtive glance. Masako's eyes were closed. Ingram spotted the gyro compass just a few feet away. Everyone was absorbed with their gauges.

Now.

Ingram rose on his haunches and stole a glance at the compass card: COURSE: 250°. Quickly, he went back to his scrubbing, his mind racing with what he'd just seen. *Two-five-zero.* If they had cleared the Malacca Straits, then they must now be cruising through the Indian Ocean, headed for the tip of South Africa. That meant they really were headed for Europe, thousands of miles away. He wondered if —

A foot nudged his rump. Looking up, he saw it was Masako. "What?"

Masako grunted something at him and waved his palm up. *Rise. "Benjo, benjo,"* he muttered.

Ingram sighed. Masako wanted him to go aft and clean the toilet. "Sure, I'll put a man right on it." Gathering bucket and rags, he stood and followed Masako aft. Passing through the galley and engine room, they stepped into the maneuvering room and walked by his bunk under the lathe. They continued past the two motormen at the main propulsion station and stepped through the hatchway leading into the after berthing compartment. Once inside, Masako checked his watch, muttered something in Japanese, and nodded toward the *benjo,* a tiny white-painted compartment no more than three by three. The deck was black and white tiled, and there was an eight-inch-diameter hole at the forward end. Close by were indentations for one's feet where one squatted to take care of business. A standard stainless steel washbasin was mounted on the aft bulkhead, and two gleaming chrome handles controlled water to a shower spigot overhead. The place invariably stank, and Ingram always gagged when cleaning in here. Which reminded him: he'd just cleaned in here this morning. Why so soon?

Masako grunted several times, and finally Ingram got the idea. Washdown. Good. He carried the stink of the past six days on him. Taking off his clothes, he stepped into the *benjo* and patiently waited for Masako to blast away with a hose as he had in the past.

Masako held out a straight razor, a bar of soap, and shaving cream.

Ingram was stunned. "On the level?"

Masako nodded and pointed to the two shower faucets. He leaned in and turned on the basin faucet, testing the water. With another grunt, he waved toward it and tapped his watch. *Hurry.* Then he closed the door.

Ingram quickly lathered his face with the shaving cream. The razor was pleasantly sharp, removing fifteen days' growth in two minutes. Flipping on the overhead shower spigot, he luxuriated in . . . fresh water, he realized. Hot water! Steaming! It cascaded over his knotted hair and down his body, his first real shower in over two weeks.

Suddenly, the door flew open. It was Masako shouting and pointing to his watch.

"Okay, okay."

Masako slammed the door and Ingram quickly soaped up, rinsed, lathered, and rinsed again, his skin tingling as if he'd just rolled in fresh snow. He tried the door but it was locked. "Hey!" He knocked. Nothing happened so, enveloped in steam, he sat on his haunches and waited . . .

The door crashed open. Again it was Masako, a towel in his hand. But Ingram had fallen asleep and pitched out onto the deck. Luckily, he caught himself with an outstretched hand. Rising to his feet, he accepted the towel and dried off, while Masako leaned against the bulkhead with crossed arms. Wrapping the towel around his waist, Ingram asked, "My clothes?"

Masako nodded forward.

"My clothes, please."

Masako yelled, gesticulating to move forward. When Ingram hesitated, he doubled his fists and moved close.

"You want me to walk around like this?" Ingram asked.

"No, Commander, that is not his intention." Martin Taubman stepped through the hatch. "Seaman Masako merely wants you to wait at your berth until your clothes are done."

"What?" Ingram tucked the towel.

"Here's a comb, Commander. Compliments of the Kriegsmarine. Your clothes will be done in" — Taubman checked his watch — "another twenty-five minutes. Then you and I are to have lunch with the captain." Taubman headed forward. "See you shortly."

"I don't know if this is a good idea."

"Why?"

"I may try to kill the sonofabitch. You, too."

"I'm sure you'll remember your manners." Taubman walked off.

Ingram was amazed when, thirty minutes later, a seaman walked down the passageway with his clothes in hand, freshly washed, mended, and starched. Likewise, the man handed over Ingram's shoes, which, although still damp from tramping around the Georgetown docks, had been brought back to somewhat of a luster. Ingram accepted them with a bow. Returning the bow, the sailor reached in his pocket and held out Ingram's silver commander's collar insignia.

He was tying his shoes when Taubman walked in. Looking at him with approval he said, "Very nice, Commander. Are you ready?"

Ingram stood. "Whose idea is this?"

Taubman waved Masako away with the back of his hand. "Mine, actually. Don't you think it's time for a little cultural exchange?"

Ingram rubbed his chin. "Well, if you guys want to surrender to me, then I'll be glad to think it over."

Taubman chuckled. "This is not a good attitude, Commander Ingram. Captain Shimada sincerely wants to give you a pleasant meal, officer to officer. I thought you would be agreeable to this."

Ingram's jaw stuck out. "After that, it's back to sleeping under the lathe and cleaning toilets? If that's the case, then I'd rather not."

"I see, Commander. And you are negotiating from a position of strength?" Taubman took a step back and jammed his hands on his hips.

Ingram opened his mouth for a snide retort. *Shut up, Todd. Maybe you'll learn something.* "Okay, Herr Taubman. Lead the way."

"That's better. I think you're in for an enjoyable time."

Taubman knocked. After a guttural reply, he parted a red curtain and waved Ingram through. Ingram couldn't help gaping. Except for its size, he could have been at the Crown Room of the Hotel del Coronado. The wardroom was a space perhaps six by twelve, done in deep wood paneling. Brass hardware gleamed on the cabinetry, and the table was set with sparkling crystal and china. The wall-to-wall carpeting was a deep maroon, and the chairs were finished in a soft black leather. The compartment smelled of a richly patronized restaurant, including cigars and fine wine. Wearing a dress tunic with ribbons, Shimada stood at the head of the wardroom table with eight place settings. Five other officers stood with him and bowed in unison.

Open-mouthed, Ingram nudged Taubman. "What?"

"Military protocol prevails here, Commander. Now, you may return the bow to the officers as a group, then you should bow to the captain."

"You sure? I don't want my head ripped off." Ingram did as he was told.

"It's all right." Each bowed again as Taubman made introductions. "You've met, I believe, Lieutenant Commander Shigeru Kato, the ship's executive officer."

Ingram had been ordered not to look anyone in the face from the earliest point of the voyage. It seemed strange now to look at their faces, their eyes. "Er, Martin, I'm not supposed to have met any of these people," said Ingram as he bowed. He was surprised when Kato returned the gesture.

"Forget that for now." Taubman ranged on down the table: "Lieutenant Keisuke Takamatsu, the first lieutenant . . . Lieutenant junior grade Domei Hayashi, assistant first lieutenant . . . Lieutenant Koki Matsumoto, engineering and diving officer. And here is Lieutenant junior grade Fumimaro Ishibashi, the communications officer, whom I believe you've met."

"I believe so," Ingram said with a bow, noticing one of Ishibashi's eyes was black and a large bandage covered his nose.

Taubman continued. "Everyone else is on watch. Now, you are to sit at the end of the table. I will be to your right."

That put Ishibashi directly to Ingram's left. The two men glared at each other as Ingram said, "I would have thought Lieutenant Ishibashi would want to do me in."

Taubman cleared his throat. "Ah, as a matter of fact, he has vowed to do so."

Ishibashi lips formed a subtle smirk.

Ingram felt as if he'd swallowed a

bowlful of ice cubes. "He understands English."

"A few phrases, perhaps," Taubman said.

Shimada sat and they all followed suit, their chairs scraping.

Ingram said, "As a Korvettenkapitän, you should be on the captain's right."

Taubman sighed, "Actually, it should be you sitting to his right. But Captain Shimada filled out the place cards, not I."

Ingram said, "What do we talk about?"

"That's up to the captain."

Shimada looked at Ingram for a full twenty seconds, then gave a thin smile and said something to Taubman.

"With your shower and clean clothes, he says you look every bit the captain of the destroyer U.S.S. *Maxwell*, Commander Ingram."

Unable to control himself, Ingram sat bolt upright.

Ishibashi raised his hand and made a sinking gesture. Matsumoto shook his head slowly.

"Are you sure? How the hell did you —"

"Tokyo filled us in on the details, Commander," said Taubman, elaborately spreading his napkin in his lap. "Our condolences on the loss of your ship."

Shimada said something to Ishibashi, who gave a short laugh.

With great effort, Ingram composed himself as two sailors entered, carrying a large tray with several dishes. The *Maxwell* gone? Unless something catastrophic had happened, she couldn't have sunk. The last time Ingram saw her she had plenty of fight. He traded glances with Ishibashi. *Bullshit.*

Ceremoniously, the messmen placed bowls and plates on the table, Taubman narrating each time a new one arrived: "This is *katsuboshi,* a salami-shaped stick of dried bonito. And here we have *zenzai* beans, which are cooked using the captain's special recipe."

Taubman leaned over one of his plates and drew a long, exaggerated breath. "Ahhh. This is a real treat," he exchanged nods with Shimada. "We took this aboard at Georgetown. It's *tai,* a traditional redfish cooked in a light lemon sauce, again prepared according to the captain's recipe. To help round things out, there is *mochitsuki,* or rice cakes." Taubman waved a palm toward the table's center. "Last, those are a special kind of chestnut called *kachi kuri,* or victory chestnuts."

"I think I'll pass on those."

"Mind your manners, Commander."

"Sorry." *Shut up, Todd, or these guys will throw you to the sharks.*

They ate in silence while the messmen

poured tea. Ingram found the food very good. Doubtless, anything would have tasted good after what he'd been through, but even so, this was a meal worthy of a five-star restaurant. He was just about done when Shimada turned to him and asked a question. Taubman interpreted. "Captain Shimada is interested to learn anything you can tell him about the European invasion."

Ingram took a last bite of *tai* and said, "As I explained before, I have no idea about an invasion."

"Perhaps you can reconsider, Commander. It's important to us, since we're headed, as you know, for the Continent. It would be nice to know what, ahhh, could or couldn't be awaiting us. Do you understand the subtlety here?"

Ingram dabbed his lips, trying to look nonchalant. The others had finished, but he could have eaten another twenty pounds.

Ishibashi produced a pack of cigarettes and offered one to Matsumoto, who accepted. With obvious reluctance, he offered one to Ingram, who waved it away with a "no thanks." Taubman did the same. Then came the lighting ritual, with Ishibashi producing a shiny American Ronson lighter. Others, including the captain, lit up as well, and they sat back and ceremoniously blew smoke in the air, Ishibashi looking fidgety.

Apparently, there would be no seconds, so Ingram said, "I couldn't help you even if I knew, Martin."

"Ah, yes. I see. We're on our own, then."

"Afraid so." Ingram stared as Shimada adjusted his red-checkered scarf.

Taubman said, "You like that scarf?"

"He wears it a lot. Sort of non-reg for a ship's captain, don't you think?"

"Actually, Hajime Shimada is his own man. On his own ship, he doesn't worry about idiosyncracies."

For some reason, Ingram thought of Jerry Landa.

"And I particularly appreciate his wearing the scarf," Taubman continued.

"Oh?"

"Yes, I gave it to him. A Scotch House, you see, pure wool. I took a trip to Hong Kong last year and bought it from an English tailor there. Well, the shop was English, the tailor Chinese." Taubman chuckled. He looked up to Shimada, who must have figured out what they were saying, for he bowed. Taubman returned the bow. "The captain wears it on special occasions."

"So I've noticed," Ingram muttered.

Then Taubman and Ishibashi talked

animatedly. Taubman turned and asked, "Are you aware your forces invaded Guam?"

Ingram stiffened, his air of casual indifference again up in smoke.

"That's why we were out there. They interrupted our voyage to France and sent us to become part of a submarine barrier east of Guam. But there was no activity, so we were detached to proceed on our original mission. But now, it sounds like you caught us off guard. There was a terrific naval battle."

Ingram couldn't help himself. "What happened?"

With an eye to Shimada, Taubman tipped a hand from side to side. "Not sure. Results are sketchy so far. But there were many ships and airplanes involved."

Ingram didn't know what to say. "I see. Well, thanks for the nice lunch." He folded his napkin before him, wondering if they now planned to pound something out of him.

An uncomfortable silence settled, with everyone's gaze fixed on the white tablecloth.

Taubman broke it. "Is there anything you'd like to ask, outside of a military nature, of course?"

"I've been curious."

"Yes?" said Taubman.

"Why didn't you let me stay in Penang with my own people?"

Taubman pursed his lips and translated. After Shimada's reply, Taubman focused on Ingram and said, "Captain Shimada's father was a samurai. Do you know what this means?"

"A warrior of some sort. They wear that crazy bandanna with the funny writing and whack off your head."

"That's putting it crudely. The funny writing is Kanji, and it says, *'Shichi sho ho koku.'* "

"Translation?"

" 'Seven lives to serve one's country.' "

"Sort of like a cat."

"I wouldn't press that point with them. Captain Shimada, or Mr. Ishibashi here, just might take off your head."

"Some warrior."

"Well, it's more than that. They believe in the Bushido code."

"Which is —"

"Bushido means 'the ways of the warrior,' thus it's a code of conduct for the warrior class. Captain Shimada's legacy from his father is one of loyalty, courage, truthfulness, compassion, and, above all, honor. Further, a samurai has a deep respect of life and death, the latter an element so inevitable that it completes one's being."

Ingram could see where this was going. He's seen enough of the Bushido code first hand on Corregidor. In spite of his predicament, he sat stiffly, his bile rising.

Taubman prattled on. "With a stoic appreciation for death, a samurai more acutely appreciates life, especially things that are transient. Take for example, one's father or mother, precious things to us. When they are gone, they're gone. A samurai appreciates the transient elements of our lives more while they are here with us. And when they are gone, they are still connected."

"To one's ancestors."

That earned Ingram a nod from Ishibashi.

"Precisely," said Taubman. "Loyalty, honor, are critical elements to the code. It all enhances their sense of belonging, a national purpose, so to speak."

"Do you follow the ways of the samurai and their Bushido code?"

"Good God, no. I am a simple Lutheran returning to Germany."

"What does Commander Shimada have to do to become a samurai, or" — he waved a hand at Ishibashi — "the lieutenant here?"

Taubman shook his head.

"No?"

"The samurai class was abolished in

1868 with the Meiji restoration. A new military system was established; cities grew by leaps and bounds, as did western culture, thanks in large part to your Commodore Perry, who secured a foothold in the Japanese national psyche." He leaned back and sipped tea. "But it is hard to let go of the old ways. Indeed, many of them have been retained."

Ingram raised his eyebrows.

"Deeply ingrained in the Bushido code of the samurai are the ways of Zen Buddhism, Confucianism, and Shintoism."

"I'm sorry, I don't know anything about —"

"Well, you've seen a bit of it."

"Yes?"

Taubman nodded outside. "That shrine in the passageway. Have you really examined it?"

"All I see are a few pieces of rock and wood."

"Those are mementos from the great Shinto Ise Grand Shrine. Emperor Temmu had established Ise as the primary cult shrine of Imperial Japan. Its main shrine is one dedicated to Amaterasu Omikami, the sun goddess."

"Where is it?" asked Ingram.

"On the Isuzu River in southern Honshu."

"Do the rock and wood really mean something?"

"Yes. The rocks are gathered from the sea and represent the dwellings of deities. And the trees on the grounds of Ise are also sacred, especially the cryptomeria trees. The most divine plant of Shinto, however, is the *sakaki,* a shrub of the tea bush family." He waved a hand toward the passageway shrine. "Thus the rocks and bits of wood."

Ingram said, "Thus the Bushido code."

Taubman said, "In essence, yes."

"You haven't answered my question. Why am I not with my fellow prisoners in Penang?"

Taubman spoke to Shimada at length. Then he turned to Ingram and said, "He wants to see if you are a warrior. The fact that Americans freely surrender is objectionable to him, to all samurai for that matter. They believe you should fight to the death."

"How can I fight a submarine when I'm on a piece of flotsam with nothing but a monkey? Pretty poor odds, I'd say."

"You could have refused rescue."

"What?"

"You could have swam away from the submarine. They would have understood. That would have been an honorable thing to —"

"I tried, Martin, but they started shooting at me."

Taubman waved it off and continued. "But your fight against Lieutenant Ishibashi the other day impressed the captain. You could have been killed. Instead, you fought bravely. That's why you are here. He wants to find out more about it. As does Lieutenant Ishibashi."

Ingram's eyes shifted from Shimada to Ishibashi. "To not give up. Death before dishonor?"

"Yes."

Ingram placed his hands flat on the wardroom table. "Tell them I've seen their Bushido code in action on Corregidor and on Mindanao. I've seen tortured civilians. I've seen old men bayoneted just because they were old; I've seen wounded Filipinos hanging by their feet from a tree branch to be slowly roasted over a low fire; I've seen young women gang-raped and then crucified upside down. My own wife . . ." Ingram pointed at Shimada. "Your esteemed countrymen tortured her nearly to death. She still has cigarette burns over most of her body. And the nightmares, they . . ." Ingram waved a hand in the air. "Tell them this, Herr Korvettenkapitän: If I can suffer capture and live to fight these dirty bastards again, then I'll do it. And one of the guys at the top of my list is that sadistic sonofabitch back at the Penang docks who bayoneted Baumgartner."

Taubman sputtered, “Commander, please. I can’t —”

Ingram rose and pointed at Ishibashi. “And tell him I’ll be glad to take him on anytime. Maybe Commander Shimada would care to shoot me first, like Mr. Abe did to Baumgartner back in Penang. That’ll make it a fair fight. Now translate that, Herr Korvettenkapitän.” He turned and walked out.

FIFTEEN

22 JUNE 1944
IJN SUBMARINE *I-57*
INDIAN OCEAN

Guttural shouts followed Ingram as he stomped out of the wardroom and headed aft. Just before reaching the control room, he was thrown facedown on the deck. Masako and Ishibashi were on him first, beating the hell out of him as others poured out of the wardroom and jumped on the pile. Fortunately, the constricted passageway saved him from a worse mauling. Someone shouted, he thought it was Shimada or Kato; and he recognized Taubman's boots three feet away. He knew he was beyond pain when someone kicked him in the stomach. His mind whirled and she came to him . . . Helen. He reached for her but she disappeared into blackness.

It took several days for Ingram to recover, and he spent it under the lathe, groaning and doubled up in pain. It hurt to breathe and he felt like he had a broken rib. Elsewhere, he had two black eyes and a broken nose. Masako brought him food and water twice a day, and eventually he was able to move about. Eight days later, he was again cleaning the *benjo,* accompanied by his watchdog Masako.

Fortunately, the seas grew calm, the days balmy. Now, out of aircraft range, the *I-57* transited the Indian Ocean on the surface day and night at a flank bell doing nineteen and a half knots. It was just before noon on June 27 when Ingram finished polishing the stainless steel fixtures in the crew's *benjo* in the after berthing compartment. Groaning, he rose and looked to Masako, wiping his brow. *I'm finished.*

Masako poked his head in for a cursory inspection, nodded, and checked his watch. Arriving with the split-second punctuality of the three melodic chimes on NBC radio, the odor of baked fish sifted through the compartment. Masako's nose wiggled from side to side, and he grunted for Ingram to return to the maneuvering room. It was time to be chained to the lathe so Masako could go to the mess compartment and stuff his face.

Taubman appeared on the other side of the hatch. "Good morning, Commander." He stepped back, letting Masako and Ingram pass.

Pain ran up Ingram's back as he bent to ease through. He straightened beside

Taubman and Superior Petty Officer Kenryo Shimazaki, the sole watchstander on the control station. Ingram nodded, remembering that this was the only man aboard this ship who, by offering him tea a few days ago, had shown any compassion. He'd later learned that Ishibashi had disciplined him for it. But that didn't stop Shimazaki from giving Ingram mugs of tea and rice cakes during his recovery from the beating.

Ingram hadn't talked with Taubman since the day of the wardroom lunch. "You ready to surrender yet, Martin?"

"Only if you checkmate my king, Commander. You up for a game of chess?"

"I thought you'd be at chow."

"I've already eaten. And if you're a good boy, I can arrange to have something —"

The diving alarm, a strident combination of a high-pitched whistle and a rumbling foghorn, blasted into the compartment. The intercom over Shimazaki's panel screeched. Shimazaki quickly reached up and yelled, *"Hai."* Deftly, he threw a series of long shiny levers on the control board. Actually, they were large knife switches for shifting the electric motors to battery power, since the diesels would soon be shut down.

Once done, Shimazaki grabbed Masako and shouted a rapid command. Masako gave a quick bow and glanced from Ingram to Taubman, his eyebrows raised.

"Go. I'll watch him." Taubman pointed toward the engine room.

Masako dashed off as air roared from the ballast tanks. He barely made it through the engine room hatch when it was slammed shut. The hatch to the after berthing compartment behind Ingram crashed shut as well, giving Ingram a closed-in feeling. The rumble of the diesels ground to a halt and the *I-57* took a down angle. Quickly, Shimazaki threw the switches to disconnect the diesels from the motor-generators. Even though he couldn't read Japanese, Ingram could see the engine order telegraph was still set to All Ahead Flank. "We're diving?"

With a nod, Taubman cocked an ear to the intercom and said tersely, "Aircraft sighted, four-motor type. Possibly a Liberator."

Shimazaki twirled a large rheostat as Ingram checked an inclinometer mounted on the port bulkhead. The down angle was now six degrees. "What's with Masako?"

"They're minus a watchstander in the engine room, and they need him to help secure the diesels and rig for depth charging," said Taubman. The angle steepened, making him stumble. He reached out to grab a handrail.

The submarine groaned and creaked with the inclinometer bubble now reading twenty-one degrees. A tea mug slipped off a shelf and shattered on the deck as an unperturbed Shimazaki checked his motor settings.

Quickly, Ingram checked a bulkhead mounted chronometer: 1627. Plenty of daylight topside, and they were under attack by fellow Americans. His own countrymen, or maybe Brits. If Taubman's information was correct, they were flying a B-24, a big four-engine long-range bomber with enough speed, bombs, and machine guns to make mincemeat out of the *I-57*.

Suddenly, Ingram couldn't catch his breath. He wanted to race for the hatch, throw it open, and scramble topside. He wanted to stand on the deck, wave and yell at the B-24 crew. With enormous self-control, he fought the impulse as the *I-57* continued her plunge.

It's too late to go out there anyway. A hell of a samurai I'd make. Just call me chickenshit Joe. But, by God, I've got a baby to bounce and a wife to kiss. A lot to live for. No, I don't want a bunch of Army Air Corps jockeys blowing me up just now.

More loose gear tumbled from shelves and lockers and shattered on the deck; shards, tools, and odd bits of clothing cascaded forward and crashed into the bulkhead. The submarine shuddered, with Ingram, Taubman, and Shimazaki reaching to brace themselves on the control board.

Twin, almost simultaneous, explosions rocked the submarine. She vibrated, and her down angle increased another ten degrees.

"Poor aim," muttered Taubman.

"Too bad," said Ingram.

The sarcasm was lost on Taubman as sweat broke out on his forehead. His knuckles went white, and he clutched a pipe overhead.

Another pair of depth charges roared, shaking the submarine violently. A blue bolt of electricity arced across the compartment. Cork dust spewed about, and Ingram could hardly see more than a few feet.

The lights flickered. Then they went out, plunging the compartment into darkness.

Someone yelled on the intercom. A lone emergency light of low wattage went on. Shimazaki yelled, and in the gloom Ingram saw him flip a switch.

"Gott," swore Taubman.

"What?"

Taubman said, "Stern-plane stuffing tube ruptured back there. They're taking on water."

"No!" Once again, the closeness and the

odors and the opaque cloud raged at his senses. *Get out!*

"Worse."

"What?"

Taubman's voice shook. "The stern planes are jammed at full dive."

"Good God." *What the hell do we do?* Ingram's heart thumped in his chest like a raging bullfrog as the *I-57* dived deeper. He could only imagine the physics outside as ever-increasing water pressure compressed the hull, making it groan and pop in protest as metal grated against metal. Her down angle increased to thirty-five degrees, and he braced a foot on a deck-mounted stool. About him the sounds of loose gear, crockery, cabinets, and tools clanged and crashed. Something swished past Ingram's head and shattered on the console. Another blue-white bolt of electricity zapped across the instrument panel, outlining Taubman's and Shimazaki's faces in a hoary luminescence. The odor of ozone overwhelmed them, ripping at their nostrils.

Suddenly, the hatch to the berthing compartment slammed open. A figure lurched through, flashlight in hand, and reached in a cabinet for tools. Ingram glanced aft, realizing he was looking up into the berthing compartment. Their lights were also out, jiggling beams of flashlights producing the only illumination. Seven or so men were on their knees, clustered around a deck-mounted assembly of some sort. A thin, two-inch pipe extended from the device all the way to the overhead at an obscene angle. Something shrieked, ripping at his ears. Suddenly, Ingram realized the pipe was not a pipe. It was a cold stream of water, blasting into the compartment under enormous pressure. Ingram covered his ears, the shrill noise of the water leak raking his eardrums. Two men slipped on the deck and tumbled forward, their bodies glistening as they slid down the deck and slammed into the bulkhead, where they lay groaning.

The man from the aft compartment grunted and, apparently satisfied, stepped through the hatch and pulled it shut.

Quiet. Blessed quiet, except for the hull's groaning and creaking. Ingram uncovered his ears and blinked with the certain knowledge that he'd just had a glimpse into hell. Unlike the uncontrolled mayhem in the aft berthing compartment, here he discerned what was going on. But it was a false sense of security, he knew. Their problems could rapidly become his problem. Especially if that leak got away from them. And especially if they didn't fix the stern planes.

How deep is it here? he wondered. *Six*

thousand feet? Ten thousand? Dead is dead, no matter whether it's 125 feet or 3,000 fathoms. Oh, God. Please, no, dear God.

To his left was another swish, a thud, and a groan. Intuitively, Ingram knew Shimazaki was down, but he couldn't see in the darkness. He yelled, "Shimazaki is hurt."

"Was?"

Ingram reached over his head, found a battle lantern, and flicked it on. Its beam stabbed down through cork dust and floating bits of insulation, illuminating a ghost-white Martin Taubman. He threw his hands across his face. *"Mein Gott,"* he yelled, reaching out to the console, slipping and falling to the deck.

Ingram reached down and found Shimazaki's head covered with a sticky wetness. "Come on, Martin," Ingram yelled. "Do something." His eyes darted to the inclinometer and his heart thumped: the down angle was forty-two degrees! Both feet were braced on the side of the maneuvering station console as if it were the deck. Only the battle lantern illuminated the compartment, and it was hard to pick out familiar objects. He realized he was looking down at the forward bulkhead and the engine room hatch.

The intercom screeched again. Ingram yelled, "Martin, what's he saying, for Pete's sake?"

Taubman's lips quivered.

"Martin. You're the submariner. Do something. Shimazaki is out." That wasn't quite right. Shimazaki was groaning and trying to sit up, a horrible gash across his forehead. Blood glistened on his face, his left eye completely covered.

The intercom came to life again, the caller's voice hoarse with frustration. Terrible thuds and crashes echoed in the background, while in the maneuvering room the lights flickered in a kaleidoscopic dance.

Ingram chanced another look at the inclinometer: fifty-eight degrees. Then he took a sharp breath: the depth gauge read forty meters, more than 120 feet. His mind raced with the math. This submarine is about 350 feet long. If the depth is 120 feet at the maneuvering room, then the bow must be poking through 350 feet!

Ingram didn't know what crush depth was on this submarine, but he would have laid odds they were close to it. *God!* He reached over to Taubman and shook his lapel. "Martin, we gotta do something. It looks like we're in an uncontrolled dive of some sort. I'm thinking the motors need to be reversed. How do we do it?"

Taubman looked up as the *I-57*'s hull gave a long ranging groan, almost as if a ghost were wailing somewhere in the bilges. Tears ran from his eyes and he mumbled and sputtered.

As Taubman sniveled, Ingram heard the frantic hiss of air coursing from the high-pressure air flasks and into the ballast tanks.

"Martin! They're blowing ballast tanks." Just then he noticed the engine order telegraph was still in the All Ahead Flank position. "That doesn't make sense. What the hell's wrong? Shouldn't we be backing down?"

Taubman sputtered, "Power to the engine telegraph synchro must be out, just like these damned lights. I think you're right. They don't want an Ahead Flank bell. They need an All Back emergency bell."

"Well then, what the hell do we do?"

"I . . . I . . ." Taubman's lips quivered, and he reached for Ingram.

"No!" Ingram pulled himself free as his eyes quickly darted about the control board. Then he spotted two large handles with arrow signs pointing forward and aft. Positioned next to those were smaller handles with numerical graduations running to 30.

Here goes. He yanked what he hoped were the motor speed regulators to the 0 position. He was rewarded to hear the motors wind to a stop. *Next.* He pulled the direction levers through the neutral position to reverse. Then he eased the motor speed regulators forward to 15. The motors spooled up slowly.

"All right."

I-57 began to shake and rattle as the screws bit the water. "Okay!" Ingram shoved the power handles all the way to 30. The motors wound up faster as the screws churned in reverse. His eyes flicked to the depth gauge: ninety meters! Inclinometer: seventy-one degrees. Nearly twenty degrees to straight up and down. But the *I-57*'s plunge seemed arrested while air hissed, blasting a path from the air flasks to the ballast tanks.

The depth meter stopped winding. In fact, it began rising. "Martin. Look!"

"Ahhhh!" Shimazaki rose next to him, wiping a rag over his bloody face. But he seemed alert as he reached up to match pointers on the engine room telegraph. But it was still in the All Ahead Flank position, so he flicked on the intercom button and shouted at the officers in the control room. A heated exchange followed as the submarine shook and vibrated, her screws frantically pulling her from being crushed like a watermelon. At the same time, the down angle decreased from 71 degrees to 65 . . . to 55 . . . 40 . . . 25 . . . 15.

The submarine was nearly level when Shimazaki muttered, *"Bako."* Throttling down the motors, he disengaged them, threw the motor reversal switches forward, then set the power at 15.

Ingram nearly shouted for joy as the down angle rapidly became an up angle. Like a drunken whale, the *I-57* lurched toward the surface, the up angle now twenty degrees. Then the angle increased to thirty degrees and loose gear that had plunged to the forward bulkhead now soared on a new journey to the aft bulkhead, crashing about him and Taubman and Shimazaki, the cacophony worse than before.

The *I-57* blasted through the surface, her bow crashing back onto the water. She slid back under for a moment, then shook herself back to the surface and rolled in a glassy sea, water spilling from her decks and limber holes. As she wallowed back and forth, the conning tower hatch opened. A lone figure crawled out and, lacking the strength to stand, lay with his back to the bulkhead.

He drew in a sharp breath. Looking aft, he saw a thirty-foot section of the teak main deck had been ripped away as if by the gnarled hand of Susanoo, the storm god, brutal brother of Amaterasu, the benign sun goddess. The starboard screw guard was twisted like a pretzel, with stanchions and other topside gear bent to obscene angles. In the distance, he saw a lone B-24 circling a smoke float, perhaps fifteen kilometers down sun: a miracle. Another miracle was just two kilometers ahead: a rainstorm approached. A third miracle was that the port engine coughed into life, pulling oxygen-rich air through the stricken *I-57*. In the maneuvering room, Superior Petty Officer Kenryo Shimazaki threw his switches.

The *I-57* staggered to safety.

SIXTEEN

27 JUNE 1944
IJN SUBMARINE *I-57*
INDIAN OCEAN

At first glance, Commander Hajime Shimada thought that he'd soiled himself. No! It was seawater that darkened his crotch, not urine. He'd been drenched when he popped the hatch to the bridge, soaking half his body. Grabbing a handrail, he lurched to his feet, glad for these few moments by himself. The *I-57* was making close to fourteen knots and they'd halved the distance to the rain clouds, lightning crackling in its midst. Only a few hundred meters to go.

Perfect.

Aft, he saw the Liberator still flying lazy circles over the smoke float. Then it straightened and came in low, two black specks falling from its belly. Thirty seconds later, two enormous geysers spewed up as the four-engine bomber pulled up and out.

The storm cloud swooped over them. Safe! It was raining, and it felt wonderful.

Shimada stepped over the hatch and

yelled down, "Lookouts, up."

"On their way, Captain." Shigeru Kato, the executive officer, stood in the conning tower, looking up, his fatigue cap splotched with oil.

"Who's listed for junior officer of the deck?" Shimada barked.

"Ensign Kintomo, sir."

"Well, get him up here or I'll slap him under hack."

"His leg is broken, Captain. The doc has him lashed to his bunk."

Shimada seethed with the memory of the report from the forward torpedo room. The one remaining torpedo had broken loose just as they passed the sixty-five-degree down angle. Three men, including Ensign Kintomo, were seriously injured trying to secure it. *How did they ever do it?* he wondered. "All right then," he said to Kato, "you'd better get up here as OOD. And find a new JO to help you."

"Yes, sir."

"Do you have damage reports?"

"Yes, sir." Kato began his climb. "That's why I was coming up."

The more Shimada thought about the fact that they'd almost died for nothing, the angrier he became. "Hurry up!"

"Yes, sir." Kato scrambled up and saluted.

Shimada returned the salute. "Go ahead."

Pulling a grease-smeared sheet of paper from his pocket, Kato began, "The stern planes are still jammed in the hard-dive position."

Shimada whisked off his cap and held his face to the rain, letting the water run down. "What happened?"

"The hand-tilting shaft bound against the pressure hull with the second depth charge attack. Then the coupling shattered and nothing worked. Worse, the stuffing tube on the starboard side gave way, setting up a major leak in the after berthing compartment. Half the place flooded. But it's almost pumped dry now, and the coupling should be repaired in another thirty minutes. Then we can zero the stern planes."

The rain became a downpour, and the water felt wonderful. Shimada took off his shirt, letting the fresh, cleansing water cascade over his body. "What about the starboard engine? When does it come on line?"

"As soon as we fix the 500-pound air-starting line. It ruptured in several places with that one depth charge."

"Kato, I asked you when."

"Yes, sir. Fifteen minutes."

Shimada nodded and wrung out his shirt. "Now solve a mystery for me." His gaze found Kato's eyes.

"Yes, sir."

"Where's the damned chief engineer. Why haven't I heard from him?"

"Lieutenant Matsumoto was in the engine room when the attack occurred. He slipped on the deck, then fell against the bulkhead and was pummeled with flying debris. He was unconscious until a few moments ago. Now he's with the work party on the starboard engine."

Shimada nodded. "Another mystery. What happened in the maneuvering room? Why didn't they answer the backing bell? Shimazaki is our top electrical NCO. You would have thought he would have figured what to do."

Kato shrugged. "I don't know about Shimazaki. What I do know is that the a/c auxiliary power motor-generator circuit breakers tripped with the depth charging. So the engine room telegraph was inoperative. It was still set at All Ahead Flank, even though you had ordered an All Back Full bell on both motors."

"And?"

"And reports are that Shimazaki didn't answer the verbal command because he was unconscious. To what degree, I don't know yet. But apparently he was out for a while. Also, Korvettenkapitän Martin Taubman was out."

"Where was the prisoner?"

Kato shrugged.

"Right there with Shimazaki and Taubman?" Tiny embers flared in Shimada's eyes. "What about the guard?"

"Well, uh, yes, sir. They sent Masako forward to the engine room to help rig for depth charging."

Shimada stood to his full height. "You're telling me that with Taubman and Shimazaki unconscious, the American was at liberty to move about the maneuvering room?"

"It looks that way. Yes, sir."

"And throw us into a suicide dive?"

Kato said, "I'm not sure yet, Captain. But that certainly could have happened."

"I see." Shimada jammed his cap on his head. "What else?"

"Topside main induction for the starboard engine is dished in. But we can fix that. Also, the master valve for main ballast tank six is jammed open. That's going to take some doing, that and the stern diving-plane stuffing boxes." He waved a hand aft. "And the decking back there is ruined, but that's a yard job. The biggest thing now is cleaning up the litter down below, which is considerable — everything from rice cakes to socket wrenches — replacing lightbulbs, and getting the ship looking more like a ship than a whorehouse." Kato turned red. "Excuse me, sir."

"Injuries?"

"Ensign Kintomo. That's the most serious. Then the two men in the forward torpedo room have various sprains and contusions. After that are minor injuries to Shimazaki, Herr Taubman, and Matsumoto." After a polite cough, he added, "We should be ready for full operational capability in no less than two hours."

Anger boiled within Shimada, but he did his best to not let it show. He waved a hand at the rain falling around him. "Very well. Take the deck and the conn now. Keep us in this rainstorm, no matter what. That Liberator is out there sniffing for us, but they can't find us in here. We'll stay in this until dark, then proceed on our normal course. Remain at fourteen knots and put the starboard engine on charge when it comes on the line."

"Yes, sir." Kato saluted. "I relieve you, sir."

Returning the salute, Shimada said, "I stand relieved. Now I'm going below to inspect the damage." Shimada watched as the lookouts scrambled to the bridge and took their places in the periscope shears, Lieutenant (j.g.) Hayashi joining them as JOOD.

After everyone had passed, Shimada descended through the conning tower and into the control room. He had business aft, all right. But first he walked forward to get something from his stateroom.

Circuit breakers for the auxiliary power system were reset, which allowed the electricians to turn on the lights and air conditioning, giving everyone else a sense of normality. Fervently, men dashed about fixing leaks, unclogging drains, sweeping up broken glass, screwing in lightbulbs, and returning material to shelves and brackets. In the engine room, Ingram was on hands and knees wiping hydraulic oil off the deck plates. A drum had broken its lashings and had caromed about the compartment, spewing the rich-smelling red stuff like a child flinging ice cream at a birthday party. Already, two men had slipped and hurt themselves, giving Ingram's job a high priority. Several feet away, a shirtless Martin Taubman helped with restoring 500-pound air to the starboard diesel starting line.

In retrospect, the hideous mess in the engine room seemed nothing compared to what they'd faced with a seventy-one-degree down angle. The *I-57* had been headed for crush depth, and somehow they had escaped. After broaching, Shimazaki, blood running from his forehead, grinned and clapped Ingram on the back. Strangely, Taubman was silent.

The rumble of the port engine starting was like a call from heaven, and even more so as Shimazaki threw his switches to engage the port diesel to the motor-generators. After that, Ensign Shigeaki Morimura, the assistant engineering officer, relieved him on the control board. Shimazaki walked forward to the temporary hospital on the messdecks to have the jagged cut on his forehead sutured and bandaged.

Men scampered fore and aft, carrying parts and tools, as Ingram scrubbed. It got so that he didn't rise, only watched their split-toed sandals dashing past in other important errands.

Suddenly, a pair of split-toed sandals stopped before him. Looking up, he saw that they belonged to Commander Hajime Shimada. He also wore his dress tunic, and a samurai sword was attached to his belt.

"What?"

Masako and Lieutenant (j.g.) Ishibashi grabbed him from behind and began tying his hands with leather thongs. "What the hell are you doing?" Ingram exclaimed.

They were soon done and stepped away. Suddenly, Ingram felt like the victim jumping from a burning building, spectators below backing away lest they be spattered with the mess. "What's going on?"

With a flourish, Shimada unsheathed his sword and ran a hand along the blade.

Ingram's heart beat faster. Desperately, he spotted a wide-eyed Martin Taubman half hidden behind a cluster of enginemen. "Martin, can you tell me what this is all about?"

Taubman slipped behind an engineman, his face completely hidden.

"Martin!"

Shimada growled and shoved Ingram's head down.

"Bow, you pig," yelled Ishibashi.

"Why?"

Ishibashi spat. "You tried to kill us. Now you're going to die."

"I did not. I — Martin, tell them what I did!" Frantically, Ingram looked for Taubman, finally finding the top of his head behind a large engineman. Instinctively, the men backed away, leaving Taubman exposed.

"Martin, come on. Tell them what happened."

Everyone sensed Taubman would have something to say. Even Shimada looked at him and barked a question in Japanese.

Taubman shook his head slowly and mumbled something back.

They all looked back to Ingram, hate in their eyes.

Ingram nearly shrieked, "No! You can't! Martin! Tell them!"

Ishibashi kicked the back of Ingram's

head. "Bow, you stupid bastard!"

Shimada raised his sword.

"No!" Shimazaki lurched into the compartment, the right side of his face bandaged. With a hand to his head he grunted some Japanese and pointed at Taubman.

Taubman yelled at him.

Shimazaki pointed and yelled back, *"Baka!"*

Ingram closed his eyes. *Helen. Oh, God, my dear, sweet Helen. I'm not going to make it. I love you, honey. You and our child, yet to be born.* It was the best he could do. He opened his eyes and raised his head.

Taubman and Shimazaki glared at each other. Then Shimada sheathed his sword with a loud *clank.* The captain of the *I-57* turned once again to Ingram, his face flush with contempt. With a final glance toward Taubman, he walked out of the compartment.

SEVENTEEN

28 JUNE 1944
NBC RADIO STUDIOS
HOLLYWOOD, CALIFORNIA

The conductor's hand swooped boldly, making Laura's heart thump. The radiant tones of Respighi's *Pines of Rome* burst from the NBC Symphony Orchestra's West Coast Division, filling the room with the grandeur of the ancient metropolis. Only fifty-five instrumentalists from the main NBC studios in New York's Radio City were present. The other twenty-five were pickups, mostly movie people, including Laura on the piano. This was their first full rehearsal. Even at that, their blend was at the top of the profession, captivating, and Laura felt as if she were dancing on air.

They fearlessly rolled through the first movement, "The Pines of the Villa Borghese." It was the finest Laura had heard from such a large orchestra, and she was proud to be part of it as she bore down on her music, biting her lower lip in concentration. Laura was nervous since she would solo today in the third movement,

"The Pines of the Janiculum." But never mind. With each note the orchestra played, she became more confident, more at ease. *This is music at its best.*

It was all due to the spellbinding leadership of the man who stood no more than twenty-five feet away. He knew every note, every bar, every grace note, and every rest by memory. Some of the time he conducted with his eyes closed; elsewhere, he would open them, skewering a violinist or nodding enthusiastically at the harpist. But that was for a different reason, she'd heard. Evelyn McCormick, the harpist, was a stunning blonde with the New York contingent and was the maestro's latest in a long line of mistresses. So what? The man was a genius. He had a broad face, a square jaw, a mustache, and white wavy hair. But what set him apart were the darkest eyebrows mounted atop the most intense eyes she'd ever seen.

He was Arturo Toscanini, reputed to be in his midseventies, yet judging from his vitality and focus, the man, wearing a black turtleneck and dark slacks, would have easily passed for a fifty-year-old.

"Stop!" Toscanini yelled, rapping his baton loudly on the rostrum.

Obediently, the orchestra quit playing, as if a giant had lifted a needle off an enormous phonograph player.

Sliding off his stool, Toscanini pinched his fingers against the bridge of his nose. At length, his eyes fell on one of the French horn players. "Mr. Shackleton, are we boring you?"

Shackleton, one of the California pickup players, looked from side to side.

"Yes, you, Mr. Shackleton."

"I don't understand, sir."

"Damn you!" Toscanini roared, kicking over his rostrum and scattering his sheet music. He pointed to Shackleton. "I ask, where are you?"

Shackleton's eyes went wide as Toscanini's sheet music fluttered in the air and fell to the ground. Helplessly, he looked around and said, "Uh, Hollywood, I suppose, sir."

Toscanini stomped a foot and screeched. "No, no, no. A thousand times no. Not Hollywood. You are supposed to be in the Villa Borghese."

"Where?"

Half the orchestra groaned while Toscanini threw up his hands in frustration. At length, he smiled and said softly, "Mr. Shackleton, perhaps it's better if you go back to playing barroom music or whatever it is that you do." He waved a hand at the door.

"No!" Shackleton said.

Toscanini's eyebrows lifted on his forehead and he stood to his full height. Drawing a breath, he said, "You'd better —"

"I mean, I'm sorry," the man said meekly. "I know, I know. This Borghese business. It's the first movement. It's beautiful, but —"

"Mr. Shackleton, you come highly recommended, but your head is not in this." Toscanini pitched a hand toward the door, more forcefully. "Please go."

"I need the job, sir. My wife is pregnant. And my son has the measles."

"Then you should be doing something where you can properly support them. What do you expect me to do?"

"Please, sir, I'll try."

Toscanini sat back on his stool, again pinching the bridge of his nose with thumb and forefinger. Without looking up, he said, "All right. I'll make you an American deal."

"Anything, sir."

Laura exchanged glances with Roberta Thatcher, West Coast orchestra manager.

Finally the maestro spoke. "You do have public libraries in this town, don't you?" His eyes opened and he found Shackleton.

"Er, yes, sir."

"I want you to go to a public library, check out a book on the Villa Borghese, and write a full report on it for me: its history, a description of the grounds, size, flora, birds, everything. Do you understand?"

"But I —"

"And I want it in forty-eight hours. Is that clear?"

Shackleton's shoulders slumped. "Yes, sir."

"Go then."

"What?"

"Go check out your book. Time is wasting." Again Toscanini pointed to the door.

"Yes, sir." Shackleton packed his French horn and walked toward the exit.

When Shackleton was close to the rostrum, Toscanini roared at the top of his voice, "You all sound like you're playing from the Hollywood Zoo. The Villa Borghese, the Catacombs, the Janiculum, the Pines of the Appian Way, must be in your hearts. You must know these places as if you've lived there all your lives." Toscanini doubled a fist before his face. "Feel them. See the magnificent buildings; smell the odor of death in the catacombs; hear the nightingales at midnight on scented air; hear the slaves triumphantly driven into Rome before conquering masters aboard magnificent, gilded chariots. How can you play Rome if you've never been there? How can you play Rome if you have no passion for it?"

After a scathing glance, he bent to pick up his rostrum. The first and second violinists scrambled to help with the music. Suddenly, he turned to Laura and said, "Miss West?"

If there ever was a paragon for sitting at attention, Laura was it, her heart pounding in her chest. All eyes were on her, she knew, as she squeaked, "Yes, sir?"

"Play a little louder, please. I can't hear you."

"Yes, sir." Laura silently expelled her breath.

Toscanini's eyes lingered on her for a moment. Then he checked his watch and tossed aside the baton, saying, "This is as good a time as any to take an hour for lunch." Chairs scraped and musicians yawned loudly, while Toscanini was lost among a number of sycophants and assistants, Roberta Thatcher among them.

Laura spent a few moments checking her music and making notes. Then she looked for the exit and caught Evelyn McCormick's eye. The NBC Symphony's top harpist didn't look happy. In fact, her glare was downright murderous as she stood near the exit, her arms crossed. Laura decided to head for another exit when she felt a tug at her elbow.

It was Roberta Thatcher.

"Hi."

"I have a message for you."

Laura had no idea what she meant.

Roberta didn't look happy with what she was about to say. "The maestro would be most happy to have lunch with you."

"Oh." Laura's stomach tightened a bit. "Oh, so that's it." She looked over to Evelyn McCormick, obviously spurned by the maestro, at least for now. "Roberta," Laura nodded to McCormick, "what do I do about her?"

"I can take care of her. Will you do it? The maestro would like an answer."

Laura turned to see Toscanini had left the room. "I don't know. Does he know I'm engaged? What do you think I should do?"

"Dammit, Laura," Roberta hissed. "Don't ask me. I don't like being his pimp. Just go to lunch with him and make sure you flash your ring every chance you get."

"Okay."

Roberta, always stately, swooped away. "Back entrance. Now. His car is waiting to pick you up."

She emerged from the rear entrance, finding a black Cadillac limousine waiting, its engine running. Toscanini himself held the left rear door for her. "It's so good of you to join me. I hate eating alone."

"Thank you. This is very nice."

He followed her in, settled beside her left side, and picked up a microphone, saying something to a uniformed chauffeur sequestered behind a sliding glass window. Silently, the Cadillac eased through the alley and made its way to Vine Street and turned south under dark, overcast skies. Toscanini waved a hand outside. "Is California always like this?"

"They call it 'June gloom.' "

"I anxiously await our Mediterranean climate." He reached over to pick up her left hand, covering her engagement ring with his massive right. "Listen to me, dear. Your playing is good. You're all good technicians. I have no complaints in that department. Except here, everyone here seems to be making movies, not music. You should know all about what you're playing. For if you don't, our selection has no passion, no vitality." He patted her hand, let go, and smiled. "Spirit. That's what Respighi was trying to show us. The spirit of a fine old Rome. Don't you see?"

"I'd love to see it sometime."

"And I'd be glad to take you there." He frankly surveyed Laura up and down.

"And soon, too, now that they have a new landlord." The Allies had liberated Rome from the Germans on June 5.

"Did you grow up in Rome?"

"Oh, goodness no. I'm from Parma. Up

north, near Milan. Have you ever had Parmesan cheese?"

"I love it."

Toscanini shook his head slowly. "Sadly, Parma is still under the Nazi boot." He tilted his head and waved. "Those fools will soon get what's coming to them. Do you know that I once spurned Hitler?"

"No." She turned to him, mouth open.

Toscanini moved close and grabbed her hand again. "It was when he was elected chancellor in 1933. That was it for me. I hate those Nazis so much that" — he clenched his fist — "it's like compromising with the devil. So I canceled my engagement to play in the Bayreuth Festival."

"Was he angry?"

"Very. It was a major embarrassment for Herr Schickelgruber. It hit all the newspapers, as I'd hoped."

"What did you do?"

"He wrote a beautiful letter to me on Reich stationery. I refused to answer it. Before long I could see the handwriting on the wall. Mussolini grew angry with me. Stupid fascist, called me into his office and sat at his desk screeching at me for forty-five minutes. Half the time, he sat back, his slick boots on the desk, while I was not invited to sit. Finally, I was excused without having said a word. Then, that idiot Hitler . . . started sending dark emissaries around. That's when I made up my mind. I moved here, to the Land of the Free." His hand flopped on her knee.

Casually, she brushed it away. "And will you go back?"

He gave a wisp of a smile. "Of course. The day is almost here when we will march triumphant and drive those brainless fools into the ground." Then he continued, "I hope you don't mind, we're going to the Brown Derby and will be lunching with David Sarnoff."

"What?" David Sarnoff was the president of RCA. Absently, she sat straight and patted her hair.

"He'll be introducing our concert Saturday night."

"My God."

"This could be good for your career." He slid close and his hand went on her shoulder.

She slid away, letting his hand drop. "My God, Mr. Sarnoff."

EIGHTEEN

28 JUNE 1944
OLSEN'S RESTAURANT
SAN PEDRO, CALIFORNIA

The sun was poised to set over Palos Verdes, leaving San Pedro bathed in a golden glow. Los Angeles Harbor was crammed with warships of all sizes, their gray hulking masses swinging at anchor in a light breeze. An occasional whistle tooted or a clanging of steel-on-steel could be heard from shipyards grinding out vessels of war. Powerful steam locomotives rumbled and clanked onto the piers, delivering the tools of battle to cargo ships, their gaping hatches yawning to the evening sky.

The blue Plymouth coupe pulled in front of Olsen's, an upscale restaurant near the corner of Ninth and Grand. Wearing dress khakis, Captain Jerry Landa got out and walked around to open the passenger door. Helen Ingram, feeling every bit of her full-term pregnancy, pulled herself up, using the door to steady herself.

"Easy," said Landa. "Ummm, perfume tonight." He inhaled deeply, taking in her

Chanel No. 5. In spite of the change in her center of gravity, he marveled at how she'd blossomed with the mask of pregnancy, her face absolutely dazzling. *Ingram, you lucky bastard.*

"I don't get to wear it very often."

"I'm glad you did." He took her hand. "You look like you're going to pop."

"Thanks for the encouragement."

"No, I mean —"

"I know what you mean, and actually, I feel like I am going to pop. Say" — she pointed to a 1941 light green Cadillac convertible two stalls away — "she beat us to it."

"Well, then we're all here."

Helen stiffened when they stepped inside. Laura West sat in the corner booth, her left hand casually flipping through the menu. In her right was a glass of dark amber liquid. She took a long swig — and then spotted them. With a Cheshire cat grin, she scooted out and said, "Hi, everybody." She patted Helen's belly. "Looks like four for dinner." She pecked Helen on the cheek.

"Thanks," said Helen.

"Hi, honey." Landa lightly kissed his fiancée and took his place in the middle, Laura on his left, Helen on his right.

Laura looked into his eyes. "Good day at the office?"

He was temporarily assigned to an intelligence staff in Long Beach. They knew he was killing time and they treated him like dirt. He hated every moment and she knew he didn't like to talk about it. Worse, he knew she was needling him. But what caught him was Laura's inflection. She slurred a bit, and the stark reality of what she'd been doing hit Landa like cold ocean breezes whirling through San Pedro in the middle of winter. Disgust, then anger, surged through him. He fought the impulse to walk out. "Not bad. How was your day? Weren't you to play for his nibs?"

"Toscanini," Helen corrected, kicking Landa under the table.

"I did, and guess what happened?" Laura said.

The waiter stepped up. Helen ordered a Shirley Temple, Landa a beer. Laura ordered "the same," which, Landa guessed, was a double scotch. When the waiter left, Laura continued, "He took me to lunch at the Brown Derby."

Helen broke into a broad smile and clapped her hands. "Laura."

"Did you see anybody?" Landa asked.

"You bet I did."

"Who?" Perching her chin on interlaced fingers, Helen leaned close to Landa, her perfume tickling his nostrils.

"Jascha Heifetz and Miklos Rosa sat in

the booth next to us. The maestro introduced us."

"Who?" said Landa.

"Heifetz is a violinist; Rosa composes music for films."

"Oh," he said.

"And I saw Joe E. Brown. He's as funny as he looks. And a nice man, I'll bet."

Landa crossed his arms. "Did you meet him, too?"

"No, but that's not all. We sat with David Sarnoff."

"Really," said Helen.

Even Landa was impressed. "The RCA guy? What's he like?"

Laura's next sip was immediately followed by a hiccup. "Sorry. David — Mr. Sarnoff is a very nice man. Very conservative. Very, very direct about things. You know where you stand right away. And he knows everybody, even FDR."

"Wow," said Helen.

"He told us about his house in New York. That is, he called it a house, but it sounds like a mansion to me. Toscanini's been there many times. And they invited me."

"Great," said Landa.

Laura pouted. "Well, then we got down to brass tacks and talked about programming." She reached for her glass.

Landa casually laid a hand on her wrist

before her hand got to the glass.

Laura jerked away, her eyes flashing. She opened her mouth with a retort, but then her eyes flipped to Helen. "What's wrong, hon?"

"I feel weird." Helen put a hand on her forehead. "Must be the Shirley Temple."

Landa turned. "You okay?"

"I go through these spells. It's all part of, well, you know what." Running her purse strap over her shoulder, she slid out of the booth.

"You want me to go with you?" asked Laura.

Helen waved her away. "Just going to freshen up. Won't be a minute." She walked off.

Laura waited until Helen disappeared down the back hallway. "That was low," she hissed. "Right in front of one of my best friends."

"I didn't mean to —"

"You embarrassed me."

"I was only trying to help. Your glass was empty."

She looked over, seeing that it was true. "I don't give a damn, Captain Boom Boom or whoever you are. Don't ever do that again." Her face turned red.

Landa sat stiffly. "I will, if you've had too much."

"What the hell do you mean, 'too much'?"

"Honey, almost every time I see you, you're drinking. Now that I recall, I can't remember when I haven't seen you reaching for a glass. I'm getting worried. It's like Luther all over again. Maybe you need help or something."

Laura's voice went to full pitch. "So now you're counting my drinks, you bastard."

"Shhhh." Landa looked around, seeing people avert their eyes. *God, this has gotten out of control.* "I'm sorry. I only meant —"

"I suppose you think I was drunk when you came in tonight?" she demanded.

"No, I didn't say that."

"No, you didn't. But it's in your eyes."

Landa felt himself flushing, which he knew meant he was beyond the point of no return. He snapped, "No, it's not in my eyes. But it's in your face and your voice. You sound like the village drunk. Why don't we take a look at the bill and see just how much you've had tonight."

Laura slid out and stood.

Remorse swept over him. "Honey, I'm sorry." He started to follow, but she blocked him.

"You're the village" — she searched for a word — "dunce. Ha! Jerome Landa from Brooklyn. Who do you think you're fooling with, you stupid jerk?" She twisted off her engagement ring and flung it on the table. "You don't like your job? They treating you like dog crap? So what? Go take out your frustrations on someone else."

She turned and walked out.

For a moment, Landa sat in shocked surprise, not believing Laura was already out the front door, its soft tufted red leather gleaming in the pale light. "Damn!" He scooted out to run after her.

"Jerry." It was Helen in the hall, her hands gripping the doorway molding.

He went to her. "You okay?"

"Let me sit for a minute," she said breathlessly. "How about you?" She nodded toward the front door.

Landa helped her over to the booth and eased her onto the cushion, noticing she looked pale, her hand clammy. "You don't look too good."

The engagement ring had landed on her bread plate. She picked it up and handed it over. "You don't either. What happened?"

"Ummm." He pocketed the ring. Slowly shaking his head, he said, "I think I really messed up. I lost my temper." He quickly explained what had happened. When she didn't respond, he looked at her, noticing beads of perspiration on her forehead. "Hey, what's up? Seriously."

Helen asked, "Seriously?"

"That's what I said."

"Okay, Boom Boom. Here it is with both

barrels. My water broke."

"No shit?"

She nodded.

"That means —"

"Right now, I'm having contractions. Nothing heavy. But we have to get going."

"Where?"

"San Pedro Community Hospital."

"Where's that?"

"Sixth and Walker."

"Okay. I'll put a man right on it. Hold on." Landa went over and spoke with the maitre d', then handed him a two-dollar bill. He walked back saying, "Okay. I got him to alert the hospital. Then he'll call Mrs. Peabody to bring your stuff over. What else?"

"Call my mom and dad."

"I'll do that when we get to the hospital. Come on. Let's get going." He reached down to help, but she stayed put. "What is it?"

"Hold on a moment."

She gripped the table, her knuckles whitening a bit. Landa watched, realizing these weren't minor contractions. Her neck reddened for a moment and, suddenly, Landa's stomach tightened.

A full thirty seconds passed before she looked up, her face pale, but serene, the mask as compelling as ever. He leaned close to take her hand, her perfume reaching up to him. "Okay?" he asked gently.

She gripped his hand with both of hers. "Ready."

Landa ran only two red lights getting Helen to the hospital. He thought his job would be done once the attendants strapped her to a gurney. But one of them, a gaunt, white-coated man of about thirty years, asked, "Are you the husband?"

"No, not me —"

Helen's breath came in short gasps, her knees raised, and she clutched the gurney rails in a death grip.

Landa leaned down and took her hand as they began wheeling her. "You okay?"

Her eyes were squeezed shut, her teeth clamped over her lower lip. Finally, she expelled a great gasp and then looked around, realizing where she was. "Dr. Gaspar here?" she asked the attendant.

"On his way, ma'am."

They wheeled her down a long hall, through two sets of double doors, and into an anteroom redolent of the sharp odor of alcohol. Around were gleaming stainless steel instruments, some in glass cabinets, others on a tray nearby, poised, ready for action. Feeling claustrophobic, Landa moved close to Helen.

She looked up clutching his hand. "Still

here?" She smiled.

I'll say it again. Ingram, you are one lucky bastard. "As long as you need me."

A redheaded female nurse in her forties walked in. Pinned to her collar were an RN badge and a Bakelite tag on her lapel that read BRUBAKER. "So Helen, what have you been up to now?" She threw a blanket over Helen, then began yanking her clothes off underneath. Landa stepped next to her head, doing his best to avoid seeing what Brubaker was doing.

He was close to her mouth when Helen said, "I think this is it, Martha."

"About time. This your husband?"

"No."

"Oh, I'm sorry." She looked up to Landa. "Captain, I think it's time for you to —"

"Let him stay for a little bit, Martha. Please. He's family."

Brubaker planted her hands on her hips. With an eye on Landa, she asked, "How far apart are your contractions?"

"About two minutes."

"Wow."

"And my water broke about twenty minutes ago."

"Better take a look." Brubaker nodded her head to Landa. "Out."

"Yep." Landa walked outside and shuffled up and down the hall. Two minutes later, Nurse Brubaker swept out, her brow deeply knit. Preoccupied, she hurtled past Landa, then stopped. "You better get in there, Captain, while we get set up."

"What's going on?" *Dumb question.*

A corner of Brubaker's mouth raised. "Why, she's having a baby."

"I know that. What else?"

Brubaker sighed. "She's about ready. Unusual for a first child. I'd say, in the next fifteen minutes or so. I gave her a shot of morphine to ease the pain." She laid a hand on his elbow. "Don't worry, she'll do fine. Helen's from tough stock."

Don't I know? "What should I do?"

"Just try to keep her feeling good about herself, confident, not afraid. Hold her hand and help her breathe. Roll her on her side and give her a little back rub, if you can. Now, I gotta go. You have the deck, Captain." Brubaker dashed off.

"Aye, aye," Landa said softly. He turned and walked into the room, finding Helen's eyes squeezed shut, her hands gripping the rails.

He peeled her fingers off one of the rails and held her hand while brushing her hair away from her forehead. "You're doing fine. Help is on the way."

"Ummmfssst!"

He rubbed a shoulder. "Try to inhale through your nose; exhale through your mouth. Ready? Begin."

"What?" she gasped.

Landa repeated it. "Now do it."

"Where'd you hear that?" And yet she did it, her breathing rapid.

He found a washcloth, squeezed it dry, folded it, and laid it on her forehead. "The Landa School of Medicine, of course."

"Where is everybody, dammit? Where's Dr. Gaspar?"

"Shhh." He made a show of looking from side to side. "Just heard they found Doc Gaspar in a cathouse in Wilmington. Sobering him up right now. Had to pump his stomach, though. And his hands are a little shaky."

"Wha . . . what?"

"Sorry. He's scrubbing up."

Helen let out a great gasp of air. In five seconds, she relaxed, still trying to catch her breath. "Who . . . who taught you your bedside manners?"

Gently, Landa took her right hand and held it to his chest. "I'm from Brooklyn, remember?"

She smiled. "Dead-end kid?"

"Just about."

She fell back, letting herself go limp. Landa wiped at beads of perspiration on her forehead and upper lip.

"Oh, Todd, where are you?" she moaned.

He almost said, "Closer than you think."

Instead, he hung his head in prolonged silence.

"Jerry."

"Yeah."

"Laura has a problem. A big one."

"The booze."

"She needs help." She squeezed his hand. "It's not your fault."

"I know." He didn't feel convinced.

"Find out what's behind the booze."

She was right, Landa knew. Right now, he didn't give a damn.

"I'm serious. She'll come around. She's basically a good person. All we need to do is — Uhhhh!" Helen arched her back and she felt like she was coming off the gurney, so much so that Landa had to hold her down.

"God. Easy, honey. Breathe through the nose and exhale through the mouth."

"Ahhh."

Brubaker swept in, wearing a surgical cap and gown. Two nurses followed. She said, "Okay, Helen, we're ready." With a nod to Landa, she said, "You can wait down the hall."

He kissed her on her damp forehead. Then quickly on her lips. "That's for Todd."

"I know."

"See you in a little bit." He walked out.

Emma Peabody worked herself to her

feet and yawned. She pulled ample forearms through the sleeves of a worn black cardigan sweater. "Tired."

Landa swore he caught the odor of the home-cooked brew on her breath.

Emma stretched. "Think I'll go home. Get the guest room ready for Kate and Frank." Looking down to Landa, she smiled. "Call me the minute you hear anything."

"You bet."

After Mrs. Peabody left, he flipped through old issues of *Collier's*, *Saturday Evening Post*, and *National Geographic*. That was it. So he started flipping through the same ones again, checking his watch every five minutes.

Nurse Brubaker, wearing a starched white uniform and cap, walked out. She looked down at him, her face impervious. "Mr. Ingram?"

"No. I'm Landa, remember?" He jumped up.

"I'm sorry." She laid a hand on his arm, her face softened a bit. "Relax, Captain. You're the proud godfather of a newborn son. Mother and child are doing fine."

"Whew." His heart surged and he felt like jumping.

"Seven pounds, fourteen ounces; twenty-one inches."

"On the level?"

"Ummm. Let me ask you. Where is the father? Overseas?"

Landa's hands went to his hips and he looked down, shaking his head.

Her intake of breath was sharp. "Not coming back?"

"No."

"She's doing so well. Does she know?"

He nodded. "Can I see her?"

"Thought you'd never ask. Follow me."

He followed Brubaker down a long corridor that teed into another. Then another, passing room after room, their lights low, the patients inside desperately trying to recover, to escape to the outside. At long last, she stopped at a brightly lighted room and nodded toward the door. "She's on the far side. I have to catch up on charts, so I'll be there in a minute."

It was a two-room suite, curtains drawn around both beds. Landa eased aside the far curtain. Helen lay there looking fresh, a newborn infant cradled in her right arm. In a flash, he was overwhelmed by the miracle of life, that a new being lay in her arms, a little life that had not been there when he'd picked her up for dinner earlier in the evening. "Hi," he whispered.

She looked up, smiling.

Ingram, this is really hard for me.

"Say hello to Jerome Oliver Ingram."

Landa, you are such a bastard. "Hi,

kiddo. Too bad you're named after me." With his forefinger, he grazed the baby's cheek, while kissing Helen on the forehead. "Mrs. Peabody went home. Your folks are on their way."

"Okay."

"Congratulations. Todd would be proud."

"I'm sure he is." She smiled again.

How the hell does she know? He held his pinky to the infant's hand. The boy wound his fingers around it tightly. "Holy smokes. What a grip."

NINETEEN

30 JUNE 1944
IJN SUBMARINE *I-57*
INDIAN OCEAN

He checked the bulkhead chronometer for the third time in as many minutes: 2216. They were surfaced; the sea detail was set and the *I-57* had been creeping for the past half hour or so. The normal relaxed atmosphere at this time of night was strangely absent. In fact, as Ingram recalled, the officers and men had been quiet and pensive since morning quarters.

The ship was not rocking, which meant the sea outside was mirror glass flat. Except for an internal vibration now and then, it seemed as if they were floating in a vacuum chamber with no sensation of movement or speed. The only indication of motion was the knotmeter, its white needle jiggling about the numeral 6.

Stranger still was that they proceeded on battery power alone, the great diesels having been shut down. There could be only one reason for that. Noise. Shimada didn't want his two thundering engines to announce their presence. For good measure, he'd even shut down the auxiliary engine. Ingram could only conclude they were near land — East Africa, he supposed. They had been at sea for thirteen days on the same course and speed, as far as he could tell. The hatches were open, and he could feel the warm blanket of land-generated humidity swirling about the ship, bringing a faint aroma of vegetation.

The day after the diving incident, six feet of chain was added to Ingram's tether, giving him more room to move. And the crew seemed less indifferent, more polite to him. Instead of a clubbing, they stepped aside when he needed to pass. Also, his rations improved. Just last night, he'd had *katsuboshi,* a salami-shaped stick of dried bonito, the protein invigorating him. He had seen Taubman only once, two days ago when the German was exiting the officer's head. Averting his eyes, Taubman headed for his stateroom without a word.

Now, he stood across from the maneuvering board, watching Superior Petty Officer Shimazaki hover over his two electricians, Samara and Takada. All three were shirtless, except Shimazaki, who had a handkerchief tied around his neck; he also wore his signature oil-splattered trousers, white combination cap, and sound-powered phones. Sweating, they quietly watched their gauges and awaited orders from the bridge, where Masako was posted as a lookout.

The engine telegraph jingled, and the arrows jumped to All Stop. *"Hai!"* said Shimazaki. The electricians threw the motors into neutral and stood back, poised for the next command. The sensation was uncanny. Aside from the ventilation blowers and the light buzzing of a small rubber-bladed fan overhead, there was no sound except for Shimazaki, his tea gulping sounding like a grenade.

The telegraph jingled again, its little arrows jumping about the dial. Samara threw levers for Ahead One-Third on the starboard screw, while Takada answered the order for Astern One-Third on the port screw. Seconds later, the arrows jumped again: Astern One-Third on both screws. After five seconds, the motors were ordered to All Stop.

The auxiliary engine coughed into life as another bell was rung up: Finished with Engines. Shimazaki sat back on a stool and lighted a cigarette. Blowing smoke through mouth and nose, he began filling in his log book as Samara put away procedure manuals and Takada pulled out a rag and shined brasswork.

Ingram wondered: *Moored? Anchored? Where? To what?* Nobody was saying anything, and he resigned himself to being patient. Then he felt a gentle thump, and the ship seemed to rise and fall a bit. Tidal surge, he guessed. *Where the hell are we?* They could be moored to another ship. Possibly to a dock. If so, there might be a chance to jump. The possibilities intrigued him, and he looked aft toward the berthing compartment, seeing a number of men scrambling up the hatch. He sniffed at the air and his skin tingled. *Freedom is up there. Just dive over the side. It's nighttime and they'll never find me. Hope for a quick swim to shore and hide in the jungle.* But then he thought, *Snakes. I hate snakes. Are there any sea snakes in this area? No matter. I'm going to do it. Just dash up the hatch and jump.*

He looked down at the chain attaching him to the lathe. *Not yet.*

"Commander." Shimazaki pulled a grease-stained pack of cigarettes from his pants pocket. With a glint in his eye, he held it up and shook out a cigarette.

"Ah," said Ingram. "No, thank you. I don't smoke."

"Uhhh!" Shimazaki's face darkened.

Masako, his duties over as sea detail lookout, walked up. Giving Ingram a hurry-up-there's-work-to-be-done look, he stooped down and began unlocking the chain.

Ingram looked toward the aft hatch. *Per-*

fect. All I need is a few seconds.

Shimazaki said something to Masako, making him rise. Then he jiggled the cigarette pack vigorously. *"Dozo?"*

Ingram had only smoked a few times, mostly cigars when friends had babies. But every time, a single puff had made him feel woozy and nauseated. And cigarettes were worse. "No, thanks." He waved a hand.

Shimazaki held the pack closer, shaking it, his eyes boring into him.

This is an international incident? Hell, this is war. "Afraid not."

Shimazaki thrust the pack almost under his nose. Samara, Takada, and Masako edged in a bit closer, Masako smirking openly.

"All right." Gingerly, he took a cigarette. They watched intently as he turned the little white cylinder over in his hand for a few seconds. Unable to delay any further, he raised it to his mouth.

Shimazaki lifted his foot, and with a loud scratch, lit a wooden match on his sole. With a flourish, he leaned forward, holding it to Ingram.

What the hell? Holding the cigarette between thumb and forefinger, he wrapped his lips around it and puffed a couple of times to get it lighted. Sitting back, he took a big puff and held the smoke in his mouth. Looking as casual as possible, he blew the smoke slowly, over their heads.

Perceptibly, they relaxed. Samara smiled and went, "Ahhh."

That's when Ingram broke out in a paroxysm of wheezing and coughing. Turning red, spasms racked his chest. He felt as if his throat were on fire. "What the hell's this thing made out of, ground glass?" he gasped.

A chuckling Shimazaki relieved him of the cigarette as Takada raised a thermos and filled a paper cup with water.

"Thanks." Ingram gulped while the others laughed. Shimazaki reached around and pounded his back. Still wheezing, Ingram held out the cup for more water. With a nod from Shimazaki, Takada poured and Ingram drank, some of the water dribbling down his chin. Suddenly, he grew dizzy, and his stomach rumbled mightily, making him feel as if a gopher had crawled in there and died.

The general announcement loudspeaker squawked. After exchanging glances with Shimazaki, Masako pushed Ingram against a bulkhead and stooped, letting out an ingeniously fashioned grunt, which, Ingram was sure, was half Japanese and half Uzbek. As Masako fumbled with the chain lock, Ingram tried to catch Shimazaki's eye. "Thanks, Chief, for the good-will butt," he said sarcastically, his stomach still racked with convulsions.

But the fun was over. The superior petty officer turned back to his logbooks, his face intent, the cigarette dangling from his lips.

Finished with Ingram's chain, Masako stood and gave a push that sent him stumbling toward the engine room. Casting a longing glance at the after hatch, he vowed to try again before the night was out.

Stepping into the engine room, he was hit with a blanket of heat from the yet uncooled engines, the cracking and popping sounding like .22-caliber pistol shots. The dull-gray engines were massive. With ten cylinders, they were about eight feet tall, twenty feet long, and seven feet across.

Twenty or so men stood in the now-cramped engine room stripped to their waists, mostly junior ratings, a few third-class scattered among them. Hands on their hips, they watched as four machinist mates unbolted the deck plates between the two engines. Five or six officers, some shirtless, stood on a catwalk running athwartships, next to the forward hatch. Ingram was surprised to see Commander Shimada there as well, in dress uniform with medals and sword. Next to him was Korvettenkapitän Martin Taubman, hands clasped before him, also wearing dress blues with medals. And the man had the temerity to wear Ingram's Naval Academy ring. Ingram was dismayed the two had apparently reconciled. Even now, they were talking animatedly. Something else caught his eye. Standing on the catwalk were two Japanese naval officers in dress uniform he'd never seen. They spoke casually with Shimada and Taubman, who occasionally motioned toward the engine room. *Where the hell did they come from?*

How poignant, Ingram thought; these four elegantly dressed thugs, arrogantly displaying their authority over these shirtless souls, directing them in the name of two of the most despotic regimes on earth.

Lieutenant Matsumoto, the engineering officer, stepped through the forward hatch and spoke with Shimada for a moment. Then he took off his shirt and climbed down a ladder to the bilges, joining two grease-stained men between the engines. Five minutes later, the main engine room deck plates were unbolted and strapped aside, exposing a wide chasm between the mighty diesels.

"Iko, Iko!" Matsumoto waved his hands. Two petty officers at the deck level took up the shout, and the men, like ants, began crawling down ladders to the bilges.

Masako, stripped to the waist, gave Ingram a push. The message was clear, so Ingram quickly took off his shirt and crawled down with the others. He alighted among the twenty men or so, their body heat mingling with that of the diesels, creating a sweltering atmosphere. There was little room, and some jostled against the still-heated engine blocks, crying in pain. Worse was the bilge odor: salt water mixed with pungent fuel oil, hydraulic fluid, and cooking grease, something that would never have been tolerated on Ingram's ship or on any U.S. naval vessel. Ingram's stomach churned. The others were having difficulty, too. Seasoned submariners' eyes darted; their Adam's apples bounced as they tried to hold down their bile. Several tied handkerchiefs over their noses and mouths. Ingram grabbed a wipe rag and did the same. But the stench persisted, and he felt himself on the verge of nausea.

Like the upper-level deck plates, the bilge gratings were pried up and strapped aside. Matsumoto kneeled down, his light khaki trousers splattered with a black muck. He plunged his hands into the dirty water and fumbled for a moment. Rising up, he yelled over his shoulder. Immediately, a rating handed over a crowbar.

Leaning down, Matsumoto again plunged his hands in the bilgewater, working the crowbar at whatever it was. He took a strain and his tongue stuck out, veins on his forehead bulged, and his face grew red. Grunting, he leaned farther down and yelped, "Ahhh."

Matsumoto signaled for a man to kneel in front of him. Together, they reached beneath the black, oily surface. Gritting their teeth, they raised an oblong wooden carton up to a cross beam, bilgewater running off it. At either end of the carton were woven rope handles. They grabbed the handles and, snarling and growling, heaved the carton to two men positioned at the ladder. Groaning loudly, those two heaved it up to another pair at deck level. Then the carton was passed through the aft hatch and into the motor room, its destination topside, Ingram supposed.

Matsumoto stooped and waved a hand under the starboard diesel. Then he motioned to the port side. Both spaces were about ten feet wide, with only about eighteen inches or so of crawl space between the crankcase and cross beams. And the crawl space was complicated by a number of pipes, hoses, and hydraulic lines running to and fro.

Matsumoto spoke for a moment, then waved the men beneath the diesels.

They started crawling, except for one man who groaned and vomited just as he began his trip beneath the port diesel. Matsumoto walked over and kicked him in the rump. With a cry, the man vomited again, the smell infiltrating the engine room. Matsumoto yelled and kicked harder as the man wailed in terrible pain. He flipped on his back just as Matsumoto wound up for a third kick. Waving his hands, he wiped spittle off his chin and scrambled beneath the diesel.

Matsumoto, his face flushed with anger, stood upright, his hands on his hips, daring anyone else.

Masako pushed Ingram. *Go!*

Ingram kneeled and crawled beneath the starboard diesel. It was tricky going. He balanced on the structural I-beams, working his way around a variety of pipes and hoses. Some were hot, the others cold, there being no way to predict which was which. And the voids between the I-beams contained at least eighteen inches of the odorous bilgewater. This close to it, he had a hard time to keep from gagging and retching. Occasionally, he brushed his shoulder against the black greasy crankcase. Fortunately, the engine had cooled enough so his skin didn't blister. But it still hurt like hell. In desperation, he splashed bilgewater over his arms, putting out of his mind how polluted it was.

A pair of men had crawled all the way under the engine and shoved a crowbar in the water. Soon, they fished out a carton just like the one Matsumoto had found. Grunting and heaving, they pushed and shoved it to Ingram and Masako, who passed it on to another pair of men positioned amidships. He was astounded at the weight. After the second or third carton, he estimated each at between sixty to seventy pounds. Fortunately, the rope handles were sturdy, making it easy to gain a purchase to drag the cartons across the I-beam.

After passing a dozen or so cartons, Ingram was dog-tired. A look at Masako's oil-splattered face told him he felt the same. Fortunately, a whistle blew and the men stopped in their tracks. Some rolled to their backs, their chests heaving. With all this, Ingram had the impression they were expecting this, that they'd done this before.

Masako kicked Ingram and waved amidships. "*Iko.*" Go!

Ingram crawled out, bumping arms and shoulders against pipes and hydraulic lines to emerge into the midships passageway. He looked up, finding Matsumoto pointing to a little wooden bucket. With more greed than he cared to admit, Ingram grabbed the wooden spoon and ladled in a mouthful of sweet, cool water. Smacking his lips, he began his trip back under the engine.

When he drew close, Masako grabbed the bucket, raised it to his mouth and gulped and gulped, water dribbling down his chin.

"You little jerk," Ingram growled. Masako was still gulping when Ingram yanked it out of his hands.

Masako raised his hand to strike but Ingram gave him a malevolent "Try me" look.

Masako backed away and Ingram finished the bucket.

The whistle blew, making the five-minute break seem like five seconds. Over the next two hours, they worked at the rate of about one carton a minute, with the pair ahead digging them out and passing them back. It seemed forever in between breaks, but finally, the whistle blew. Ingram flopped on his back and splayed his arms out. "Your turn."

Masako gave him a long, dreary look and nodded to a grease-stained carton balanced precariously on an I-beam.

"Got it." Ingram flopped a hand on top of the carton to steady it.

With a grunt, Masako crawled off, dragging the empty bucket with him.

Too exhausted to move, Ingram lay there, staring up at the black crankcase, just inches from his eyes. It was quiet, the men too tired to talk. The heat pressed in. He shook his head, more to keep his wits than to stay conscious. Someone whimpered nearby. Across the way, a sailor moaned and urinated loudly into the bilge.

Ingram shook his head again, his mind drifting to home and Helen. He wondered if they would move to her father's avocado ranch near Ramona, a town forty miles northeast of San Diego. Frank Durand had offered him an equal partnership, explaining there would be a boom in avocados after the war. "Get in on the ground floor," Frank said. "Great place to raise kids, too."

Kids. He racked his brain. When is Helen due? Not yet, he decided. Another two weeks at least for the baby. He wondered if there was a way he could contact the Red Cross to let her —

Something splashed beside him.

"Damn." He rolled to his side, realizing the carton had tumbled end first into the bilge. Masako would be mad. He didn't feel like arguing with a greedy Masako when there was a bucket of water to split. The little jerk could just as well keep it all for himself. He rolled over and reached for the carton. Grunting and gritting his teeth, he raised it and once again had it on the I-beam. A corner was bashed in. A sizable chunk of wood had come loose and he tried to push it back into place. Instead, it fell out.

"What?" He raised himself on an elbow for a better look. He moved aside slightly, and a little more light fell on it.

"Damn."

It gleamed. It shone a deep, rich, compelling color. This was the stuff of endless greed throughout the ages. Gold. All these cartons contained giant ingots of gold.

TWENTY

30 JUNE 1944
IJN SUBMARINE *I-57*
ANTONGILA BAY, MADAGASCAR

"Dammit." The carton tipped precariously, nearly sliding back into the murk. He grabbed it quickly and balanced it on the I-beam. *Good God. It really is gold!* Its deep, lustrous beauty seemed so out of place in the stink and filth around him.

"Uhhh."

Ingram jumped. It was Masako returning with the water bucket. Then he realized he could be killed if caught tampering, no matter how accidental it seemed. *Do something.* He clawed deep in the bilge and found a greasy claylike silt on the bottom. Scooping up a handful, he quickly slapped it on the corner of the carton, then stuck the chip of wood back in place. *Please, God. Make it stay.*

"Ahh, Ingram-san." Masako peered over his back with cobralike eyes.

The chip fell in the water with a tiny *plop.*

Smiling from ear to ear, Masako bared

gleaming teeth. “Bad, bad.” He waved a finger from side to side, leaned back, and opened his mouth to yell. But Matsumoto’s back-to-work whistle obliterated his words.

On the verge of panic, Ingram reached for Masako, but the sailor wiggled away.

Someone shouted. A flashlight beam swept over oil-smeared bodies and Masako yelped in pain. He yelped again, and Ingram realized that Matsumoto was out there with a sharp prod of some sort. Others yelped. Matsumoto must have been jabbing them also.

Trying to avoid the prod, Masako wiggled back toward Ingram. That’s when Ingram doubled his fist and smacked Masako full in the nose.

With a groan, the seaman clamped his hands over his face. Rolling to his side, his upper body almost pitched into the black bilgewater. Once again, Matsumoto nailed Masako with the prod, making him cry out more from surprise and indignation than from pain. With blood seeping between his fingers, Masako clutched his face and loosed a string of Japanese over his shoulder. After blinking a moment, he focused on Ingram with a look of abject hatred.

Matsumoto called out in a calm tone.

Nowhere to go. Ingram was trapped on an

enemy ship, under a multiton engine, thousands of miles from home. Desperately, he looked for another way to get to the aft hatch.

Kill Masako! He reached for the crowbar and was ready to swing when he heard scraping and grunting. Two men slithered toward him. One he recognized as a heavyset torpedoman, the other a wiry little quartermaster. *Damn.* Ingram backed away a bit but kept his arm cocked.

Reaching Masako, the two men barely glanced at Ingram. Instead, they grabbed Masako's feet and arms and dragged him to the midship passageway. With those two engrossed with Masako, Ingram reached in the bilge and scooped up a large, dripping glob of silt. He spread it liberally on the corner of the carton and pasted on the chip. This time it stuck.

The torpedoman crawled back to him and gave a dull stare. Soon, the quartermaster joined them; by contrast, his eyes darted wildly. The torpedoman jabbed a thumb amidships. "Go!"

Needing no further encouragement, Ingram quickly crawled from under the engine, grateful for freedom from the oppressive heat and slimy darkness. Men about him were blackened with greasy bilgewater. Grunting and straining, they pulled cartons from under the engines, heaving them up the ladder. There were three teams under each engine passing the cartons across. It looked as if they'd been working from outboard toward the center. What remained were the cartons in the midship area and the work there appeared to be going quickly. At the three ladders, a yeoman checked each carton's serial number before it went up and out the motor-room hatch.

After a rest break, Matsumoto and his CPOs walked about, shouting at the blackened men who lay there too tired to move, their mouths hanging open. They lay sprawled on the beams, half in the bilges, not caring, their bodies and clothes soaked in putrid water. Among them was Masako, propped up against a toolbox, his head in his hands, a bloody rag clamped over his face.

Feeling like the rest, Ingram lay sprawled on an I-beam, cooling off, trying to catch his breath. Matsumoto walked up and yelled down to him. When that didn't work, he kicked Ingram in the ribs.

"Ouch, dammit." Ingram tried to rise, but grew dizzy and stumbled.

Matsumoto grabbed his elbow, yanked him abruptly to his feet, and shoved him toward the ladder. Then he turned, blew his whistle, and shouted a string of orders. Soon, more men crawled from under the engines and were replaced with a new group who'd been milling about. It hit Ingram that he'd never seen these men. Yet they were Japanese and wore the same working uniforms.

Matsumoto braced his hands on his knees and yelled at the crew splayed on the deck. Some nodded, rose to their feet, and began crawling up the ladders. Then Matsumoto turned to Ingram. "You, too, Joe." He pointed to Masako.

"Okay," Ingram grabbed Masako's trousers, yanked him to his feet and shoved him on the ladder. At the same time his eyes darted about the compartment looking for a way to escape aft to the motor room. There were just the forward hatch and the aft hatch, nothing else. *Get out of here!* He shoved Masako aside and started up the ladder.

Masako snarled and batted Ingram's hands away.

"Hey, Joe!" Matsumoto pointed at Masako.

Dammit! Ingram backed down the ladder and made room for Masako. Except for blood and oil smeared over his face, the Japanese sailor seemed all right. With a sullen look, Masako mounted the first rung and started up behind a line of exhausted men.

"Commander Ingram." Taubman beckoned from the athwartships catwalk. The other officers were gone.

"What?" Ingram replied.

"Come." Taubman beckoned again.

Turning sideways, Ingram squeezed past blackened and oily men and made his way to the forward bulkhead. "Yes?"

"Terrible down there."

"Depths of hell," Ingram agreed. "But I don't need you to tell me that."

"No, you don't." Spreading his hands on the rail, Taubman leaned down and said, "They can't decide whether to take you on to Europe or send you back to the Pacific."

"I don't understand the either-or part of what you just said."

Taubman pointed to starboard. "A sister ship is out there. She's going back to Penang. This submarine is going on to Lorient, France. What would you like to do?"

"Another submarine," Taubman had said. That's where all those Japanese had come from. He'd also said the other submarine was going back to Penang, this one to Europe. A full-color image of Baumgartner's tarp-covered body flashed before him: Baumgartner screaming as the Japanese soldier plunged the bayonet into his chest.

"Commander?"

"Think I'd like Europe since —"

Someone yelled. A sickening thud. Men

gathered around a prostrate figure. It was Masako. He'd fallen backward and lay on his back, eyes wide open, his head dangling at an obscene angle over an I-beam. The place grew quiet as Matsumoto knelt and pressed Masako's carotid artery, then thumbed an eyelid. He slowly shook his head. Thoroughly spooked, the men scrambled up the ladders and worked their way aft and out the hatch to the motor room as if the place were on fire.

"Too bad. Must have slipped," said Taubman, looking down with a thin smile. "Interesting. I heard what he said to Matsumoto. But I don't think anyone listened to him. One would have thought you pushed him; but then you were right here chatting with me, weren't you? Well, your secret's safe with me. Just don't get any ideas about what you saw."

Ingram drew a thumb and forefinger across his mouth as if zipping it shut.

"Good."

Masako, dead. Ingram couldn't believe it. With a twinge of guilt, he felt as if he'd pushed him. *Wait. The man's an enemy.* Masako had beaten and kicked him so many times that Ingram was beyond forgiving him. But in a way he felt sorry for him. Masako was just a kid, eighteen, maybe nineteen years of age; his whole life had been before him. He looked up to

Taubman. "Are you serious about Europe?"

Taubman's eyes flicked from Masako back to Ingram. "Yes."

"Count me in."

"Very well."

They watched as two men cut a length of Masako's hair and stuffed it in an oil-smeared envelope. Then they rolled him in a sheet and secured it with a length of line.

"It'll be a pleasant cruise. Perhaps we can play some chess," Taubman said.

"Sure. All you have to do is to break through the ASW barriers. That'll be a trick."

"Another reason why I would like you to accompany me. You would be invaluable in that department."

"I doubt it. That's all Atlantic Fleet doctrine. I have no idea how they do things there."

"Better than what we have now."

Ingram jammed his hands on his hips. "Martin, I thought you were avoiding me."

"I'll explain. It came over a broadcast; Cherbourg fell to the Americans on the twenty-sixth."

Ingram had no idea of the date. "When was that?"

"Four days ago. This is June thirtieth."

"Why do I care? More power to them. I hope they overrun Europe by next week and kick Hitler's ass all the way back to Berlin."

"That's what I'm trying to do, make you care. With Cherbourg in Allied hands, they will now drive down the western coast of France with a vengeance and try to take the U-boat pens. You must see my point. If the *I-57* is going to Europe, we need a friendly port." He rubbed his chin and looked down. "I feel sorry for my countrymen defending the U-boat pens. It will be a hard battle for them."

"Martin, can you really feel sorry for your countrymen while they stand on someone else's soil?"

Anger flashed across Taubman's face. He opened his mouth to speak.

Ingram continued, "Now let me ask you something. Are you really a submariner?"

Watching them lug Masako's body up to the deck level, Taubman said, "Of course not." He gestured to the shrouded corpse and said, "Is it true?"

"Is what true?"

"That you hit him in the face? And that you saw gold?"

Ingram looked from side to side. "Gold? Jeez, Martin. Have you blown a fuse?"

"That's what Masako was prattling. But I don't think Mr. Matsumoto really listened. He was simply too preoccupied." Taubman leveled his eyes on Ingram.

"Quite frankly, I don't care about Masako. But I do care about a safe transit through the North Atlantic and getting safely in and out of Lorient." He looked at his watch. "I'm due topside. We'll meet then and talk about it more." He walked off.

Watching Taubman disappear through the forward hatch, Ingram knew that the man had heard everything Masako had said. He could be dead by sunrise. *Shit, shit, shit. What have I done?*

TWENTY-ONE

30 JUNE 1944
IJN SUBMARINE *I-57*
ANTONGILA BAY, MADAGASCAR

The deck plates were bolted in place, the last carton on its way topside. Next, Masako's shrouded corpse was handed up. Waiting until last, Ingram clambered up the ladder and shuffled aft behind a line of oil-smeared sailors. The starboard diesel rolled and thundered into life as he stepped into the motor room. The port diesel started soon after, the engines mercifully pulling cool air through the motor room, making him feel as if he had stepped into a spring-time evening.

He stopped behind a knot of men as they wrestled Masako through the after berthing compartment and up the hatch. At the maneuvering board, Shimazaki, Samara, and Takada had been replaced by two new electricians he didn't recognize. Stepping through the hatch, he found more new sailors gathered about, tossing their gear on bunks. Strange, it was almost as if he were aboard another ship.

Nervously, he waited for the *I-57* sailors to ascend the ladder topside. Dark thoughts ran through his mind. *Did Matsumoto really not hear? Does Taubman really know? Maybe someone's coming after me. Oh God, let me up there. Give me time to jump.*

A second-class petty officer gave him a "you're next" jab in the ribs. Quickly, he scrambled up the hatch into sweet, cool night air. The sky was overcast, the blackness nearly overwhelming. His eyes adjusted. As Taubman said, another submarine lay alongside to starboard, her silhouette similar to the *I-57*. The bullion cartons were stacked near her after hatch, where a group of sailors stood, passing them down. Both submarines' engines were turning over, and even at idle, the unmuffled noise would carry for miles, Ingram figured.

Where do I jump? Where is land? Looking from starboard to port, he saw only inky blackness, much like the sky overhead. They could just as well be twenty or even fifty miles from land. *The hell with it. Just go.* He started for the port side.

A dark figure loomed next to him. "That you?" It was Taubman.

Ingram's heart sank. "What ship is that?" He pointed to the submarine next door.

"The Imperial Japanese Navy submarine

I-49. Now, place your hands behind your back, please."

"What the hell —"

"Are you familiar with the Luger pistol?"

"Yes."

"Well, right now, one is trained on your back. So?" Taubman prodded Ingram's ribs with a pistol muzzle. "Unlike submarines, I am qualified to use this."

Ingram tried to edge to the port side.

"Now! I don't have any time to fool with you, and I'm trying to save your life, you fool."

Ingram did as instructed and the handcuffs soon clicked home. Gamely, he said, "I heard that submarine was sunk months ago." *Can I jump with these darn things on?*

Taubman nodded. "That is as it was intended."

"Where are we?"

"Madagascar. We're anchored in Antongila Bay."

That was why they'd boarded an anchor in Penang. "Where's that?"

"Must you know everything?"

"Try me."

"East side of Madagascar. Very remote," Taubman snorted.

"Are we actually in the bay?"

Taubman chuckled. "That we are. But don't get any ideas. You're too far from land to make it. Believe me."

Dammit!

"There are some things you should know."

Water lapped against the hull. So damned near. He wondered how far they really were from land. He took a deep breath. It was there all right, a land breeze carried the beckoning soft scent of vegetation. Was Taubman agile enough to pull the trigger if he jumped? He kept his silence and tensed.

"Don't try it." Taubman pushed harder. "Even if we don't shoot you, you'll be unable to swim ten kilometers without the use of your hands.

"Now, about Cherbourg —"

"Martin, at this point, I don't care if Tijuana has fallen."

Taubman pressed on. "I need to get out of Lorient."

"Good luck."

Taubman's voice dropped a notch and he looked from side to side and hissed, "You're being stupid. Listen. I don't have much time. These people want to take your head off. You're no longer a sideshow, a curiosity. They'll do it, especially if they discover you know about the gold."

"Martin, what is a sane man supposed to conclude after working in that sweatbox down there?"

"I see your point."

"Then take off the cuffs and let me jump."

"I need you to help me get across France."

"What?"

"You can do it. Look, here it is in a chestnut. I can make you rich. Very, very rich. All you have to do is pass me off as a U.S. naval intelligence officer and help me get to my own lines."

"How the hell could I do that?"

"We'll think of something."

Ingram was fascinated. "Where are you going? And how rich are you going to make me?"

"I'll let you know. Is it a deal? You have five seconds." He pushed again with the Luger's muzzle.

"You think they really want to kill me?"

"They're going to give you to Ishibashi."

"Okay."

Taubman nodded. "Very good. To repeat, the *I-57* is going on to Lorient. You'll remain aboard with me. I'll guarantee safe passage. The *I-49*," he nodded to the submarine next door, "returns to Pacific waters. The *I-57* transferred sixty tons of fuel oil to her for the trip."

"What for?"

"Yakuza gold."

"Whose gold?"

"They've given up."

"I don't understand."

"These people are going to disappear. They've —"

Someone shouted from up forward.

"They want us for something. I'll tell you later. Just keep your mouth shut." He prodded with the pistol.

With Taubman guiding his elbow, Ingram stumbled among khaki-clad figures on the *I-57*'s deck, his mind racing. *What the hell is Yakuza? And who is giving up? These two ships?*

Working slowly around the deck gun, he made out the vague outline of the after part of the conning tower, a group of officers gathered underneath. Two of them wore swords; one was Shimada, the other was the officer who had stood with Shimada in the engine room, the skipper of the *I-49*, he supposed.

The familiar shape of Lieutenant (j.g.) Ishibashi materialized beside him.

Taubman said, "Stand right here, Commander, while I say good-bye to Captain Shimada. In the meantime, they've sent Lieutenant Ishibashi to entertain you with his little Nambu pistol." His voice dropped to a whisper. "Don't try anything. He may not speak English, but he understands it."

"Okay."

Ishibashi poked a pistol in Ingram's ribs the moment Taubman stepped away.

They're going to kill you, Taubman had said. In the pale light, Ingram risked a glance at Ishibashi. His eyes were like dark, ebony pools. Way beyond a poker face, it was the masque of death.

From their stance, the conversation between Taubman and the two submarine captains looked less than casual. At one point, Shimada stood nose to nose with Taubman and repeatedly poked a finger in his chest. Soon, all three were gesticulating. At one time Taubman looked at Ingram and shook his head. As soon as that happened, Shimada resumed his finger jabbing. Stepping back, Taubman waved his hands and pranced around a bit, at one point stumbling and nearly falling overboard. After a while, they were quiet. A decision seemed to have been made. Shimada handed over a leather briefcase. A chain was attached, which he cuffed to Taubman's wrist.

With that, all three shook hands, stepped back a half pace, and saluted. Shimada turned and barked an order to Ishibashi, then marched across a wide plank rigged between the two ships.

Ishibashi prodded with his pistol. "Go."

"Hey," said Ingram. "Taubman said I'm supposed to stay here."

Ishibashi said, "German has no authority. Go."

"Martin," Ingram called over his shoulder. "What's going on?"

Taubman walked up and shrugged. "Shimada changed his mind. I'm sorry."

"Why?" Ingram protested.

Taubman raised his arms and then dropped them. "You know too much. They didn't count on you seeing all this," he waved toward the *I-49* and stepped close. "They can't afford to let you go to Europe and blab about what you've seen."

"I won't talk."

"They don't believe you. And now that I think of it, why should I believe you? Especially when you boast about kicking Hitler's ass into Austria?"

Ingram kept silent.

"I didn't think so," said Taubman. "Even with that, they are very angry."

"About what?"

"The fleet broadcasts have confirmed the Japanese suffered major losses in the Philippine Sea two weeks ago. They lost at least a fleet carrier, with some other capital ships, and over four hundred airplanes."

"No kidding?"

Taubman paused and then said, "You are not to be killed. Captain Shimada gave me his word to treat you fairly. He'll take you back to Penang."

Penang! Baumgartner and that sadistic Captain Abe. Dammit! He had truly counted on going to Europe and making a break for it.

"I'll miss our little chess games." With a nod, Taubman dropped the handcuff key in Ishibashi's outstretched hand and started to walk away.

"Martin, you're such a phoney."

Taubman paused and then turned. "What did you say?"

"You don't care about Hitler's ass being kicked into Austria, do you?"

"What are you talking about?"

Ingram pushed past Ishibashi. "You don't care about Germany or your fellow Germans. You don't care about me or these fine folks here on these two pleasure cruisers, do you?"

In the gloom, Taubman looked hurt. "I'm sorry. I thought we were really friends."

"Baloney. All you want is your damn gold."

Taubman studied the water lapping between the hulls. "You'll never know."

"I hope you choke on —"

"Iko!" Ishibashi racked his Nambu down the side of Ingram's head.

"Oww."

"You'd better head over there, Commander. They want to clear the area before the British patrol boat shows up." Taubman held out his hand.

Ignoring Taubman's hand, he said sarcastically, "And my ring? I was hoping you'd give it back to me."

"Good luck."

"Rot in hell, Fritz." With Ishibashi behind, he stepped carefully over the plank and walked to *I-49*'s conning tower.

The plank was pulled aboard the *I-49*. Shouting from the bridge, Shimada called for the mooring lines to be taken in. That done, the *I-49*'s engines increased in pitch. Water swirled under her screw guards. She backed clear as sailors catcalled back and forth.

Taubman's voice echoed over the water. "Perhaps we'll play chess after the war, Commander."

"When pigs fly," Ingram shouted back.

The banter increased as the *I-49* gained sternway. Then both crews began cheering and waving their caps over their heads. Blending with the night, their voices carried on an easterly breeze to Manambolosy, a fishing village twelve kilometers away. A few dogs raised their noses toward the ocean and barked, but the villagers didn't wake.

TWENTY-TWO

1 JULY 1944
TWELFTH NAVAL DISTRICT HEADQUARTERS
SAN FRANCISCO, CALIFORNIA

Someone knocked. Lieutenant Commander Oliver Toliver III spilled his coffee. "Awww, shoot!"

A muffled reply came from outside. "Sir?"

"Enter," Toliver said irritably, wiping at the spill with paper towels. He'd been up late last night with Jerry Landa, and now he'd been here since 0515 this morning. Three hours' sleep. He didn't know if he felt good enough to make the *I-57* presentation to COMTWELVE and his staff at 0800. But Toliver had no doubts about Landa, who would also attend. The man had the constitution of an ox.

Wearing dress khakis with black tie, Hank Wellman stuck his head around the door. The balding chief warrant officer puffed an enormous black cigar and asked, "Everything okay, sir?"

"What is it?"

A trumpet player in the U.S.S.

Oklahoma's band on December 7, 1941, Wellman was subsequently recruited to COMTWELVE's security section to assist with breaking codes. Cryptographers had discovered that musicians, with their sight-reading skills, were well suited to code encryption, decryption, and analysis. Wellman was no exception. The fact that he'd lived in Japan as a boy for eight years made him a sought-after decryptographer-translator, a rare combination. His deep voice rumbled. "COPEK message from HYPO, Commander." He handed over a red-banded white folder marked TOP SECRET — MAGIC.

"You're up early," said Toliver.

Wellman looked at his watch. "Took me a while to break that one, Commander. Thought you would want it before this morning's brief."

"You're right about that." Accepting the folder, Toliver checked the time: 0547. He entered it in the log, signed for the message, and handed back the folder. "Thanks, Henry."

With a nod, Wellman took the log, puffed twice, and closed the door wordlessly.

It was an *I-57* message forwarded by the Hawaiian radio intercept station HYPO to San Francisco (Station FOX), where Wellman had broken it. Scanning the message's work-up, Toliver was continually amazed at the Navy's radio intelligence system. By 1940, there was a ring of more than twenty listening stations around the Pacific set up to intercept Japanese radio signals. The Navy had most of the stations in the Pacific. But the Army had a handful, as did the British. The network was described as a "splendid arrangement" by then Chief of Naval Operations Admiral Harold R. Stark. Indeed, Toliver reflected, the raw data-gathering power alone gave the Americans a leg up. These stations not only intercepted Japanese radio signals, but used them for direction-finding broadcasts originating at sea.

When a Japanese radio message was intercepted by one or more stations, it was forwarded in COPEK, a superenciphered Navy code, to one of two regional centers: HYPO in Hawaii or NEGAT in Washington, D.C. HYPO got the job if the message was related to JN-25, the Japanese Fleet Naval Code. Messages in the Japanese diplomatic Purple, J, LA, and PA codes were sent to station NEGAT.

Under the Director of Naval Communications, who reported to the Chief of Naval Operations, NEGAT's activities were directed by OP-2O-G, the communication security section in Washington, D.C.

But seven thousand miles away, close to

CinCPac headquarters on Makalapa, the Intelligence Center of the Pacific Ocean Areas (ICPOA), was the main intelligence gathering and analysis unit. ICPOA was divided into five units: The first was the Fleet Radio Unit (FRUPAC — listening station HYPO), which did the actual intercepting. Next was the decryption and translation section, which enjoyed the use of some of the most modern and innovative equipment available, computing machines manufactured by International Business Machines using the Hollerith code (the British called their equipment Hollerith machines). IBM keypunch machines were used to enter information on punched cards that were loaded into tabulators, sorters, and printers, devices that could make thousands of calculations per second, drastically reducing the trial-and-error time required to break the enemy's codes. On top of that, the Navy trained skilled Japanese translators to convert the messages to English. Other ICPOA sections were photo intelligence, objective data, special projects, and a special unit titled Combat Intelligence, which analyzed and disseminated intercepted signals to relevant commands.

But in this case ICPOA had forwarded the decrypted message to Station FOX in San Francisco without comment from the

Combat Intelligence Unit. Toliver quickly scanned the message. Stations BELCONNEN (Melbourne, Australia), SAIL (Seattle, Washington), and KING (Dutch Harbor, Alaska) had each picked up the *I-57*'s broadcast, then forwarded it on to HYPO — ICPOA for decryption. Odd, Toliver reflected. Due to "skipping" of radio waves, some stations halfway around the globe picked up the *I-57*'s transmissions, even though she currently steamed in the Indian Ocean. Just four days ago, HYPO in Hawaii, ITEM in Imperial Beach (San Diego), California, and SEVEN, an Army station in Fort Hunt, Virginia, picked up the same message.

Most of the *I-57*'s messages were position and fuel reports. And this seemed to be no different, except . . . Toliver looked again. Something was out of place. The *I-57* reported about 120 tons less fuel then she had since the last report. Amazing consumption, he pondered. Reaching into a cavernous safe, he pulled out a top secret pub containing performance data for American fleet submarines. Flipping through it, he found that *Gato*-class submarines using four Fairbanks Morse 38D8 engines generated 1,535 horsepower each and consumed, on the average, about eight gallons of fuel oil per mile. With a slide rule, he quickly worked out that 120 tons would have yielded about four thousand miles for an American submarine. He didn't have performance data for Japanese submarines, but it couldn't be that much different. How could they have used that much fuel?

Scratching his head, he read on, finding the *I-57*'s position was far different from what she reported on the last intercept, two days ago. He stood and went to a wall-mounted chart of the Indian Ocean and western approaches to the South Atlantic. In this message, the *I-57*'s position was 27.6 S, 52.2 E. But he'd been keeping a track on her from previous position reports and checked. Finding that using the same course and speed, she should have been at 36.2 S, 49.6 E.

Toliver rubbed his chin. An error of nearly five hundred miles. This report indicated the *I-57* was up near Madagascar, when, according to previous reports, she should have been preparing to round the Cape of Good Hope. Also, Wellman had added a note that the *I-57*'s operator was new, that whoever sent this message had a different fist than the two others who had been sending the past few weeks.

Toliver was tempted to call his counterpart at NEGAT in Washington, D.C. But the *I-57* affair had been discounted as low priority. NEGAT had too many fish to fry, including all the intelligence gathering and dissemination connected with the European invasion. Same thing with the people at HYPO; they were busy ironing out the ramifications of the Battle of the Philippine Sea.

Worse, personnel at HYPO and NEGAT hated each other's guts. Toliver and the rest of the Twelfth Naval District Intelligence staff went to great lengths to keep out of the firing line. The two staffs openly dueled like the proverbial Hatfields and the McCoys. It began with raw feelings about who should shoulder the blame for Pearl Harbor. In Hawaii, the two local commanders, Admiral Husband E. Kimmel, CinCPac, and Lieutenant General Walter C. Short, of the U.S. Army, were sacked, and exhaustive investigations followed: the Roberts Commission, December 1941 to January 1942, and the Hart Inquiry, February 1944 to June 1944. And now, July 1944, Congress was planning to conduct two more inquiries: the Army Pearl Harbor Board and a naval Court of Inquiry.

The Roberts commission found that the Army chief of staff, General George C. Marshall, and the naval chief of operations, Admiral Harold R. Stark, had properly discharged their duties up to the time of the attack. However, Admiral Kimmel and General Short were censured for failure to take appropriate action in light of warnings received before the attack. But the Roberts Commission and subsequent Pearl Harbor investigations were hindered because of the extreme sensitivity of the United States' code-breaking capabilities. Very few were privileged to know about it. For example, the newer Japanese diplomatic "purple" (its predecessor was "red') code had been broken in August 1940 when American cryptographers duplicated the Japanese Type 97-*shiki O-bun Injiki* (alphabetical typewriter 97). Eventually labeled "Magic" intercepts, the decoded material was limited to only the president, his secretaries of state, navy, and war, and selected operational department heads in the War and Navy Departments. Morsels were occasionally sent to area commanders like Kimmel and Short, but most of it was held in Washington, D.C. Instead of a tool to keep area commanders informed, access to Magic became a path for ascension to the top of the heap; a backbiting power tool to shunt others away from the decision-making cycle; an award signifying a concomitant rise in rank. So Kimmel and Short were made scapegoats while others bailed out, only to backbite at a later date.

What worried Toliver more was the case of Commander Joseph J. Rochefort, the hero of the Battle of Midway. In March

1941 Rochefort took over what became Hawaii's ICPOA. His objective was to break the critical Japanese naval operating code JN-25. Initial versions of JN-25 had been broken in 1940. But a follow-on version, JN-25-B, was installed in December 1940, making decryption so difficult that only fragmented parts were readable up to November 1941, a crucial time. However, Rochefort kept at it, and much of JN-25-B became readable by May 1942, just days before the Battle of Midway. In fact, Rochefort had broken enough of JN-25-B in time to provide information for his boss, Chester Nimitz, commander in chief of the Pacific Fleet, to outguess the enemy and position his ships so that the Navy sank four irreplaceable Japanese fleet carriers on June 4, 1942. Ironically, a new Japanese follow-on code, JN-25-C, became effective on June 1, 1942, too soon for Rochefort to break, but Japanese forces were already committed.

Then Rochefort ran into a political morass. Before the war the director of naval communications in Washington, D.C., Captain Joseph R. Redman, set a personal goal of assuming "active coordinating control . . . of all intercept stations, D/F nets, and decrypting units," including control of naval intercept work at station HYPO. By early 1942, Captain Redman had achieved his objective and secured his flank by placing command of OP-20-G, which included NEGAT, under his younger brother, Commander John R. Redman.

During April and May, preceding Midway, Admiral Ernest J. King was under enormous pressure from the Joint Chiefs of Staff, who were concerned about the allocation of men and material, to provide accurate predictions of Japanese intentions in the Pacific. To get his information, King walked down the hall and pressured the Redman brothers. Burning the midnight oil, John Redman's staff concluded, incorrectly, that Admiral Isoroku Yamamoto's fleet would strike to the south, toward Fiji, Samoa, and New Caledonia — not Midway, as Rochefort had been predicting. Accordingly, King announced to the Joint Chiefs that Yamamoto's plan was to the south, in order to cut the U.S.-Australia lifeline. Worse, King fired off blistering messages to Nimitz, casting grave doubts on CinCPac's plans to defend Midway. Fortunately, Nimitz kept faith in Rochefort, and the U.S. Navy achieved a marvelous victory. King was embarrassed.

With King's tacit permission, the humiliated and power-hungry Redman brothers did everything to cover up their blunder. For openers, they insisted on taking credit for the Midway victory. King saw to it that the Redman brothers were promoted to rear admiral and captain. In turn, the Redman brothers cut orders recalling Rochefort to Washington, D.C. There they pulled him through a bureaucratic knot-hole. First, they relieved him of command of ICPOA. Over the ensuing months, they forestalled his promotion to captain, nullified a recommendation that he be given the Distinguished Service Medal, and, sadly, forever sidelined one of the great cryptographic geniuses of the time.

Kimmel and Short were caught in the same meat grinder. People at the top, covering up and watching their backsides, kept operational commanders in far-flung bases off key intelligence distribution lists unless it meant promotion for themselves.

In a way, the infighting was worse in Washington, D.C., than in the Pacific, where Toliver had been the gunnery officer under Todd Ingram aboard the minesweeper U.S.S. *Pelican* (AM 49) in Manila Bay. After escaping with Ingram in an open boat, he became gunnery officer of the U.S.S. *Riley* (DD 452). In the battle of Cape Esperance on October 11–12, 1942, Toliver received his debilitating hip wound; the *Riley* sank when hit by a Japanese Type 93 torpedo. Toliver had more than enough to keep busy; he stayed well clear of Station NEGAT's political vindications, a continuing effort to whitewash their complicity with the Pearl Harbor debacle and to sweep their Midway blunder under the rug. *Put your head down and do your job,* Toliver swore to himself. Why worry about it? He didn't plan to make a career of the Navy, anyway.

He checked his watch: 0644. Almost time to get together with Wellman and go over some notes. But first, he had to wake Jerry Landa. They'd had dinner at Wong Lee's last night. After a few drinks, Landa starting calling Oliver Toliver III, "Ollie Triplesticks." Soon, it was around the bar. Even Wong Lee and his daughter Suzy called him Commander Triplesticks.

Wouldn't Dad love that?

Time for retribution. He picked up the phone to wake Landa at the St. Francis Hotel.

TWENTY-THREE

1 JULY 1944
ST. FRANCIS HOTEL
SAN FRANCISCO, CALIFORNIA

The phone rang; Landa fumbled for his watch: 0714. "Hello," he croaked.

"Captain Landa?" It was a woman's voice.

"Later." He slammed down the phone and rolled over.

Thirty seconds passed. The phone's strident bell once again ruptured Landa's sleep.

"What!" he growled.

"Captain Landa, it's Roberta Thatcher. Forgive me for calling you so early. I —"

"Roberta who?"

"Thatcher, Captain Landa. The NBC Symphony Orchestra."

"Yeow!" Landa sat up in bed, running a hand through his hair. His watch read 0715. Actually, Roberta had done him a favor. Toliver had made a wake-up call nearly a half hour ago and he'd gone back to sleep. His head pounded. After dinner at Wong Lee's café, they'd driven around in his 1942 Oldsmobile. "Mrs. Thatcher, I'm sorry. How are you?"

"I wish I could say better."

A feeling of dread washed over Landa. "What is it?"

"It's Laura. I'm afraid we've had to let her go."

"Aww, sh—" He cut it short and said instead, "It's her drinking." A statement.

"Exactly. We feel terrible about it. But Laura is in a destructive mode. She doesn't concentrate and has become belligerent. I think she's taken on every section leader."

"By that you mean . . ."

"It's been going on for weeks. Bitter arguments. And not just artistic flings. These are intense, mudslinging, backstabbing, spittle-flying arguments. Even the maestro got pulled into one. And you know how that goes."

"Frankly, I don't."

"That doesn't matter. What matters is that she has alienated everybody, including me. And that's pretty hard to do."

That was true, he realized. Roberta Thatcher stood up for her people. A prude at the outset, she was basically a caring person; the orchestra was her life. He checked his watch, heaved out of bed, and stood, looking out the window. It was overcast. "When?"

"Yesterday at the end of the day. I

handed over her final paycheck."

The line was silent for five seconds.

Quietly, Landa offered, "She hates my guts. Won't return phone calls. I tried till I was blue in the face." That wasn't quite true. After flying back to San Francisco, he had tried to reach her at NBC. He couldn't get through, so he phoned her house, leaving a message with Trudy, her housekeeper. That was it. She hadn't returned the call. And now, his pride was stretched; she should crawl back to him. But she needed help, he realized. A rush of guilt swept over him.

"I know that. First things first, Captain. She's a marvelous talent and a wonderful human being."

"That she is. If it weren't for the damned booze." Another rush of guilt. Landa hadn't helped Laura with her drinking problem. Just the opposite. They'd been blitzed many times together. But he just shook off hangovers and went back to work. Last night, for example. He and Toliver had really pasted one on; that's why his stomach was rumbling now. But Laura. She often became angry when she drank. Something was buried deep inside that made her mean. "Maybe I better call again."

"Can I suggest something?"

"Shoot."

"Mrs. Ingram. Maybe she could call. Has she tried?"

"Don't know. Frankly, I hadn't thought of that. But she's in the hospital."

"What?"

"She had a baby boy, two days ago. Jerome Oliver Ingram," he said proudly. Longing for a cup of coffee, he stifled a hiccup. "But you know, Mrs. Thatcher, that's a damn good idea. As soon as I can get a line to San Pedro, I'll call Helen and see if she will give it a try. Tell me, do you think Laura has a shot at returning to the orchestra?"

"Between you and me, anything is possible. The maestro left it up to me. But I must see a vast improvement. I'm not going to take any more chances."

Landa exhaled. "Thank you."

"Don't thank me until you get her on the wagon and straightened out."

"Mrs. Thatcher, may I remind you that it was Laura who walked out on me."

"That's no excuse." Roberta Thatcher hung up.

"And they're sending you home tomorrow?" asked Landa. Toliver's chair creaked as he leaned back and plopped his feet on the desk. His stomach growled. He hadn't had time for breakfast after rushing from the St. Francis Hotel to the Twelfth

Naval District Headquarters, where Toliver had set up a line to San Pedro.

"No reason to keep me here. They need the bed." Helen had just awakened, her voice husky.

"And Mrs. Peabody will —"

Toliver walked in and said softly, "They're waiting." He crossed his arms and stood before the desk.

"Right away, Triplesticks." Landa waved him off.

"Pardon?" asked Helen.

"I said, is Mrs. Peabody all set?"

"As much as she can be." She sounded wonderful.

"Is she sober?" Landa looked up and winked at Toliver.

"How can you say that?" Helen laughed.

Landa closed his eyes. After a moment, he said, "Look, hon, I need a favor." He told her about Roberta Thatcher's call early that morning. "Could you try and talk some sense into her?"

Toliver pointed at the door, threw his hands in the air, and flopped them to his side.

"Do my best," said Helen. The connection wavered; he thought she was gone.

"Thanks," Landa yelled. "Gotta go. Say hello to little Jerry."

Toliver stood close and shouted, "He means 'little Ollie.' "

Helen said, "Tell Ollie his little boy is doing just fine. He has beautiful gray-blue eyes, just like . . . just like . . ." Her voice broke.

"It's okay, hon," said Landa.

"Oh-oh. The nurse just walked in with a bunch of forms. I better go. I'll call Laura and let you know."

"Thanks." The telephone company did the job for them and broke the connection. "Bastards." Landa looked at the phone, cradled it, and looked up to Toliver. "Thanks for putting me through. It would have been an all-day wait on a regular line."

"She okay?" asked Toliver.

"Going home tomorrow. Kid weighs eight pounds. Can you believe that?"

"That's great." Toliver straightened up a bit. "Captain, its ten past eight. Those people in there are wondering what the hell is going on."

Landa shot to his feet, straightened his tie, and donned his blouse. "Well, Commander, let's not keep them waiting."

"One thing, Jerry." Toliver waved across the hall. "There's a guy in there from OP-20-G."

Landa's eyebrows went up. "All the way from Washington, D.C.?"

"You bet. A Navy captain named Bunker. He's a hired gun, so keep your

. . ." Landa's face flushed a bit and Toliver dropped what he was going to say: *So keep your trap shut.*

"Hired gun for what?"

"Not what. Who. He works for the Redman brothers. They're on another witch-hunt."

"What the hell are you talking about?"

Toliver checked his watch. "No time now. Just follow my lead, Captain. All you have to do is tell 'em about the *I-57*. Did you read this morning's intercept?"

Landa pointed to a red-banded folder marked TOP SECRET. "Got it right here."

"What do you make about the fuel oil and position discrepancies?"

"It's a surprise to me. But the D/F had them at the Madagascar area. So I don't know what they're trying to pull." Landa rubbed his chin. "That and the new 'fist' aspect. All I can say is that we should watch her progress closely. So let's see what they say in tomorrow's posit report. But since this is all new, I plan to leave it out of the presentation until we see what gives."

"Makes sense to me. You about ready?"

"Up and at 'em."

"Your tie is loose."

"What would I do without you, Triplesticks?" Landa adjusted his tie.

Toliver waved a hand at the door. "After you, sir."

TWENTY-FOUR

1 JULY 1944
TWELFTH NAVAL DISTRICT HEADQUARTERS
SAN FRANCISCO, CALIFORNIA

They walked across the cement hall. Limping ahead, Toliver opened the door, allowing Landa to lead the way into the conference room.

The last time Landa had been here, the room seemed cold and distant, the photographs of FDR, King, and Nimitz austere and detached. Now the room was warm and steamy, the radiator heaters clanking and rattling merrily. Landa blinked, wondering if his vision was failing him or if the hangover was that intense. It seemed as if he couldn't see across the room, the photographs a blur. But his next breath told him why; the room was thick with cigar smoke. He recognized Henry Wellman, Toliver's hotshot chief warrant officer, sitting at the table's far end, puffing an enormous black stogie. In the middle stood a large carafe of coffee and a pile of doughnuts on a silver tray. His stomach growled again.

"Gentlemen, I'd like to introduce Captain Landa," announced Toliver.

There were five naval officers gathered around the table, all resplendent in dress khakis. At the head was a silver-haired vice admiral who looked as if he'd stepped from central casting. Landa recognized Jonathan Sorrell, a three-star flag officer bedecked with medals whose career had gone sideways after the Pearl Harbor attack. A star of the 1920s and 1930s, Sorrell had been a staunch member of the "battleship club," whose supporters were thinned drastically after December 7, 1941. But he still retained enough credibility to be tombstoned into his current billet.

Sorrell rose and grabbed Landa's hand, pumping it furiously, "Well, if it isn't Jerry 'Boom Boom' Landa, commodore of DESDIV 11. Welcome, Jerry."

"Nice to be here, Admiral. Thanks."

Sorrell asked, "And how's the destroyer business?"

"The destroyer business is fine, sir."

"Can we do anything for you?"

"Just keep sending Japs, sir. We'll take care of the rest." Landa flashed his signature Pepsodent smile.

While the others chuckled, Sorrell began introductions. On his right, he nodded to a tall Navy captain wearing impossibly thick glasses. "Meet Dick McCann, my district intelligence chief." They shook, with Sorrell next waving at a thin Army major at the end of the table wearing a dark brown Eisenhower jacket and parachute wings. "I believe you know Howard Curtis?"

Recognizing the jagged facial scar and unlit cigar, Landa reached across and shook. "Good to see you again, Major."

At the end of the table was Wellman, nearly consumed by a black cloud. Sorrell said, "Henry, dammit, can you cut that out long enough for us to see what you look like?"

That brought another chuckle from the group as Sorrell moved to a lieutenant on Wellman's right, wearing aviator's wings on his breast and aiguillette around his left shoulder. "That's Bill Villafort, my aide, dog robber, and right-hand man."

To Sorrell's left sat a thin, mousy-faced commander with slicked-back black hair. Except this man wore his uniform stiffly, and his blouse was without ribbons, looking as if he'd just picked it off the rack. "Please say hello to Warner Bunker, assistant director of OP-20-G. He's traveling through all the naval districts, looking for ways to increase office production."

As they shook, Bunker said in a strong baritone, "Pleased to meet you, Captain.

Forgive me for asking, what does 'Boom Boom' mean?"

Long ago, Landa had learned that when people asked that question, they already knew the answer. "I received several citations for fleet gunnery exercises a while back. Guess the name stuck."

"Oh." Bunker's eyes narrowed just a bit, telling Landa he knew that was not the reason for the nickname.

"Office production. Does that mean efficiency expert?" countered Landa, reaching for a doughnut. He wolfed it in two bites.

"Well, we like to say we just look for ways to streamline operations. Make things work more smoothly." Bunker flicked a finger at imaginary dust on his sleeve.

"Is that what you did in civilian life?" Landa asked.

"Well, yes. I'm a senior partner with Thorp, Thorp, and Collins. Then Admiral King asked me to come in and help straighten things out."

"When?"

Toliver eased close to Landa and lightly elbowed him.

"Uh . . . three months ago," said Bunker.

"I see. And how long —"

". . . Let's take our seats and get started, gentleman." Sorrell waved Landa to an empty chair between Bunker and Villafort;

Toliver sat just across between McCann and Curtis. Clearing his throat, Sorrell remained standing. "Welcome, gentlemen, to this special briefing on the *I-57* matter. There's good news. For once, I can say that we're all cleared for Magic. So we have a level playing field and don't have to hide behind rocks half the time." Apparently, Curtis had come up in the world. Last time Landa had seen the paratrooper, he wasn't cleared for Magic.

After clearing his throat again, Sorrell said, "What I'd like to have us do is to hear an update about the European situation. Then there have been developments in the Pacific you should know about. After that, we'll hear about Operation Neptune from Captain Landa and look for recommendations we need to act upon. Without any further adieu, Major Curtis."

Curtis stood, walked to a large easel and flipped off a black cloth, revealing a map of northern Europe. Northwestern France was obscured with slashing arrows, circles, and double rectangles. "Progress is steady, gentlemen. Cherbourg fell on the twenty-sixth, but it's going to take a while to get ships in there. The Krauts did an ingenious job of wrecking the place. They blew buildings into the harbor, destroyed the cranes, sank ships in the channels, bridges, everything. They even planted pressure-sensitive mines that count twelve ships before going off. That means our minesweepers have to sweep the same area at least thirteen times. They decorated the Kraut in charge of it all. His name was —" Curtis snapped his fingers.

"Yes, yes," said Bunker.

"I beg your pardon?" asked Curtis.

"The German responsible for Cherbourg's destruction." Slouching in his chair, Bunker steepled his fingers under his chin and said, "His name is Konteradmiral Walter Hennecke. And even though he was captured by American forces, Hitler still decorated him with the Knight's Cross."

Stuffing an unlit cigar in his mouth, Curtis jammed his hands on his hips. "Thanks for refreshing my memory."

Bunker's gaze flicked to Landa, their eyes locking for a moment. Landa knew about the Redman brothers and wondered why this little efficiency expert was here. Without any fruit salad on his chest, it was obvious the man had received a direct commission. Such people, Landa knew, were highly placed in civilian life and were adept at pulling strings with congressmen, who assured them noncombatant safe billets. But why would OP-20-G want to be involved in a piddly little backwater intelligence operation here, he wondered? He grabbed another doughnut.

"You may continue, Major," said Sorrell.

Curtis said, "That's about it for now. Rommel and Rundstedt have been counter-attacking our Normandy perimeter with tanks, trying to split our lines and drive to the beach. But we've landed enough equipment to hold them off. Having air superiority doesn't hurt, either. The next big battle will be here," his pointer slapped the map at St.-Lo. "Once that's captured, our southwestern flank is anchored and then we begin Operation Cobra, our breakout into central France."

"How about Paris?" asked Villafort.

"That's a French operation which starts pretty soon. We see Paris back in our hands no later than the end of August."

"Wow," said Wellman. "Had a girlfriend there once. Wouldn't it be nice if —"

"What about the U-boat pens?" asked Toliver.

Curtis shrugged. "Two, three months. There's a very tight ring around each one. It'll be tough. Plus, we have to capture Brittany first."

"How big is your Normandy perimeter?" asked Wellman.

"It's expanded to about sixty miles long by fifteen miles deep, ranging from Lion-sur-Mer in the east to Cherbourg in the west."

"That's pretty good, I'd say," said Wellman.

"Anyone else?" asked Sorrell.

When they shook their heads, the admiral nodded to Captain McCann on his right. "Dick will now give us the Pacific Island summary. I believe he has some interesting news for us. Take it away, Dick."

McCann rose and walked to a second blanket-covered easel. "Hot in here, Admiral." His eyebrows went up.

Sorrell glanced at the clanking wall radiators. "Can't shut the damn things off. Like the sorcerer's apprentice. Of course. Blouses off, everyone."

They all removed their blouses except, Landa noticed, Bunker, who still slouched. McCann said, "Thank you, Admiral. Now," he turned to his chart and whipped off the blanket, "last week we learned of the Saipan invasion by Howlin' Mad Smith. So far, he's secured most of the southern end of the island. The Jap's forces are split, and he'll soon begin his campaign to drive north. The Marines expect to secure the entire island by the fifteenth, thus giving us our first strong foothold in the Marianas."

"About time," said Wellman, puffing mightily.

Sorrell cleared his throat. "Thanks, Dick. Now we're saving the best for last." He waved to Villafort. "There's been a great victory in the Philippine Sea, gentlemen —

an aerial victory with minor losses for us. So, Lieutenant, since you're the token zoomie, could you summarize for us, please?"

Landa felt himself growing red with jealousy. Rumors had been flying around about the Philippine Sea fracas ten or twelve days ago, but these would be the first specifics he would hear. He admitted to himself that he appreciated being home and out of danger's path, especially if it meant saving Todd's life. But another part made him regret giving in so easily to Arleigh Burke.

Villafort walked to the opposite wall and flipped a black cloth off a board. This guy was no ordinary dog robber, Landa could see, as he examined his battle ribbons. He had the Distinguished Flying Cross, Purple Heart, and five battle stars.

Villafort said, "Admiral Spruance finally broke radio silence with a detailed report. And thanks to another release from COMSUBPAC, we've pasted together a broader picture as well. Here's what it looks like."

He held up a flimsy. "Spruance set a trap on June 19 and the Japs fell into it. Basically, what he did was keep his Big Blue Fleet close to Guam, denying the Japs the chance to shuttle bomb off their carriers. This sucked them close to Task

Force 58 and Admiral Mitscher, who had already wiped out their Guam airfields, along with the bases in the rest of the Marianas. Mitscher hit the Japs with everything he had. Over the next two days, he shot 'em all down. Nearly four hundred." Villafort looked up and grinned.

Landa ran his finger around his collar again, cursing Arleigh Burke for sending him stateside during one of the greatest naval battles of all time. But then he reminded himself of Ingram and what the Japs were doing to him. *Torture? Get hold of yourself, Jerry.*

"Three hundred ninety-five planes to be exact," snapped Bunker.

Villafort stared at Bunker. "You're right, Commander. Three hundred ninety-five plus another fifty land attack bombers situated on various runways in the Marianas."

Landa sat back as the meeting broke into a minor hubbub.

"And that's not all," said Villafort, gaining control. "The Japs lost three flattops. Submarines *Albacore* and *Cavalla* got the fleet carriers *Taiho* and *Shokaku*, and that's confirmed by COMSUBPAC. So is the fact that *Belleau Wood* TBFs got the carrier *Hiyo*." McCann rubbed his chin. "Goes on to say that the Jap flattop *Zuikaku* was heavily damaged along with the battleship *Haruna* —"

"Big Blue caught 'em with their pants down," said McCann.

"Also damaged were the light carriers *Chyodo* and *Ryho*, heavy cruiser *Maya*, destroyers *Samidare* and *Shiguri* —"

Wellman and Curtis puffed heartily, the cloud nearly obscuring a hacking Toliver.

"— and the hermaphadite carrier *Hayasui*."

"What's a hermaphadite?" asked Curtis.

"Who cares? As long as it's headed for the bottom. Soooo solly, Cholly," said Wellman.

Villafort waited for quiet and then said, "There's something else." He paused again. "To accomplish all this, Admiral Mitscher was forced to launch planes late in the day on the twentieth. They hit their targets but had to find their way back in full darkness."

"What?" They stared at Villafort.

"It says Mitscher turned on the lights to guide 'em back. Had every ship in the fleet turn on her lights, searchlights, running lights, breakdown lights, Boy Scout flashlights, the works. Planes landed on any deck they could find. He recovered a bunch of them that way. And not one ship of Task Force 58 got hit by a Jap sub. Some planes ran out of gas on the way back, though. Others crash-landed alongside ships in Task Force 58."

"Wow," said Wellman.

Villafort shook his head slowly. "I'll tell you, the guys of Task Force 58 are true heroes in my book, from cooks to pilots. I hope Admiral Nimitz gives every last one of 'em medals." He looked at Landa and smiled. "Even the tin can sailors."

Landa had crammed a doughnut in his mouth. "Umfff. Glad to be of service."

Bunker sat up and said, "Our losses were 130 planes, most of it due to Admiral Mitscher's, ah, nocturnal ramblings."

Villafort clenched his teeth. "Commander. I don't think —"

"Thank you, Lieutenant, you may be seated," said Admiral Sorrell.

"Admiral, I don't think this man —"

"I said sit."

It became quiet as eyes bored into Bunker, who nonchalantly doodled on a notepad. At length, Sorrell asked, "Captain Landa, could you fill us in on Operation Neptune, please?"

"Neptune. Yes, sir." Landa explained the *I-57*'s progress and finished with, "As of this morning, we have word that the *I-57* is preparing to round the Cape of Good Hope and head into the South Atlantic. So now, we're moving into the finesse phase where I'll be working with a Task Group 26.3, which consists of the escort carrier U.S.S. *Purvis Bay* and eight destroyer escorts. Turns out the group commander is Pete Hutchinson, an old friend. We served together aboard the U.S.S. *Golden* back in the early thirties. We'll fix it so the *Purvis Bay* gets the *U-497* after she refuels the *I-57*. Then we help the *I-57* make it through the North Atlantic to Lorient. And we'll do this by working with two other HUK groups stationed up there." Landa dropped the pointer in the tray. "That's about it. Any questions?"

"Admiral?" said Bunker.

Sorrell said, "Yes?"

"I'm curious. Do you think we are getting the best out of our resources?"

"I don't understand," said Sorrell.

Bunker waved to the table's end. "This man, Wellman. He's the cryptographer assigned to this operation, right?"

"Yes."

"Also, he reads and writes Japanese. Is this true?"

"Yes, Howard's a very talented man," said Sorrell. "Spent eight years in Japan, right, Howard?"

Wellman pulled a cigar out and said, "My dad was in a traveling circus. We went everywhere. Got stuck in Japan when he went Asiatic and married a Japanese girl. I finally got out when I turned fifteen. And that's where I learned to play the trumpet."

"And then you joined the Navy?" queried Bunker.

Wellman thumped his fist. "Yes, sir, I did."

"At the age of fifteen. You lied about your age."

"Where are we going with this, Admiral?" Landa asked bluntly. Toliver kicked him beneath the table.

Sorrell waved Landa's question aside and looked at Wellman, who continued, "Well . . . the Depression was on. And the recruiting chief liked me and told me to put down a different birth date."

Sorrell sighed and looked at Bunker. "What are you getting at, Commander?"

Bunker rubbed his hands together. "This man has a unique talent, Admiral. It's obvious he's underutilized here. We'd like to transfer him to OP-20-G where his true capabilities can be put to work."

"To Washington, D.C.?" gasped Wellman.

"Exactly."

"But my wife and kids are here." Wellman turned to Sorrell. "You promised, Admiral."

Bunker said, "I thought we were supposed to serve at the pleasure of the United States Navy, rather than the other way around."

"Is this what you mean by streamlining?"

Landa asked quietly. "Like how you did things at Thorp, Thorp, and Schmidlapp?"

Bunker said, "Thorp, Thorp, and Collins. Yes. It's strictly a question of resource allocation. This man is far more valuable in Washington."

"What about the *I-57*?" asked Landa. "What about Todd Ingram?"

"Actually, it looks as if the *I-57* was sunk three days ago," said Bunker.

"What?" said Landa.

"We have a report from the Royal Air Force Indian Ocean Command. One of their B-24s out of Trincomalee, Ceylon, claims a Japanese submarine sunk on June 27. Big oil slick. It occurred right along the *I-57*'s projected track."

"Bullshit," growled Wellman.

Bunker shot his cuffs. "I beg your pardon, Chief?"

"The guys at HYPO say the same fist sends her posit reports. I talk to them on the phone every day, and what's good enough for them is good enough for me. That sub is still alive. And so is Mr. Ingram."

Bunker leaned forward and jabbed a forefinger on the table. "Mr. Wellman, you have to recognize that —"

"Fifteen-minute break, gentlemen," said Sorrell. "Mr. Toliver, Mr. Wellman, I'd like to see you in my office, please."

Tight-lipped, the three left the room. Villafort and Curtis coughed politely while McCann poured coffee, each taking the remaining doughnuts. But Landa noticed McCann didn't offer coffee to Bunker. After a moment, Bunker rose and walked out. Landa accepted coffee from McCann, then excused himself, carrying his coffee. He walked down the hall to the men's room and shoved open the door.

It was empty except for Bunker zipping up his trousers and walking from the urinal toward a washbasin. Landa made a show of working his own zipper as he walked past Bunker. Then he faked a stumble, lowered his coffee cup, and pitched the steaming contents onto Bunker's crotch.

"Oww, hey!" Bunker protested. "What the hell?" He looked down, seeing the crotch of his khaki trousers splattered with coffee.

"Oh. I'm so very sorry." Landa ripped a half dozen towels from the dispenser and handed them over.

Bunker grabbed the wad and wiped furiously.

"Here." Landa grabbed another wad of towels, soaked them under the faucet, and handed them over. "Please forgive me."

Bunker looked at the wad, then at Landa. "What is this?"

"I'm just trying to help."

"I know when I've been had, Captain. What do you want?"

Landa braced his hands on his hips. "Such a good cup of coffee, too."

Bunker stared.

"All right. Here it is, Commander. That's my buddy's life you're screwing with."

"But he may be dead —"

"I'm not going to fool around with you anymore, you little goldbricking, backwater turd." Jabbing his finger into Bunker's shoulder, Landa said evenly, "That's Todd Ingram out there on that Nip sub. And you want to foul up this operation in order to build your little kingdom in Washington, D.C.?"

"You don't realize what you're doing. I can have you thrown in the brig, like that!" Bunker snapped his fingers, then furiously wiped wet towels at his crotch, making the contrast more vivid.

Landa's fury was mounting. It was all he could do to keep from smacking Bunker in the mouth. "I'm sure you could do that. Especially if you're brownnosing everybody like you say you do. And you know what? You'd get away with it, except you won't have the satisfaction of seeing me in Leavenworth."

"What?"

" 'Cause if you screw this operation up,

you little bastard, then I'm coming after you. And I swear to God, I'll kill you."

Bunker swallowed, his Adam's apple bouncing up and down.

"I repeat, if you take apart this operation, then I'm coming after you. And you'll end up under a freight train, all sliced to pieces. Now get out of here," Landa said with barely controlled rage.

"You . . . you . . ."

"Out," Landa roared.

Bunker walked out.

Landa expected Bunker to run down the hall to Sorrell's office. Instead, he walked for the front door, grabbing his cap off a tree before he exited. Landa was surprised that the Marine sentry saluted him, coffee-stained crotch and all.

Landa walked back into the head and braced himself on the sink for a couple of minutes, catching his breath. *Shit, Jerry, what have you done?* He waited until the water ran warm, then washed his hands over and over. Five minutes later, he walked back into the conference room, finding them all gathered. "Sad news, gentlemen." He shook his head slowly and said, "Commander Bunker became ill. Won't be able to rejoin us."

Admiral Sorrell jogged papers and said, "Shall we continue?"

Nobody asked questions. So Landa took

a chair and said, “We’ve got a problem with this operation. We’ve overlooked the RAF in the Indian Ocean. Dammit. It’s my fault.”

“Well, maybe Bunker did us some good after all,” said Sorrell.

Landa sat forward, “Possibly. Here’s what I think we should do.”

TWENTY-FIVE

2 JULY 1944
IJN SUBMARINE *I-49*
INDIAN OCEAN

Midshipman Yuzuru Tsunoda weighed just 140 pounds and stood just to the top of Ingram's collarbone. But at twenty-two years of age, he was a good-looking young man with dark, intense eyes and good muscle definition. In another era, he would have been a movie star. For such a gregarious young man, it was Tsunoda's misfortune to be assigned in Masako's place as Ingram's watchdog. He was forced to wear a duty belt and carry a pistol that Ingram was sure he didn't have the slightest idea how to operate.

Tsunoda talked incessantly to whoever was around and constantly besieged Ingram with questions about English. With Taubman's departure, Ingram gladly accommodated him, but after a few hours the midshipman's demands became monotonous. Even so, it was a welcome break from scrubbing decks and cleaning toilets.

Aboard the *I-49* Tsunoda was bunked in

the forward torpedo room. This torpedo room had only six torpedoes, the rest of the space being given over to storage for canned and packaged food. Ingram slept on the deck, this time chained beneath a massive Type 93 torpedo. Tsunoda enjoyed a bunk atop the torpedo, which was clear of bare-chested torpedomen who sweated heavily, spoke in grunts, and shuffled about the space in greasy trousers, smelling of hydraulic fluid.

Before acquiring Ingram, Tsunoda's normal duties had been as the executive officer's assistant, meaning he was a glorified yeoman. The young midshipman liked that, since it meant the bulk of his days were spent in a closet-sized office pecking at an ancient typewriter. With the help of sign language, Tsunoda told Ingram he spent most of the day asleep in there. So much for Commander Kato, he would say in a false basso, rocking on his feet from side to side, his hands on his knees.

Thirty-six hours out of Madagascar, they cruised at twenty meters beneath a relatively calm sea. They had been under all day, and the air in the boat was becoming foul with the day's activities, further complicated by a highly seasoned evening meal of *kaya*. At the moment, the officers and crew were finishing dinner in anticipation of surfacing in two hours, starting the engines to charge batteries, and drawing fresh air through the boat.

Having not yet eaten, Ingram and Tsunoda were in the control room. Lieutenant Seiichi Onishi, torpedo and gunnery officer, was the officer of the deck and spent most of his time bent over the chart table or reading thick operating manuals. Ingram was scrubbing the deck near the chart table and pushing a bucket of soapy water before him. Tsunoda sat perched on a linoleum padded bench next to the stern planesman, a third-class quartermaster. With furtive glances around the space, they leafed through one of the girly magazines making the rounds of the boat. Aside from Tsunoda's and his friend's stifled giggles, it was quiet; the watchstanders' eyes were heavy with fatigue, doing their best to stay open.

Something rattled as Ingram scrubbed. He stopped and looked up. Yes, there it was again, pencils rattling in a tea mug. His ears picked up. Odd. It was a motion, a sensation he couldn't pin down. He flattened both palms against the steel deck. Yes, there was something. He felt it. It was a vibration, a sound. He jammed his right ear to the cold steel deck. There. He heard it clearly: *thrum, thrum, thrum*. It was definite, predictable. There it was again: *thrum, thrum, thrum*. With each repetition of three, it would go away. But then it would return and he could feel it again: *thrum, thrum, thrum.* He could feel more than hear it, and after a while, he knew it came from back aft: a prop shaft. The starboard side was out of alignment: *thrum, thrum, thrum.*

Ingram looked up, finding Tsunoda casting a malevolent look in his direction. *Back to work.*

Scrubbing with a vengeance, Ingram was thankful Masako wasn't around. Instead of just a dirty look, Masako would have been kicking him. As he worked, Ingram's mind ranged over differences between the *I-49* and the *I-57.* Both had the same basic configuration, but inside, things were different: the galley was on the starboard side instead of the port, and the crew's mess in the *I-49* had one more table than the *I-57.* The motors in the motor room seemed much larger, and her diesels were a different shape altogether and made a lot more noise when operating. But this submarine seemed not as clean as the *I-57.* The main question: Why swap submarines? And what was with all that gold? What does *Yakuza* mean? He decided to ask Tsunoda.

Captain Shimada stepped through the hatch, a toothpick clenched between his teeth. He walked to the chart table, carrying an armload of books and rolled-up charts. Onishi barked, and the men more or less stood or sat at attention at their stations. Waving them down, Shimada bent over the table and unrolled a chart.

After a moment, Shimada walked over and began talking to Onishi. Curiosity getting the better of him, Ingram rose on his knees to check the compass repeater over the chart table: their course was 090°. It confirmed what Taubman had said; they were headed east, back into the Indian Ocean, away from the South Atlantic. But oddly, the course, directly east, was not the route to Penang, which should have been a bit north by east. He recalled their course on the way out was 250°. Thus they should have been on the reciprocal for Penang, a course of 070°.

Odd. Where the hell are we going?

Still huddled with Onishi, Shimada leafed through a manual, jotting notes as he went. Pushing his bucket, Ingram worked around to the starboard bulkhead so Shimada and Onishi were between him and the chart table. Again, he rose on his knees. The chart Shimada had been working on was labeled in English. It read: SOLOMON ISLANDS TO VANUATU. He was familiar with this chart and quickly picked out regions he had steamed through when aboard the *Howell* and, more recently, the *Maxwell*.

Someone bellowed. It was Shimada, his face in a rage, his finger pointing directly at Ingram. To his horror, Ingram found that he was on his feet, in full sight of everyone, hunched over the chart. It felt so natural bending over a chart. It was almost as if he were back in the *Maxwell*'s pilothouse, scanning coastlines, seeking safe passages and dangerous shoals, plotting courses and speeds.

"Jeez, I forgot. I'm sorry." Quickly, he dropped to the deck and began scrubbing.

Shimada quickly dashed around the chart table and kicked Ingram, the blow connecting with his upper arm, sending him on his back.

Screaming loudly, Shimada kept at it, his kicks going wide as Ingram flailed his hands parrying the blows. Shimada's kicks became more fierce. He stepped closer and drove a foot down on Ingram. The blow connected with the side of Ingram's head, nearly knocking him out.

In a rage, Ingram caught Shimada's foot as he kicked again and twisted, hard.

Arms flailing in space, Shimada lost his balance, tripped on the bucket, and fell over. His head hit the chart table with a sickening crunch. Then he fell to the deck in a crumpled heap, the bucket's dark contents sloshing about him.

"Oh my God. Forgive me. I didn't mean

to . . ." Ingram rose to his knees. Shimada lay on his side, groaning and holding his head, blood gushing between his fingers.

Ingram stood, looking into the vehement eyes of men gathering around him. "I swear, it was an accident."

Shouting, they pushed in, pinning him against a fuse panel on the starboard bulkhead. Officers in the wardroom piled in, as well. He ducked as fists whooshed past his head. He yelled, "I didn't mean to. He was kicking so hard. I couldn't —"

A blue light flashed though Ingram's head, followed by a hot bolt of intense pain. "You bastards," he yelled just as another blow connected. This time he didn't feel the pain, but simply collapsed on the deck.

Water trickled down his neck. Wind whipped over his face as if he were in a tunnel.

"Uhhh." He raised a hand to wipe his face, but he couldn't move it. He discovered it really was a tunnel and they had him trussed with a heavy piece of line. And going up! Warm liquid ran over his eyes as he thumped against the cold, sleek, hatch wall. The *I-49*'s engines grew louder as he rose to the top. With a final yank, they pulled him out, set him on the deck, and untied the hoisting rope.

He blinked blood from his eyes, finding it was overcast. Just past sunset, the sea was a calm slate gray broken by a few feathery whitecaps as water gushed down the *I-49*'s flanks, leaving a broad greenish-white foaming wake. The tone of the engines was deep, intense; his sailor's eye told him they were doing at least fifteen knots. He stood in the middle of about twenty sailors, wind ripping at their hair. They'd left his hands tied and try as he might, Ingram couldn't budge. Worse, the more he struggled, the deeper the bonds bit into his flesh.

They were behind the conning tower. The bridge watch looked down upon them with detached curiosity. Lieutenant Commander Kato, the ship's executive officer, was wedged among them.

Standing before him was Captain Shimada, a crude blood-soaked bandage wrapped around his forehead. Beside Shimada was Midshipman Tsunoda, his eyes wide open, his mouth opening and closing.

"Arrrrgh." Ingram lunged for the side, only to be caught by strong arms and thrust back into the middle of the group.

Commander Shimada stepped up and barked a few clipped sentences. Some sounded like questions, but he had no idea what the man was saying. Then, with great force, Shimada slapped Ingram across the mouth. He stepped back into the circle and crossed his arms.

"Same to you, shithead."

Shimada spit, the wind whipping it high in the air and aft.

Again, Ingram lunged for the side. Anticipating his bid, strong hands once again found him and thrust him back in the circle's center. And this time they shoved him to his knees. With all his might, Ingram tried to rise, but someone delivered two quick blows to his head. Someone else kicked him in the ribs; pain caroming about his thorax in white-hot jagged scythes. With a groan, he fell over, but someone yanked him back to his knees.

Lieutenant (j.g.) Fumimaro Ishibashi stepped into the group, taking a place alongside Shimada. Shirtless, he wore spotless trousers and classic split-toed sandals. Strapped around his waist was a samurai sword, and on his head was the *hamchimaki* — a white bandanna with the kanji ideographs. What had Taubman told him they meant? *Seven lives to serve my country.*

"I've waited a long time for this," Ishibashi said.

"What the hell are you doing?" Ingram sputtered through pain.

"You're not surprised that I speak English?"

"Not really."

Ishibashi stepped to Ingram's left and drew his sword with a clang. "Your German friend had it little wrong."

"What are you talking about?"

Ishibashi pointed to his forehead. "My *hamchimaki.*"

"Didn't Taubman say, 'Seven lives to serve my country'?"

"He was wrong. Actually it means, 'Born seven times to serve the homeland.' There are subtle differences." Ishibashi stared at him as if it were really important. "Do you see what I mean?"

Ingram's teeth chattered and he shook all over. "No, I don't."

Shimada barked, slicing a hand through the air.

Ishibashi bowed to Shimada, then turned and said, "This debate could be interesting, but we're out of time. Yours will be an honorable death. I could shoot you or strangle you, after all." He stepped behind Ingram.

The men before Ingram moved back two paces. The sword swished as Ishibashi took a couple of practice swings.

"This is bullshit!" Ingram tried to rise but someone clubbed him on the head.

Helen. I love you. God keep you and our

child safe and happy. I love you.

Through a fog of pain, Ingram saw the sailors' eyes tracking the blade in fascination, as Ishibashi swung it back and forth. Finally, they looked up as the sword was raised to the sky. But one of them focused on something distant. He screamed and pointed.

Gunfire. Ten-foot-high waterspouts raced toward the *I-49* and across her deck. Metal clanged on metal. Something screeched past Ingram's ear as deck wood chips flew into his face.

A shadow flashed overhead, starboard to port. Except there was no sun. *How could that be a shadow?* In the men's faces, he saw their anticipation of his execution suddenly change to dark, cold fear. Their heads whipped to port, watching the apparition go.

Wham! Wham!

Nearly simultaneous, the savage twin concussions knocked Ingram over. The men around him fell, too, their faces pale with disbelief. Shimada shouted. As Ingram struggled against his bonds, the men about him quickly rose and scrambled for the safety of the engine room hatch, Shimada yelling as they went.

The diving klaxon sounded as the half-panicked men leaped, one by one, down the hatch like Rumanian acrobats. But two weren't making the trip. A petty officer lay on his back, a giant red splotch across his chest, arms thrust out. Within two feet of Ingram lay Lieutenant (j.g.) Fumimaro Ishibashi, staring with dull, lifeless eyes, a giant hole in his belly, smoke trailing out.

The men who had surrounded Ingram were gone in thirty seconds. The hatch was slammed shut, and the dogging wheel spun as the diesels ground to a halt. Air blasted from the *I-49*'s ballast tanks as she lurched into a down angle. When the ballast tanks stopped roaring, another sound took its place: airplane engines. The plane was coming in on another run, its nose erupting with machine-gun fire. Again waterspouts raced for the submarine, finding her conning tower. Bullets clanged and ricocheted, throwing great chunks of metal and deck grating into the air. Red-hot pieces of shrapnel and wood fell about Ingram as he lay on his side, frantically trying to work his feet between his wrists.

The plane, a Wellington bomber with British roundels, ripped overhead, its twin engines growling.

Water gushed around the conning tower. Cascading down the deck, it lapped at Ingram as he kicked and groaned. Suddenly, white foamy water hit him at the full force of the *I-49*'s surface speed. Suddenly, Ishibashi's body swept from his sight.

Ingram was shoved down the deck. He slammed into the deck-gun pedestal. Desperately grabbing at space, he bounced away, slipping farther down the deck. Pain ripped through him each time he crashed into chocks or stanchions, so he rolled into a tight ball, smashing his way along. One collision gave an electrifying, painful boost, and his legs came through. His hands were before him and suddenly, he was swirling in white aerated water, rolling over and over. It happened so fast, he hadn't taken a complete breath before he found himself underwater, kicking for the surface. A part of the *I-49* swished past, a last farewell, as she clawed for the safety of the deep. With no sense as to which way was up, Ingram kicked, his lungs near bursting.

Let it go. It was a voice, his own.

"Todd. I'm here," she said.

It's okay. There's comfort down there. It's beautiful, the voice said.

"I love you," Helen said.

"Me, too," he gasped, breaking the surface. Frantically, he pulled in great lungfuls of air, kicking his legs and bound hands in a mushy dog paddle. At length, he looked about and saw he was alone in the Indian Ocean. Three-foot windblown waves lapped at his face, carrying him up and easing him down into troughs. Except for the sound of waves tumbling about, it was quiet. And this time there was no wreckage to cling to, no Dexter to keep him company.

"Oh, God," he called to the darkening overcast.

"You have a wonderful child," she said.

God, she's beautiful.

Let it go, said the voice from below.

The silence was broken by whining twin engines. Ingram jerked his head around to see the bomber coming right at him, no more than thirty feet off the deck, propwash mist trailing far behind.

"Yea! Rule Britannia!" he shouted, throwing his bound fists in the air as the plane roared closer. "God save the King." But then a long, black object fell from beneath the plane and hurtled right for him.

"No! You can't!" He turned and paddled furiously. Two seconds later the plane streaked overhead. Something smacked the water no more than ten feet away.

"You dirty —" Instinctively, Ingram ducked beneath the water and grabbed his legs in a fetal position. He waited for the blast. And waited, holding his breath as a series of waves flung him about, bubbling above. Finally, he raised his head, gasping for breath, just as the plane flew away, wagging its wings.

"Todd. Turn around," she said.

He turned, seeing a slick black rectangular object, perhaps two by four, bobbing no more than fifteen feet away. Writing, in yellow letters down the side announced: PULL HERE.

"I must be nuts." Furiously he paddled, the waves slapping at him. And the water was icy; the last water-injection temperature reading he'd seen aboard the *I-49* was fifty-two degrees. The cold sucked the warmth from him; his arms ached terribly, his legs felt like lead. Suddenly, pain shot into his right calf and his leg doubled up. Holding his breath, Ingram bent over and kneaded it with his fingers, working out the knot. It took five long minutes in the wind-tossed chop, which seemed to be gaining in strength. The cramp gone, he looked up and caught his breath.

The raft was a tantalizing five feet away.

But his strength was gone.

"Keep going, my love," she said.

Finally, he was there, the PULL HERE legend right before his face. It was a life raft, and all he had to do was to yank the damned stainless steel D-ring that dangled before his eyes. But he couldn't raise his arms. Biting his lip, he tried, but only his right hand broke to the surface. It flopped back and he gasped, ". . . can't."

In the distance, the Wellington flew about him in circles, its engines growling monotonously.

Let go, Todd. It's warm and safe and comfortable down there.

"Uh, please." He tried again for the D-ring. No luck.

"Todd, you've got to for our sake." Helen sounded the way she did the first time he met her in Corregidor's Malinta tunnel, dressing horrible gangrenous wounds, giving comfort to the sick and dying and to the doctors and nurses around her. She was a beacon of strength.

"I love you, honey." He raised both hands and found the D-ring. It seemed easy. He yanked with all of his might. There was a pop and then a loud hiss. As if by magic, a four-man life raft unfolded before his eyes.

The plane blasted over his head, waggling its wings, then disappeared. Ingram watched it go. "Thanks, buddy."

The top of the raft stood fourteen inches above his head. It might as well have been fourteen feet. *How do I get aboard this damn thing?*

"I love you, too," she said.

Summoning the last of his reserves, he pulled himself aboard and fell unconscious.

PART TWO

He has placed before you fire and water: stretch out your hand for whichever you wish. Before a man are life and death, and whichever he chooses will be given to him . . .

— ECCLESIASTICUS 15:16–17

TWENTY-SIX

2 JULY 1944
IJN SUBMARINE *I-49*
INDIAN OCEAN

"Make your depth seven meters," called Hajime Shimada. Then he looked at Ensign Kintomo, who sat hunched over his sound gear, hands pressed to his earphones. "Well?"

Kintomo raised a hand. "Still checking, sir."

"Just make certain. We —"

A wrench clanged on the control room deck; someone cursed.

Shimada looked at Kato on the other side of the periscope well. "We're jumpy, Shigeru."

Kato, a man who had ascended up the enlisted ranks, shrugged. "It's not every day we lose two men." Red lights in the conning tower mirrored their mood. Shimada thought about how close they'd come to being obliterated. Everyone, including the damned lookouts, had been mesmerized by Ishibashi, especially when he raised his sword to behead the American.

That was two long hours ago and Shimada had stayed down just to make certain. He had a healthy respect for the British Wellington bomber. Especially the one that had nearly sunk them. No doubt she was based in Madagascar and, according to an intelligence summary, was adaptable to many purposes, including antisubmarine patrols. Powered by twin Hercules radial engines of 1,610 horsepower, the bomber carried a payload of 2,300 kilograms and had a range of 2,900 kilometers. Twin .303-caliber machine guns in the nose were what had ripped into Ishibashi and Shinozaki. But what worried Shimada was that later models were fitted with 10 cm. radar and the new Leigh lights of extraordinary brilliance. She could still be up there now, scanning the surface for them. Circling. Waiting.

But now the boat again smelled foul. And they hadn't had a chance for the battery charge.

Time to go up. "Ummm?" His gaze darted from Kato back to Kintomo, whose hands were pressed to his earphones. "We don't have all night, Ensign," Shimada said dryly.

Kintomo looked up. "All clear as far as I can tell, sir. Do you want to do an active sweep?

"I'd rather not let the British know we're

about, if you don't mind." He nodded to his quartermaster. "Up periscope. And stay with me, Kintomo. Tell me the instant you hear anything, even a shrimp farting."

"Yes, sir."

The periscope hissed in the well, the eyepiece rising before Shimada. Quickly, he did a full sweep and then, slowly, another 360° sweep. Keeping his eye to the lens he ordered, "Lookouts to the conning tower." Shimada did a third sweep, then ordered, "Surface."

The klaxon sounded; air roared into the ballast tanks, and the *I-49* took a shallow up angle. "Come with me, Kato," said Shimada as he reached up, undogged the hatch, and threw it open. Water cascaded down, soaking his face, neck, and shirt. But it felt wonderful as he scrambled up the rungs and into the black, humid night. Kato and the lookouts followed as the submarine pitched gently in a smooth sea, her diesels growling into life.

Shimada called down the hatch, "Steady on course zero-nine-zero; make turns for fifteen knots." Kato stepped beside him as the *I-49* gained speed, plankton-saturated water swirling down her flanks. A rich, whitish-green glow illuminated Kato's face, reminding Shimada of a Dracula movie he'd seen in Tokyo. Within a minute, the lookouts called their sectors clear as Kato and Shimada kept scanning. "Looks okay," said the executive officer.

Shimada lowered his glasses. "We lost a good man today. It shouldn't have happened."

"Can't let it get to you," said Kato.

With a shake of his head, Shimada said, "I know Ishibashi's parents. Fine people. They've lost two other sons in this damned war."

"Ummm. All for the emperor."

"The damned emperor. Ishibashi could have had a better life. He deserved one. So did his mother and father."

Kato raised his binoculars for another sweep.

Shimada said, "Take over, and make sure these lads keep their eyes open. Those Brits are everywhere, and I'll be damned if I'm going to be caught flat-footed again."

"Especially since we've come this far."

"I think we're all right for now. I am going to do the right thing for once. Using the *I-57*'s call sign, I'm going to report Ishibashi's loss to Tokyo. His parents must know."

Scanning dead aft, Kato said, "You might as well do it up big and report all of them, including the American's."

"So be it." Shimada started down the ladder. His head was level with the deck when he called up, "Since we now play

Yukota's game of lying around Madagascar for two or three months, I'm going to draw some charts. I rather liked his description of Antongila Bay. Hardly any people, lots of fresh water and fish to catch. What do you think?"

"As long as we don't see any Tommies."

"All up north, apparently." He fixed Kato with a look. "Call me."

"Sir?"

"Call me if you see anything. The slightest scintilla."

"Yes, sir."

The cab pulled before the main gate on Treasure Island. Grabbing his B-4 bag, Landa paid, jumped out, and walked up to the Marine sentry, showing his ID.

The Marine saluted and said, "Car waiting for you, Captain." He nodded to a gray Plymouth sedan with Navy markings, a dungareed sailor standing at the front bumper.

"Thanks." Landa climbed in. Two minutes later, he was fighting his way through various doors of the Twelfth Naval District Headquarters, flashing his ID to a myriad of guards.

He found them in the conference room. Dropping his B-4 bag with a thump, Landa said, "Your messenger jerked me off the plane. Engines were started and they were closing the door. What's this about, for crying out loud?"

Wellman chomped an unlit cigar. McCann looked into the distance as Toliver steepled his fingers under his chin.

"Ollie, give, dammit."

Toliver snatched a sheet of paper and held it out. "We got the message at two this morning. It's a long intercept forwarded from HYPO. Took Hank six hours to crack it."

A look at Wellman's red-rimmed eyes confirmed that he'd been working at it. His sleeves were rolled up, and a fine band of perspiration stretched across his forehead and above his lip.

It was an *I-57* status report signed by Shimada. Landa's eyes jumped over the sentences. It was banal stuff: tons of fuel on board, ammunition on board, number two generator needed a new bearing, two sailors had yellow fever. Landa was ready to say, "So?" when his eyes froze:

> . . . STRAFED AND BOMBED BY BRITISH BOMBER. NO DAMAGE EXCEPT LIEUTENANT (JG) FUMIMARO ISHIBASHI, TORPEDOMAN SECOND CLASS TOSHIO SHINOZAKI, AND AMERICAN POW COMMANDER ALTON C. INGRAM, ALL KILLED IN THE ATTACK.

"No!" Pushing his hat back on his head, Landa sat heavily.

Wellman looked up. "Captain, I'm sorry. I've checked it six ways from Sunday. Some of this message was garbled, but I recovered about eighty percent. And Commander Ingram's name was very clear. Clear also was that his title was assigned in the proper order. I even had another guy come in from the *New Mexico*'s crypto gang and verify it for me. And . . . and . . . then I . . ."

"I'm sure you did your best, Hank." Landa's eyes again ran over the line. It burned into his brain: "Ingram . . . killed in the attack."

Landa raised his head and saw tears welling in Toliver's eyes. "Ollie, I'm sorry."

Toliver lowered his head. "I was his gun boss on the *Pelican*. Then we had this thirty-day canoe trip: Corregidor to Darwin, all expenses paid. You . . . you get to know a guy."

"Steamed a few miles with him myself," said Landa. "None better."

Toliver rose and kicked over a chair. "We should have talked to the Brits. We" — his eyes bored into Landa — "should have worked more closely with the damned Brits. What the hell are we going to tell Helen?" he roared.

"She already knows, Commander, in case you've forgotten." Landa stood.

Toliver paced the room. "She was with us. Todd saved her life. Saved all of our asses," he said shrilly.

"That's why they gave him the Navy Cross, son," said Captain McCann.

"Otis DeWitt, Leon Beardsley, Forester, Yardley, Sunderland — shit — we were planning a reunion. What am I going to do now?" Toliver's fist thumped the table.

Landa said, "I'll tell you what you're going to do. For starters, Commander, shooting off your mouth and wetting your diapers isn't going to bring Todd back."

"You — shit," growled Toliver.

Landa held up a hand. "Hey, Ollie. Whose side are you on, anyway? He was my buddy, too."

Toliver ran his hands over his eyes, and his shoulders slumped. With some difficulty, he reached down, upended his chair, and sat.

"Okay, Triplesticks?" said Landa.

Toliver pulled out a monogrammed handkerchief and blew his nose. "Sorry."

Landa sat beside Toliver and clapped his shoulder. "Okay, so Todd's gone. Nothing we can do about that. But the *I-57*? Let's finish the Brit's job and sink the sonofabitch."

TWENTY-SEVEN

20 JULY 1944
IJN SUBMARINE *I-49*;
KRIEGSMARINE SUBMARINE *U-497*
SOUTH ATLANTIC
10°05.7'S, 19°56.2'W

Wind howled through the periscope shears as the *I-49*'s bow climbed up a huge wave. Thirty meters to starboard, the *U-497* rose with her. Side by side, the submarines crested and plunged into the trough, their forward sections buried under angry seas as foaming white sheets of water crashed into their conning towers. Commander Norito Yukota, the *I-49*'s commanding officer, watched the *U-497* rise again, shaking off tons of water. Amazing, he thought. One's own plight didn't seem so bad when you saw someone else going through the same thing.

Two hours before, they had rendezvoused with the *U-497*. She was a milch cow: a submarine converted to replenish other submarines with fuel, food, and torpedoes. And now they were connected by a life-giving fuel hose. Yukota marveled that the rig hadn't carried away in this tumultuous sea.

The weather wasn't bad when they first rendezvoused. It was only in the last thirty minutes that a front had roared through, turning the ocean into a cauldron with whitecaps atop enormous whitecaps. Everything had taken so long: first, there was the personnel transfer, bringing two German communication specialists over to the *I-49*. Then they had to ship a moaning Korvettenkapitän Taubman, doubled up in pain, back to the *U-497*. It looked as if his appendix was ruptured. Luckily, the *U-497* had a doctor.

Yukota checked his watch: 0607. Sunrise pretty soon. Time to get under way. He yelled down the conning tower hatch, "How much longer?"

"Sir?" echoed the reply from inside the conning tower.

Water cascaded about Yukota as yet another wave inundated the bridge. Barely controlling his temper, Yukota kneeled over the hatch, watching buckets of water swirl down. "Kosuga? Where are you? Get over here where I can see you."

The sailor stepped under the hatch. Wearing slickers, his face was drawn tight, his blue lips stretched over chattering teeth. Water splattered on his face as he looked up, pulling an earphone off his right ear. "Yes, sir?"

"Wake up, you damn fool. I want to know how the fuel transfer is going."

More water spilled down the hatch. Kosuga's ankles were awash, but he didn't seem to realize it.

"Call the control room and tell them to activate the drain pump," Yukota yelled.

"Sir."

Suddenly, the *I-49* pitched into a trough and rolled thirty degrees to port in a bizarre, corkscrewing motion. A greenish-black mountain reared above Yukota's head. It grew and thundered toward him, poised to rip him off the bridge. Yukota kicked the hatch shut and frantically wrapped his hands around the periscope shears. Locking his fingers, he took a deep breath just as the wave hit. Tons of fifty-degree seawater pounded Yukota, threatening to tear him off the ship. Angry water penetrated his slickers and two layers of clothes and soaked his skin.

The wave subsided, tugging at his boots in white, seething swirls. Yukota could breathe again and he opened his eyes, finding it a bit lighter.

Everybody still here? Lieutenant (j.g.) Koyama, his OOD, hung to the starboard bulwark, watching the *U-497* pitch and crash. Aft, three motor machinists were hunkered around the fueling trunk, ensuring that the hose connection remained secure. Above, Yukota made out the dim shapes of Watanabe and Kazaki, his two lookouts, strapped into their positions. *All present.*

Yukota reached down and pulled open the hatch. "Kosuga!" he yelled.

Another face filled the void. It was Lieutenant Inichi, his engineering officer, in dark, oil-splotched overalls. "Fueling complete, Captain. Ninety-six percent on board." The wind howled so loud, it nearly ripped the words from Inichi's lips.

Yukota kneeled and shouted back, "About time. We'll break away the hose and clear the bridge as soon as possible. Secure the diesels now and tell the control room to prepare to dive in two minutes." He stood and called to his officer of the deck. "Koyama!"

Koyama turned and said something, but it was obliterated by screeching wind. Yukota staggered across the bridge and shouted in Koyama's ear, "Tanks are full. Shifting to electric propulsion. Signal the *U-497* to secure pumping and give them our thanks. Then let's break away and get the hell below. I'll send down the lookouts and fueling crew now."

"Yes, sir!" Koyama raised his portable signal lamp, braced it on his left forearm, and began clicking his message to the milch cow.

Yukota beckoned up to Watanabe and Kazaki. Quickly, they unstrapped themselves, scrambled down the rungs, and disappeared through the conning tower hatch.

"*U-497* signals pumping secured, Captain," shouted Koyama. "She adds, 'Good luck.' "

"Very well. Break away," yelled Yukota to the men at the trunk.

The engineers unlashed the hose and cast it into the sea, happy that the wildly snaking umbilical was free of the ship and was now the *U-497*'s problem. With that, they secured the fueling trunk, dashed past Yukota, and scrambled down the hatch.

"Come on!" Yukota yelled at Koyama. "Clear the bridge. Get down there and take the dive."

"Sir." Koyama climbed down the hatch.

For a moment Yukota lingered, mesmerized like a deer caught in the headlights. In this lifeless dawn there were only grays, enraged greenish-whites, and menacing blackness, deep in the troughs. Yet there was the sheer power of it all. Howling winds roared and threatened to tear paint off the *I-49*'s hull as mountainous anthracite waves built to impossibly high peaks, poised to crush anything in their paths.

To starboard, the *U-497* rode a wave sluggishly, dug her nose into the next, and was gone. Yukota threw a mock salute.

Good-bye, Martin. Get well soon. And take care of those greenbacks you have in that briefcase chained to your wrist. Spend it wisely, and there will be plenty for all of us on the other end. He hoped Taubman could keep his mouth shut with all the drugs the doctor would pump into him. The German had been nearly delirious with his pain.

Europe. They were only going to the outer reaches of the Bay of Biscay to meet the fishing trawler, transfer the crew, and scuttle the boat. To bring this off, Yukota and Shimada had to make it look good and do the fueling.

He sensed it first. Then it grew in his vision: a rising blackness of immense power. He drew in his breath. An enormous wave built before the *I-49*: at least twenty-five meters high. It quickly became a greenish-white malevolent apparition dominating the entire horizon. Yukota's whole world seemed to ascend with the wave as it rose and rose. And above the screeching wind, Yukota heard it, coming alive, groaning with tons of water ready to smash anything in its path. Louder it came, blocking the wind, creating a bizarre calm.

Yukota hadn't felt real panic until this. Quickly, he dashed down the hatch. Yanking on the cord, the hatch thumped shut above his head. "Dive! Dive the boat," he yelled as he twirled the dogging wheel.

"Captain?" Koyama's voice echoed up from the control room.

"Get her down, dammit! Make your depth forty meters." Even as he said it, the wave rumbled overhead, making the submarine pitch sickeningly.

"Yes, sir. Forty meters," said Koyama, his voice thick with tension. Men cursed in the control room; they were having trouble with the dive.

Hands braced on his hips, Inichi asked, "Everything okay, Captain?"

Yukota dropped to the conning tower deck and pulled off his slicker. Water dribbled on the deck as he said, "You should have seen that wave, Inichi. Why does man insist on going to sea? We must be crazy."

Inichi grinned. "Most are not after what we are, Captain." He reached for the slicker. "Here, let me take that to the engine room and dry it out for you."

"Thank you." He handed it over.

The *I-49* rolled thirty-five degrees to starboard. Yukota and Inichi grabbed overhead pipes and swung with it. When she straightened out, Yukota kneeled over the control-room hatch and roared, "Dammit, Koyama, get on with the dive. What the hell's wrong with you?"

"Working on it, Captain."

TWENTY-EIGHT

21 JULY 1944
U.S.S. *PURVIS BAY* (CVE 88)
SOUTH ATLANTIC
08°21.7'S. 16°13.2'W

The Grumman TBF was designed by an advanced team under the lead of Bob Hall, one of Roy Grumman's best engineers. The midwing, single-engine torpedo bomber was selected by the Navy over rival designs on April 8, 1941. Hall flew the first of two prototypes on August 7, 1941. The plane featured the new 1,700 horsepower R-2600 Wright-Cyclone, double-row, fourteen-cylinder, radial engine — the same engine that powered the twin-engined Army Air Corps B-25 that raided Tokyo on April 18, 1942. At 14,500 pounds, the TBF proved to be the heaviest carrier-based aircraft in the U.S. Navy. Even so, she had a top speed of 271 miles per hour at 12,000 feet. However, the engine seemed lost in a hulking configuration that some dubbed the Pregnant Beast or the Turkey, neither of which, fortunately, proved true. She had a crew of three, including a pilot, who sat in a large cockpit close to the wing's leading edge. Besides flying the airplane, he aimed the torpedo and fired a fuselage-mounted .30-caliber machine gun through the propellor. In the enclosed rear compartment sat a bombardier-radio-operator who doubled as a ventral gunner. Seated just above him was the rear gunner; his all-glass turret was electrically powered by an amplidyne generator that aimed a .50-caliber machine gun with great precision. With a payload of 2,000 pounds, the TBF was initially built to deliver the Mark XIII aerial torpedo. But later on, the Avenger, as she was officially dubbed, was adaptable to many missions, including bombing, depth charges for antisubmarine work, rockets for air-to-ground support, and reconnaissance.

In the Atlantic, TBFs were adopted for a purpose well served by their specifications: antisubmarine warfare. Many were fitted to carry a Westinghouse APS-4 radar mounted in a pod under the right wing. A common payload was four depth charges or two five-hundred-pound bombs combined with one of the most innovative weapons developed in World War II: the Mark 24 acoustic torpedo. When dropped from a TBF, the seven-foot, 684-pound FIDO, as it was code-named, had four hydrophones in each quadrant surrounding the nose, allowing it to passively track a submarine at speeds up to twelve knots. When it hit the target, a contact fuse detonated its warhead of ninety-two pounds of HBX, plenty of explosive for inflicting catastrophic damage to a submerged submarine.

The front had blown itself out. It was cold and crisp, with stars glistening in the South Atlantic predawn sky. With an air temperature of fifty-five degrees, the wind had moderated to fifteen knots blowing out of the west. Seven ships steamed in a circular formation at twelve knots on course two-seven-oh. In the formation's center was the light carrier U.S.S. *Purvis Bay*. Stationed in a protective screen around the carrier were eight destroyer escorts: U.S.S. *Cheffer*, U.S.S. *Fisher*, U.S.S. *Moody*, U.S.S. *Grady*, U.S.S. *Foreman*, U.S.S. *Simpson*, U.S.S. *Anslow*, and the brand-new U.S.S. *Bunyan*.

It was a half hour before dawn when two TBFs rose on the elevator and were spotted in tandem on the *Purvis Bay*'s deck. Wings still folded, they were gassed, loaded, and ready to go. Their crews had climbed aboard and were strapped in, finishing their checklists, fidgeting with last-minute items. After running up the engine for two minutes, Lieutenant (j.g.) Ralph Kenrich switched it off and sat back in the cockpit of the aft TBF, the name *Big Lug* painted on either side of the nose. Brisk ocean air washed his face, whisking away the sharp odor of 100 octane gas and hydraulic oil.

Destroyers abeam of the *Purvis Bay* blinked at her, which usually meant an acknowledgment for a change in formation course and speed. They were already steaming into the wind, so this time it was just a change of speed. Sure enough, Kenrich felt the ship vibrate as she worked up to her top speed of eighteen knots, the wind whistling a bit stronger. Kenrich keyed his intercom mike: "Bishop, you have those recognition codes?"

"Lost 'em in a crap game."

"Dammit, Bishop!"

"Yes, sir. I have them. Double-checked with Chief Asher just before I came up."

"That's better. What's our call sign today?"

"Hopscotch four-one, sir."

"And Lieutenant Boyd?" Lieutenant Tommy Boyd, the group leader, was in the TBF just forward.

"He's Hopscotch two-six, sir."

"Okay. Now, no screwing around this time. We have a live one out there."

"They've been saying that for the past four months . . . sir."

Bishop's insolence was not lost on

Kenrich. They'd had a lot of dry runs lately. Everybody on the ship was frustrated. But the air boss, Commander Tomlinson, sounded pretty convincing at the briefing this morning. Uncharacteristically, he kept looking from side to side, saying, "Keep this to yourself." He went on to explain exactly where the target was, what it was, and when they could find her on the surface, details that Kenrich wasn't used to. It gave him an eerie feeling.

But Tomlinson had sworn him to secrecy, so Kenrich merely said, "What can I tell you? This is what we get paid for. If you don't like sitting in your nice little warm compartment back there, then turn in your wings and I'll get someone else."

"Sir . . . come on."

Bishop knew Kenrich didn't mean it. They'd been flying together for the past thirteen months. Radioman Second Class Everett Bishop was one of the best in the bombardier-radio-operator business. Plus, he was a wizard on the APS-4 radar. Kenrich was lucky to have him, and he didn't mind cutting a little slack. With a grin, he decided to leave it alone and let Bishop squirm a little.

Again, Kenrich keyed his mike. "Donoho. You okay?" Aviation Ordnanceman Third Class John Donoho was his rear gunner.

"As long as Bishop remembered the sandwiches and coffee, sir," replied Donoho.

"Sorry, Crapper. Just enough for me and the skipper," chirped Bishop. Donoho loved to play dice, thus his nickname "Crapper."

"Where's my bag? They had it next to yours," Donoho complained.

"Couldn't find it," replied Bishop. Donoho was well known for a massive appetite. Bishop loved playing tricks on him.

"Dammit, Bishop. You couldn't find your ass with both hands," said Donoho.

Kenrich cut in. "Knock it off, you guys."

Donoho said, "Skipper. He's saying I'm stuck in this little turret, flying for four hours without anything to eat, while he sits down there on his dead ass slopping up my food. I ought to go down there and pound some sense —"

"Pound sense into who?" Bishop interrupted. "You're that strong?"

"I'm that strong, wise guy."

"Oh," said Bishop in falsetto. "You're so strong, I'll bet you have muscles in your shit. The thing is you're just too fat. That's why you don't get lunch today. Too much weight. We need to save gas. Good for the war effort."

The PA system screeched, "Pilots, prepare to start engines."

"Hey, you two," said Kenrich, "time to get serious."

"You're the one with the fat butt, Bishop," said Donoho. "Hell, you can't even climb through the door down there. Hell, you need ten pounds of grease just to —"

"Start engines," bleeped the PA.

"Pipe down, fellas," Kenrich growled as he set the fuel mixture to auto-rich and clicked the fuel priming switch a couple of times. "Here we go." He leaned over and caught his plane captain's eye. "Clear!" he shouted. When his plane captain gave a thumbs up, he flipped the starter switch. An electric motor whined and the prop began turning. Kenrich counted blades as they whipped by his field of view. He was glad for something to do. Sometimes it was hard to tell when Bishop and Donoho were serious. Trouble was, both were very sharp kids with completely different backgrounds: Bishop spent three years at the University of Virginia; Donoho had a well-defined athletic frame and an inquisitive mind seasoned by a youth spent in the ghettos of Detroit. The only times things went wrong was when they had nothing to do.

Six . . . seven . . . eight . . . nine blades rolled past, three complete turns. Kenrich twisted the magneto to BOTH and the R-2600 caught with a mighty roar, belching thick smoke from its twin exhaust stacks. The engine coughed, backfired loudly, and settled into a steady rumble, the smoke finally clearing.

Ahead, Tommy Boyd's plane, Hopscotch, was started, with sailors now at each wing tip, pulling them forward and out, extending them for flight.

Kenrich looked down to his plane captain and gave the sign for wings unfolding. Two airmen at each wing grabbed a corner and ran it forward, sliding the wings into place. Kenrich pulled the T-handle, setting a hydraulic locking pin in each wing. With a thumbs-up to his deck crew, he eased in the throttle and Hopscotch 41 began waddling to the *Purvis Bay*'s starboard side. His earphone clicked: Tommy's signal to check in and say hello.

Kenrich clicked back twice. That was all that was needed. He and Tommy knew each other well enough to know that each was ready. And out here radio silence was important. No telling if their target was monitoring the radio waves.

Two minutes later, Hopscotch 26 roared down the deck and cleared the bow. Kenrich watched her go, then put in full flaps, lined up with the bow, stepped on his brakes, and locked the tail wheel. "All set, fellas?" he called on the intercom while setting the prop to flat pitch.

"Yes, sir," they answered in unison.

Barely visible in a white sweater and white canvas cap was the Fly One officer who stood off to Kenrich's right. Soon, Fly One shot his fingertip over his head and twirled it in the air. *Wind her up.*

"Okay," Kenrich muttered to no one in particular. Yanking the stick back into his lap, he stomped in right rudder and moved the TBF's throttle all the way to full power. Pulling forty-eight and a half inches of manifold pressure, the R-2600 engine roared in its mount, the whole plane vibrating and protesting, every joint, every fitting shouting, "Please, please, let me fly."

Thirty-eight knots of wind rippled Fly One's clothes. His finger kept twirling over his cocked head as he listened to Kenrich's engine, making sure it sounded all right.

Aboard Hopscotch 41, Kenrich strained against his harness, waiting for the launch signal, anxious to urge his TBF into the air.

Fly One whipped down his hand.

Kenrich popped off the brakes. The TBF lunged forward with Kenrich easing the stick to neutral. The tail wheel rose, and from the corner of his eye he saw the deck edge flash past. By that time *Big Lug* had flying speed and was already five feet above the flight deck. She dropped a bit and

Kenrich pulled back the stick just a little, eased into a shallow right turn, and slapped the landing gear handle to the up position, all at the same time, not really thinking about it. Next, he began milking up the flaps, setting the cowl flaps, pulling *Big Lug* into a climbing turn to join up with Tommy Boyd. Datum was a hundred miles out; course 300° magnetic.

"You sure you don't have my sandwich?" asked Donoho.

"Call me later. I'm taking a nap," said Bishop.

"Three more degrees right, Skipper." There was a captivating timbre to Bishop's voice. It was quiet, level, every syllable pronounced precisely.

"Check," said Kenrich, steering the new course. The sun wasn't quite up, but the sky was much lighter. Kenrich flew lead since he had the radar; Boyd, who had sonobuoys and listening equipment, flew wing position. Kenrich had two five-hundred-pound bombs and the FIDO; Boyd carried four depth charges.

At one thousand feet, the angle was perfect as they came up on the target nearly out of the sun. "How's the echo doing?" asked Kenrich.

"Strong, sir. Just six miles now," said Bishop.

"Bomb doors coming open," called Kenrich, tripping the handle. Wind whistled in the compartment as the TBF's bomb doors opened.

"Five miles! Directly ahead. Strong echo. You see anything yet, sir?"

"Question is, do *you* see it, Bishop?" retorted Donoho.

"Lemme take a look." Bishop eased from his radar receiver and pressed his face to the bombardier's window, which now had a clear view out the open bomb bay. "Just waves," he muttered. "Go back to sleep, Crapper. You can — Sheeeat! There he is!"

Kenrich twirled in his seat, looked back at Boyd, and chopped a hand across his throat. Boyd acknowledged with the same motion. With that, he retarded the power to idle and dropped the nose. Wind whistled though the airframe as *Big Lug*'s engine popped and backfired softly. Ahead, Kenrich picked a speck out of the ocean, twin white exhaust plumes trailed past the submarine's fantail, hanging over its wake.

"Bingo!" Kenrich shouted.

Boyd clicked in. "Dead duck," he said. "Go get 'em, Ralph."

"Three miles," said Bishop.

Misty air spewed above the submarine, its motion seeming sluggish. "Dammit. She's diving!" said Bishop.

Kenrich punched in some throttle and keyed his mike. "Tommy, let's both salvo."

"You got it," replied Boyd.

Except for the periscope, the submarine was gone by the time Hopscotch 41 flashed over. Bishop salvoed both bombs. Then he added power and eased into a shallow climbing turn while behind them, twin bursts rose in the air. "What do you think, Donoho?"

Looking aft, Donoho said, "You straddled his wake. Can't tell anything else. No Krauts swimming around. No — Hold on."

Four depth charges burst around the target, throwing great columns of smoke-charged water into the air. Donoho continued, "Mr. Boyd straddled the target, too. Still no Krauts running around."

"Maybe an oil slick?" asked Bishop. "What do you think, Mr. Kenrich?"

Kenrich pushed into a steep left bank and leveled off at five hundred feet. All he could see was dissipating mist. "Can't tell." Kenrich keyed his mike, "Tommy?"

"Let's drop sonobuoys," was Boyd's terse reply.

"I got the smoke," called Kenrich. He punched his intercom and said, "Bishop, drop smoke on my command." He hauled into a tight turn, then leveled out, eased the nose down, and headed for water still swirling from the explosions. It was an arbitrary point called datum: the last position where the submarine was detected.

Bishop grabbed a smoke cannister and got it ready. Above, the little hatch to the turret opened. Donoho peered down between his knees, his face screwed up. "You serious about my lunch?"

"I got your damned lunch. Wait until I toss the smoke," said Bishop.

"That's better." Donoho smiled. "You'll live to see another day."

"Yeah, yeah," said Bishop.

Ten minutes later, the sun was up, glistening bright yellows off bouncing wave tops. Boyd called over, "We got him, Ralph. Two-four-zero, twelve hundred yards from datum. Possible submarine. Lots of noise. Sounds like he's cranking up full turns." Hopscotch 26 peeled into a tight turn, headed over datum, and seconds later dropped another smoke float. "Right there," said Boyd. "Drop it right there."

Kenrich felt a rush of blood to his head. "On my way." Easing his TBF around, he lined up the two smoke floats, pulled the throttle almost to idle, and put in twenty degrees of flaps. When the TBF had dropped to fifty feet off the water, he cranked in the throttle and aimed for the smoke floats. By the time *Big Lug* flashed over the first smoke float, he was perspiring. Without thinking, he rolled the canopy open. Then his hand went for the torpedo-release handle as *Big Lug* floated along at a hundred knots.

Keep her level, keep her smooth. Don't even blink. Don't even think of blinking. "Now!" Kenrich yanked the handle. Free of the 684-pound missile, *Big Lug* jumped five feet. The FIDO fell free behind them and plunged into the water, leaving a tall white waterspout where it hit.

"Bingo! About ten feet at two o'clock from the smoke, Skipper," Donoho shouted.

Big Lug's engine growled as Kenrich jammed in the throttle and pulled into a climbing turn. Settling into a shallow circle about five hundred feet around over the smoke float, he keyed his mike and asked, "Anything, Tommy?"

Boyd answered, "Screw noises. FIDO's running hot all right. There's something, but it's jumbled. I think — Whoa!"

"What?"

"Big pop. Damn! Bubbles. Lots of cracking. Oh, shit."

"Tommy?"

"A big whap! Breaking-up noises. He's going down. Scratch one Kraut."

Kenrich flew for a moment, looking down at the sea, now bathed in sunlight. "You sure?"

"Positive kill. I'll call home and report it. Let's head on back."

Boyd and Kenrich climbed to five thousand feet and lined up on course one-two-oh, Kenrich assuming the wingman position for the trip home.

Ten long minutes passed as the crews sat with their thoughts. Finally Bishop asked, "Skipper?"

"Yeah."

"You know how deep it is back there?"

Big Lug droned for a moment. Kenrich answered. "Chart says twelve thousand one hundred."

Thirty seconds passed. Bishop called up. "Hey, Crapper. You ready for your sandwich?"

"Think I'll wait awhile."

TWENTY-NINE

22 JULY 1944
TWELFTH NAVAL DISTRICT HEADQUARTERS
SAN FRANCISCO, CALIFORNIA

It was cold and windy when the cab lurched to a stop before the dimly lit sentry post. Toliver's words on the phone still rang in Landa's ear as he eyed a crowd of sailors around the gate. "I've got something for you, Jerry." He checked his watch: 2342. Two hours to go before the gooney bird took off for Terminal Island.

The driver cursed and honked, but the sailors, intent on checking in before midnight, didn't budge. Many had red-rimmed eyes and rumpled dress whites, merit badges attesting to their Saturday night on the town. Some dug in their pea coats, nervously fingering liberty cards. Others propped semiconscious buddies between them, smelling of sweat and cheap beer. A group stood off to the side, slurring the words to "On Moonlight Bay."

"Hold on." Landa jumped out and drew up behind an enormous sailor with dark, curly hair. "Can we get through?"

The man ignored him.

Landa tapped him on the back. "Sailor?"

The sailor twirled: a burly first class boatswain's mate with powerful forearms. "What the fu— ? Oh, 'scuse me, sir." He stepped to the side. "Hey, you guys," he called in a deep baritone, "make a hole — er — gangway for an officer. Jeez, a captain."

Muttering and grumbling, the crowd parted, one sailor whipping off his hat and waving the cab through with an exaggerated bow.

Landa climbed back into the cab. "Go!"

With another horn honk, the cab driver popped the clutch and moved ahead, drawing to a stop at the gate. A Marine corporal stood on one side, a private on the other. As Landa cranked down the window, the corporal, his cap the requisite two-finger width above his eyes, stooped and looked in. "Captain Landa?"

"That's right." He flashed an ID card.

The corporal threw a smart salute and said, "They're expecting you, sir. Go right on ahead."

"Thanks."

The cab went through the gate and was at the headquarters building in two minutes.

"Wait for me here." Landa jumped out

and rushed in, winding his way through a maze of guards. Three minutes later, he rapped on Toliver's door.

"Enter."

Toliver and a cigar-chomping Wellman sat at a small side table, poring over notes. Their coats were hung on a tree, their sleeves were rolled up, and every horizontal surface, including the deck and floor, was covered with books and papers, half of them wadded and tossed where they lay.

Wellman shot to his feet. "Evening, Captain."

Landa waved Wellman to sit. "You guys are working late."

"Want some?" Toliver pointed to a coffee service.

"Thanks." Landa grabbed a cup and poured. "What have you got, Ollie?"

"Henry?" Toliver cocked an eye.

Wellman fished among a pile of flimsies. He found an envelope marked OPERATION NEPTUNE — TOP SECRET and silently handed it to Landa.

Landa accepted it and absently sipped while pushing piles of papers toward the center of Toliver's desk with his buttocks. The message read:

TOP SECRET
DTG: 22071362Z
TO: COMTWELVE

FM: COM TG 26.3
INFO: DESLANT
CINCLANT
CINCPAC
COM TG 58.3

1. TWO TBF ATTACKED AXIS SS 21070937Z; 09°16.3' S; 16°45.8' W
2. SONOBUOYS INDICATE FIDO HIT TARGET AFTER SUBMERGING. BREAKING UP NOISE FOLLOWED FOR THREE MINUTES.
3. TG 26.3 SUBSEQUENT SEARCH 22070822Z. FOUND OIL SLICK AND WRECKAGE. FOOD CARTON WITH IDEOGRAPHS INDICATE JAPANESE ORIGIN.
4. EVALUATED AS KILL, JAPANESE SUBMARINE.
5. THANKS FOR THE TIP. PLEASE SEND MORE BUSINESS.

BT

Landa snorted. " 'More business.' " He looked up, catching Toliver's eye. Both looked away with the same thought. The *I-57* was their last tangible connection to Todd Ingram. Now the submarine was junk, littering the bottom of the South Atlantic. "Guess that's it," Landa said. Somehow, the satisfaction he thought he would derive wasn't there. In fact, Landa felt pale and empty, the office's cold cement walls pressing in.

Toliver stood, hobbled over to the carafe, and refilled his cup. "It's . . . it's . . . you spend twenty-some-odd days with a guy in an open boat. He saves your life. You save his." He looked up. "What's it all mean?"

"Need a fresh cigar. Back in a minute." Wellman walked out, closing the door softly.

Toliver fell into his chair and ran a hand over his face. He looked up to Landa, his eyes glistening. "Helen must be used to it by now. Now it's our turn." He smiled ruefully.

"He's gone, Ollie." Landa turned away. "Don't know if I can get used to it, either. I thought he had a great chance. I don't know what the hell went wrong. But it's not your fault, it's not mine. So buck up."

"Maybe so, maybe not."

"I'm ordering you to forget it, mister. It's not your fault. What did Todd used to say? 'Let the dead bury the dead.' " Landa turned and held out a hand. "Cab's waiting. Got a red-eye for Terminal Island. I say good-bye to Helen tomorrow. Then I shove off for . . ." He waved a hand toward the Golden Gate.

"Out there?"

"Somebody has to fight this war." Toliver flushed a bit, and Landa was sorry the instant he said it. "That doesn't mean you, Mr. Triplesticks. You've paid your dues."

Toliver stood. "I don't miss it one bit." With a sigh, he said, "Tell Helen I'm sorry for not getting down there right away to see her and little Ollie."

"You mean little Jerry," said Landa.

"Ollie."

"Whatever."

"Please let her know I'm really swamped. And then next week I'm off to Washington, D.C."

Landa gathered his things. "What for?"

Toliver lowered his voice. "School. I'm being transferred to ONI. A ton of courses."

"My God, Ollie, that's really swell. But they don't usually send reservists to naval intelligence, do they?"

"Well . . ."

Landa's smile gleamed. "You mean you're shipping over? Career Navy?"

"Ummm."

"Welcome to the club, you damned fool."

They hugged and clapped shoulders. "Thanks, Boom Boom," said Toliver.

"Watch it. I could have you busted for that."

"Probably the best thing that can happen to me. Then I'd be reporting to Wellman.

And I'd be running his butt off instead of vice versa." He held out a hand. They shook.

"Be well, Commander," said Landa.

"Give my best to Helen."

The R4D, the Navy version of the venerable DC-3, landed at Terminal Island a little after five a.m. By six Landa had checked into the Long Beach Naval Station BOQ and was fast asleep by six thirty. The sun streamed through his window at two that afternoon, waking him. Yawning, he rose and padded down the hall to a pay phone, dropped in a nickel, and dialed the number.

Helen answered on the second ring. "Hello?"

Landa mustered a high falsetto. "This is the social services department, ma'am. Can you give us any information as to whether or not young Jerome Oliver is being cared for properly?"

"It's hard to tell."

"Huh?" said Landa.

"I can't say until he gets back from his golf game."

"You sound great." He meant it.

"You're here in town?"

"Just for three, maybe four days."

"And then?"

"Bye-bye."

The line crackled for a moment. Helen said, “How ’bout dinner tonight? Mrs. Peabody and I pooled our ration cards and got some real hamburger. We’re planning to barbecue outside. Corn on the cob, baked beans, a little salad. How does that sound?”

“No kidding?” He looked out the window. Warm, with clear blue skies, it was a beautiful afternoon.

“I think she’s going to serve her beer.” Helen giggled.

“Damn! So she admits it. I knew she brewed her own. You have enough of everything?”

“Plenty.”

“Okay. Sure I’ll be there. What time?”

“Say six-thirty?”

“I’ll be there. What can I bring?”

“Just an appetite.”

Mustard, ketchup, mayonnaise, and other condiments were laid on a redwood table in Mrs. Peabody’s backyard. The sun had drifted over Palos Verdes and shadows stretched. Landa sat in a massive wooden lawn chair, Helen in a chair beside him, feeding a bottle to her son. He sank back, overpowered by the aroma of two gardenia bushes in full bloom, just three feet away. Off to the side and brimming with fruit were orange and lemon trees. He took a deep breath, relishing it all. "Beautiful," he said. Helen looked delectable wearing a light black sweater and slacks. A large orange scarf was gathered around her neck.

"What?" said Helen.

"Beautiful. Emma's trees are just beautiful."

"Leo planted those just after we bought this place."

"Leo?" asked Landa.

"My dear Leo, my husband. I lost him four years ago. But he planted these back in 1922." She raised a frosted pitcher. "More?"

"Don't mind if I do." With two gulps, Landa downed the rest of his beer and held up the glass.

"What do you think?" She poured.

The beer was a bit green, and there was some pulpy material that hadn't filtered out. But she had chilled it well, and even one glassful had a hell of a kick. "Great stuff."

"You're not going to tell anyone?"

"Emma. I've known about you for years. Your secret's safe with me."

"I'm not sure . . ."

"As long as you keep pouring this firewater, my lips are sealed. After all, I'm cleared for top secret." It slipped out. He wished he hadn't said that, even in jest.

"Fire's about ready, Jerry," said Helen,

nodding to the barbecue and boosting the baby to her shoulder. She began rocking the baby and patting him on the back.

"Say ah," said Landa.

The baby burped.

"That's my boy," said Landa, rising. "Duty calls. And to tell the truth, I could eat a horse. Where's the stuff?"

"Get busy." Mrs. Peabody pointed to three thick hamburger patties.

Ceremoniously, Landa tied an apron around his gabardine khaki trousers, rolled up his cuffs, and played chef. He had just put the buns on to toast when Mrs. Peabody produced another chilled pitcher of beer. "Is this okay?" she asked.

"Why, Mrs. Peabody, do you think I'm just another sailor?" He poured, drank, and smacked his lips. "Ahhh. This stuff really grows on you." He turned to Helen. "Like one?"

"How's it taste?" She was a teetotaler.

"Just hold your nose and swallow fast. You won't know the difference," said Landa.

Emma Peabody glared while Helen said, "Okay, I'll try a glass."

"That's my girl." Landa poured her a glass.

It was near dark and a full moon was rising in the east by the time they finished dinner. Even with the city and harbor blacked out below, they could see dark, hulking men-of-war swinging at their anchors in Long Beach Harbor, the water glistening with the last tiny wind waves of the day. Mrs. Peabody brought out a portable radio, and the disk jockey played "Harbor Lights" while they sat back, drinking Mrs. Peabody's beer, watching the moonrise in silence.

Helen sat up. "Jerry?"

"What?" said Landa.

"No. I mean him." She pointed to the crib. "It's his bedtime."

"Let me," said Mrs. Peabody. "You kids relax." She rose, leaned over the crib, and picked up the baby. "Say good night, everybody." Both stood as she offered the baby to Landa for a peck on the cheek. "I'll be there in a few minutes," said Helen.

"Take your time," said Mrs. Peabody. She walked off to Helen's house.

They stood for a few minutes, listening to the radio and watching the moon climb higher in the sky, a silvery-gold disk. On an impulse, Landa reached and was surprised when she took his hand. He deliberately thought things through. *He's gone,* he said to himself.

The phone rang next door.

"Uh," Landa said.

"She'll get it," said Helen.

The disc jockey announced, ". . . And now, we dedicate this to all of our boys overseas. Here it is, folks, America's favorite, 'You Belong to My Heart.' "

The song began, and seconds later, they were dancing to the ballad on the concrete walkway. After a moment, Landa pulled her close. She felt wonderful and moved with him, slow step by slow step. He luxuriated in the gardenia and orange blossoms and lingering hamburger and even beer and wished he could somehow freeze the moment forever. Then, remembering Helen's perfume, he took a deep breath, expecting Chanel No. 5. Instead, he snorted.

"What?" She looked up to him.

God, she's beautiful. "I smell baby." He looked down at her, his grin flashing in the moonlight. "Talcum."

When she smiled back, he bent to kiss her. But she turned her head a bit, so he buried his face in her neck and wrapped both arms around her. Then he reached up, untied the scarf, and let it fall to the ground. He kissed her neck, then rose and brushed her cheek with his. He drew back to kiss her again. When she turned away again, he said, "I'm sorry." He held her tighter. They swayed in place.

"I'm sorry, too. I'm not being good. It must be the beer." She hiccuped. "It just doesn't feel right."

Landa ran his hands up and down her back. "Feels right to me." *He's gone, Helen. Don't you know that?*

She looked up to him. Again he tried to kiss her and she covered his mouth. "Jerry, I —"

The back door slammed open and something rustled on the walkway. They turned to see Mrs. Peabody rushing up to them. Wheezing horribly, she braced herself on the table for support.

"Emma, what is it?" Helen turned from Landa and took Mrs. Peabody's hands. "Are you all right? Come. Sit." Helen sat with her, then said with alarm, "The baby! Is that it?"

"No!" gasped Mrs. Peabody, her hand to her chest. ". . . Fine . . . fast asleep." She looked at Helen. "Go!"

"Go where?"

Taking a deep breath, she said, "The phone. Western Union. A cable from your husband, Todd. They read it to me. He's alive!"

"What!" Helen jumped up.

". . . Australia," she said. "Oh, mercy me. He's alive." Looking to the sky, she clasped her hands together. "Thank you, God."

Wordlessly, Helen ran for her house at full tilt.

"I'll be damned," said Landa, watching Helen disappear.

Mrs. Peabody dropped her head onto her arms, sobbing quietly. Landa sat beside her and put his hand on her shoulder, patting her.

Next door, Helen yelped with joy.

"It's all so . . ." Mrs. Peabody was still out of breath. "I'm sorry. I didn't mean to interrupt. But my, oh, my . . ."

"It's fine, Emma. Just fine. What great news." *Jerry Landa, you are one dirty son of a bitch.* Three minutes later, he thanked a teary-eyed Mrs. Peabody, excused himself, and drove to the Long Beach Naval Station Officers Club, where it took five shot glasses of scotch before he could look another human being in the eye. Just before tossing off each shot, he slurred, "Jerry Boom Boom Landa. You are one dirty son of a bitch."

THIRTY

10 AUGUST 1944
KRIEGSMARINE SUBMARINE *U-497*
PASSE DE L'OUEST
LORIENT, FRANCE

Kapitänleutnant Conrad Blücher had no neck. His head was round as a pumpkin, and when the tension was up, his eyes were as wide as if they'd been propped open with toothpicks. No wonder the crew called their Kaleun (short for Kapitänleutnant) Soccer Ball. But that was always behind his back, not to his face. Standing beside him on the bridge, Taubman watched as Blücher jammed binoculars to those enormous eyes, doing his best to see through this damned early-dawn fog. Thick hairy fingers twirled the fine focus, his white captain's hat rippling in a soft breeze. A man of the sea, Blücher had served on sailing ships in his youth. Step by step he had worked his way up, and now he was a submariner's submariner. His Ritterkreuz, dangling from its black, white, and red ribbon, proved it. Short and powerfully built, his girth had been trimmed by eighty-six days at sea.

When he wasn't exhausted or drinking schnapps, his eyes were a clear blue, and his jowls bounced when he laughed, making him look avuncular. But that could be disarming. Taubman found out the hard way, ten days after his surgery. Feeling better, he decided to climb to the bridge and sniff the fine ocean breeze, the boat rolling lazily through a ten-degree arc. But he forgot to ask permission. As a Korvettenkapitän, Taubman outranked Kapitänleutnant Blücher by one grade. But that didn't stop Blücher from shouting at Taubman before everyone on the bridge, and later in the control room, and even later at the evening meal. After that run-in, it became clear to Taubman that the way Conrad Blücher did business with people was to beat the hell out of them at the first opportunity, trusting that would hold for the duration.

But Blücher didn't bear grudges; when it was over, it was over. And as before, he would greet his men with a broad, gap-toothed smile, thumping them, officer or enlisted man, on the back. As far as Blücher was concerned, all men of the Dönitz Volunteer Corps were brothers, a dark distinction, since the U-boat mortality rate was approaching seventy percent.

After the Normandy landings, the bombing attacks on Lorient had been stepped up to a daily basis. Thus, everyone on the bridge was outfitted with binoculars, and Blücher expected them to be put to use. That included Taubman, along with the engineering and torpedo officers Hartmann and Mecke, six enlisted lookouts, and the four men on the Oerlikon flack gun. Of necessity, there were watchstanders in the control and engine rooms, but since it was too shallow to dive, Blücher had the rest of the crew turned out on deck, their gray-green overalls blending into the mist. Life jackets were jammed at the base of the conning tower, the men shuffling back and forth, casting nervous glances at the sky.

What good do binoculars do? Taubman wondered as he peered into the fog. The entrance to Lorient and the French coast lay just four kilometers ahead, and yet he couldn't see in this stuff. Nor could he hear, except for the pounding of his heart, which attempted to keep pace with the *U-497*'s thundering diesels.

"Time to turn, Herr Kaleun." Boemke, the navigator, popped up the hatch. "Recommend course zero-six-zero."

"Very well," rumbled Blücher. "Come left to zero-six-zero." He took out a cigarette, lit it, and turned to Taubman. "Welcome back to Europe, Martin. Excited?"

Taubman couldn't tell whether he was scared or excited. "It's been close to three years, Herr Kaleun." He waved toward the French coast. "It would be nice to see Europe without the Tommies jumping down our throats."

"Don't worry. Our escort is well-armed and E-boats are stationed on either beam. The last thing Uncle Karl wants is for his boys to get bloody noses on their way into port." Blücher referred to the armed escort *Altair* steaming two hundred meters ahead. They'd rendezvoused with her off the Ile de Groix two hours ago. Bristling with antiaircraft guns, she was a converted trawler that doubled as a minesweeper and antiaircraft vessel. An hour ago, the *Altair*'s silhouette was visible. But as the *U-497* drew abeam of the Ile de Groix, fog poured over them like cream from a pitcher. The *Altair* and the E-boats disappeared. The only evidence now was a small trailing line of foam from her wake in the early morning grayness.

Suddenly they were out of the fog, and France sprang at them, the predawn horizon razor-sharp under a brilliant yellow sky. Barrage balloons hung over the city like a herd of cockroaches. Off their port bow was Port Louis, its ancient citadel guarding the main entrance to Lorient Harbor. What immediately struck Taubman was the utter devastation of the city. Except for the massive U-boat bunkers, the town had been blasted by Allied bombers. Here and there a decayed wall or a lone chimney reached to the sky, testifying where homes and shops once stood. Closer in, smoke wisped up from a wooden structure that looked as if it had been a warehouse. The water was littered with oil and debris and dead birds. "Dismal," said Blücher. "Worse than when we left. What do you think?"

"Never been here," said Taubman. "I went from Germany to Vladivostok in May 1941 via the Trans-Siberian railway."

"Pity the Führer ruined your travel plans." Blücher referred to Germany's attack on the Soviet Union in June of that year. A slight against Hitler that Taubman knew wouldn't be tolerated ashore. "But some things never change. Take a look at that, for example." Blücher waved a hand to port.

"Yes?" Taubman trained his binoculars to his left. Atop a hill, about five kilometers distant, stood a three-story Victorian building with a tall, peaked roof.

"That's Kernéval," said Blücher. "Command Headquarters of our esteemed Grand Admiral Karl Dönitz." Flashing a toothy grin, Blücher's eyes grew wide with sarcasm as he referred to Germany's Chief Flag Officer of U-boats, his title: Befehlshaber der U-Boote (BdU). "The

Tommies haven't figured out a way to bomb out BdU, yet. Although I'm sure he's gone now. Probably hightailed it with the rest of those cowards before —" Knowing he'd gone too far, Blücher cast a nervous glance at Taubman.

Taubman lowered his binoculars, doing his best to keep a stone-faced expression. He even flared his nostrils a bit to make the little bastard sweat over his political slur. He didn't care if Blücher and his boys were pro-Nazi or pro-Churchill. But why not use this opportunity to get back at this sanctimonious little toad?

A signalman called from the cigarette deck. "Message, sir, from port commander."

"Well, read it, dammit."

" 'Welcome home. *U-497* is assigned to Kéroman III, berth eleven, starboard side to.' "

Blücher straightened his Ritterkreuz and said, "Good. Straight in. Very well, time to get into work." He cupped his hands around his mouth and yelled to the crew on deck, "Right, men. Fall into ranks for entering port." He called down the hatch, "Set harbor stations. Stand by to shift to electric propulsion and shut down the diesels. Make turns for five knots."

Boemke's head popped up though the hatch. "Time to turn, Herr Kaleun. Recommend course zero-one-six." Then he disappeared.

"Very well." Blücher yelled down the hatch, "Port engine stop. Starboard engine slow ahead. Rudder to left fifteen. Steady up on course zero-one-six."

When *U-497* settled on her new course, he rasped to Taubman in a low voice, "Martin?"

"Yes, Herr Kaleun?"

"Conrad, please."

"Conrad."

"You're not going to report me, are you, Martin? I was only joking."

As Germany piled up her conquests, the Todt Organization, an enormous paramilitary construction company, built military bunkers and other facilities throughout Europe. In so doing, Todt used immense quantities of raw materials and employed slave labor on a large scale. The biggest projects were concrete bunkers protecting U-boats from bomber raids. The first two were completed in Hamburg in 1940 and 1941. Soon after, one more was finished in Trondheim, Norway, with another under construction. With the fall of France, thirteen more bunkers were built during 1941 along Hitler's Atlantic Wall, all completed in an astonishing eleven months. Headquarters to the Seventh U-Boat Flotilla,

Lorient was the largest facility, with six bunkers. St.-Nazaire, La Pallice, and Bordeaux, each had two submarine bunkers. Brest had one.

Lorient's rather soporific name was derived from the word *L'Orient,* "the East." Founded in the eighteenth century, it had its beginnings as a trading and warehousing village for goods arriving from East Asia. But gradually Lorient lost its eastern trade to larger cities and was reduced to a fishing village. It grew again when the French navy moved in during the early twentieth century. By the time the Germans occupied France in 1940, Lorient had a population of 46,000, employed either by the navy or the dockyards or the fishing industry.

U-497's berth was Kéroman III, one of three bunkers sitting on the Kéroman promontory overlooking the Port Louis roadstead. It was a "wet pen," with a capacity for docking twelve U-boats. By comparison, the other pens — Kéroman I and Kéroman II, Dombunker East, Dombunker West, and the Scorff (River) bunker — were "dry pens," where the submarines were hauled from the water on massive dollies and slotted into one of the well-protected pens for overhaul.

Huge armored blast doors guarded the entrance to Kéroman III. Inside, thick concrete columns supported a concrete roof, which was a staggering seven meters thick. Like the other complexes, Kéroman III was self-sufficient; it housed communications offices, medical facilities, administrative offices, transformers and diesel generators, antiaircraft gun emplacements to counter low-flying aircraft, munitions, fuel tanks, a water purification plant, and machine and repair shops.

U-497 approached Kéroman III at dead-slow speed, the bunker looming before them larger and larger, massive, cold, rectangular, and functional. Armored blast doors were closed to the other pens, except for a cavernous berth 11 that yawned open, waiting. Inside, three U-boats were moored, an empty-berth nearest the exit. Within fifty meters Taubman could see officers in dress uniforms pacing on the quay. Behind them, against the wall, light glinted off a uniformed band and their brass musical instruments. "A welcoming committee, Herr Kaleun?" Taubman asked.

Blücher's eyebrows shot up. *"Jawohl."* Straightening cap and Ritterkreuz, he became all business, shifting to electrical power and shutting down the diesels. His slur forgotten, Blücher jumped from side to side of his little bridge, shouting orders down *U-497*'s hatch. Bouncing about, he carved a wider and wider area on the bridge as he conned his ship under the bunker's massive entrance. Eventually, Taubman, Mecke, and Hartmann were jammed against the lookouts and the gun crew at the aft end of the conning tower.

As the sub passed under the bunker's roof, the glory of the sunlight and the pure morning air abruptly changed to a cacophony of saw blades chewing into steel, compressors thumping, air hissing, and acetylene torches sparking and throwing off great clouds of smoke. In the slip ahead, enormous Jupiter lamps beamed a hoary brightness on a submarine's bent and twisted conning tower, where dark overalled figures worked with cutting torches and crowbars.

Mooring lines snaked through the air and were caught by *U-497* crewmen, the submarine gliding no more than two meters alongside the quay wall. As the first line hit the *U-497*'s deck, a whistle blew and the band struck up "Deutschland über Alles." On deck, sailors shouted greetings to men on the quay, while against the walls, in shadows, mute workers wearing drab overalls and carrying toolboxes stood in groups, their faces devoid of expression.

U-497 eased into her berth and was snubbed to a gentle stop. "Double up all lines," Blücher bellowed. Then he cupped his hands around his mouth and shouted down the hatch, "Finished with engines." With a churlish glance at Taubman, he nodded at the officers gathered on the quay wall and said quietly, "Admiral Dönitz is not here to greet us like in the old days. Too bad." Then he stepped high on a bracket and, jamming his fists to his hips, looked forward, then aft. Satisfied, he yelled, "Welcome home, men. Liberty in thirty minutes. Now, come on. Let's look sharp." Waving a hand at the quay wall, he said, "Gangway coming aboard. Standby to receive flotilla commander." He waved at Mecke and Hartmann. Obligingly, they scrambled down the ladder and joined the other officers of *U-497* standing in ranks just forward of the conning tower.

The banging abated enough for Taubman to hear the band strike up a mournful ballad. He cocked an ear and listened.

"How moving," Blücher stepped down from his perch and raised an eyebrow. " 'Lili Marleen.' Beautiful, don't you agree?"

"Enchanting," Taubman said. He had the record in Japan and had worn it out.

"Did you know that 'Lili Marleen' was put on the forbidden list by Reichsleiter Joseph Goebbels?" Blücher gave a crooked smile.

"No, I didn't know." Taubman followed

Blücher down the ladder. When he drew next to him on the main deck, he said, "How could he? It's so beautiful."

"Because Rommel played it for the Afrika Corps. Then the Tommies quickly picked it up, then the Americans and all of their crowd. Now the whole world loves it except Goebbels and his rabble." Blücher threw his head back and laughed. "What do you think of that?"

Taubman waved a hand in frustration as the band played the song.

Blücher said, "What can they do to a band that plays 'Lili Marleen' while surrounded by Americans. Shoot them?"

"I don't know, Herr Kaleun."

Blücher shook his head. "Me, neither. Come, you must meet Rudy before that blasted pounding starts again." He started walking forward.

"Rudy?"

"Fregattenkapitän Rudy Krüger. Our flotilla commander. He's one of us."

Taubman raised his eyebrows, wondering what Blücher meant by "one of us." But Blücher turned and walked past the conning tower to join his officers lined up at the head of the gangway. Taubman eased off to the side and stood against the conning tower.

Blücher barked and his officers came to attention. With that, the Fregattenkapitän started for the gangway. At first glance, he seemed full of youth and vitality. Wearing a summer tan uniform, he was blond with clear gray eyes, and his face was clean, as if he'd never shaved. But he stumbled a bit as he mounted the gangway, and holding the wooden rails tightly, he limped. The Fregattenkapitän saluted the flag, then Blücher, and stepped aboard unsteadily. Like Blücher, the Fregattenkapitän also wore the Ritterkreuz, this one with oak-leaf clusters. On his left breast were four rows of campaign ribbons. Beneath that was a Wound Badge. Immediately following the flotilla commander was a Kapitänleutnant carrying a thick briefcase in his right hand, a cane draped over his left arm. After exchanging salutes, the flotilla commander and Blücher bear-hugged and clapped shoulders. Amongst the noise, Taubman heard the grinning flotilla commander say, "Good to see you, Soccer Ball."

Then he took Blücher's elbow and walked him slowly forward, where they stood off by themselves, speaking quietly for two or three minutes. Blücher's eyes grew wider and wider until the flotilla commander threw his hands in the air and looked up, saying, "Ach!"

With a nod, Blücher led the flotilla commander back to the rank of officers and began introductions. As youthful as he looked, the flotilla commander seemed fragile as he drew closer. His limp was more pronounced, he leaned on his cane now, and his left hand shook slightly.

"Psssst, Martin." Blücher motioned Taubman to line up at the end of the rank. While the flotilla commander was deeply engrossed with Mecke, Blücher walked over and said in a low voice, "Shit to pay. We have to be careful now."

"What?"

Blücher nodded over his shoulder. "See those people waiting on the quay?"

Taubman quickly glanced over to four black uniformed SS officers gathered in a group, their hands on their hips. "What about them?"

"Interrogation."

"What the hell for?"

Blücher spat, "The Führer. Rudy tells me somebody tried to knock him off while we were gone. And it seems the fools bungled it." With a slight smile, Blücher threw a hand over his mouth. "Oh, excuse me. You didn't hear that from me."

"Conrad, you really are a pill."

Blücher leveled his eyes on Taubman. "I'm serious, you idiot. July twentieth. Count von Stauffenberg. Did you know him?"

"I'm afraid not."

"Well, the damn fool is dead now. He

set a bomb in Rastenburg. The thing went off, but somehow Hitler survived. Now his henchmen are out skewering everybody. So be careful. Rudy tells me hundreds have died so far. And remember. You don't know where you heard this, all right?"

"What the hell? I've been out of the country for three years."

"Martin, I'm going to do you a favor, a big one. I don't know what your game is, but what you said under the anesthetic could land you in big trouble."

Taubman jerked his eyes to Blücher, wondering if the damned fool had tried to look in his briefcase. The key was around his neck. It wouldn't have been too difficult. Worse, he hadn't thought about blabbing under the anesthetic. His blood rushed and his heart pounded.

"Don't worry," Blücher said. "The doc will keep his mouth shut. And nobody else heard your ramblings. I don't care what you and the Japs are doing. Just don't piss off about me to those idiots over there." He nodded to the SS officers.

So that's what Blücher had been fishing for. It sounded as if he hadn't heard much. Just enough to arouse suspicion. But then SS interrogators were experts at putting things together. Taubman forced himself to breathe slower. "Of course."

"Good."

"Now, can I ask another favor?"
"Just ask."
"Get me through the gate and into the countryside. Away from those people."
Blücher looked him up and down. "There's a problem."
"Yes?"
"If the Frogs or the SS don't kill you, the Americans will."
"What?"
"Rudy just told me. We're surrounded. Some damned, crazy American general has driven through western France. We're all cut off. Brest, Lorient, La Rochelle, St.-Nazaire. All of us. Fifteen-kilometer perimeter around here. Shit! Nothing to do but sit around waiting to go out again."
Taubman raised the briefcase in the air, the chain rattling. "There must be a way. Berlin is expecting this. It's of the utmost importance."
Blücher shrugged. "Let's talk to Rudy." He turned and led Taubman to the Fregattenkapitän and introduced them.
"Welcome to Lorient, Korvettenkapitän." The flotilla commander offered his hand. Krüger's voice was a deep baritone and rang with confidence, despite his fragile appearance. "You've been gone for how long? Two years?"
"Three, Herr Fregattenkapitän," said Taubman.

"Please call me Rudy."

"Yes, sir, Rudy. It's been much too long." It seemed Krüger was in pain, but he had a genuine, youthful grin. Taubman liked the man.

Krüger turned to Blücher. "*U-684* made it in. She sank 17,000 tons." *U-497* had refueled *U-684*.

"Wonderful," said Blücher.

"So have *U-395* and *U-781*. But both came back with zero tonnage sunk, all torpedoes expended." Likewise *U-497* had refueled these U-boats and had also given them food and torpedoes.

Blücher's eyes went wide. "No tonnage. How could that be?"

Krüger's voice dropped. "Torpedo malfunction." His eyes jerked toward the SS officers. "They're trying to make a case for sabotage. I'm afraid I'll have to hold your officers aboard until they're —"

"Shit, interrogated?" Blücher jammed his hands on his hips. "Is this how we treat our boys who have been at sea for eighty-six days? They're horny as two-peckered goats. They'll mutiny."

Krüger's voice was sharp. "What the hell can I do about it, Conrad? The town is wrecked. Only two or three cathouses left. And the Americans are fifteen kilometers away on all sides. Our backs are to the sea."

"So what do we do?" asked Blücher.

"Turn you around and send you to back to sea within two weeks."

"Rudy. I —"

Krüger held up a hand. "It's either that or they give you a rifle with just five rounds, shove you into a truck, and send you to the front lines to fight the Americans. That's exactly what they did to the crew of *U-474*, you know."

"Shit."

"Precisely," said Krüger. He turned to Taubman. "There's other news. Not all of *U-497*'s brood made it back."

Krüger's eyes said it. But Taubman automatically asked, "I don't understand, sir."

"The *I-57*. She was due in last week. We've lost her, I'm afraid. Gave a position report shortly after you transferred off. That was it." Krüger snapped his fingers. "No more radio transmissions. Disappeared." Steel-gray eyes fixed on Taubman. "I'm sorry."

Chipping hammers clattered. An overhead crane clanked above as dockyard workers shuffled across the gangway carrying tool kits. Behind them, the SS officers lined up, waiting to come aboard.

"Gone?" Taubman said, trying to look flushed, doing his best to hide his elation.

"I'm truly sorry for your shipmates, your

friends," said Krüger. He took Taubman's hand. "What a stroke of luck for you to have a ruptured appendix."

"Ja . . . Gott," Taubman muttered and turned away. He was afraid Fregattenkapitän Krüger and Kapitänleutnant Blücher would see his face, see the grin spreading from ear to ear. He couldn't stop it. He had to turn away and compose himself. He hadn't felt so exhilarated for a long time. What luck! If only there was a way to get out of here.

Krüger lay a hand on his shoulder. "My condolences."

"Thank you, sir," Taubman muttered.

"Sir, what about my men? Is there anywhere to send them on liberty, besides to lice-ridden cathouses?" demanded Blücher.

"To the barracks ship for the time being. They can take hot showers and have decent food," said Krüger.

"Thank you, sir," said Blücher. "Also, Korvettenkapitän Taubman has a request."

"Yes?" asked Krüger.

Taubman held up the courier pouch. "Sir, this is dated material from the Imperial Japanese Government. Berlin is expecting it immediately. And I'm under orders to get it there." He drew a paper. "If you need authentication, this will —"

"No, no, I believe you, Martin," said Krüger. He rubbed his chin. "We're sending *U-689* to Kiel next week with a load of wounded and excess Seventh Flotilla staff. Perhaps . . ."

"Thank you, sir. But if there is anything more immediate, I would appreciate it."

Krüger pawed at the concrete with his boot and looked up. "Well, there is another way. But I'd still recommend going with the *U-689*. It's much safer."

"What's the other way, sir?"

THIRTY-ONE

10 AUGUST 1944
SAN JUAN CAPISTRANO, CALIFORNIA

Ingram stared out the train window, seeing nothing but white. The fog parted as they clanked though San Clemente and he caught a glimpse of the ocean: very quiet, like its name, the Pacific looked like a pond. Nice to be home. Nice to be on this side of the Pacific rather than on the other.

The fog clamped down again, as if someone had drawn a sheet over the window. That's why he couldn't fly today. Everything was socked in from San Diego to Santa Barbara. Through the graces of a sympathetic Navy PB4Y crew, he'd flown yesterday from Honolulu, reaching the North Island Naval Air Station in San Diego at three in the morning. Dead tired, he walked into base operations, grabbed the nearest phone, and called Helen.

Helen's voice, her shouts of joy, cascaded upon him. A promise fulfilled, a promise of tomorrow, his son, Jerry, gooing in the background, all combined to bring him out of a malaise. They agreed he would take the 8:52, leaving San Diego in three hours, and they would meet in San Juan Capistrano when it pulled in at 10:17.

Ingram hung up. The light in the booth was out, and no one was around. He dropped his head in his hands and sobbed uncontrollably for what seemed forever. A minute later, the accordion doors squeaked open and he walked away.

He found the base OOD, who took him down the hall to the dispatcher, a crusty chief aviation ordnance mate. Bellowing in a foghorn voice, the chief roused a driver who took him on the Coronado ferry to the Southern Pacific train station in downtown San Diego. Ingram jostled his way aboard the second car of the very crowded 8:52, a fifteen-passenger-car train stuffed with sailors and Marines bound for Los Angeles.

They rumbled into San Juan Capistrano's little Spanish mission-style station, where the engineer laid on the brakes at the last possible moment.

There she is! The train rushed past Helen. Her ebony hair, pulled back and gathered into a band, flowed down her back. She wore a black beret, a dark green overcoat, and black mittens. In her arms was a bundle in a light blue blanket. Beside her stood a naval officer. A full captain. Landa.

I'll be damned. Then they disappeared in the fog.

The train finally slowed. Ingram jumped off, B-4 bag and all, before it ground to a halt. It was so misty he couldn't see more than three cars back. He hoisted his B-4 bag and started trudging back toward the depot as the engineer yanked the whistle twice and cracked his throttle. The engine's big drivers spun and caught; the couplers clanked all the way to the back of the train as it slowly pulled out, chuffing against an uphill grade.

The mist parted. "Todd!" She ran toward him, the baby cradled in her arms.

Sailors and Marines leaned out the windows, cheering and hooting with lopsided grins. "Go get 'em, Commodore," thundered a bemedaled Marine gunny. His garrison cap was pitched back on his head; his blouse was open, and he tipped a half-finished bottle of Schlitz in Ingram's direction. "She's a peach, all right!"

"Smoothest piece of satin I ever saw," yelled a sailor as the train picked up speed.

The last three cars clanked past, every open window filled with cheering sailors and Marines. "Owwwuuuh!" they howled. "Hubba-hubba."

Cheers crescendoed as Helen ran into his arms, her beret falling off. Oblivious to everything, Ingram kissed her, held her — a dream fulfilled, her warm mouth, her perfume, the baby grunting and cooing. He felt like crying again. "Can't," he muttered.

She cupped his chin, her brow furrowed. "You've lost weight."

He was afraid to talk. "Goes with the job." He pulled her to him and kissed her again and again.

At long last, Helen said, "Say hello to your little boy." She held up the bundle.

He took the baby and raised the blanket. Red skin, doubled fists. The baby opened his eyes. "My God, he's got your eyes."

"Uh-uh," Helen said. "They're gray, like yours."

Ingram looked again. The baby's eyes were gray. "Guess so. What's this? He's bald."

"It'll grow."

"He's beautiful. Look, he's even smiling at me."

"That means he's passing gas."

"No kidding? Chip off the old block. Someday, this kid's going to —"

"Welcome home, sailor." Jerry Landa walked up, his shimmering white smile beaming through the fog.

"Jerry — er, Captain. This is great." They saluted, shook hands, and clapped each other's shoulders. "How the hell are you, Boom Boom?"

Landa threw a fake punch, "Careful, sailor, I'll toss you in the brig."

"Oh, would you, please. Please?" Ingram reached down and picked up Helen's beret.

"Getting cold, you two," said Helen, adjusting it on her head.

"Yeah, how's that for the middle of summer." Landa jabbed a thumb at the parking lot. "Come on. Just pretend I'm the taxi driver. You guys ride in back and make out."

"Jerry!" said Helen.

The baby burped.

Ingram grinned. "Kid knows his name."

Landa grabbed Ingram's B-4 bag. "Lunch is on me. Perfect place, called the Hurley Bell." They started walking.

"Where's that?" asked Ingram, wrapping his arm around Helen.

"Over on the coast."

Old English in style, the Hurley Bell was a comfortable half-timbered restaurant in Corona del Mar, a sleepy hamlet just south of Newport Beach. Inside, the bar was dark, publike, with a small fire glowing in a corner. The restaurant was open and homey with leather booths and the lingering odor of cooked beef and fine cigars.

They ordered, and Landa filled an eager Ingram in on the war news. After a pause, he said, "We're sending you back to the

Maxwell. That okay with you?"

Ingram buttered a roll, his second. "I was hoping you'd say that. What's her status?"

"Nouméa. Still undergoing repairs. Should be done in about a month?" His eyes flicked between Ingram and his wife.

Ingram said, "You're saying I could have more time off."

"Probably another thirty days."

Helen reached over and whispered in his ear.

Ingram nodded slowly. "Okay, Jerry. You got me."

"Thanks, Helen," said Landa, leveling a gaze at her. "You're a good sailor."

She returned the look with one as powerful. "Just make sure you send him back to me."

Ingram looked around. "Where's Ollie hiding?"

"Sends his best, but for the moment he's indisposed."

Ingram's eyebrows went up.

"Washington, D.C. He's turning into a spook. Going to ONI school."

"You're kidding."

"And get this," Landa added. "He's shipping over. Going career Navy."

Ingram rubbed his chin. "I'll be damned. But, you know, I think that's a great thing for him. His only option after the war was going to law school and then joining his dad's law firm."

"What's wrong with that?" asked Landa.

"Scared the hell out of him. I never met his dad but I think he must be a pretty powerful character back in Manhattan. Certainly overbearing as far as Ollie is concerned."

Landa nodded. "That can happen. Anyway, he promised to call."

An awkward silence followed. Ingram broke it with, "How about you, Jerry? What's your next stop?"

Landa said, "Any day now, I'm expecting orders back to DESDIV 11." Then he said, "We haven't heard how you ended up in Australia."

Buttering a third roll, Ingram said, "*Duke of Salisbury.*"

"Which is?"

"A six-thousand-ton square-tailed tramp filled with tanks and airplane engines, part of a ten-ship convoy. She was crewed by a bunch of crazy Brits who pulled me out of the drink off Madagascar. And without skipping a beat they pressed on for Perth. They took great care of me. Even had my own stateroom. They let me take three showers a day."

Landa sat back and folded his arms.

"Don't you want to know how I came aboard the *Duke of Salisbury*?"

Landa felt a rush to his head, and he knew he was blushing. He hadn't given any thought to the fact that he would have to do some acting before these two. To Ingram and Helen, he was not supposed to know what happened. He wondered if it would ever come out. How would Toliver handle it? Maybe he should go up there and talk to him. Maybe —

"Jerry?"

"Of course, I'm all ears." *What the hell did happen?*

"I was blown off the *Maxwell* and spent the night in the drink with a monkey."

"What?" said Helen.

"Dexter. Our mascot."

"Oh."

"Next morning, a Jap sub surfaced and picked me up."

Helen's mouth formed an O. "My God."

Act surprised, you jerk. "Sonofabitch," said Landa.

"But those bastards shot the monkey. Wouldn't let him come aboard. In many ways, I think he saved my life."

Landa said, "You'll be happy to learn that Dexter is alive and well, once again terrorizing the decks of the U.S.S. *Maxwell.*"

"You're kidding!"

"Found him clinging to wreckage a few hours after the Japs picked you up, I heard."

Ingram grinned. "Dexter." Then he focused on them. "They shoved me down a hatch and submerged."

Steaks were laid before them, sizzling on their platters. They ate in silence. Helen and Landa cast sideways glances at Ingram as he wolfed his food, washing it down with draught beer. He caught them looking and said, "It's been almost five months since —"

"Go ahead, hon." Helen laughed and patted his sleeve. "Want the rest of mine?"

"You bet."

Coffee came, and without prompting, Ingram sat back and continued with details of the voyage. Landa found himself leaning forward, nearly on the edge of his chair as Ingram described Shimada, Taubman, and the horror aboard the *I-57*.

With a glance at Helen, Ingram said, "That jerk has my academy ring. It's probably in Europe by now."

Landa shook his head slightly.

Ingram looked up and said, "No, it's not?"

Landa blinked, sorely tempted to share his secret with Todd and Helen. What justice they would have felt to learn that the *I-57*, Herr Taubman, and the rest of those Japs were twelve thousand feet down. He finessed the question. "I'm just astounded at what you've been through."

Ingram's eyelids were drooping. The exhaustion from the flight and the beer, his first in a long time, had put him close to the edge.

Helen saw it, too, and stood. Massaging his neck, she said, "Time to get my boys home. You both need naps."

Ingram looked at Landa and winked, his eyes saying, *The nap comes later.*

Landa dropped Todd and Helen off at the Alma Street house in San Pedro and drove to the BOQ at the Long Beach Naval Shipyard. A large manila envelope was in his in box. He opened it when he got to his room.

FROM: COMMANDING OFFICER,
DESTROYERS PACIFIC
TO: CAPT. JEREMIAH T. LANDA,
416232, USN
DATE: 8 AUGUST 1944
SUBJ: ORDERS
INFO: COMMANDING OFFICER
DESTROYERS, TASK FORCE 58
COMMANDING OFFICER,
DESTROYER
DIVISION 11
COMMANDING OFFICER,
TWELFTH NAVAL DISTRICT
COMMANDING OFFICER,
U.S. NAVAL STATION,
TREASURE ISLAND

1. UPON RECEIPT, YOU ARE DETACHED AS PROGRAM LIAISON TO COMTWELVE.
2. YOU ARE ORDERED TO PROCEED TO PORT IN WHICH TASK GROUP 58.3 MAY BE AND RESUME COMMAND OF DESTROYER DIVISION 11.
3. UPON RECEIPT, YOU WILL PROCEED TO SAN FRANCISCO AND REPORT TO THE COMMANDING OFFICER U.S. NAVAL STATION, TREASURE ISLAND, FOR TRANSPORTATION.
4. ACCOUNTING DATA 3629454.7728 152 73/2177440.

BY DIRECTION
M. L. RILEY

Landa sat back and tipped his hat back on his head. "Sorry, Ralph. I'm coming back." Actually, he didn't feel sorry for Ralph Sorenson, the man whom Arleigh Burke had assigned as his temporary relief. Landa's job was done. Time to get back to work. Mission accomplished.

Two drinks later in the O Club bar, Landa decided that the mission was not yet accomplished. Something tugged at the back of his mind, and he headed for a phone booth. A late Thursday afternoon, it was quiet at the club, and all three booths were empty. He dialed the operator, asked for the number, and dropped in three quarters, a dime, and a nickel.

Laura's phone rang ten times. "Sorry, sir, no answer," said the operator.

Dammit. "Try again, please."

"Certainly, sir." Again ten rings. "No answer, sir. I'm sorry."

He caught her before she rang off. "Try another number, please?" He fumbled at his little black book, found the number, and told her.

The phone rang three times. "Hello."

"Ahem."

"Who is this?"

"Mrs. Thatcher, it's Jerry Landa."

"Oh, good evening, Captain."

So it's Captain, is it? "How you doing, Roberta?"

Now it was her turn to pause. "What can I do for you?"

"Have you heard from Laura?"

After a long pause, she said, "Captain, I —"

"Roberta, please. I'm shipping out tomorrow or the next day."

"You're going back out there?"

"Way the hell out there. Listen, I don't want to leave it like this. I must talk to her." Landa was surprised to hear himself beg. "So if you know where she is, please tell me."

"I've been keeping loose tabs on her, but she doesn't know it."

"Good. What's up?"

"She's working at a piano bar. And it sounds like she's making progress."

"That's swell. Doing what?"

Roberta Thatcher raised her voice to the clipped tone that was signature Roberta Thatcher, Queen of Pretense. "Playing the piano. Singing, I suppose."

"Where?"

"Studio City. A little place on Ventura Boulevard called Dominic's."

"Roberta, you're a doll."

"Just be careful, Captain. She's damaged goods. It's going to take a while."

"Don't I know it! Thanks."

THIRTY-TWO

10 AUGUST 1944
STUDIO CITY, CALIFORNIA

Landa wolfed down a ham sandwich for dinner, drew a Ford from the car pool, and headed up Sepulveda for the San Fernando Valley. Three hours later, he was traveling down a surprisingly busy Ventura Boulevard. There were bright lights, lots of people and cars rushing about on a ninety-five-degree August night. Dominic's was about five doors east of Laurel Canyon, the name over the door done in plush red, diamond-tufted leather. The street was crowded, and he drove down the alley to find a parking spot behind the restaurant. He got out and stood against the car for a moment, rubbing his hands. Sweaty. *Why the hell am I so nervous? She dumped me, didn't she? And then I went off and tried to move in on Helen. Stupid. Stupid.* Landa shook his head, thinking of that evening under the stars mixed with joy for Helen and guilt for himself. He felt so sheepish. Even Mrs. Peabody had seen him at his worst, acting like a horny tomcat. *Stupid.*

Stupid. But Laura and Helen hadn't talked. *So what?*

The back door to Dominic's stood wide open, a fan in the doorway vainly trying to shove the heat of the kitchen into the heat of the night. Kitchen utensils clanked, a dissonant counterpoint to the strains of "Basin Street Blues" drifting from the dining room along with sounds of laughter and tinkling glass.

"Forget it," he swore to the sky. "Laura's hair will be hanging in her eyes, and she'll be so plastered, she'll be playing the piano with her elbows while a bunch of draft-dodging Hollywood types hang all over her, fumbling at her clothes."

He stepped back in the car and began sorting his keys.

The band inside had changed to "Twelve O'Clock Jump."

Not bad.

"What the hell?" He'd driven all this way. Better check and see how she was. But he vowed to keep his distance, not let her see him, and turn right around and go home.

He stepped out and slammed the door. Mounting the steps to Dominic's, he walked into the kitchen. Four cooks rushed around while waiters burst through a set of double doors, paying not the slightest attention to a full Navy captain in dress khakis standing in their path.

Landa pushed through the doors and walked into a fog of cigarette smoke. It was dark, and he sensed more than saw people jammed about him. On his right was a packed dining area, each table with a small brass low-wattage light fixture. The ceiling was done in glittering plaster with stars and a three-quarters moon illuminated by a soft spotlight. To his left was a dance floor surrounded by palm trees softly lit by green lights. On a stage was a ten-piece band in white dinner jackets: their logo, ACES HIGH. But, he sighed thankfully, the room was air-conditioned.

An odor of heavy perfume engulfed him. Someone tugged at his coat.

"Huh?"

It was a hatcheck girl in a short dress. "I said, 'Take your hat, sir?' " She nodded to a small vestibule with coats on hangers.

"Yeah, sure." Landa absently handed over his hat and walked toward the stage.

Again, the girl tugged at his coat. "No room out there, sir." She pointed. "I think you'll find a stool at the bar."

"Okay, thanks." Landa edged his way to his right. People were everywhere, and the place was very dark.

A waiter plowed into him, softly cursing.

"Sorry," Landa muttered.

The bar was three deep with a mixed

crowd, half civilian, the rest servicemen, mostly Army Air Corps. Gratefully, he discovered an empty stool and sat.

"Hey, Captain! How you doing?" A civilian stood before him.

"I'm sorry. Is this one yours?" Landa got up.

"Hell no," the man said. "Sit, sit. This is your lucky night."

"Pardon?"

"Please let me buy you a drink. Why" — he looked Landa up and down — "a real war hero. I tried to sign up four times, but I lost a kidney as a kid. They wouldn't let me in. Whadda ya say, Captain?"

The man had a friendly smile.

Another civilian turned and handed the first one a martini with a single olive. "Here, George. Next time, it's your turn. Well, hello."

George took the glass and said, "Meet Captain . . ."

". . . Landa. Jerry Landa."

"Jeez, Gordie. Look at all those ribbons," said George.

Gordie, a thin, balding man in his late forties, leaned close and peered at the campaign ribbons on Landa's chest. "Damn right. This guy's got the Distinguished Service Medal, two Purple Hearts. Holy smokes." He looked up. "Is this the Silver Star?"

Landa nodded. "You know your stuff."

"Torpedoman aboard a four-stacker in the first war."

"Jerry Landa, Gordie . . ."

"Collins. And this here's George Klosterman."

They shook.

"Well, what will it be?" said Gordie. "They make great martinis here."

"Well . . ."

"Captain, jeez. You're saving our ass out there. You can at least let us repay the favor," said George.

What the hell? Landa burst out with his trademark grin. "Okay, just one. Thanks."

"That's swell." Gordie reached in and thumped his fist on the bar. "Hey, Lyle, dammit. Set 'em up! Three double martinis, one for a real Navy hero. Chop-chop."

The martinis were delivered and Landa sipped. "Wow!"

"Okay?" said Collins.

"It really *is* a double," gasped Landa, his throat on fire.

Collins laughed. "Like I said, they make 'em great here."

"Yeah." Landa sipped again and turned toward the band. They played music he understood. Right now, they were doing a takeoff on "Tea for Two" that was half Spike Jones slapstick, the rest fantastic jazz with a rolling base that had the crowd clapping in time. Landa got to know Klosterman and Collins above the din and learned they worked at Lockheed-Burbank building P-38s.

He looked at his watch. "Jesus."

"What's up, Captain?" said Collins.

"Forty-five minutes I've been here." Landa slid off the stool. It puzzled him that he landed rather heavily. "Must be in the wrong place. I thought Laura West played here."

"Yeah, she does. What a number," said Klosterman, checking his watch. "Comes on in five minutes."

Landa shook his head. "Fellas, we better settle up." He reached for his wallet. "How much do I —"

"I thought we had an understanding. Your money's no good here, Captain. You ready for another?" said Collins.

Landa blinked for a moment, then recalled he'd had three, no, four martinis. *Doubles. Jeepers! I'm bombed. Time to . . .* "Fellas, thanks very much. Gotta go." Landa shook their hands and backed toward the front door.

"Come back anytime, Captain," they said.

"Right."

Just then there was a drumroll and the place went dark. An announcer loudly built up the introduction and a single spot flicked on, illuminating Laura West at the piano.

"I'll be damned," Landa muttered.

The spotlight captured Laura in a way he hadn't seen in a long time. Her mouth was parted in the same wide, easy smile that drew Landa to her the first time they'd met. No, he reminded himself, the *second* time they'd met. The first time, she was dead drunk. Now, she wore a blue sequined dress and a simple pearl choker. *Gorgeous. Simply gorgeous.*

Laura arched an eyebrow, started playing softly, and said in a low voice, "Thanks, Randy Stone, for that nice introduction. And tonight I think I see more of our boys in uniform than usual. It's really nice to have you with us. Let's hear it for them!" She shot a hand into the air and the civilian crowd applauded appreciatively.

"Drinks on the house?" she shouted.

The waiters and bartenders booed. Everyone laughed.

"Okay, okay," Laura played a few more bars. "I guess we have to make a living, too. What do you say we begin with this one?" The spot narrowed to her face as she launched into a rendition of "Always."

"This is for you, sir." A waiter stood beside him, a martini balanced on a tray.

"What?"

"They ordered it for you. 'One for the road,' they said." He nodded over to a grinning Collins and Klosterman.

"Thanks." Landa took it, waved at them, and sipped. Then he concentrated on Laura once more.

Applause crescendoed as Laura sang the last bar. She stood and bowed, her dress shimmering. Her hair was combed to perfection, and her eyes and smile were as beautiful as he'd ever seen. She sat, lowered her mike, and asked, "Okay, boys. What'll it be?"

" 'Bless 'Em All,' " roared the crowd.

"It's not too early?" She gave a pout, her face closely framed in a spotlight that followed her tiniest movement.

Landa checked the radium dial on his watch. It was almost eleven-forty-five. He burped and leaned against a column. *Time to amscray.*

" 'Bless 'Em All,' " they yelled again.

"You sure?" Her smile was electric.

The applause rose again. Laura turned to the piano and arranged herself. A waiter, barely visible, just off to her left, leaned over with a glass and bottle on a silver tray. Carefully, he set them down and poured.

Landa squinted through his malaise. *I'll be damned! Ginger ale. She's drinking ginger ale.* It suddenly hit him. *Jesus. She's sober as a judge.*

". . . bless the long and the short and the tall . . . ," the crowd sang.

He turned and found he'd downed his martini. *My God. What have I done?* He ran his hand through his hair and tried to recall how many of these things he'd consumed. At least four, plus this one; he looked at the glass, a lonely olive in the bottom.

". . . there'll be no promotion this side of the ocean, so come on me lads, bless them all . . ."

He picked up the olive then put it back in the glass. *What did I have for dinner? Nothing, a damned ham sandwich.*

Suddenly, he started weaving his way to the hatcheck booth.

"Hey, watch it," a waiter protested as Landa elbowed his way past. A glass crashed to the floor, and Landa pressed on, not looking back.

Hurry. Landa's stomach raged as he pushed through roiling cigarette smoke and the crowd. They were winding up the song as he lowered his head and kept pushing.

". . . so come on me boys, bless them all . . ." The crowd held the last note for a long time, then cheered and clapped. The main lights went up as Laura stood and walked off the stage. They dimmed again and the band started playing a soft rhumba, with couples taking the dance floor.

The girl was inside her booth, her perfume invading his nostrils, crawling in him, making his stomach feel as if a force-six storm rumbled inside. Clamping his hand over his mouth, Landa fumbled in his pocket and gave her the ticket.

Her eyebrows went up. "You all right?"

"Ummmmfff." *Hurry up, Tilly, before I puke all over you.*

He didn't have a tip, and her pout let him know immediately how she felt. Reluctantly, she handed over the hat.

"Thanks." He turned for the door.

"You leaving without saying hello?" Laura West stood close.

"Oh, my God. How did you —"

"Kind of hard to miss when you blew past the waiter. Reminded me of a Rose Bowl game I once saw. You know, a fullback charging the line, people flying through the air. I mean it was —"

"Oh, I'm so sorry." Landa's arms went around her, and he buried his head in her neck.

"Jerry." Laura's hands ran through his hair and down the back of his neck.

"I'm . . . so sorry."

"It's okay."

They kissed. Servicemen hooted and whistled as Landa kissed and kissed her again.

She pulled away. "Whew. Where have

you been? You smell like either the City Morgue or a Sixth Street gin mill." She made a show of wiggling her nose. "Haven't made up my mind."

"Oh, God. I'm sorry." Quickly, he told her about Collins and Klosterman.

Laura jammed her hands on her hips, a smile crossing her face. "You should all be ashamed of yourselves."

"You still love me?"

"You came all the way out here to see me, didn't you?"

Landa nodded, the storm in his belly suddenly abated. "I sure did."

"Well, then, you bet I do."

He pulled her close and kissed her again. "Man oh man. I've been such a sap. Can we . . ."

"Look, Boom Boom, I've got one more show to do, then I'll fix you up. Right now, coffee first, talk later."

THIRTY-THREE

11 AUGUST 1944
SEVENTH U-BOAT FLOTILLA HEADQUARTERS
LORIENT, FRANCE

Lorient was dead, corrupted, a city of the past. Artillery rumbled to the northeast as Taubman checked his watch: almost nine-thirty. He and Krüger stood on a broad thoroughfare under a balmy, full moon. Beside them was Krüger's Kübelwagen, its top down. In the backseat wearing headphones was Krüger's aide, an Oberfeldwebel, or warrant officer, named Kaufmann, who twirled dials on a transceiver. Krüger said, "Flying conditions are good. That Storch can land, refuel, and take off in fifteen minutes. You'll be in Tours no later than three a.m. That is, if the Americans aren't out with their night fighters. Then it gets a little dicey. But Hauser is a good pilot. He can set that thing down in a barnyard, if need be."

Taubman turned his face away and bit his lip. Blood coursed through his veins like river rapids, and his clammy hands were jammed deep in his pockets, his fists balled. The last thing he wanted to do was to putt around the countryside in a little Fieseler Storch, a three-seat, single-engine observation plane that looked like an overgrown grasshopper. With this moonlight, they would be fish on a fork for every dallying American or British fighter.

Except, his mind raced for a moment, *I wonder if the damn thing can get me to Switzerland? Now that would be something, wouldn't it?*

Squeezing the bridge of his nose between his thumb and forefinger, Taubman began thinking ahead as he looked about at his surroundings. Trees not already blasted to splinters had been cut down on both sides of the thoroughfare, making a landing strip of, perhaps, one hundred meters. Soldiers with flashlights were stationed on either side of the street waiting to flip them on at Krüger's command.

"You will be in Berlin by tomorrow afternoon," Krüger clapped Taubman on the shoulders.

That's it! Switzerland tomorrow. Eureka!

"Martin? Are you here?"

"Yes, of course, sir. Sorry."

Krüger bent close and reached in his coat. "A favor, please?"

"By all means."

"Could you post a letter to my wife? She lives in Munich."

Taubman held out his hand. "When was the last time you saw her?"

"Thirteen months, one week, three days, five hours, and seventeen minutes."

"An honor to do so, Fregattenkapitän."

"Rudy."

"Rudy, I wish I could deliver it personally." Taubman pocketed the letter, cleared his throat, and then asked, "How long can you hold out here?" As if to emphasize his point, an artillery round landed two hundred meters away, throwing up a blue-black cloud of dust and rubble.

"The U-boats are snug in their bunkers, safe from . . ." Krüger waved at the billowing cloud. "The real danger is the perimeter collapsing. We have enough tanks, food, and ammunition to hold out for six months, if need be." With a smirk he added, "The Führer has assured us relief is on the way." He raised a finger in the air. "Let no man shirk from his duty. We must hold out to the last round —"

Three meters away, a man on a stretcher groaned. He was a Hauptgefreiter, a seaman first class, whose uniform was blackened and shredded in spots. The man's head and hands were wrapped in bandages, a hole left for his mouth. Two corpsman knelt beside him, doing their best to soothe him. In spite of what he'd seen on this voyage, it made Taubman feel uncomfortable. He nodded at the man and raised his eyebrows.

Krüger said quietly, "Yes, that's Ott. He was terribly maimed by a battery explosion aboard *U-329* yesterday. Thank God for the Storch. He's going out with you. It's his only hope."

Just then Kaufmann said, "Hauser reporting in, sir. Says he just passed over the perimeter."

"Good, the Storch is here." Krüger cupped his hands over his mouth and shouted, "Lights on, you men. Stand by to receive the Storch."

In response, a dozen flashlights flipped on, their beams stabbing the sky.

Taubman looked about. "Nice visibility. He shouldn't have any trouble."

"This is the fourth night," said Krüger. "Seems to be going all —"

An SS Colonel walked up, the death's head insignia gleaming on his cap. "Excuse me, are you Fregattenkapitän Krüger?"

Krüger and Taubman gave a military salute. *"Jawohl, Herr Standartenführer,"* Krüger replied.

Returning a casual Nazi salute, the man said, "My name is Schroeder. I was told to report to you." With a perfectly cut uniform, Schroeder looked as if he'd stepped from a recruiting ad. He was handsome, too. But he had that piercing stare Taubman associated with the SS. He hadn't been this close to an SS officer since he was last in Europe. They had terrified him then, and this one terrified him now. This man, Taubman noticed, had suffered a split lip, probably as a child. Scar tissue ran from beneath his nose to his upper lip, giving his appearance a strange combination of the near-comical and the demented.

"What for?" asked Krüger.

Taubman cocked an ear, hearing a soft whistling in the distance, the Storch gliding in for a landing.

"I am to ride on that plane," said Schroeder.

"I'm sorry, Standartenführer. That is impossible."

"What?" Schroeder jammed his fists on his hips.

"We have a critically wounded sailor going out, tonight, a Hauptgefreiter named Ott who —"

"Who else?" demanded Schroeder.

Krüger gestured to Taubman. "This man, sir. Korvettenkapitän Taubman."

Schroeder snapped his fingers a few times. "Taubman . . . Taubman . . . hmmm. Ah, yes." He looked up. "Martin Taubman, the appendicitis case. The courier." He folded his hands, fixed his gaze on Taubman and said to Krüger, "You'll bump that sailor over there." He nodded to Ott, lying on his stretcher. "I must be in Berlin by tomorrow. It's very important." He held a sheaf of papers in the air.

Krüger protested, "But, sir, that man has very serious burns." He lowered his voice. "He may die. One eye is gone. We may be able to save the other if we —"

Schroeder stood to his full height. "Put him on the next plane."

"That won't be until tomorrow night."

"I order you. And must I remind you that I'm under the direct authority of Reichsführer Himmler?" Schroeder smirked. "All I have to do is make one phone call."

A putrid odor swept across the three.

From the corner of his eye, Taubman watched Krüger's fists ball. Casually, Schroeder's hand went under his overcoat.

This is getting out of hand. Taubman stepped away just as a shadow zipped overhead. All three turned their heads as the Storch's tires chirped on the roadway.

Krüger beckoned. "Kaufmann?"

"Sir." Krüger's orderly stood to attention in the back of the Kübelwagen.

"There's a change in the manifest. Please remove Hauptgefreiter Ott from the list and insert —" Krüger spat. "Insert Standartenführer Schroeder in his place."

"But —" said Kaufmann.

"Do it!" barked Krüger.

"Jawohl, Herr Fregattenkapitän," said Kaufman. He sat and began scribbling on a form.

"You see, Herr Fregattenkapitän," said Schroder. "That wasn't too difficult, hmm?" He bent to pick up a larger bundle and walked toward the Storch, its engine now still.

Krüger watched him go. "What a turd." He looked up to Taubman. "And I can't take you off the list, either."

With a flash of guilt, Taubman said, "I'm afraid not, sir."

"That man, Schroeder. He made us watch movies."

"Movies?"

"Hitler is having people killed. Hundreds, I've heard. Maybe more."

"Why . . . why?"

"He's killing people suspected of taking part in the bomb plot against him last month. Generals, admirals. Hitler's henchmen had these people stripped of their clothes and hung by piano wire tied around their necks. The bastards filmed it, and we were forced to watch them die, dangling from meat hooks."

"My God."

"The rumor is that even Rommel is implicated. Can you believe that?"

"No. Impossible."

Krüger shook his head slowly. "I don't see how they can ever prove that, but there you have it. Anyway, that's Schroeder's job. Flying from station to station, forcing people to watch movies."

"I thought he was here for that torpedo investigation."

"Oh, that's beneath Standartenführer Wolfgang Schroeder. He's doing just one thing. Touring the countryside on a pass from Himmler, making sure the Führer's officer corps watches the movies. How's that for the most efficient, morale-boosting use of our time?"

"My God."

The Storch's pilot was a small, tight-lipped Stabsfeldwebel, or flight sergeant, named Dieter Hauser, who hovered over the fueling crew like a mother hen. When that was complete, Hauser hobbled over to Krüger, gave a military salute, and asked, "I'm ready to depart, Herr Fregattenkapitän. My orders, please?" My God, Taubman marveled. The man is ninety if he's a day. White, close-cropped hair bristled from under his garrison cap. And he was slight and stooped. Perhaps that's why he hobbled, stooped with arthritis, Taubman thought. And small; he almost looked like a boy. Perhaps his superiors had calculated it that way, he mused. More payload on the Storch.

"Good God, it's Dieter Hauser," grinned Krüger. He extended his hand. "Dieter, how was your flight?"

Hauser shook and bowed stiffly. "Very good, thank you, Herr Fregattenkapitän."

Krüger turned to Taubman. "Dieter will take good care of you. He flew Fokkers in the Big War. Lost a foot and kept flying. How many Tommies did you shoot down, eh, Dieter?"

A shell landed two hundred meters away, throwing rubble high in the air. Hauser waved at it, saying, "Apparently not enough, sir."

Krüger lowered his voice. "Dieter, do you have room for a fourth passenger?"

"I'm afraid not, sir," replied Hauser. "Plus, we have a bit of mail and some cargo, I see." He waved to some boxes and luggage piled at the Storch's door.

"Where'd —"

"That's mine, Herr Fregattenkapitän," Schroeder walked up to them. "Priority material."

Krüger hobbled over to the plane, and called back. "Looks like two cases of Kriegsmarine commissary wine."

Schroeder shrugged.

"And what's this?" Krüger's cane tapped a large cardboard box.

"Official films of the Reich," said Schroeder.

"This is what you showed to us?"

"Yes."

"Why don't you leave it here and let me ship it instead. My men would be very grateful."

An artillery shell landed closer; fifty meters this time. Schroeder whipped around, then threw his hands over his head. "In a pig's eye. Now let's get going." He started walking to the plane.

Krüger shook his head slowly.

"Sir?" Hauser called to Schroeder.

"What?" snapped Schroeder.

"I don't have room for all that. Where do I store your box of film?"

The box was dumped in Taubman's lap, with Schroeder insisting it be tied down lest it lurch into Schroeder's back in the event of a crash landing.

Hauser goosed his Argus-inverted V-8 engine, and the overloaded Storch staggered into the sky, the flashlights and brilliant moonlight guiding his way. The air was smooth, and light shimmered off the Blavet River as Hauser settled on an easterly course for Tours, keeping his little plane fifty meters above the deck.

Schroeder turned and shouted over the engine's noise, "I heard about your trip from Japan, Herr Taubman. A hazardous voyage. Welcome back."

"Umff." The box of film weighed on Taubman's legs, cutting off his circulation. In spite of that, his heart raced unaccountably. Just speaking to the man made his blood run cold.

"What?" yelled Schroeder.

"I said, 'Thank you, sir'," said Taubman, hoping that would be the end of the conversation.

Schroeder's head turned further. His teeth gleamed as he hollered, "How are our little yellow friends doing?"

Think of something! "Holding on, sir. But it's becoming harder and harder for them."

"Are they having torpedo problems?"

"No, sir. Their torpedoes are the finest in the world."

"Impossible," Schroeder yelled.

Taubman bit his lip. *How can I get rid of this man? If he keeps asking questions, surely he'll figure me out.*

When Taubman didn't reply, Schroeder continued, "Let me put it another way. As a naval liaison officer, wouldn't you think that our torpedoes should be as good as the Japanese's?"

"What?" said Taubman. Looking forward, he noticed Hauser's head was cocked slightly.

Schroeder raised his voice. "Our torpedoes. They've been sabotaged. Surely you've heard."

"Frankly, I haven't."

Schroeder turned all the way around. "Surely you have. What the hell have you been doing out there all this time besides screwing geisha girls?"

"I . . . we . . ."

"Our U-boats, you idiot. They're having failure rates of over fifty percent. All due to incompetence. Where have you been?"

"Japan, sir."

"Did anyone check your papers when you landed?" Schroeder asked suddenly.

"Of course, sir," Taubman lied. *Do it!* Blood pounded in his head as he leaned forward and reached down to his belt.

Schroeder took another tack. "Fregattenkapitän Krüger, for one, is implicated. His record is the worst. Upon arriving at Tours, I plan to file my report and recommend his arrest. How close are you to Fregattenkapitän Krüger?"

Working frantically, Taubman eased his Luger out of its holster, transferred it to his left hand, and flipped off the safety. Bile rose to his throat with the realization that he'd never done anything like this before. "Standartenführer Schroeder."

"Yes?"

"You are an ass."

"What?" Schroeder's head whipped around.

Taubman jammed the pistol to Schroeder's forehead and pulled the trigger. A loud report followed as brain matter and blood splattered on the cabin's starboard side. The acrid coppery odor of blood flooded the cockpit.

Taubman threw up.

"What was that?" yelled Hauser.

Still retching, Taubman began untying the knots securing the box to his lap. "Can we open this window in flight?" he asked.

"What did you do?" Hauser shrieked.

Taubman yelled back, "Shut up, you old fart, and answer my question."

Hauser turned all the way around. His eyes bulged when they settled on Schroeder. "What — what — what the hell have you done?"

Taubman leveled his Luger at Hauser. "Open this cabin window. Now."

"Shit!"

Taubman pulled out a handkerchief and wiped vomit off his chin. "That's what you'll be doing if you don't do what I tell you."

Hauser reached back and unlocked a series of latches. Wind whistled in as the window popped open a quarter of the way. Taubman reached in the box and began tossing out film reels stamped with the official seal of the Third Reich. "How much more range will we have if we dump Standartenführer Wolfgang Schroeder and his cargo?"

"Why?" Hauser yelled.

"We're going to Switzerland." Taubman tossed out another can of film. "Now, answer my question, you stupid *schwanz.*"

"All I have to do is set her down in Tours and you'll be arrested," said Hauser.

Aiming carefully, Taubman squeezed off a round that grazed Hauser's left ear, the bullet exiting through the windshield and clearing the Storch's propellor. Somehow, the pistol's report made him feel better; the nausea left him.

"Ow, ow, shit!" Hauser clamped a hand on his ear. "Listen. I don't have anywhere near the gas we need to get to Switzerland."

"Then think of something. Look, how would you like to make five thousand dollars?"

"What?"

"American."

Hauser spun again in his seat, forcing his eyes away from Schroder's face. "How much did you say?"

That's more like it. "I said five thousand dollars American, payable the minute you land me in Switzerland."

Hauser returned to checking his controls.

"That'll take some doing."

"And?"

A minute passed while Hauser rubbed his chin and looked out the windows, checking for enemy aircraft. "I suppose I can do it."

Taubman finished cleaning himself with the handkerchief and tossed it out the window. "What do you have in mind?"

THIRTY-FOUR

11 AUGUST 1944
TOURS,
FRANCE

Taubman couldn't recall a time in his life when he'd felt so vulnerable, not even aboard the I-boats. Against his better judgment, he'd allowed Hauser to talk him into landing the Storch at the airfield outside Tours. It was a night fighter base, and they had to dodge around Ju-88Gs on the taxi strip as they picked their way to the fueling station. Finally Hauser shut down his engine and flipped open the door. He waved a hand over his face and shouted, "Wheeeeow!" They'd poured a bottle of wine over Schroeder for two reasons: One was to cover up the sharp odor of blood; the other was for their charade.

Taubman drew his pistol.

Hauser cocked an eyebrow. "Don't get cold feet now, you damn fool. The guards would have you for breakfast."

"Stay where I can see you or we'll both be had for breakfast."

"Do your part, trust me, and everything

will be fine," Hauser said, alighting from the Storch.

Taubman held the pistol low. "Move more than five meters away and you'll have a bullet up your bung."

"You are our ticket out of here, Herr Standartenführer." Hauser reached in the cockpit, grabbed Schroeder's shoulders, and propped him upright. Then he tipped Schroeder's cap over his face, letting it rest on the corpse's nose. "Hmmm, sleeping like a baby, all right."

In the blink of an eye, Hauser grabbed Taubman's pistol by the barrel and yanked it from his hand. "Who are you calling *schwanz,* you phoney little shit?" With a lopsided grin, he said, "I suppose I could take the money from you and turn you over, but then again" — he nodded toward the hangar where guards strolled back and forth — "these animals would probably steal it from me. In any case, keep your mouth shut, *schwanz,* and do your part. You may get to Switzerland yet." He tossed the pistol in Taubman's lap. "And put on the safety before you blow your balls off." Shaking his head, Hauser limped away.

"Shit," Taubman muttered. He wiped sweat off his forehead, tipped his head back, and opened his mouth as if he were asleep.

One of the corporals pulled up a fueling hose and nozzle and called out, "Sir, how much?"

Hauser replied, "All you can give her."

The man's hands went to his hips. Then he quickly stooped and stuck his head in the cabin. "Wheeeoow."

Taubman peeked from under an eyelid, his heart jumping as the corporal's eyes flicked over the two human forms.

"Officers: the pride of the Reich," the corporal muttered as he backed away and stood. "Herr Stabsfeldwebel," he called. "You have all this weight and —"

"Shut up, you damned fool. Do you want to wake them?"

"But I only —"

"Shhhh," Hauser said in a hushed tone. "That is Standartenführer Wolfgang Schroeder of the SS."

"I can see that."

"And I'm under his orders. Don't worry. I've flown these things many times before. So don't worry, Sonny. We'll make Paris. That is, unless you wish to wake the Standartenführer and ask him yourself."

Cursing under his breath, the corporal stammered, "*Jawohl,* Herr Stabsfeldwebel."

Hauser casually wiped the blood off the starboard window with a soaked rag as the corporals refueled the plane.

Taubman watched, and when the corporal's head bobbed out of sight, he whispered, "Hauser."

"Shut up," the pilot hissed.

"See that mail chute over there?" Taubman nodded toward the hangar.

"Shut up. Do you want to ruin everything?"

Slowly, carefully, Taubman eased the envelope from his inside coat pocket. "Take this over there and drop it in." He handed it over.

"Who the hell do you think I am? Your personal delivery boy?"

"It's from Krüger to his wife. I promised I'd mail it."

"Oh, why didn't you say so?" Hauser took the envelope over and dropped it in the mail slot.

When he returned, the corporal reported, "All done, sir. How about the oil?"

"That's it. Stand back." Hauser climbed in and started the Storch's engine. The corporals stepped away as Hauser gunned the engine, stomped on the right brake, and turned the little observation plane back toward the runway. "All ready for takeoff, Herr Standartenführer? Your seat belt buckled up nice and tight?" he called.

"Ha-ha," replied Taubman.

Hauser waited behind a Ju-88G as its pilot ran up his twin Junker Jumo 213E V-12 engines, the noise, incredible, ripping at the night. Finally, the Ju-88, its nose bristling with radar antennae, took off. Hauser guided the little wobbling aircraft onto the airstrip and gunned the engine. "Here we go, sonny. Keep your seat buckled and your arse puckered. This may take some time."

The plane was very sluggish at first. Finally, they gained speed and the tail lifted. Taubman felt the Storch trying to fly. He yelled over the engine's roar, "How much runway do we have?"

"A thousand meters, if you don't count the bomb craters. That's where it gets dicey."

As the Storch stumbled into the night, Taubman heaved a sigh of relief and forced himself to breathe. Now he could give some thought to their next task, a grisly one.

Hauser found a deserted country road forty kilometers southeast of Tours, near the village of Veigne. They landed under a full moon and, working quickly, hoisted Schroeder's body from the Storch and laid it under a nearby sycamore tree, the head propped up against the trunk. Carefully, Hauser positioned Schroeder's cap over his eyes, then stood and gave a Nazi salute. "*Wiedersehen, Herr Scheisskopf.*" Good-bye, shithead. Then he limped back to the airplane.

Taubman kneeled and folded Schroeder's hands over his belly. Then he searched for a moment and found a daisy. He picked it and stuck the stem between Schroeder's fingers just as Hauser staggered back with the two cases of wine.

With a grunt, Hauser set the cases beside Schroeder and said, "Poor bugger looks peaceful. Probably for the first time in his life." Then he turned. "Come on. Let's get out of here."

With Schroeder and his cargo gone, the Storch seemed incredibly nimble in spite of the fuel load. The night grew cooler, the air denser. They picked up a tailwind, with Hauser setting them on a near-easterly course, the brilliant moon showing their way over a quiet French countryside.

Taubman slept for a while, until turbulence shook him awake. He checked his watch. Nearly four a.m. "Where are we?"

Hauser pointed. "See that?"

Taubman craned his neck, finding a faint glow on the horizon at about one o'clock. "What is it?"

"Dijon. Looks like they don't believe in blackouts."

Indeed, the glow was a beacon. "Thank you, Dijon."

"We're ahead of schedule."

Taubman's pulse quickened with the realization his objective was close. “Can we make the border?”

“No.”

Taubman raised himself in his seat and looked over Hauser’s shoulder. “Your fuel gauge says a quarter.”

Hauser whipped around. “Listen, *schwanz*. I’m in this all the way. I need fuel not only to take you to Switzerland, but then get me back to Lyon.”

“Lyon?”

“Once I’m there, I’m okay. I have friends in the south of France.”

“What will you do?”

Hauser pondered the question. “Something I’ve wanted to do for a long time.”

The glow from Dijon came into focus. It looked like a cluster of lights over an intersection. “What?” Taubman said.

“Spain.”

“What the hell’s in Spain?”

“My son, Adolph. An Me-109 pilot; he lost a leg in a crack-up. Adi bought a small vineyard down there. He has a wife. I think she’s pregnant.”

And Hauser had lost a foot in the first war, Taubman recalled. He thought that one over, sensing there was more, and waited patiently.

As Dijon slid past their right wing tip, Hauser added, “Lost my wife and daughter in an air raid. I’d planned to join Adi all along. Your little offer just accelerated things a bit."

"Glad I could help."

"We'll see." He nodded to his left. "Look over there."

"What?" said Taubman. The countryside looked dark and mottled.

"An airdrome is right down there. We need fuel, don't we?"

Taubman couldn't see a damn thing. "This time we don't have the Standartenführer." Blood roared in his head. Things had been going so well. Now this. And he was terrified of descending into a dark nothingness.

Hauser cut the throttle and eased his Storch into a gentle bank to the left. "Ready to try your luck again?"

Hauser had eyes like a cat and found the heavily camouflaged runway on the first try. It was grass, and the Storch bounced high, with the old man fighting for control. Finally, the little plane rolled out and, as before, Hauser taxied up to a hangar where a fuel truck was parked.

A lone soldier stood near the truck, a Schmeisser MP-40 machine pistol hooked over his shoulder. No one else seemed to be around. The soldier smoked and watched as Hauser shut down the Storch. Eventually, he flicked the cigarette down, ground it under his boot, and strolled over.

"Just like before, act like you're asleep," muttered Hauser. Then he jumped out, meeting the soldier at the engine. "Hi, there. Where is everybody?"

"All gone. We just closed down. My captain is in town getting last-minute provisions before we take off." He nodded to a lone Ju-52 trimotor transport squatting nearby.

"Your captain?"

"Base commander."

"Getting provisions at this time of night?" chuckled Hauser. "What's her name?"

"Daphne. Now, what do you want?"

"Fill 'er up, check the oil and tires, and don't forget the windshield."

Taubman raised in his seat to see.

"Who are you?" The soldier was a Feldwebel, a sergeant. And he didn't sound like a fool.

"Drifted off course on a cross-country mission. Training hop." Hauser jabbed a thumb over his shoulder. "That's my student pilot. Now, we need fuel."

"Where did you come from?"

"Bar-le-Duc. Who the hell do you —"

"Bar-le-Duc was evacuated and closed three days ago." He unlimbered his Schmeisser and thrust out his other hand. "Your papers."

"I — I know, I was there," stammered Hauser. "They made us fly a triangle from Montargis to Bar-le-Duc to —"

"Hands up, old man!" the sergeant roared. "Who the hell do you think you're kidding? Montargis was closed two weeks ago. What's going on here? Tell that man to get out of there and stand beside you. Where the hell are your papers?"

Hauser raised his hands. "Top pocket." Then he said, "I swear, we got into Bar-le-Duc."

Carefully, the sergeant reached and pulled out Hauser's papers. "Bar-le-Duc is closed. We're closed. All of France is shut down. Where the hell have you been?"

"You're closed? You don't have any fuel?" Hauser gasped.

"Just what's in the truck. And that's for our plane. What's left over we torch with the truck." The sergeant lowered his Schmeisser. "Your papers look all right. You may take down your hands. But I'll need to see your trip manifest along with —"

Taubman climbed out and walked up to them. He shouted, "What's going on here?"

"I'll have to see your papers, sir," said the sergeant.

"How's this?" Taubman drew his pistol and jabbed it into the sergeant's temple.

The sergeant's eyes bulged.

"On your knees," Taubman ordered. "Now, when does your captain return?"

The sergeant shook his head.

"No time for this crap," Taubman muttered. With a swift motion, he clubbed the sergeant across the head. The man fell over with a groan.

Hauser's hands were still in the air. The man gulped, looking down at the prone sergeant.

It was quiet. A zephyr rustled a treeline fifty meters away. "You heard the sergeant, you old *schwanz,*" said Taubman. "Take down your hands and dig up some gas while I tie this bastard up."

With the Storch refueled, Hauser took off and headed east again. With the monotonous drone of the Argus and the still of the night, Taubman fell asleep. But ten minutes later, the Storch bounced and pitched. "What?

Hauser yelled, "Tighten your buckle, *schwanz*. We may be in for a hard ride."

"What the hell are you doing?" Yanking his buckle tight, Taubman looked about, seeing nothing. Not a headlight, not a village street lamp, as the plane jiggled violently. For comfort, he raised up a bit to see the green backlighted instruments on the pilot's panel.

"Just turbulence. We're over the Jura Mountains. Go back to sleep."

"Are you sure?" Taubman ran his hand over his pistol. For some reason it made him feel better, although he knew it was useless up here.

"Twenty minutes, half an hour, then you can stop peeing your pants." Hauser laughed loudly.

Taubman gritted his teeth. After a minute, it grew calm. Two minutes later, he felt himself nodding off. He relaxed his grip on his pistol and went back to sleep.

It was near daybreak, and Taubman's heart soared as they crossed the Swiss border. Hauser found the road Taubman wanted: a little stretch of country lane southeast of St.-Cergue. The Stabsfeldwebel cut the engine, letting the plane roll to a stop under a grove of trees.

Leaves and a bit of dust swirled about the aircraft.

Hauser broke the silence. "All out."

Taubman snapped his briefcase shut and climbed out. Retrieving his duffle, he leaned in and dropped a bundle of money in Hauser's lap.

"What?" he said, quickly thumbing the neatly wrapped stack. "There's more than —"

"That's ten thousand, Dieter. I decided you needed a bonus. Something to remember me by. Now go buy yourself a decent suit. You look like shit."

Hauser's eyes went wide. "Thank you."

"You have enough fuel for Lyon?"

"Barely."

"Where will you go in Spain?"

"Why?"

"I may want to look you up after the war."

Hauser rubbed his chin, trying to decide. "Lumbrales. It's a village near the Portuguese border."

"Sounds beautiful."

"It is, I'm told."

"Well, then, good-bye." Taubman reached in and they shook.

"Hals und bein bruch, schwanz," said Hauser. Literally, "Break your neck and your legs," meaning "Good luck." He started his Storch, spun around, and gunned the engine, the plane bouncing into the air after rolling just thirty meters.

Taubman stepped deep into shadows and reached into his duffle, pulling out a dark gray suit he'd bought in Hong Kong six months previously.

The Storch circled, wiggled its wings, and flew west, its drone quickly fading. Taubman yanked off his Kriegsmarine tunic and threw it into the bushes, saying softly, *"Hals und bein bruch, alter Mann."*

THIRTY-FIVE

12 AUGUST 1944
THREE KILOMETERS SOUTH OF ST.-CERGUE, SWITZERLAND

Taubman had picked a remote spot to land, six kilometers inside the border, which put him well behind security guards and fences, the gangly Storch landing and taking off without a hitch. But Geneva was eighteen kilometers away. What if some self-serving, crooked border agent happened along and took him in? He'd heard stories of Swiss border guards turning suspected fugitives over to the Germans for a price. Now that he was out of uniform, he could be shot. Looking occasionally over his shoulder, he walked the four kilometers to the main road without incident. Checking carefully for police and military vehicles, he turned right and headed toward Geneva, sixteen kilometers to the south.

Five minutes later, a Geneva-bound fire truck stopped. They'd been out for a test run after an engine overhaul and thought nothing of giving a neatly dressed civilian a lift into town.

By eleven that morning, Taubman had checked into the Hotel Maurice and took a penthouse on the eighth floor. It cost $500 a night, but he needed to be up high. After a three-hour nap, he yawned, stretched, and stepped into the shower, luxuriating in steam and the strong flow of hot water. Putting his head down, he let it gush over his head, neck, shoulders, back; he hadn't felt so relaxed in a long, long time. Not even in the German embassy in Tokyo, where the piping was abysmal.

Turning, he let the water cascade over his face. His mind wandered . . . the *I-57*.

"*I-57*," he muttered aloud.

In Lorient, Krüger had said, *"The I-57. She was due in last week. We've lost her, I'm afraid. Gave a position report shortly after you transferred off. That was it. No more radio transmissions. Disappeared. I'm truly sorry for your shipmates, your friends."* Then he took Taubman's hand. *"What a stroke of luck for you to have a ruptured appendix."*

"Stroke of luck," Krüger had said. With *I-57*'s loss, it certainly was a stroke of luck that there were far fewer people to share the gold. Right now, his share was about one-forty-seventh, far better than the one-ninety-fifth before the *I-57* was sunk.

He was getting scalded, so he turned off the shower and stepped out, still turning things over in his mind. He toweled off and ordered lunch sent to his room: roast goose. While waiting, he sat at the desk and doodled on Hotel Maurice stationery. The *I-49* was now loaded with 142 one-thousand-ounce gold bars weighing nearly seventy pounds each. At the U.S.-pegged price of $35 per ounce, each brick was worth U.S. $35,000. Therefore, five tons of gold was worth $5,072,382. Before the *I-57* went down, they were going to split it a hundred ways, which equaled U.S. $49,700 per share. Taubman ground his teeth. Shimada, the idealistic samurai, insisted on an equal share for everybody, whereas Taubman and the senior officers wanted to take fifty percent, giving the rest to the crew. At any rate, the split was now forty-seven, or U.S. $105,745 per man.

Better. A man could do a lot with U.S. $106,000.

Still muddling, Taubman finished his goose and dressed. He took the elevator down and walked through the Maurice's ornate lobby onto the sidewalk. Turning right, he trekked three blocks to the Merchants Bank of Geneva. There he set up a numbered account and deposited all the cash in his case: $100,000, less the $10,000 he'd given the old Storch pilot, less another $10,000 he kept out for himself. Completely unburdened and armed with a checkbook, he walked across the street and headed for the Montreux Bank des Switzerland, feeling invigorated.

The lobby of the Montreux Bank des Switzerland was done in marble with oversized heavy mahogany furniture and deep green potted plants. But what struck Taubman was that it was quiet and a sense of gloom and intimidation pervaded the understated elegance. Two men in dark coats and ties sat in back, one using the phone, another poring over a document. A large desk dominated the lobby's center; a neatly coiffed receptionist worked on a folder. Her glasses conveyed a professorial image, but her hairdo, shimmering green eyes, and beauty mark told a different story. Her smile was dazzling. "May I help you, sir?"

"Walter Taubman, please," he smiled back.

She looked over her shoulder at a large clock with roman numerals. Clasping her hands, she said, "Mr. Taubman is in a meeting. Is he expecting you?"

"Yes."

"Oh? At what time, sir?" She looked down and made a show of scanning a large inked register.

Taubman smiled again. "Dear girl, Walter is my brother. He's been expecting me for several days now."

She looked puzzled. "I see. And your

name, please?" She picked up a phone.

"Martin Taubman."

She turned to the side, covered the mouthpiece, and spoke softly. Hanging up, she waved a hand at a deep leather sofa. "Someone will be out. Please be seated. Would you like tea? Something stronger, perhaps?"

"No thank you." As a naval attaché, Taubman knew enough about lobbies to know that one never sat while waiting. Nor did he accept a beverage. For sitting and balancing a cup of tea, or whatever, put one at a disadvantage when the person he was calling for walked in. Instead, Taubman circled the coffee table like a hungry cat, looking down at a number of neatly fanned American and British magazines. It was tempting to sit and leaf through one of them, but he resisted and kept his pace, occasionally catching the receptionist's glance.

He was on his fifth circuit when the phone rang. "Yes?" she said. After a nod, she replaced the receiver and waved to a bank of elevators trimmed in glistening white marble. "Mr. Taubman will see you now. Please take the elevator to the third floor."

"Thank you." Taubman stepped in to find a uniformed operator looking straight ahead. Nothing was said. The operator closed the doors and whisked them up. They stopped at the third floor; the doors slid open.

A thin, balding man with a reddish Vandyke stood before him. He was only six years senior to Martin, but Walter Taubman looked far older than his thirty-four years — and far different compared to the childhood photograph Martin kept in his suitcase. "Martin," the man said, extending a hand. "Welcome. How are you?"

"I'm well, Walter. You're so kind to see me." They shook as Taubman stepped out into a reception area. There were just two desks. Secretaries sat at each, concentrating on typing.

"Not at all, Martin." He looked Martin up and down. "You look fit. The Kriegsmarine must be treating you well." He waved a hand. "Come, please join me for tea."

They walked into Walter's office. Desk, credenza, and side table were furnished in Monte Verde. A large leather couch and two deeply stuffed wing chairs flanked a black slate fireplace. Walter walked to the side table and fussed with a silver tea service. He waved Martin to a leather chair before his desk and said, "How do you like it?"

Martin sat and looked around, taking in the deep wood paneling and original artwork. Aside from his hotel room, it had been a long time since he'd seen such comforts. It all seemed incongruous, especially when he thought of the hell he'd been through the past few weeks.

"Martin?" prompted Walter Taubman.

"A little sugar, that's all." Beside him was an ornate table with a number of silver-framed photographs. The largest showed Walter seated with a woman wearing glasses, her hair done in a tight bun. Flanking them were two boys, six and nine. "Is this —"

"My family, yes. My wife, Stella. My sons, Fritz, he's the big one, and Gert, our budding pianist." Walter chuckled and handed over a cup of tea. "Who was that girl you were dating, the glider pilot?"

Martin flushed. He hadn't thought of her for years. "Trudie, yes. She did like to fly."

"I thought she was quite enchanting. Whatever happened?"

Martin shrugged. "The war." His eyes snapped to a photo near the table's rear edge. It was of a uniformed German officer, a colonel. Slightly yellowed, it had been taken ten years ago. Taubman had the same photograph packed with the rest of his luggage back in Japan. It was Manfried Taubman, their common father. He'd divorced Walter's mother, Gerta, in 1914, who returned to her native Switzerland to raise Walter. Then Manfried married Martin's mother, Hilda, in 1916. In 1918, at the end of the Great War, Manfried Taubman ran off with a Spanish flamenco dancer. But each month, he sent an allotment to Hilda, who raised Martin in Munich. Martin always wondered if Walter's mother received a similar allotment. But now was not the time to ask.

With their father either carousing or off with the Wehrmacht, the two boys grew up in different countries, Martin staying in Germany with his mother, Walter in Switzerland with his mother. Thus, the boys grew up separately, not maintaining close ties. Except for the summers of 1930 and 1931, when Manfried made a Herculean effort to be with his boys and took them camping. But at war's outbreak, they lost touch altogether — Martin in the Kriegsmarine and posted to Japan; Walter safely ensconced in Switzerland as a banker. One day the embassy duty radioman handed Martin a message announcing his father was killed in a tank battle near Rostov, Russia, in 1942.

Walter joined his half brother in gazing at the photo. "A pity."

"Yes. When did you find out?"

"Just last year. And you?"

"Same."

Walter sipped his tea and raised his eyebrows. "It's been — what? Three months since I received your telegram from Tokyo. I'd expected you two weeks ago. Then . . . I was worried. So this is very good. I trust your, ah, journey went well."

"It was awful."

Walter averted his eyes for a moment, then looked back. "Brother, what can I do for you?"

"I need a bank account. Discreet, of course."

"Of course." Walter issued a thin smile and sipped his tea.

"I need to draw on it from anywhere in the world."

Walter leaned forward. "Within reason, of course." After a drawn-out silence, he said, "Forgive me for asking, Brother, but we have a minimum requirement here at Montreux. How much do you plan to deposit?" He held out a mahogany box and flipped it open. Inside were American cigarettes: Chesterfield.

"No, thank you."

Walter's eyes darted over his inventory and finally selected one of the cigarettes as if it were a long lost bottle he'd misplaced in his abundantly stocked wine cellar. Sharply, he tapped the cigarette on the desk three times, then lit it with a gleaming silver Ronson lighter. After exhaling a huge cloud, his eyes settled on Martin. *Well?*

Martin waited until Walter was well into his second drag, then said casually, "Five tons of gold. Will that be enough?"

Walter's eyes bulged just a bit. He stopped in mid-inhale and rasped, "What?"

"I said, 'Five tons of gold.' "

With some effort, Walter composed himself and expelled the smoke in his lungs.

"Walter?" Martin prompted.

"Yes, yes, we can help you." Stubbing out his cigarette, Walter Taubman reached in his top drawer and pulled out a form. He scribbled for a moment, then looked at Martin, an eyebrow raised. "Brother, we do need a deposit to activate the account."

"How much?"

"Well. Three thousand Swiss francs should take care of it." Both of Walter's eyebrows were up.

"How about thirty thousand American?"

The expression on Walter Taubman's face was evident. *Where would Martin Taubman, a common Kriegsmarine sailor, most likely on the run, get thirty thousand dollars American and five tons in gold?* "Yes, that's all right."

Martin took out his checkbook from the Merchants Bank of Geneva, wrote a check, signed his name with a flourish, and handed it over.

"Thank you." Walter must have pushed a button somewhere because a secretary entered silently and stood beside Walter while he signed another form and handed everything over to her. Once done, she walked out.

"Brother, to activate an international account, the, ahhh . . ."

"Gold?"

"Yes, the gold needs to be delivered to a triple-A-rated correspondent bank. Where would this be?"

"Chile."

"But where in Chile?"

Martin shrugged. "I was hoping you would have a suggestion."

"I see." Walter picked up a thick book and thumbed pages. "How about the Viña del Mar branch of Banco Santiago? It's just three kilometers north of Valparaiso."

"Oh?" Martin sat back. Viña del Mar. He'd heard rumors about Viña del Mar. Along with many little towns in Argentina and Brazil, Viña del Mar was marked as a bolt-hole for high-ranking Nazi party officials. Stories of the Casino del Mar drifted back to him. High-rolling gamblers played there. It was one of the hottest spots in South America. He looked up. Walter's eyes glistened. *Yes, Walter knows all about Viña del Mar. I bet he's financing a lot of other Nazis there right now.* "All right. Viña del Mar."

"Right. Once the gold is delivered to

Banco Santiago, I can wire funds to you almost anywhere in the world at any time. Well" — Walter coughed politely — "at least a place that's not at war, I mean. Now, would you like suggestions for code numbers for your account?"

"Please."

The next ten minutes were absorbed with Martin and Walter signing a number of forms. At length, Walter stood, reached across the desk, and extended his hand. "On behalf of Montreux Bank des Switzerland, let me express our appreciation for the trust you have placed in us. It is our great honor to serve you."

They shook and Walter remained standing, as if dismissing Martin.

Instead, Martin said, "I have three other requests, ah, just little ones."

"I see." Walter sat. "Please, anything."

"First, I need a Swiss passport. Second, I need a radio, a transceiver, a good Telefunken with worldwide range. Third, I need clearances and documentation for transport to the South Pacific."

"South Pacific? Where?"

"Nouméa, New Caledonia."

"And you speak French?"

"Oui, Monsieur."

Walter nodded. "Well, then, that's very good. Had you said Davao or Manila or Singapore, I would have had doubts. But a

Swiss passport? I'm afraid that's impossible." He held up a hand to cut off Martin's protest. "But," he smiled, "I think another country might be possible."

Martin drummed his fingers.

"Belgian? Irish? British, perhaps. I might even be able to get an American passport for you. But Swiss? We're just too tightly controlled here."

Martin's English was too heavily accented for British or American passports. "French, then."

"Excellent. Nouméa is French, so it all fits."

"How much?"

"Five thousand American."

"Shit." Taubman saw his expense money flying out the window.

Walter Taubman pouted as if the word had never sullied his wood-paneled office. "I'm sorry. I act only as an intermediary in a matter like this."

Martin was sure Walter would have draped black velvet over his family photo were it next to him. "All right. Five thousand."

"Do you wish to use your real name?"

Walter knows all the questions. He's done this many times. "No. Use Henri Dufor."

Walter made notes. "Henri Dufor it is." He tore off a piece of paper and handed it over. "So. Go to this address tomorrow morning at ten o'clock. They will take the photo and deliver the product to you by four tomorrow afternoon. Will that do?" He sat back and steepled his fingers.

Five thousand? Martin Taubman wondered. I'll bet that's at least twice the cost. "How much for the radio?"

"Five thousand."

Martin dropped his head into his hands. "Shit."

This time Walter didn't miss a beat. "I can have it delivered to your hotel room, if you wish."

Martin looked up. "Discreetly?"

"Very. Where are you?"

"The Maurice."

"Very, very good. We know the Maurice staff very well."

"Is it going to cost me anything?"

"I'd say another two thousand."

"And how about the transportation to Nouméa?"

"I'll have a French diplomatic visa rigged up for you. Red Cross, possibly. I've done it before, and it seems to work all right."

"Will it be Vichy?"

"No."

"Good. All right. And how much is that going to cost me?"

"Well, you'll have to go by ship. If you don't mind me saying so, fewer questions asked that way. Is that all right?"

Taubman had been hoping for air transport, but he knew it would be impossible with all the American security. Instead, he was faced with a long sea voyage, four, five weeks possibly. Shimada would be going crazy with the waiting. But the irony struck him that he would be voyaging through the Suez Canal this time, not the long way around the Cape of Good Hope. "Yes, that's all right. What's *that* going to cost?"

"Well, after greasing the skids to get you manifested, I'd say about ten thousand American."

"Shit!"

It was a cool and clear night in Geneva. With great caution, Taubman uncrated Walter's Telefunken and carefully rigged the antenna. Thoughtfully, Walter had included a bottle of schnapps and two crystal glasses. *Does he expect me to have company?*

Martin sipped until five minutes to midnight, then donned his earphones and got ready. At the stroke of twelve, he took a deep breath and tapped out the call letters JTT/ITN . . . JTT/ITN . . . JTT/ITN.

At ten to one, he'd about given up. Then his heart jumped when he heard a weak response: ITN/JTT.

Taubman gulped a glass of schnapps,

fully energized. Carefully, he tapped out the message in a simple checkerboard code to Shimada.

1. MISSION ACCOMPLISHED.
2. AIR XPORT NOT AVAILABLE.
3. BOOKED MARIE LORRAINE, DEPARTS MARSEILLE 08142000.
4. ARRIVE NOUMEA ABOUT 0926.
5. PLS RNDZ 0929.
6. 50 METERS OUTSIDE REEF POUM 0500.
7. IF RNDZ MISSED WILL TRY 10010130, THEN AGAIN TWO NITES LATER.
8. WILL GUARD SAME FREQUENCY AS AGREED.
9. CONFIRM.

MT

He heard them trying to transmit but static was heavy, the *I-49*'s signal very weak. He asked them to repeat. Finally, it came through.

GOLDEN KITE

Taubman settled back. Shimada and his damned medals. He wondered what Shimada's reaction would be when he told him of the loss of Yukota and the *I-49*. He hadn't seen the two together very long, but his take was that the two submariners were close. Taubman poured one last glass of schnapps, flipped the power off the Telefunken, and put his feet up. *So what?* Six weeks to get to Nouméa and put it all together. Walter's papers had better be good.

The crystal glasses gleamed. *Company*. That's what Walter was suggesting. Not a bad idea. It's been a long, long time. He donned a coat and walked out.

PART THREE

The Captain

Only a seaman realizes to what extent an entire ship reflects the personality and ability of one individual, her commanding officer. To a landsman this is not understandable, and sometimes it is even difficult for us to comprehend, but it is so.

A ship at sea is a distant world in herself and in consideration of the protracted and distant operations of the fleet units, the Navy must place great power, responsibility, and trust in the hands of those leaders chosen for command.

In each ship there is one man who, in the hour of emergency or peril at sea, can turn to no other man. There is one who alone is ultimately responsible for the safe navigation, engineering performance, accurate gunfiring, and morale of his ship. He is the commanding officer. He is the ship.

This is the most difficult and demanding assignment in the Navy. There is not an instant during his tour as commanding officer that he can escape the grasp of command responsibility. His privileges in view of his obligations are almost ludicrously small; nevertheless command is the spur which has given the Navy its great leaders.

It is the duty which most richly deserves the highest, time honored title of the seafaring world — Captain.

— ATTRIBUTED TO JOSEPH CONRAD

THIRTY-SIX

5 SEPTEMBER 1944
SAN PEDRO, CALIFORNIA

Unlocking two locks and a deadbolt, Emma Peabody opened the door to her basement. Casting another glance over her shoulder, she clutched the handrail and walked down the steep stairs to her basement. Snapping on the light, she looked around with pride. Years ago Leo had converted it to a workshop complete with bench, vise, table saw, drill press, and lathe. Leo had even poured a concrete floor and laid black-and-white checkered tile on top of that. Leo had retired from the Southern Pacific seven years ago, and, in addition to puttering in his basement, he had taken an interest in photography. Opposite the workbench was another one of Leo's achievements, a tiny darkroom and photo lab with developing and enlarging equipment. Leo's photos still hung throughout the house, many of them showing trains rumbling through rugged California mountains, the engines gloriously belching smoke and steam. Leo had been an engineer, and the two-by-three photo hanging over the workbench was Emma's favorite: it showed a long, lanky, sandy-haired Leo standing before number 4242, his "baby." It was an AC-10 class, cab-forward, 4-8-8-2 locomotive, at 6,000 horse-power one of the most powerful on the Southern Pacific Line. The photo had been taken in Truckee, California, near the Donner Pass, at nearly seven thousand feet. It was winter, the shot dominated by stark blacks and whites. Snow lay everywhere; old 4242, a big, black, sinister locomotive, steam rising around her, filled much of the picture, while a switching engine and two other cab-forward AC-10s puffed and snorted in the background. But there was Leo, resplendent in heavy winter overcoat and mittens, leaning against 4242 with his signature lopsided grin. He still looked like the teenager Emma had fallen in love with in high school back in Indianapolis.

She looked up at it and smiled. *I love you, Leo. We'll be together again. Sooner than later.*

Leo had died four years ago, but not before he'd installed their pride and joy, a project both shared. Wedged between his workbench and the photo lab was another simple bench with a deep sink. Tucked underneath was a six-and-a-half-gallon bucket with lid and airlock, a five-gallon carboy, a five-gallon boiling kettle, and two wooden crates of glass bottles. Above the bench were shelves containing racking tubes, a scale, a thermometer, a Pyrex pitcher, and a hydrometer. Leo had even found room to fit in a refrigerator. Emma opened the door, her eyes scanning the ingredient boxes, all neatly stacked and correct. There were only twelve bottles of beer left; it would soon be time to brew another batch. She grabbed a bottle, uncapped it, and tipped it toward Leo's photo. "Here's to you, sweetheart." Then she took a long, satisfying swig. Wiping her mouth, she gave a thunderous, ripping belch, just as Leo would do. She sat in a chair, closed her eyes, and shook her head, reveling in the fact that this stuff was far better than the cheap swill offered at Carmenelli's grocery store down on Gaffey Street. *Ah, Leo, who's to say a couple of old beer drinkers like us didn't have a happy life together, even though we didn't have children?* And the sad part was that they could only drink alone. Home-brewing beer was illegal in California.

She finished off the bottle, set it down, reached in the refrigerator, and uncapped another. Tipping it to her grinning Leo, she drank deeply. Not bad for a pale ale. Then she thought of the imperial stout she and Leo had made at one time. Now that was a beer with a real kick, brewed by Leo, who kept meticulous records and proceeded as if he were cooking up a batch of nitroglycerin. Everything clean, measured precisely, poured impeccably. *Even if I could get the ingredients, I wonder if I could handle that?* Her eyes drifted to the drawer containing Leo's notes. She reached in the refrigerator, uncapped another bottle, and took a long swig. *I wonder if —*

"Mrs. Peabody? Hello in there?"

Damn! Todd Ingram. She'd forgotten to close the basement door.

"Knock, knock," Ingram called.

Quickly, she put the half-empty bottle in the sink and headed for the stairs. "Right there."

She snapped off the light just as Todd Ingram's head popped in the doorway.

"Hi. Sorry to bother you. I need a favor."

She started up the stairs. After the fifth step, her head started to swim and she stopped for a moment, clutching the handrail. *How much of that stuff have I had?*

"Ah, is this where you brew your concoctions?"

"Never mind," she muttered.

"You all right?" Todd stood at the top of the landing, a bundle in his arms.

She did her best to stifle a belch. But some sneaked out anyway. "I'm fine."

"Had lunch yet? Maybe I'd better . . ."

She gained the landing and forced him into the kitchen. Turning and locking the door, she said, "Not yet. I was just down there checking my canned goods supplies."

" 'Canned goods'?" Ingram's eyes puckered in mirth.

" 'Canned goods,' I said. Say, I have tomato soup. Would you like some? And I have a little bit of ham for sandwiches." Having caught her breath, she vowed never again to touch her beer in the daytime. It would become an activity reserved strictly for late evening.

"Thanks, I can't. I just got a phone call from Terminal Island saying my orders are in. So, could you watch Jerry for about an hour while I go and pick them up?"

"Oh, yes, thank you." She reached out and accepted the bundle. The face was covered with a corner of a blanket. "Oh, darling sweet Jerry." Another belch leaked out as she rocked him.

"Okay. He's been fed. Here's two extra diapers. And do you have Helen's number at Fort MacArthur?" He headed for the door.

"Of course." Then she said, "Orders. Does that mean . . ."

"Ummm." He nodded.

"By the way, tell Helen I have her scarf."

"You do? Which one?"

"The orange one." She walked into the

dining room, then came back with a bright orange scarf. Handing it over, she said, "She left it here the night that . . . well, she and Jerry were here for a barbecue. And then we got the telegram from Australia and —"

"Australia? Bar-be-cue?" Ingram held the scarf to his face. It was a gift from Laura West. Helen wore it only when she was in a vampish mood. He sniffed, "Chanel No. 5. That's Helen, all right." He looked up. "She told me she and little Jerry and Fred were listening to the radio when the telegram came."

Another belch was on the way. Mrs. Peabody did her best to muffle it. "Well, I guess she forgot. I answered the phone. And what a marvelous surprise it was."

"Bar-be-cue?" Ingram carefully folded the scarf and put it in his pocket. "Well, thanks for the . . . scarf."

She blurted out, "They were just, you know, slow dancing. None of that boogie-woogie business."

"Dancing? Where was Jerry?"

"At your house, of course. I was —"

"How long had they been doing that?"

A look of horror swept over Emma Peabody. They'd all thought Todd Ingram was dead. Everybody was just trying to have a good time on a beautiful moonlit evening. They'd been drinking her beer, later dago red. "And then the telegram . . ."

Ingram's hands were on his hips, reading her mind. "Thanks," he muttered. "Back in an hour." He walked out.

Helen felt the ice the minute she walked in the door. Todd's greeting, a cheek brush, bordered on somewhere between civility and barroom brawl. And he was drinking a bottle of that cheap beer from Dominic's. Two empties stood on the counter. She was ready to ask, "What's wrong?" when she saw the flat manila envelope lying on the little dining table. Her heart sank. "Orders?"

"Yep." He grabbed a bottle and took a long swig.

"Damn this war." She pitched her purse and valise on the counter and threw her arms around his neck. "They keep taking you from me."

His arms hung loosely around her. She drew back. His eyes were misty, all right, just the way she felt. But there was something else. "Hon?"

He turned and walked away. "Not much warning. Day after tomorrow. I'm on a plane for the blue Pacific. But they promised me a first-class cabin. Lots of hula girls, roast pig, and leis. You remember those big flowers over there? What did they call them? Did they ever smell?"

Her eyes darted about the room as he rambled. "What's gotten into you?"

"Moonlight cruises on the blue Pacific. Dorothy Lamour undulating beneath a palm tree to the strains of 'The Moon of Monokura.' "

On the table, next to the flat envelope, was her orange scarf.

"Where'd that come from?"

A faint cry rose from the other room.

Ingram drank again. "Kid's hungry. Maybe you ought to feed him." He walked into the living room and sat heavily in the armchair.

She followed, absently picking up the scarf. "What's with this 'Moon of Monokura' stuff?"

"You know, Jon Hall running around in a tight bathing suit and a captain's hat. Dagger clenched between his teeth. Two grenades sizzling in each hand, ready to blow sharks out of the water if they come within ten feet of where he's pearl diving . . ."

The baby cried louder. Helen looked toward the bedroom, asking, "When did he last eat?"

Ingram raised a hand then dropped it on the arm. "Two o'clock. Mrs. Peabody gave him a bottle."

"Well, he's overdue."

"Have at it."

"Todd!"

"Try the fridge." Ingram took a long swig, finished the bottle, and plopped it on the coffee table.

She stalked off to the kitchen. Opening the refrigerator, she pulled out a bottle, poured water in a pan, and began to heat it.

The baby began screaming. "Todd!" she shouted.

"Yeah, yeah." Ingram got up and a moment later, walked into the kitchen, the baby on his shoulder. "Dry diaper. Must really be hungry." He bounced the baby and kissed him on the cheek. "So solly, cholly. Me no realize you so hungry. Mama fix you up, chop-chop."

"Just about ready." Helen squeezed a bit of milk on her wrist. "Here." She reached for the baby.

"I got it," said Ingram, grabbing the bottle.

"But —"

"Go change." He sat at the dining table and gave the bottle, the baby sucking loudly.

Helen turned the scarf in her hands. "What's wrong?"

Ingram's eyes riveted on the scarf.

"This?" Then it hit her. The last time she'd worn it was that night. The barbecue. The night of the telegram. They'd been dancing and Jerry Landa was getting frisky. They'd had wine and — "My God, Mrs. Peabody."

"Loose lips sink ships."

"What'd she tell you?"

"Seems you were having a moonlight serenade."

"Todd! For crying out loud. Nothing happened."

"Yeah." He held the scarf to his face and took an exaggerated breath. "Ummm, I remember that. Chanel No. 5." His eyes rested on her. "You told me you were listening to the radio when the telegram came."

"Well, she —"

"Is Jerry a good dancer?"

"Todd, stop it. Oh" — she ran her fingers through her hair — "this is all so stupid."

"You're calling me stupid?"

She leveled her gaze at him. "You *and* Jerry."

"I guess that's right, now that I think of it. A stupid friend can hurt you more than a smart Jap."

"Stop this."

"I repeat. Is Jerry a good dancer?" Ingram stood and yelled.

The baby spit out the nipple and started crying.

"Oh, God. I'm sorry. Nothing happened. We were just . . ."

"Just what?"

"We didn't know. We thought you were dead," she yelled back.

The baby screeched.

"It's okay, little fella," Ingram soothed. "I'm sorry." He stroked the baby's forehead and finally got him to take the nipple. The baby began sucking again, his little fists balled out into space. "Good boy."

He looked up at Helen. "Next time I'll try harder to get killed."

THIRTY-SEVEN

6 SEPTEMBER 1944
SAN PEDRO, CALIFORNIA

"Sure you don't want me to come?" Helen asked.

Ingram tucked the blanket around the baby and wheeled the perambulator through the front door. "No, thanks. Just us boys." He walked out.

"You won't be long?"

"Around the block," Ingram called over his shoulder as he disappeared into the mist.

Dammit. He's so distant. The phone rang and she picked it up.

"How's everything in sunny San Pedro this morning?" It was Kate Durand, Helen's mother.

"Hi, Mom. San Pedro is foggy and damp. And I have to work today."

"Todd's leaving tomorrow?"

"Uh-huh."

"They wouldn't let you off?"

"Flu epidemic. Seems like everybody's down. But they've given me this afternoon and evening off. And . . . tomorrow when I have to drive Todd to the . . ."

"Airport."

". . . the airport." Helen twirled the cord and sat. Fred jumped in her lap. She scratched his ears and he purred. "You sound good, Mom."

"That's what mothers are for. Why don't you bring little Jerry out here for a few days after Todd ships out?" Helen's mother, Kate, and her father, Frank, had an avocado ranch near Ramona in northeast San Diego County. It was where she grew up.

"Can't. Not with this flu epidemic."

"There's always something. How's Todd taking it?"

"He wants to go and he doesn't want to go."

"What does he tell you?"

"He clams up."

"Helen, what's wrong?"

"What do you mean?" A tear ran down her cheek. She looked about for a handkerchief.

"Honey."

"Everything's wrong, dammit," she spat, wiping the tear with the back of her wrist. "There's a war on and my husband's been out there too long, and those bastards are taking him again, and he doesn't know when to quit." With that, Helen bawled for thirty seconds.

When she eased off, Kate asked, "You okay?"

"Never better."

"You sound like your husband. Tell me, what is it?"

"We had a fight."

"What?"

Helen told her mother about Mrs. Peabody spilling the beans about the night with Jerry Landa.

"But nothing happened?"

"Of course not. I must admit, Jerry was getting frisky. And now that I look back on it, I could well have been . . . well, I mean, I could have aroused him romantically."

"Is that why you wore the orange scarf?"

"I felt like having fun, being festive, enjoying an evening with friends. That's why I wore the scarf." She sniffed, and the phone was silent. "Mom?"

"I'm here."

"I mean, I was supposed to be a widow — no longer married — and a lot of things were there that night to put Jerry and me together. But you know, Mom. I just couldn't. It's like we've always been. Todd was supposed to be dead, and yet . . . Do you know what I mean?"

"That's how we are. You felt in your heart he wasn't dead."

"Something was there all right; I just couldn't let go. And then that night, when

Jerry was getting, well, you know, it just didn't seem right. And then Emma Peabody saw us, and that didn't help much."

"Maybe I should talk to her."

"God, no, don't do that. She's a great lady. She just drinks too much beer."

"And where is the good captain?"

"Gone. He shipped out three weeks ago."

"Well, at least you've been without distractions from that sector."

"Well, that's something else. I'm afraid Todd is going to hold this against Jerry when he goes back out there. And they're supposed to be best friends."

"Helen, they're grown men."

"That's what worries me. I know them both, and I think it'll be like two tomcats meeting for the first time."

"Don't be silly. Give them a chance."

"I suppose so, but —" Helen looked up to see Ingram materialize out of the fog. "Here he comes, Mom. Gotta go."

"Helen."

Ingram fumbled at the screen door.

"Yes?" she whispered.

"Love your husband."

"I'm trying to, dammit."

"No, I mean love your husband. Goodbye, hon." Kate Durand hung up.

Ingram walked in. "Thought you were going to work."

"Yep." Helen donned her coat and grabbed her purse and valise off the couch. "Half a day. I'll be home at lunchtime." Then she walked up to Ingram, threw her arms around his neck, and gave him a long, wet kiss. She took a half step back, tapped his nose with her forefinger, and winked.

Ingram rubbed his chin. "What was that for?"

"See you at lunch." She leaned over, kissed the baby on the forehead, and walked out the door.

"Damn!" The odor of her hair and her freshly bathed scent lingered. He ran his hand over his mouth, bringing away a red smear of lipstick. He was aware of the Plymouth pulling out of the driveway; he wasn't aware that a corner of his mouth had turned up.

Helen stopped by her cubicle for a quick cup of coffee. Sunlight streamed in the dirty little window, telling her the fog had burned off. Wistfully, she looked outside to brilliant blue skies, a beautiful day. She checked her watch: 1030. An hour and a half to go. What worried her was that she had the whole afternoon off. The evening, too, and then tomorrow morning she was due to deliver Todd to the Terminal Island Naval Air Station for his flight to San Diego.

Leaning at the desk pensively, she folded her arms and stared out the window, wondering what to do about her husband's attitude, his gloomy indifference.

Then the phone rang.

The traffic on Sepulveda Boulevard was light, the drive to Dominic's in Studio City taking two hours and fifteen minutes. It was a pleasant seventy-five degrees as they drove mostly in silence, deep in their thoughts, both reluctant to speak. The Plymouth huffed and puffed its way through the Santa Monica Mountains in second gear, finally emerging into the San Fernando Valley via the Sepulveda Tunnel. Suddenly, they were greeted with an additional fifteen degrees of dry heat. Both cranked open their wind-wings, the blast of warm, dry air ruffling Helen's hair as Ingram fought bumper-to-bumper traffic down Ventura Boulevard. The temperature was down to eighty-five when they drove past Dominic's at ten past seven. Ingram found a parking space and, switching off the engine, said, "Nothing better to do than drive into the devil's cauldron the night before I ship out. You think it's air-conditioned in there?" He opened the car door for her.

"Let's hope so."

"Still can't figure out why we're here."

Ingram reached in the backseat, struggled into his khaki blouse, and donned his hat.

"Laura promised."

"Promised what?"

"A big surprise. Can you think of anything better to do?"

"Nope." They walked in the door and were greeted by delicious, cool air, along with the mixed odor of fine food, leather, and tobacco smoke. The lighting was low and accented with subtle tones of greens, reds, and blues; starched white tablecloths covered each table, all having low-wattage lamps fixed in the middle. Dominic's was almost full, more than half the crowd in uniform.

A tall, thin waiter caught them. "Commander and Mrs. Ingram? Please, right this way." He led them to a booth off to the side with a fine view of the bandstand, dance floor, and dining area. Snapping on the table light, he said, "Here you are." He seated them and handed over menus. "Dinner is on us. Anything you see here. Ah, libations, too." He walked off.

Ingram stretched his arms and shot his cuffs. "Might have been a long drive, but the price is right."

"Not bad." Helen picked up a menu.

The waiter returned, two martinis expertly balanced on a silver tray.

"Who ordered those?" Ingram demanded.

The waiter said, "Miss West, sir. Perhaps I can get you something else?"

Ingram looked at Helen. Her eyes twinkled. "Seems like a good place to start," he said. "Thanks."

"Of course. I'll let Miss West know you are here." The waiter walked off.

They clinked glasses. Helen's eyebrows went up.

She knows what I'm thinking. "Don't look at me like that."

"Why not?" Helen's gaze was intense, thoroughly focused. But there was something else there, too.

"I feel like a potato bug on an ice pick," he said.

"You can do better than that."

"Okay. Simply put, you're beautiful."

She looked away quickly.

"Hey, what was that?" He cupped a hand under her chin, seeing her eyes welling with tears. "Honey, what is it?"

"What do you think it is, you damn fool? In case nobody told you, I'm about to become very lonely again."

He scooted close and wrapped an arm around her. "I wish there was something I could —"

"Hi, everybody." Wearing a red sequined strapless cocktail dress with matching over-the-elbow gloves, Laura West pecked them both on the cheek and slid into the booth.

"Why so solemn?" she asked, pulling off her gloves and laying them aside.

Ingram raised his glass. "Laura, this is great. Thanks very much."

Laura cushioned her palms under her chin and leaned on her elbows, batting her eyes and wiggling her fingers.

Helen and Ingram exchanged glances. Ingram grinned. "You ever know Laura to be tongue-tied?"

"No. And I — Oh, my God." Helen pointed at Laura's left hand. "Is that —"

"Jerry," peeped Laura.

"That's swell," said Helen. "It's . . . the ring . . . well, you know —"

"Exactly. The same ring. He sent it by mail, via a courier pouch. Then he called me last night from Hawaii. We're engaged!" She thrust her hands in space as if singing the last bars of "Oklahoma." "Again. For keeps."

"I'll be damned," said Ingram. "Boom Boom Landa strikes again. This is really solid."

"He sends his best to you two. Says he's leaving today for . . . wherever." She waved a hand.

The waiter walked up and raised his eyebrows.

"The usual, thanks, Mario," said Laura.

Moments later the waiter produced a cut-crystal glass of ice water and a bottle of ginger ale and then walked off. "He knows me too well," Laura muttered. Then she looked up. "There's more."

"What?" they both asked.

"Well, Roberta Thatcher called, and they're giving me my old job back at NBC. I start Monday."

"Wow!" said Ingram. "Toscanini and all?"

"When he's in town, I head for the exit," she laughed. "No, actually, I just won't accept any more Hollywood luncheon invitations."

Helen reached across and squeezed Laura's hand. "That's great, Laura. I'm proud of you. This is a wonderful surprise. Thanks for letting us share."

"Now that I'm back, I intend to stay back."

Helen and Todd knew what she meant. He raised his glass. "Well, here's to the future Captain and Mrs. Landa. May you have a long and happy life together and lots of little Landas." They clinked and sipped. "Wonder why he was in Hawaii so long?" he asked.

"Something to do with training. I guess you'll know soon enough."

Ingram looked around the room, seeing the place almost full. "Really jumping now. Looks like we got here just in time."

Laura took their hands. "Thanks for

being my friends, you two. And Todd, take care of yourself. Come back to us well."

"Oh, I plan to do that. No more submarine rides." *How convincing did that sound?* Ingram wondered.

The band members began taking their seats and tuning up. Laura eased out of the booth and stood. "Due on in five minutes. Dinner's on the house. Everything. Ahhh . . ." She looked from side to side and said in a low voice, "Listen. We just got in a small shipment of filet mignon this afternoon. You won't see it on the menu. They like to save it for the movie crowd. But just say the word to Mario and he'll fix it up for you."

"Thanks, Laura." Ingram stood and hugged her. "You're very special to us, too. And congratulations again. I know you'll be very happy together. Anything I can tell him when I get out there?"

Her eyes welled with tears. "Just tell him to come back. The both of you dumb lugs." She turned and walked off.

Ingram sat and grabbed Helen's hand.

"That goes double for me," she said.

The waiter stepped up. "Are you ready to order, sir?"

Ingram smiled. "Do you have any filet mignon?"

The alarm clock read three-twenty-seven.

It was set to go off at six-thirty. Plane departure was nine-thirty. In the past, Helen and Todd never slept the night before he shipped out. Tonight was no exception. They just stayed awake and talked and made love and told little jokes. Now Helen dozed, an arm and a leg thrown over Ingram as he listened to the sounds of the night: an occasional ship's whistle, a siren, an airplane droning overhead. The sound he loved the most was little Jerry in his crib beside them. Quietly sleeping, he stirred occasionally and smacked his lips.

Sleep well, my boy. If something happens, you're all she's got.

A narrow shaft of moonlight eased through the window, lighting up the room. He looked down, finding her eyes wide open. "You're spying."

"You caught me."

She kissed him on the chin, then exhaled.

"I've been thinking," he said. "Did you know you saved my life?"

She raised on an elbow. "What?"

"When I was in the water, off Africa. That Wellington flew over and the Japs pulled the plug with me on deck. Then the water swept over me. It was cold. It was very, very lonely out there. But then the Wellington flew over again and pitched out the raft."

She kissed him on his chin.

"There were two voices. One told me to just go down, to sleep, to . . . to give up and stay there forever. It was very tempting. I was so damned tired of it all. Just go to sleep."

"I don't see you giving up. What was the other voice?"

"You."

"Come on."

"Loud and clear. I was about to give up, but you told me to swim to the raft. I made it, but I was so out of gas. God, it was all I could do to hang on. Again, I almost went down, but you told me how to pull the inflating ring. You even told me how to climb aboard when I was sure I didn't have the strength. And during this time, you told me we had a child. I saw your face. You . . . you told me you loved me . . . God."

"I do love you."

"Mmmm." He kissed her. "There's something else. I've been a real jerk the past few days."

"Forget it." She hugged him tight.

"I wish I could, but I can't. I'm sorry, honey. Maybe all this fighting is getting to me. I wish I knew."

"You could bail out, you know. Nobody would say a thing. You've done more than your share."

Ingram slowly shook his head. "I'd like to, but those are my guys out there. My shipmates." He looked into her eyes and ran a hand over her cheek and through her hair. "You've given me so much."

"You, too." She kissed his hand.

"That's just what I'm talking about."

She raised herself to kiss his chin, his forehead. "Ummm. What is it you're talking about?"

"You can give without loving, but you can't love without giving."

THIRTY-EIGHT

27 SEPTEMBER 1944
NOUMÉA, NEW CALEDONIA

Ingram's R5D landed at eight in the morning under a sultry sun. Wearing dress khakis and a garrison cap, and lugging a bulky B-4 bag, he climbed into an overloaded jeep and spent the next two hours bouncing down to the harbor on a dusty road. The fleet landing was a fifty-foot ramshackle shed where thick blue exhaust hung in the air. Launches, workboats, gigs, LCVPs, LCMs, admiral's barges, roared up to the dock, embarking and disgorging their human cargos. Ingram pushed through the tangle of hot sweaty men, looking for the *Maxwell*. She was somewhere in the middle of the inner harbor, nested with other destroyers alongside the destroyer tender *Dixie*. But it looked like a cockroach farm out there: radars twirled, antennae and guns bristled. Stately battlewagons and truculent carriers were surrounded by ships of all kinds, including World War I–era rust-streaked freighters. He took heart in the fact that traffic was not as heavy since he'd last been here, a good sign. The war had moved forward as advance bases were captured and the Allies pushed across the Pacific closer to their objective, the most recent examples the invasion of Peleliu and Morotai.

He also was aware that his quick heartbeat and the sweat running down the inside of his shirt just wasn't from the sun or the oppressive humidity. Nor was it from lack of sleep or lack of a decent meal. He'd felt this way ever since he'd awakened that last gray morning in San Pedro. Helen had seen it in his eyes. Ingram covered her mouth, lest she say something like "Don't go," or "They can't do this to you." Had she said it, he surely would have stayed. He'd done his job. He had enough medals. Let somebody else do the dirty work for a while. Let somebody else chase down Shimada, wherever he was, or that bastard Taubman. Instead, he kissed her, long and deep. Helen drove him to the airport after walking next door and handing his infant son over to Mrs. Peabody.

Now his stomach churned. His head swirled as a wave of nausea passed over him. He closed his eyes, then opened them to look upon the turquoise-blue waters of Baie de la Moselle. Twenty feet off the dock, a pelican dived for its meal as gum-chewing sailors in dungarees milled about, laughing, elbowing each other, their sleeves rolled up, white hats pitched back on their heads. He made a mental note to ask Bucky Monaghan, *Maxwell*'s chief pharmacist's mate, to prescribe belladonna the minute he stepped aboard. What else could he —

"Sir? Captain?" someone called.

Falco, the blond, curly-haired third-class boatswain's mate, stood in the stern sheets of a gray, double-ended, twenty-six-foot gig. Numbers on her bow stood out: DD 525.

"Yo." Ingram hardly remembered him. Falco had joined the ship just before they shipped out from Majuro Lagoon. Shortly after that, Ingram was on his odyssey aboard the *I-57* through the Indian Ocean.

Suddenly, Hank Kelly walked up, saluted, and pumped his hand. "You look great, Todd."

A grinning Jack Wilson was right behind, his right arm in a sling.

Ingram grabbed his left hand. "Jack, glad to see you're on the mend."

Wilson said, "The quack tells me full mobility in two weeks."

Falco handed the B-4 bag down to the gig, then climbed in.

Kelly threw out a palm. "Last one in's a rotten egg."

It was an old joke. But Ingram was glad to hear it as he waited patiently for everyone else to scramble aboard according to tradition.

The lines were cast off and Falco rang four bells for full speed. The wind on his cheek and the boat rocking under his feet did something to him. The water seemed bluer, the ships brighter, the humidity tolerable. He turned to Kelly. "Everything shipshape?"

"Not bad, Captain," said Kelly. "But we do have a little business as soon as you step aboard."

"Certainly. What is it?" The thought of immersing himself in his ship made him feel even better.

"Captain's mast," said Kelly.

"What? Can't we put this off a little while?"

"No, sir. We gotta do it now."

"Who is it and what the hell is he up for?"

"You, Captain. You've been AWOL for three and a half months."

The *Dixie* stood anchored near the harbor entrance. The destroyers *Milford*, *Wallace*, *Cluster*, and *L. T. Smith* were nested to her starboard side. Falco swung his tiller and the gig swung under the *Dixie*'s tall transom, revealing another four destroyers nested to port. The *Morgan J. Thomas* was moored inboard, followed by the *Striff* and the *Geiler*. Ingram blinked when he saw the fantail of the outboard ship: *Maxwell*. The last time he'd seen her, it was from this very perspective; sailing away from him, afire, reeling like a punch-drunk boxer, guns blazing, Jap Zeros buzzing all around.

The boat was silent as Ingram took it in. He turned to Kelly. "How many did we lose, Hank?" He'd read the battle damage reports, but he wanted to hear it from his executive officer.

"Thirty-seven dead, twenty-five wounded, eight seriously. Two of them are Stateside in a special burn unit. Clock didn't make it."

"I remember that. Saw him just before I went over the side." Ingram rubbed his chin. "How did you keep her afloat?"

"It wasn't easy. Luckily we had full engineering capability. Even the forward fire mains stayed intact. But I'll tell you, for the first half hour or so, I thought the ammo was going up and us with her. It was a hell of a fire."

"Damage?"

"Direct hit on Mount 52. Must have been a small bomb with a contact fuse, but it didn't penetrate. Otherwise none of us would be standing here talking. But shit, who needs a bigger bomb?"

"I'll say."

"So Mount 52 was wiped out. The handling room, too. Bridge had more holes than Swiss cheese."

"What about the men in the wardroom and CIC?"

"I yelled, 'Clear the space,' and we lit out with flames licking our asses. Nobody hurt, thank God. Also, officer's country on the second deck was burned out and flooded. That's pretty much it."

"We ready for sea?"

"In all respects, except for the Mark 6 stable element." The Mark 6 stable element was a steamer-trunk-sized device that calculated the ship's roll, pitch, and yaw and sent correcting signals to the directors and five-inch gun mounts.

"What happened?"

"Bastards in the shipyard cannibalized it. Their excuse was that the ship was to be scrapped. Then I put a stop to it. That was after they disassembled the thing and took most of it. So we can't shoot. And that's not good, because we're supposed to get under way tomorrow, join up with the *Franklin* and Task Force 58."

"Well, let's figure out something. I want us to be ready, stable element or not."

"Good luck. The guns will be punching holes in the waves," said Kelly.

"Anything else?"

"Well." Kelly faced outboard and stepped away from the others. He beckoned Ingram.

"What?"

"Something's been bothering me."

"Spit it out."

"We could have gone back for you." Kelly's eyes glittered. "Shit, Skipper, I was so mesmerized with keeping the plant going and putting out the fire, I plumb lost track of you. I gotta tell you, I haven't slept well since. The happiest day of my life was when I got the message you were alive. Even then, I've felt pretty shitty about this. I should have —"

"Hank!"

"Yes, sir?"

"Command of the ship had passed to you. Your first responsibility was to save your ship and her crew."

Falco rang a backing bell and with a roar from the little four-cylinder engine brought the gig to a stop alongside the *Maxwell*. Ingram slapped her hull plates and said, "And I'd say you did that rather admirably, don't you?"

"I just wanted to get it off my chest. Look. I'm sorry. I wish I could have done a better job —"

"Dammit, Hank. Why are you —"

The 1MC squealed and the quarterdeck bell rang *ding-ding, ding-ding*. The boatswain's mate of the watch announced, "*Maxwell*, arriving."

Ingram grabbed the Jacob's ladder and looked up. "Holy cow." The whole crew, turned out in whites, manned the rail at attention. He snapped, "Is this your idea of a joke?"

Kelly shrugged.

As Ingram stepped aboard, he couldn't help but notice a little furry shape, high in the shrouds, near the radar antennae. "I'll be damned," he muttered.

The boatswain's pipe sounded and four side boys snapped to attention. Ingram gained the deck, saluted the flag on the fantail, and then saluted the officer of the deck. It was Tony Duquette, wearing tailored dress khakis. *This kid still looks like he stepped from an Esquire ad.* "Permission to come aboard, sir?"

Duquette gave a snappy salute. "Granted. Welcome back, Captain." He waved toward the fantail. "Sir, if you don't mind?"

Ingram turned to Kelly, his eyebrows raised.

Kelly said, "It was Rocko's idea. He's back there waiting to pin a medal on you. So buck up, sailor, and mind your manners."

Dammit. Ingram wanted to slip aboard the *Maxwell* quietly. "Lead the way, Lieutenant," he said to Duquette.

Duquette steered a path to the fantail. Along the way, Ingram checked the men standing at the rail and was surprised at the faces he didn't recognize: replacements for the ones who didn't make it.

" 'Ten-hut!" Men in ranks were gathered among the 40-millimeter gun tubs and depth-charge racks on the fantail. Dais and microphone were situated just under Mount 55's gun barrel. The *Maxwell*'s officers were situated before the dais. They all looked familiar except for two new ensigns and a jaygee. In ranks, port and starboard, were the captains and executive officers of the *Milford*, *Wallace*, *Smith*, *Thomas*, *Cluster*, *Striff*, and *Geiler*.

Play the game. At the dais was Rear Admiral Theodore R. Myszynski, newly selected commander of Destroyer Forces, South Pacific. Ingram hadn't seen the thick-necked, fireplug-shaped Myszynski since he'd been selected for rear admiral and bumped upstairs. The admiral looked fit. His face wasn't as drawn compared to those horrible days a year ago at Guadalcanal, when he was squadron commander of Destroyer Squadron Twelve.

Standing at stiff attention beside Myszynski was Jerry Landa, staring into the distance, his face expressionless. And — Ingram did a double take — on Landa's left was Lieutenant Commander Oliver Toliver, leaning on a cane. "I'll be damned." He fought the impulse to walk over and shake Ollie's hand.

"Is there a problem, Commander?" asked Myszynski.

Ingram drew to attention and saluted. "No, sir."

"Well, then, we can begin." Myszynski pumped his fist once, and a band standing on the *Dixie*'s 03 level struck up "The Star-Spangled Banner."

When it was over Myszynski said, "Mr. Kelly, if you please?"

"Aye, aye, sir." Hank Kelly stood on the dais and pulled a notepad from his pocket: "Attention to orders." The loudspeaker squealed horribly, and Kelly, after glaring at the sailor manning the control console on the deck, began: "Whereas, Commander Alton C. Ingram, commanding officer of the U.S.S. *Maxwell* (DD 525) on the evening of 7 June 1944 was thrown into the water after a particularly vicious attack by Japanese dive-bombers . . ."

Ingram stood before Myszynski as Kelly droned on. After a while, Myszynski's eyes twinkled, and he whispered, "Seems like I'm throwing a medal around your neck as often as that monkey craps, Mr. Ingram." Myszynski nodded toward the mast.

Ingram looked over Myszynski's shoulder. Dexter was still up in the rigging. "From now on, I'll stay out of trouble, Admiral. Promise."

"See that you do."

Ingram tried to catch Landa's eye to say hello. But Landa just stood at attention, feet planted to the deck, eyes fixed on the distance, lips pressed together.

Kelly finished his proclamation, stood back, and handed an oblong box to Myszynski, who said, "It gives me great pleasure to award you the Navy Distinguished Service Medal, Commander." There was an awkward silence while Myszynski pinned on the medal. Then he asked, "Any comments, Commander Ingram?"

Ingram said, "I think I'd like to, Admiral."

"Have at it." Myszynski backed away and covered the mike. "Just be brief. It's hot out here."

Ingram stood before the microphone. "I've been away for a while, and on returning just now, I noticed some new faces. So I'd like to welcome you aboard the fightingest destroyer in the Pacific. If you haven't found out already, we get things done here, as a ship and as an integral unit of DESDIV 11.

"We're here to do a job and we shove off soon to rejoin the Big Blue. Now, on any other ship, the rule is, if you do your jobs as you've been trained, you get by. But I expect better than that. You have a higher purpose just by virtue of being aboard this ship. Therefore, I expect 110 percent. The idea is, if you take care of the *Maxwell*, she'll take care of you. Remember that, and you'll do just fine. And so will the *Maxwell*.

"To the officers and men of the *Maxwell*, my heartfelt thanks for the hard work you put into getting her ready to fight again. To the officers and men of the other ships in company here, I wish to thank you for your kind thoughts and for your attendance. So the *Max* is back. Together, we'll lick the Japs all the way to Tokyo.

"That is all."

Ingram stepped back and said, "Mr. Kelly. You may dismiss the men."

Myszynski shook Ingram's hand. "Congratulations, Todd. Your stable-element parts should be here any day. In the meantime, keep your nose dry. No need to accompany me to the gangway. Enjoy your little party here while you can. Lord knows, you'll be in the thick of it soon."

"Thanks, Admiral."

Myszynski walked off and was gonged across the inboard destroyers to the *Dixie*.

Ingram shook hands with other skippers and execs who guffawed and slapped him on the back. Landa and Toliver were at the end of the line. Ingram and Landa shook hands. Landa's grip was like picking up a dead rat.

Ingram moved to Toliver and said, "So now it's Ollie the spy?"

Toliver raised his cane and whacked Ingram lightly on the hip. He said in a George Raft voice, "Better watch it, buster, or I'll have you rubbed out."

"What brings you all the way out here?"

"They want me to talk to you."

"About what?"

"About what happened. Hasn't anybody debriefed you?"

"Not that I know of." He nodded to Landa. "I told him everything. Why?"

Toliver groaned. "Unfortunately, Captain Landa hasn't been trained for this sort of thing."

Landa rolled his eyes.

Toliver continued, "I'm sure you picked up some valuable intelligence."

"All I did was ride a Jap submarine for two months. Bastards had me scrubbing bilges. You should have seen what they —"

"Can we continue this in my cabin?" asked Landa. "Say at 1600. I have an idea that Mr. Ingram would like to catch up on what's happening with his ship."

"Fine with me," said Ingram. "I'd like to make sure we're ready for sea."

Landa stood to his full height. "That's my point. How the hell can I send you to sea without a stable element?"

"But Rocko said — I mean the Admiral said —"

"He was just making nice to you. As far as I'm concerned, you'll be sitting here on your dead ass while we're out there putting it on the line for you, Navy Distinguished Service Medal and all."

"Jerry, what the hell's wrong?"

Landa pointed. "You ever heard of kamikazes, Mr. Ingram?"

Ingram remained silent. Months back, he'd been through a number of versions of the kamikaze attack. Landa, too.

"You're not getting under way, Mr. Ingram. Instead, you'll be sitting here in port acting as guard ship like any fleet tug or garbage scow. And the pathetic part is that I need you. Kamikazes are not fun. You got that, mister?"

"Yes, sir."

"Then get busy and fix that damn thing." Landa pointed up to the rigging. "And get that goddam monkey off this ship." Pulling a face, Landa said, "No need to accompany me, Mr. Ingram. See you at 1600, sharp." He spun on his heel and walked off.

THIRTY-NINE

27 SEPTEMBER 1944
U.S.S. *MAXWELL* (DD 525)
BAIE DE LA MOSELLE
NOUMÉA, NEW CALEDONIA

A lighter was moored alongside the *Maxwell*. Tons of food and supplies snaked aboard her to be stowed below or passed over to the three inboard destroyers. It was an all-hands working party. Men sweated and groaned and cursed under a hot, piercing sun as crates, boxes, and frozen cartons were passed hand to hand. Moored forward of the lighter was a self-propelled fueling barge, low in the water, pumping fuel oil into the ship's bunkers. Elsewhere on the ships, gun mounts trained about, radar antennae spun, torpedomen hauled out their torpedoes and ran checks while fire controlmen swarmed over their gun directors.

For Ingram, the afternoon was a flurry of inspections and reports. By 1500, he returned to his in-port cabin and, unloading a stack of personnel files from his in basket, began interviewing the new men.

Hank Kelly knocked on the bulkhead. "Captain, don't you have a date?"

Ingram checked his watch: 1555. "Ye gods, where does it all go?" He looked outside, seeing five men still waiting in the passageway. Grabbing his garrison hat, he said, "Back to your duty stations. I'll pick this up later."

The sailors turned away and groaned with the realization they had to leave the relative coolness of the passageway and go back to passing crates and boxes.

They headed for the quarterdeck. Ingram said to Kelly, "Lost track of the time."

"That's what execs are for."

"How's it going?"

"Provisioning about fifty percent complete. Fuel topped off. We get the ammo barge tomorrow morning just after *Thomas*, *Geiler*, and *Striff* shove off."

"Anything new on the Mark 6?"

"Just got a message from Pearl. They're flying one in."

"ETA?"

Kelly shrugged. "They didn't say exactly."

"Find out, okay?" Ingram saluted the flag and the OOD, and was gonged over to the *Geiler*. He continued over to the *Striff*, finding Russ Nelson, her skipper, a man of large proportions, up on the 01 level, talking to Rick Frey, skipper of the *Geiler*.

Nelson casually balanced a putting iron over his shoulder while Frey juggled golf balls. Ingram called up to them, "That all you guys ever think of?" The two were scratch golfers.

Nelson said, "We've laid a carpet up here in the forty-millimeter gun tub. Not bad for a putting green. Ready to try your luck? Say a buck a ball?"

Ingram knew they were watching the provisioning, making sure it went well. "Can't. On my way to see the Commodore."

Frey and Nelson exchanged glances.

"What's wrong?"

Frey leaned down. "Go easy, Todd. He's on a rampage."

"Don't I know it." Ingram walked on.

"Hey, Todd," yelled Nelson. "Wanna whack a few balls off the fantail after chow?"

"If Jerry doesn't throw me in hack."

"Make sure your teeth are brushed and shoes shined," Frey called after him.

It took another five minutes for him to wind his way around crate-burdened sailors aboard the *Thomas* and find Landa's cabin. Ingram rapped his knuckles on the bulkhead and walked in. "Afternoon."

Landa sat at a desk, Toliver in a side chair. "Where the hell have you been?" Landa demanded.

Ingram held up his watch. "Jerry, I'm four minutes late. What is wrong with you?"

Landa steepled his fingers and looked up at Ingram. "Do I have to brace you to attention, Mr. Ingram?"

Ingram's jaw dropped. And he noted a shocked expression on Toliver's face as well. *The hell with this.* Resisting the temptation to click his heels, he drew to attention. "Commander Ingram reporting as ordered, sir."

"At ease. What's the status of your Mark 6?"

"One is being flown in from Pearl, sir. Top priority."

"When?"

Ingram felt his bile rising. He began, "Why don't you take a flying —"

"Stop it, both of you, dammit!" Toliver rose to his feet. "I don't know what the hell is going on here, but I didn't travel four thousand miles to watch you two bicker like a couple of schoolboys. Now come on. You're supposed to be friends. Or was your son named after someone else, Todd?"

Landa shot to his feet. The three glared at each other. Landa shouted, "Mr. Toliver, Commander, you'd better . . . I . . ." He pinched the bridge of his nose. "Okay, dammit." He sat. "First time I've been jumped by a junior officer. I'll let it go this time."

"Your secret is safe with me." Ingram couldn't help it.

Landa's eyes flared for a moment. Then he waved them down. "Shit flows downstream. Rocko's been on me and Burke has been on him. When Burke learned of the *Maxwell*'s Mark 6 cumshaw deal, he blew a fuse." He pointed at Ingram. "I realize you weren't here, but your exec's to blame and ultimately, you."

"Baloney. Hank was on leave in the States with about ninety percent of the rest of the crew. There was one junior officer here when it happened. And the ship was a blackened, stinking mess sitting in drydock. It was outright theft. What the hell do you expect?"

Landa sighed. "Get it fixed. That's what I expect. When do you think it'll happen?"

"Soon, tomorrow maybe. That's all I can say for now," Ingram said.

Landa said, "Okay. Keep me informed. Now, Ollie wants to ask some questions. You need a yeoman, Ollie?"

"No, sir." He reached over and clicked on a machine. "Got this instead."

"What's that?" asked Ingram.

"Wire recorder. With this thing, I don't need shorthand. Okay, here we go." He pushed another button and held up a mike.

"Wednesday, 27 September 1944, aboard the U.S.S. *Morgan J. Thomas*, in Nouméa Harbor, New Caledonia. Present are Captain Jeremiah T. Landa, Commander Alton C. Ingram, and myself, Lieutenant Commander Oliver J. Toliver. Time: 1617." Toliver looked up. "Okay, Commander Ingram. Can you tell us what happened?"

Ingram whispered, "Who do I talk to?"

Toliver pointed to the mike. "Don't worry, it'll pick you up. Relax. You don't need to lean forward."

"Okay." Ingram closed his eyes for a moment, then began, "On the evening of 7 June 1944, the U.S.S. *Maxwell* was on a recon mission for Task Force 58 as an advanced unit."

"And you were skipper?" Toliver interrupted.

"That's correct. It was near sunset and we were having trouble with our air search radar . . ."

Ingram went on for over thirty minutes; his voice raced as he recounted incidents such as depth chargings or Penang or Madagascar. Finally, he finished. Taking out a handkerchief, he wiped perspiration from his forehead.

Landa leaned on an elbow. "You okay?"

"Never better." In reality, he felt as if he were going to pass out.

"Bullshit. Wait here." Landa stepped

into the wardroom and returned with a pitcher of lemonade. He poured three glasses and passed them around.

Ingram gulped the whole glass, then smacked his lips. "Thanks. Any questions, Ollie?"

Toliver thought for a moment. "Why expose themselves in restricted waters like Madagascar? And why waste all that time swapping gold? Why two submarines?"

"I've got an idea," said Ingram.

"Shoot," said Toliver.

Ingram said, "The *I-49* was their ticket to freedom."

"What do you mean?" asked Toliver.

"Pretty neat when you think about it. In February, they faked the sinking of the *I-49*. She was a cargo sub with lots of provisions, so it was easy for her to hide somewhere, probably near Madagascar, waiting for the *I-57*. When we arrived in Madagascar, we transferred the gold to the *I-49*, by then a ghost ship, one that had been stricken from the Japanese register of ships."

"Ahhhh," said Toliver.

"So now they send the *I-57* on to France, sans the gold," Ingram continued. "And that's where Taubman was to have come in. A language expert. I'll bet he was the brains to set up a system ashore to bank it. Remember, he told me he wanted to get across France. That means Switzerland."

"What about the *I-49* crew? The manifests wouldn't have jibed. The Germans would have figured that out." Toliver faked a German accent. *"Ve haf vays of makink you talk. Ver ist Captain Shimada, bitte?"*

"I think their plan must have been to scuttle the *I-57* close to shore. Close enough for Taubman to blend into the civilian population and for the crew to get to Spain or Portugal and then eventually on to where they were to meet," said Ingram.

"So now it's the *I-49* running around Madagascar?" asked Landa.

"Mmmm. With a wobbly shaft, too," said Ingram.

Landa said, "Maybe we should tell Todd about the messages that —"

Toliver's hand shot out, his face a dark mask.

When Landa went silent, Ingram said, "Tell me what?"

"Was that German really a submariner?" asked Toliver.

"Tell me what, dammit?" demanded Ingram.

Toliver and Landa kept silent.

"You guys are acting like a couple of fraternity kids."

Toliver picked up the mike and said, "This concludes the interview." Then he turned off the machine. "Don't you get it, Todd?"

"What am I supposed to get?"

"It's classified, so shut up."

"Ah." Ingram turned to Landa. "I've been jumped by the same wise-ass junior officer. Can't we put him on report or something?"

"Maybe change his orders and shove him down a hole," Landa agreed. Then he knit his brow. "But really . . . Why the gold?"

"That part's easy," said Toliver. He leaned forward and said, "With what Todd is saying, it confirms our suspicion that it's a *yakuza* operation."

"Ya . . . what?" asked Ingram.

"Yakuza," said Toliver. "It means 'eight-nine-three' in Japanese: *ya, ku, za.*"

"So what?" said Landa.

"Well, that's a Japanese card game, sort of like blackjack."

Landa rolled his eyes. "Makes all the sense in the world to me."

"Jerry, just listen, will you? The *yakuza* is Japanese organized crime. Kind of like the Black Hand or the Mafia. These guys have been around for centuries. We think it dates back to the early 1600s when a group known as the *kabuki-mono,* which means 'crazy ones,' roamed Japan. They were warriors, a samurai offshoot. But in peacetime, the *kabuki-mono* had nothing to do. So they wandered about Japan, taking up robbing and plundering to make ends meet.

"Another group of guys known as the *machi-yakko,* which means 'city servant,' rose up against the *kabuki-mono.* They were Robin Hood sort of guys who beat back the *kabuki-mono.* So now the *machi-yakko* became the bad guys: gamblers, street vendors. Quite simply, they played a lot of blackjack: *ya, ku, za.*

"Since then, they've gone into every variety of crime from dope to prostitution to all kinds of betting and gambling. Over the years, they've accumulated a hoard of cash. Some say they have backed Tojo and the Jap war machine."

"We have the *yakuza* to thank for Pearl Harbor?" asked Ingram.

"Not sure about that. But what I am sure of is that they're scared of everything falling down around them when the victorious Americans walk down the Ginza."

"Those bastards will never surrender," said Landa. "We're going to have to dig 'em out of their holes, one by one. It'll take years."

"Maybe so," said Toliver. "But smart money in Japan sees the handwriting on the wall right now."

"What's the Ginza?" asked Ingram.

"Main street, Tokyo. Now let me illuminate. People in the *yakuza* have connections everywhere, especially the military. They're trying to get their money out of the country. We've already seen Japanese gold or diamonds showing up in Peru; same thing in Argentina, even Mexico."

Howard Endicott, the *Thomas*'s skipper, knocked and walked in. "Refueling complete, supplies are all on board, Commodore. We'll be ready to get under way in all respects by 1800."

"Tomorrow at 0800 is soon enough for me," said Landa. He nodded to Ingram. "Except for our stable-element boy, of course."

Ingram shot to his feet.

Landa said, "Don't get your balls in an uproar. Just kidding. Look, you guys, how 'bout dinner tonight. The four of us. On me at the Hôtel Pacifique? Arleigh Burke's table. Say 1930?"

"Snazzy," said Endicott.

Ingram and Toliver traded glances. "Never miss a chance to flog the Old Man's expense account," said Toliver.

"You know, we just have to do something with Ollie Triplesticks," said Landa.

Endicott said, "I'm short a snipe in my after engine room. Send him over to me."

"Just kidding," said Toliver.

"Not a bad idea," said Ingram.

Endicott said, "Yeah, you got his service

record, Commodore? Ollie would fit right in. It's only a hundred fifteen down there . . ."

"Wait a minute," said Toliver.

"Perfect." Landa yanked the phone from its bracket. "Get me the yeoman and the chief engineer."

Done in French Provincial, the three-story Hôtel Pacifique stood high on Semaphore Hill. With a panorama of the harbor, one could see far out into the Pacific on a clear day. The view was especially spectacular from the expansive front veranda with its thick marble balustrade. But the place teemed with Allied military personnel, mainly American naval officers. Tobacco smoke rolled out the windows along with the sound of glasses tinkling, bawdy barracks ballads, and an occasional shout. Two beefy shore patrolmen and two Marines stood near the front entrance, clubs dangling from their belts, ready to mete out justice, it mattered not whether the offender was officer or enlisted.

A light gray jeep with U.S. Navy markings pulled up and parked in the VIP section. Ignoring protocol, Ingram, Landa, and Endicott jumped out and waited for Toliver to hobble over the hard-packed gravel. When he made it, he called, "What the hell are you guys hanging around here for?"

They walked up the stairs and across the veranda, and pushed through a set of revolving doors. The lobby was a small-scale rendition of the St. Francis Hotel in San Francisco. At the ballroom entrance stood the maître d', poring over a ledger. He had thick, bushy eyebrows. *"Oui, monsieur."*

Landa said, "Captain Burke's party of four is here."

The maître d' looked over Landa's shoulder. "And Captain Burke is . . . ?"

"Unfortunately, Captain Burke was called into a strategy session with Admirals Mitscher and Halsey. They're also unable to attend tonight. I'm sorry."

The waiter ran his hand over his chin, deciding.

Landa slid a ten-dollar bill onto the ledger.

"Oui, mon Capitaine." The maître d' signaled a waiter. "Table 42." He bowed, and the waiter led them off.

They walked into a smoke-filled room with perhaps fifty tables covered in fine linens, arranged in two levels around an empty dance floor. The patrons were men; ninety percent were in uniform. A large round table, with seating for eight, was set up across the room, and a floral arrangement with a French tricolor was set in the middle. A ten-piece orchestra wearing threadbare white dinner jackets played light dining music.

"Nice job getting us in, Captain," said Toliver.

"A little bit of French grease never hurt," said Landa.

"I'll bet Arleigh Burke is a thousand miles away," said Ingram.

"Actually," said Landa, "he's on the *Dixie* right now, talking to Rocko over dinner. They're discussing the *Franklin*'s op plan."

"All work and no play," said Ingram.

"Arleigh is a workaholic," agreed Landa. "Hey, there's gambling upstairs if you fellows want to try your luck after dinner."

The waiter cleared his throat. "Would you like something to drink?"

"Martini," said Landa. "Beefeaters."

"Make it two," said Toliver.

"Scotch," said Ingram.

"You have bourbon?" asked Endicott.

The waiter shrugged.

"What do you have?" asked Landa.

"Ummm. We do have Mount Blanc Ale."

"That's three-point-two monkey piss," Endicott growled.

The waiter gave another shrug. "Vermouth?"

Toliver pulled out his wallet and palmed a fifty-dollar bill. "Do you have something to go with the vermouth?"

"Oui, m'sieur."

He handed it over. “Then get it and it had better be good.”

“Oui.” The waiter grabbed the bill and rushed off.

“Not bad, Ollie, not bad at all,” said Landa.

“French grease, high-grade,” said Toliver.

Landa turned to Ingram and asked lightly, “Everything okay at home?”

Ingram gave Landa a look and then pulled a photo from his wallet. “Here’s your namesake. Pass it on over to Ollie.” It was a picture of a smiling Helen in the backyard, holding the baby in her arms.

Toliver leaned over. “Damn. Good-looking kid. Smart, too, I’ll bet.”

Landa held it up for Endicott. “The kid is smart. Notice, Howard, that he looks a lot like Helen. That where it comes from.”

“I can’t argue with that,” said Ingram. He lowered his voice and leaned over to Landa. “Helen sends her best.” He offered his hand. “Come on, Jerry, time to get on with life.”

“I’ll be damned,” Landa said. He took Ingram’s hand in both of his and they shook warmly. “Thanks.”

Ingram’s eyes twinkled. “And congratulations.”

“Huh?”

“Laura sends her best, too,” said Ingram.

“She told you?”

"Yeah, why not?"

"Last time we talked, she wanted to keep it a secret. Something about her career."

"Well, right now, she's flashing your rock and bragging to everyone in sight that she's lassoed this knockout Navy captain."

"What's this about a rock?" asked Toliver.

Landa said, "Lemme explain. You see . . ."

Ingram stiffened, both hands grabbing the table.

"Todd, you okay?" asked Landa.

Ingram slowly rose, his eyes fixed across the room.

Landa could have sworn he heard Ingram growl. "Todd, what the hell is it?" He looked over to the French table. Six well-dressed men in business suits were pulling out chairs and sitting. "You know them?"

"Son of a bitch," muttered Ingram. He walked across the dance floor.

Landa got up and followed. Endicott, too, with Toliver hobbling behind. They caught up with Ingram just as he reached the French table.

"Taubman!" Ingram barked.

A man looked up, his eyes wide. *"Gott."* Then he sat back, his face draining of color. *"Nein, nein. Du solst tot sein,"* he gasped.

Landa grabbed Ingram's arm. "Todd, come on. This is the French governor's table. We haven't —"

Ingram shook himself loose and walked up to the man. "You self-serving sonofabitch!" With a doubled fist, he hit him right in the nose.

Blood spurted as the man flew backward and fell to the floor. Ingram jumped on his chest and delivered two more punches while the civilians looked on, horrified.

Landa dashed around and grabbed Ingram's arm. "Shit, Todd, knock it —"

"Murderer," Ingram roared. He wrenched his arm loose and hit the man again. Endicott and Toliver rushed over, grabbing Ingram's arms, wrestling him to the floor as he growled and spat.

Suddenly, the fight went out of Ingram and he went limp. Whistles blew and the Marines and Navy SPs rushed up.

Landa stood and held up a hand. "It's under control, here, Sergeant. Go on back to your post."

The sergeant walked around and yanked Ingram to his feet, "Not sure, sir. Looks like Pierre's Bar down on the wharf."

Landa said, "A misunderstanding, Sergeant. I order you to return to your post."

The sergeant said, "I'll have to write it up, Captain. Orders is orders."

"Then go write it up. Please leave now."

"Yes, sir." The SPs walked off.

The civilians were babbling in French, one wiping blood off the injured man's face and trying to help him to his feet. Another civilian walked over to Ingram. "What the hell's the meaning of this?"

"Who are you?" demanded Landa.

"Keith Jardine, State Department. Have you people gone insane?"

Ingram waved a finger. "That man is a Nazi. His name is Martin Taubman."

"The man on the *I-57*?" asked Landa.

"One and the same," said Ingram.

"Impossible. He's dead," said Landa.

"Well, this sonofabitch somehow made it," said Ingram.

"This is all nonsense," said Jardine. "He's Henri Dufor of the French Red Cross."

"Bullshit! He's a spy," Ingram yelled.

Jardine stepped within six inches of Ingram. "You've just attacked a civilian employee of an Allied nation. So pack your bags, mister. I hope you're ready to spend lots of time in Leavenworth."

FORTY

28 SEPTEMBER 1944
U.S.S. *DIXIE* (AD 14)
BAIE DE LA MOSELLE
NOUMÉA, NEW CALEDONIA

The eight destroyers nested alongside the *Dixie* hoisted their colors smartly at 0800. Except for the *Maxwell*, the others were ready to get under way: boilers and generators on the line, rudder, electrical, and radio circuits tested. Their whaleboats were griped in, and the sea and anchor details were set on the fo'c'sles, bridges, CICs and fantails. Under an overcast sky, the air dripped with humidity as sailors smoked cigarettes and drank coffee, waiting for the order to single up lines. They shouted across the ships to one another, cracked jokes, and negotiated last-minute movie trades. Skippers paced their bridges, checking their watches, the universal question being, "What the hell are we waiting for?"

The holdup was in a compartment on the *Dixie*'s 03 level. It was the main office of Rear Admiral Theodore R. ("Rocko") Myszynski, Commander, Destroyer Forces,

Southwest Pacific. Ignoring the china and silver service carefully arranged on a side table, the admiral sat at his desk, drinking coffee from a Dixie cup. Typical of Myszynski, his office was dark; only the desk lamp was lit, and a small rubber-bladed fan whirred in the corner. Standing at attention before Myszynski's desk was Commander Alton C. Ingram, commanding officer of the *Maxwell.* Seated to the right of the desk was the pipe-puffing Captain Arleigh A. Burke, chief of staff to Vice Admiral Marc A. Mitscher. On the other side of the desk was Captain Jeremiah T. Landa, commodore of Destroyer Division Eleven. Seated on a couch behind Ingram was Lieutenant Commander Oliver Toliver III, deputy intelligence officer to the Commander, Twelfth Naval District.

"Dammit!" Myszynski sprang to his feet and smashed his fist on the desk. Pencils jumped. Coffee spilled as he thundered, "Who the hell do you think you are, Commander?"

A long silence followed. Finally, Ingram said, "Admiral — I —"

"I didn't give you permission to speak, you dumb bastard." Myszynski checked his watch. "Almost 0805, Jerry. Your boys must be getting nervous."

Landa said, "Yes, sir, Rocko . . . er, Admiral."

Burke said, "The *Franklin* has steam up and is ready to go."

"So do we, Arleigh," said Landa. "We're ready to jump."

Burke puffed his pipe, blue smoke shrouding his face. "That's nice to know. We're supposed to clear the breakwater at 1100. So we need you out there screening for us, Captain Landa." Burke represented Vice Admiral Marc A. Mitscher, commander of Task Force 58, which, in turn, was part of Admiral Raymond Spruance's "Big Blue — Fifth Fleet," part of the Central Pacific Command under Fleet Admiral Chester Nimitz. Burke puffed some more. "But then again, I'm just a visitor in these parts, Captain Landa."

Ingram noticed that Landa called Burke "Arleigh," while Burke addressed Landa as "Captain."

"Okay, we'll break this up soon," said Myszynski. He turned to Ingram. "Honestly, Mr. Ingram. What a dumb-shit thing to do. Henri Dufor is a high-ranking French official. He's in charge of the International Red Cross, Pacific Region. Does a lot for our boys in POW camps."

"He wasn't doing much for our boys in Penang, Admiral."

"Watch it, Mr. Ingram. Your slack has just about run out," Myszynski growled.

"Yes, sir. But your Mr. Dufor of the Red

Cross was right there with me, wearing a Nazi uniform, calmly looking on as the Japs bayoneted an American POW for stealing an apple. You see, a Jap Army captain shot Sergeant Baumgartner in the back with a pistol. Then a Jap guard walked up and calmly finished him off with a bayonet right through the chest. You should have heard him scream, Admiral. He —"

Landa shot to his feet. "Any more of that, Mr. Ingram, and I'll have your ass in the brig. Do you read me?"

Ingram realized he'd gone too far. He also realized that he'd already told the story and that Myszynski and Landa were, most likely, trying to keep it in the family. *Pipe down.* "Yes, sir. I'm sorry, sir."

Landa sat.

Myszynski ran a hand over his bald head. "To think I was pinning a medal on this idiot just yesterday. I'd take it away, but then we'd all look like a bunch of saps." He turned to Landa. "Has the doc seen this guy?"

"First thing I checked this morning, Admiral. Folder says he's medically qualified," said Landa.

"Send him back to the medic. They'll think of something. He's been at it too long. Shit. Corregidor, the Philippines, Guadalcanal, and the Slot. And then riding a Jap sub for six weeks is enough to scramble anyone's brains. I recommend we ship him back to the States."

Ingram squeezed his eyes closed, unable to believe they were doing this to him. *Helen was right. I've been out here too long. Look what happened after just six short hours on the job.* But the thought hit him: *that was Taubman. I'm sure of it.*

He flexed his fist, the knuckles chafed. *Not sure if I give a damn.*

Burke spoke for the first time. "Don't you think that's a bit harsh, Admiral?"

Myszynski's jaw dropped. He had reckoned Burke wanted Ingram dealt with severely. "He's one of my boys, Arleigh. And I know when a man's had enough."

Burke stood and walked up to Ingram. "Yes, sir. But we're all destroyermen here. So I'd rather see us settle this among destroyermen rather than kick him out and make him someone else's problem." He said to Ingram, "Stand at ease."

Ingram shifted to parade rest.

"I said, 'At ease,' sailor."

Ingram relaxed and looked into Burke's ice-blue eyes.

"What got into you? Were you drinking? Smoking something? Maybe overheated? I've seen sailors go crazy after half a beer. Maybe it was —"

"Sir, the man was Martin Taubman,"

said Ingram. "I should know. I know his voice. As the admiral points out, I rode with him in a Jap submarine for six weeks. We played chess, talked opera, politics, mountain climbing, our families. His father was a Wehrmacht general killed in Russia. He has a half brother in Switzerland. His dog's name was Fritz. His first girlfriend's name was Trudie. They went together when he was fourteen. She was a glider pilot and he —"

"Shipped out on the *I-57*?" said Burke.

"Yes, sir. I watched her shove off. I was supposed to go with Taubman to Europe. But the Japs changed their minds at the last minute and sent me over to the *I-49*. Turns out they wanted to kill me."

Just then someone knocked. "Enter," said Myszynski.

Hank Kelly walked in and handed a note to Ingram. Without a word, he walked out, the door clicking softly behind him.

"Well?" said Myszynski.

Ingram read the note and announced, "Mark 6 stable element's aboard, sir. They're installing it now."

"Well, that's something," said Burke, sitting down.

"Let me try something," said Landa. He stood and looked over Ingram's shoulder at Toliver. "I'm going to push the limits here a little bit, so I want everybody to just keep calm." Landa's gaze leveled on Ingram. "What I'm about to tell you is Top Secret. Do you understand that?"

Burke rumbled. "Captain —"

"It's okay, Arleigh. Trust me," Landa said. "Todd, we know for a fact that the *I-57* was sunk en route to her destination. She didn't make it to France."

Ingram gasped, "You're kidding. How? Where?"

"Got her with a FIDO in the South Atlantic. We know she's down. It's been confirmed. Nothing but fifty dead Japs and one dead Kraut in her now. Your Mr. Taubman, may he rest in peace. And that's all I can tell you."

"But . . . that's . . ." Ingram's eyes darted from side to side.

Landa said, "Speaking of FIDOs, Arleigh."

Burke tamped tobacco in his pipe and relit it. "What is it?"

"*Mount Whitney* is still six hours out." The *Mount Whitney* was an ammunition ship.

"So?"

"She has four FIDO torpedoes for you," said Landa.

Burke's eyes narrowed. "I was told they were already aboard the *Franklin*."

"A mix-up in the manifest, Arleigh. They're still aboard the *Mount Whitney* and she's not here, yet," said Landa.

"Dammit." Burke smacked a fist in his palm. "We need those things." He rubbed his chin. "Maybe send some TBFs back for them. Naw, that's slow. Can only pick up one at a time." He checked his watch. "I'll think of something. We have to get going."

Myszynski said, "Right. Time's a-wasting. We have to end this. Okay, Arleigh, let's keep it among destroyermen." He turned to Landa. "He's your boy, Jerry. Let's hear what you have to recommend."

"Just give him to me. I'll keep him on a short tether," said Landa.

"As skipper of the *Maxwell*?" asked Myszynski.

"Yes, sir. Believe me, he won't be able to drop his pants without —"

"Gentlemen, may I?" Toliver struggled to his feet.

"Ollie, stay out of this," Landa growled.

"There's another possibility," said Toliver.

"Which is?" said Myszynski.

Toliver pointed toward Nouméa. "That the man Todd took down last night was indeed Korvettenkapitän Martin Taubman."

"You're full of it," said Myszynski.

Landa narrowed his eyes. "Looks like ONI School twisted your brain."

"I have a couple of ideas," said Toliver.

"Like what?" demanded Myszynski.

Toliver said, "Didn't you notice that the guy spoke German just before Todd smacked him?"

"A lot of Frenchmen speak German," said Landa.

"Maybe so," said Toliver. "But I caught some of it. Definitely that guy said, " '*Nein, nein,*' no, no. What followed was something like, 'You're dead,' or 'You're supposed to be dead.' Now why would someone who's scared to death speak in German and not French, supposedly his mother tongue?"

"You speak German, Ollie?" asked Myszynski.

"My folks took us through France, Germany, and Switzerland during the summer of 'thirty-eight. Some of it stuck, I'm afraid."

"He said, 'You're supposed to be dead'?" Myszynski repeated.

"Ummm."

Landa said, "Admiral, maybe we should let Ollie do his stuff. Cut Ingram a little slack. After all, his career is on the line here."

"Worse than that," said Myszynski.

"Well, for the time being, I recommend we see what happens. And let me" — with exaggeration, Landa checked his watch — "get my ships under way and I'll keep a muzzle on our boy, here."

"Arleigh?" Myszynski asked.

Burke puffed. "Ummm. Fine with me."

"Hot in here." Myszynski grabbed a swatter and whacked a large fly on the bulkhead. "Need another fan." He ran a hand over his head. "Okay, Ollie. You got forty-eight hours. If I don't hear anything by then, I'm relieving Commander Ingram here and sending him to the States on a medical."

"Come on, Rocko, that's bullshit!" said Landa.

Myszynski stood. "If you don't want to join him, then I suggest you go get DESDIV 11 under way, Captain."

"Aye, aye, sir," said Landa.

Myszynski turned to Ingram. "If you think that's punitive, you ought to see what awaits me when I go ashore this afternoon. The Frogs are pissed. Really pissed. They want you arrested. They've threatened to send a boat out here and physically take you off the *Maxwell*. They want you in jail. And when the Frogs throw you in jail, they throw the key away. So while the rest of you get to go play United States Navy, I've got to go ashore with a legal rep and fight the French —; right now without much conviction. So for now, Commander Ingram, you are persona non grata here and ashore." He pointed to Toliver. "Prove them wrong, Commander."

"Aye, aye, sir," said Toliver.

"How are you going to do it?" asked Landa.

Toliver rubbed his chin. "Like I said, I've got some ideas."

"Well, they'd better be good ones." Myszynski turned back to Ingram. "As for you, Commander, get your butt back to the *Maxwell* and finish up with that damned stable element."

"Yes, sir."

Burke said, "Admiral. I have a suggestion."

Myszynski exhaled. "Shoot."

"I need those FIDOs. Why not transfer them to the *Maxwell* when the *Mount Whitney* makes port. *Maxwell* can get under way and catch up to us and transfer them at sea. That way I get my FIDOs and the *Maxwell* is no longer under the noses of our allies, the French. Out of sight, out of mind."

"Give command of the ship back to this idiot?" said Myszynski.

Landa said, "Actually, sir, it's the best of all worlds. Plus it puts DESDIV 11 up to full strength."

Ingram dared to speak. "That works with me, sir. Except, there are civilians on board right now, setting up the stable element." He held up Kelly's note. "They might not be finished."

“Take ’em with you,” said Landa.
“Can we do that?” said Burke.
“War is hell,” said Landa.

FORTY-ONE

28 SEPTEMBER 1944
U.S.S. *DIXIE* (AD 14)
BAIE DE LA MOSELLE
NOUMÉA, NEW CALEDONIA

Myszynski caught Landa's elbow just after Burke and Ingram walked out. "Jerry, could I have a word with you?"

"Certainly, sir."

Toliver tarried by the door, so Myszynski called out, "What is it, Commander?"

"My plan, Admiral. I may need help."

"Well, spit it out."

"Er, in private, sir?"

Landa and Myszynski rolled their eyes. Myszynski said, "Well, if you aren't part of the solution, then you're part of the problem."

Toliver drew to parade rest, his cane behind his back. "I'll take that chance, sir."

"Very well. Wait outside."

"Thank you, sir." Toliver walked out.

When the door closed, Myszynski muttered, "Kid has guts." They stood awkwardly as Myszynski struck a match and puffed on a new cigar. "This won't take long, Jerry." After the cigar was well lighted, he looked up at Landa. "A word to the wise, Jerry. Lay off Arleigh Burke."

"What? Sir. You don't think that I —"

"I know exactly what you think." He plopped a foot on his chair. "You think he's a stuffed shirt, don't you?"

"No, sir. I sure . . ."

"And just because he doesn't tell farting jokes in the O-club, you look down on him."

Landa leveled his eyes on Myszynski. "Admiral, that was a transgression of my youth. I haven't done that in . . . in . . ."

"Days." Myszynski's eyes gleamed. Landa had carried the evening at the officers club three nights ago.

Myszynski spit out a piece of tobacco. "Listen, Jerry. Both captains, you and Burke, are close in numbers. He was a hell of a good destroyer skipper and a great squadron commander. Jeez, who will ever forget the Little Beavers? And you are, too. No argument there.

"You and I? We're cut from the same mold. We're mutts. Navy mutts. Non–Naval Academy mutts. And someday we'll retire, have a nice pension and go fishing or something. And that's it."

"Yes, sir."

"This isn't a trade school thing."

Landa flushed. "No?"

"Absolutely not. It's beyond that. Way beyond. Burke is cut out for great things. CNO. Maybe more. People recognize that, and he's already earmarked. Works his ass off at everything he does. And he does it well. They jumped him over a bunch of shoot-'em-up airdales to become Pete Mitscher's chief of staff. Can you imagine that? A surface guy, a tin can sailor, working for Mitscher instead of another zoomie? Who would have guessed? At first, Mitscher and Burke hated each other; they bickered like schoolkids for weeks. Then Burke put aside his pride and sank his teeth into the job. And he's doing one hell of a job. I gotta tell you, Arleigh Burke is our country's future."

"No argument there, Admiral. What do you want me to do?"

"Lay off."

"I . . ."

"Jerry."

"Yes, sir." Landa looked up. Myszynski was right. He'd been treating Burke like a fraternity pledge.

"Now go out there and putter with your ships. And send Toliver back in here."

"Yes, sir."

It took Toliver just three minutes to explain his plan. Myszynski nodded, scrawled out a note, and stuffed it into an envelope.

Handing it over to Toliver, he rumbled, "Worth a try. Here, this should open some doors for you."

"We'd be doing Todd a disservice if we didn't try."

Myszynski pulled a face.

"Sir."

"Okay." Myszynski reached for his hat and headed for the door. "You want to watch 'em get underway?"

Toliver ran a hand over his mouth to hide a smile. Like a kid in a railroad yard, Myszynski loved to watch his ships get under way. He longed to be back at sea. "I really should get going, sir. I have a feeling time's a-wasting. After all" — Toliver paused — "I only have forty-eight hours."

Myszynski flashed a look at Toliver that told him the forty-eight hours was very flexible; it was meant to scare Ingram more than anything. "Very well. You have transport?"

"Thought I'd take the next shore boat, sir."

"Well, if you're in such a hurry, you'd better take my barge."

"Yes, sir. Thank you, sir."

Saluting Myszynski, Toliver hobbled down a ladder to the second deck and stepped into a large compartment marked RADIO CENTRAL. A redheaded chief looked up from his desk.

"You the duty chief?" Toliver asked.

"Yes, sir."

Toliver took out a message pad and began to scribble. "Think you can raise our naval attaché in Geneva, Switzerland?"

The chief offered a hand at the vast accumulation of electrical machinery behind him. "With this rig, I can raise Buck Rogers on Pluto, Commander."

"Good."

Ten minutes later, Toliver was scrambling down the accommodation ladder to board Myszynski's well-appointed admiral's barge. They pulled away just as the *Maxwell* sounded one long blast, followed by three shorts, and backed clear of the nest. Like a squad of Marines in a precision drill, the seven other destroyers backed clear and, in short order, formed up and headed for the main harbor entrance. Dead in the water behind them lay the *Maxwell*, three hundred yards off the *Dixie*'s port beam. Then she slowly gathered way and moved back alongside the *Dixie* to tie up, and to wait.

An hour later, Toliver had his answer. He had called on Commander Andrew Hardesty, commander of security for the Naval Station, Nouméa, and was discussing the ramifications of Myszynski's note when a young radioman striker walked in. "Commander Toliver? Message for you, sir." He handed over a sealed envelope and a clipboard.

"Wow, that was quick." Toliver signed and then pulled the flimsy from the envelope and read:

DTG: 09292132Z
FM: USANAVSERVOPS — GENEVA
TO: TOLIVER, O III, LCDR, USN
C/O SOUTHPAC INTEL
COMMAND
INFO: ONI DEPT
REF: YOUR 09290847U

1. INTERNATIONAL RED CROSS, GENEVA, VICHY, OR PARIS HAS NO LISTING FOR HENRI DUFOR, DIRECTOR PACIFIC REGION.
2. INTERNATIONAL DIRECTOR RED CROSS PACIFIC REGION IS STUART KILLINGSWORTH, MELBOURNE AUSTRALIA.
3. PLS ADVISE FURTHER INQUIRY REQUIRED.

BT

Toliver smacked the flimsy with the back of his hand. "Son of a bitch. I knew the guy was a phoney." He looked up and handed the message over to Hardesty.

"Andrew, I need a big favor."

Hardesty rolled his eyes. "Something tells me I'm not going to like this."

"Read it, then tell me."

Hardesty read the message, gave a low whistle, and then said, "Okay, what is it?"

"I have to know where Henri Dufor is staying."

Hardesty drummed his fingers. "Actually, *I* can do that. The French share listings of all military and civilians in and out of Nouméa."

"Okay, good. Next, I need transportation and some muscle."

"Right now?"

"You bet."

Hardesty looked over his duty roster. "All we have right now are two SPs and a jeep."

"Is that the best you can do?"

"Bad timing. Our security force is at a two-hour presentation on prostitution."

"When do they get back?"

Hardesty shook his head. "After lunch, I'm afraid."

The jeep headed toward the nickel plant in the northwest section of town where its tall stack could be seen gushing black smoke. Preston, a six-three, 220 pound bosun's mate with close-cropped blond hair, was at the wheel. Toliver sat in the passenger seat, and Rimini, a dark, thin, curly-haired third-class machinist's mate, sat in the back. Both wore dungarees and carried .45s in leather holsters; an M-1 carbine lay across Rimini's lap. A .45 was stuffed in Toliver's belt, under his jacket.

"So, Mr. Toliver, what did you take in college?" asked Rimini. His hat was off, his hair whipping in the wind.

"Prelaw," said Toliver. The closer they drew to the smelter, the shabbier the neighborhood became. Strange place for a Red Cross diplomat, he thought as the streets turned to cobblestone.

"Rue Descartes, here we go," said Preston, turning left. "Ummm, damn buildings all look alike. What's the number again, sir?"

"Rue Descartes 945," said Toliver.

"So, you gonna be a lawyer when the war's over, Mr. Toliver?" Rimini asked.

"Not sure," Toliver replied. Suddenly, a strong sewage odor gripped him.

"Peeeeou," Rimini said. "Ain't nothing stunk like that since I was digging *benjo* ditches in boot camp." Then he leaned forward. "So why'd you take prelaw if you ain't gonna be a lawyer, Mr. Toliver?"

"Shaddup, Benne," said Preston.

Because my father forced me to, kid. Toliver whipped out a handkerchief and clamped it over his nose. "It's okay. I don't know, Rimini. I wanted a liberal education."

"Liberal, huh? Me, I wanna be a lawyer. My dad owns a grocery store in Brooklyn, and the wholesalers are screwing him out of his profit. 'Mark up your stuff or get lost,' they tell him. Then the numbers guys move in. Then the protection guys. He and Ma don't have a day's peace that someone's trying to stick a hand in their pockets. Now me, I'm gonna be a lawyer, work for the D.A., and throw all them bums in —"

"Nine-four-five," said Preston. They drew up before a ramshackle two-story building. A faded, paint-chipped sign announced Hôtel Cap Camarat. Two old men sat in shadows near the front door while a half dozen children played a street game two doors down. Preston switched off the ignition and ratcheted the hand brake. "Nice lookin' place, huh?"

"Simply wonderful," said Toliver.

"We had trouble out here before, sir. And" — Preston slapped his forehead — "I remember now. This hotel's been off-limits to all service personnel for at least six months." Preston turned to Rimini. "You ready, Benne?"

Rimini jammed the butt of his carbine on his hip and ran the bolt, chambering a round. "Uh-huh."

"Well, set the safety, dope, so you don't blow off your damned head," said Preston, getting out.

"Uh-huh." Squaring his hat on his head, Rimini climbed out and alighted like a cat.

The clerk was a mousy unshaven man of indeterminate age who sat on a stool behind a counter reading a magazine. He wore a name tag with PIERRE scrawled in large letters. A tattered 1943 Betty Grable calendar was stuck on the wall above the counter. Toliver asked, "Do you speak English?"

The man shrugged and spread his hands. *"Non. Seulement français."*

Preston grabbed the man by the shirt and pulled him halfway across the counter. "Oh, yeah? Then what the hell are you reading, Mac?"

A copy of the *Saturday Evening Post* slipped out of the clerk's hands. The guest register and pencils clattered to the floor. "*Oui, oui.* I speak a little," Pierre squeaked.

Still holding the clerk over the desk, Preston said quietly, "Ask away, Mr. Toliver."

"Henri Dufor. What room is he in?"

Pierre's eyes bugged.

Preston shook him with both hands. "Out with it, you little turd, or I'll —"

The clerk pointed up the stairwell and

gasped, "Two-two-six."

"Is he up there now?" asked Toliver.

Looking wildly from side to side, Pierre nodded.

Preston eased the man down. "Okay, thanks, pal. Now we're going up there to have a nice little conversation with Mr. Dufor. You just sit here and read your little magazine. Now you see that guy over there?" He pointed to Rimini.

Pierre nodded.

"If you say or do anything while we're up there, Rimini is going to personally come down here and blow your balls off with that cannon. Got it?"

Pierre backed into a corner. *"Oui."*

"Fine, now please read your magazine." Preston raised his eyebrows to Toliver and nodded.

"Let's go." Toliver took the lead, his cane thumping up the stairs. The upstairs hallway smelled of urine. A man and a woman groaned in 220. They drew up before 226. Toliver knocked.

"Oui?" came a voice from inside.

"Monsieur Dufor," said Toliver, *"c'est Pierre, le concierge."* Preston's eyebrows went up. He mouthed, "Well, I'll be —"

A chain rattled, the door opened. Taubman peeked around. His eyes went wide. *"Was?"* He slammed the door, but not before Preston's thick boot jammed the doorway. Taubman tried to hold it back, but Preston put a shoulder to the door. A shirtless Taubman stumbled back into the room. Preston and Rimini followed right behind, their weapons raised. "It's okay, sir," called Preston.

Toliver walked in. A cheap valise lay open on the bed, a blood-splattered shirt and jacket draped over it. Personal belongings were strewn about, toothpaste, tie clip, cuff links, a watch.

"I'll be damned." Toliver reached down.

"What do you want?" Taubman said in English. Both eyes were black, there was a cut on his lip, his jaw was swollen, and a lower tooth was missing.

"Sheeyat! Lookie here." Rimini pointed to a half-crated radio transmitter in the corner. "T-E-L-E-F-U-N-K-E-N. Say, is that French for blood plasma?"

Preston walked up to Taubman. "Hey, buddy, did you get the license number of the truck that ran you over?"

There was a loud, concussive report. "Uhhh." Preston crumpled to the floor, the back of his shirt blossoming red.

Another report. Rimini's head snapped back, blood and gray matter spewing out the back.

Toliver hadn't reached for his .45, it had happened so fast. He stood there, looking into the eyes of hell. The man had a Luger leveled at his belly. He saw the man's finger squeeze the trigger. Toliver felt the concussion. And then nothing.

As luck would have it, the *Mount Whitney* was slow and ponderous, seeking her special berth in the ammunition area, not dropping anchor until 1745. Although top priority, the FIDOs weren't delivered by LCM until 1900. The torpedoes were secured on board the *Maxwell* by 1915, and Ingram called away the sea and anchor detail. At 1930 Hank Kelly reported to Ingram on the bridge, "Ready in all respects to get under way, Captain."

Ingram stood on a footrail on the starboard bridgewing and checked forward and aft, noting the gangway still rigged to the *Dixie*. "How 'bout the stable element?"

"Installed and calibrated, Captain. Guys are packing their tools right now."

"FIDOs secure?"

"On the quarterdeck, sir. Tied down athwartships."

"Very well." Ingram drummed his fingers. Thirty seconds later, two overalled civilians rushed across the gangway. Ingram looked up at the *Dixie*'s crane operator and whistled loudly. The operator threw a lever, the line took a strain, and the gangway was soon hauled up out of the way.

Ingram called into the pilothouse, "This is the captain. I have the conn. Tell Main Control to stand by to answer all bells."

The lee helmsman spoke into his sound-powered phone, then said, "Main control reports standing by, Captain."

"Very well. Indicate maneuvering bells," said Ingram.

The lee helmsman clicked knobs on his console and then answered, "Indicate nine nine nine turns for maneuvering bells, Captain." Moments later, he said, "Main control answers nine nine nine turns for maneuvering bells, sir."

"Very well. Rudder amidships," said Ingram.

"My rudder is amidships, Captain," answered the helmsman.

"Very well. Single up all lines," called Ingram. Looking rapidly from the fo'c'sle to the fantail, he willed his men to hurry. *Come on, come on, time to get the hell out of here.*

Admiral Myszynski walked out on the *Dixie*'s main deck and stood eye-to-eye with Ingram, just twenty feet away.

Dammit. He had hoped to get his ship under way before the old man came out. Ingram saluted. "Afternoon, Admiral."

Myszynski returned the salute. "Afternoon, Todd."

"All lines singled up, sir," said Ingram's

talker, a thin, sallow-faced, blond storekeeper first class named Vincent.

"Very well. Take in lines one, three, four, five, and six."

Vincent repeated the order in a deep baritone voice.

Ingram caught Myszynski's eye. "Any news yet, Admiral?"

Myszynski shook his head. "Last I heard the quacks had Toliver in surgery. It sounds like he'll be all right. But the two SPs are dead."

Ingram shook his head. "Anything on Taubman?"

"Lines, one, three, four, five, and six on deck, sir," Vincent reported.

"Very well."

"Just that he stole a truck and was last seen driving north." Myszynski shook his head. "How far can he go on an island two hundred miles long, for cryin' out loud?"

Kelly walked up behind Ingram and said quietly, "Captain, what the hell are we doing?"

Ingram checked aft to see the wind pushing the fantail out nicely. He wouldn't need an ahead bell after all. But he flushed a bit, knowing Kelly had caught him off guard. "Take in line two. All engines back one-third."

Maxwell's screws bit. She shuddered and

gathered sternway. "Sound one long blast," Ingram called.

The lee helmsman pulled the lever over his head, the mournful whistle blast echoing over the harbor for five long seconds.

"Line two on deck," Vincent reported.

"Very well."

Ingram turned and again saluted Myszynski as the distance between the ships grew.

Myszynski returned the salute as Ingram called, "Sound three short blasts."

After the three blasts, they were half a ship's length away when Myszynski called, "Todd?"

"Sir?" Ingram's voice echoed across the widening chasm.

"Welcome back, sailor."

FORTY-TWO

29 SEPTEMBER 1944
U.S.S. *MAXWELL* (DD 525)
19°55.2'S, 164°23.9'E
CORAL SEA

Ingram turned in in his sea cabin fully clothed. But it was his first night back at sea, and he was too keyed up for sleep. Tossing and turning, the covers scrunched beneath him as he watched moonlight stream through the porthole. It meandered up and down the opposite bulkhead like a single spot on a darkened stage as the *Maxwell* rolled easily in troughs. He dared not take a sleeping pill lest he was called to the bridge for an emergency, so he lay there blinking at the overhead. Occasionally, he heard a voice out on the bridge, the Coral Sea slapping against the hull, a hatch thumping, or laughter welling up from the main deck.

Unlike his larger day cabin on the main deck, the sea cabin was up on the third deck, just behind the pilothouse where he felt the motion of the ship more acutely. Normally, mild seas like this would rock him off to dreamland like a baby. But tonight things popped into his mind unchecked: Were they going fast enough? Should they zigzag? He clenched his fists. Maybe there was a Japanese submarine out there right now, down moon, waiting for a perfect setup. But he'd talked it over with Landa just before he shoved off in the *Thomas*. Together, they had sketched a crude map of New Caledonia on the back of a plan-of-the-day. Upon clearing Nouméa's minefield and the barrier reef, *Maxwell* would steam northwest at twenty-five knots until she reached the island's northern extremity, Recif de l'Arch d'Alliance, a fancy name for a mile-long reef. At that point, *Maxwell* would head due north to rendezvous with the *Franklin* and Task Group 58.38 at about noon on the twenty-ninth.

But Landa was in one of his moods: businesslike. None of the old Boom Boom Landa. It didn't help when Dexter ran squealing down the main deck waving a hot dog in the air. Two overalled sailors ran after Dexter, one growling, "Bring that back, you little —" He stopped when he saw Landa. "Er, excuse me, sir."

Landa looked up from his sketch. "I thought I told you to get rid of that damned monkey."

Impervious to Ingram and Landa,

Dexter, with great alacrity, braked his forward motion and disappeared down the hatch to the after engine room, the hot dog clutched high in the air.

Ingram flopped his hands to his sides. "We're trying to catch him. See?"

The two sailors drew up at the hatch and peered down. One said, "Sanders, we got him trapped. Go close up the portside hatch. Then you and me are going in for some monkey stew." The sailor rubbed his hands together.

Ingram pointed at the two sailors. "Okay, Captain?"

"Let me know when the stew is served," Landa said dryly.

Dozens of questions ran through Ingram's mind as the ship rolled back and forth. Did Myszynski really intend to sack him? And what about Ollie? Would he pull through? Damn! There was so little information on the shooting. Only that Ollie was in guarded condition and two American sailors had died on the spot. And that damned Taubman. Ingram clenched his fists, realizing he should have held his temper in check. He should have just collared the German and turned him over to the authorities rather than trying to kill him. But he'd been so outraged when he saw Taubman sitting there as if he belonged.

Someone knocked.

"Enter," Ingram croaked. The bulkhead clock read 0356.

Lieutenant (j.g.) Duquette walked in. "Sorry, sir."

"Go ahead, Tony."

Duquette cleared his throat. "Midwatch relieved, Captain. Boilers one and four, superheated, are on the line, as are generators one and two. Surface and air search radars operating normally, as is the sonar. No contacts, no IFF, no sonar, no nothing. We're at condition III with a fuel load of ninety-five percent. Condition Yoke is set throughout the ship. Course three-zero-five; speed twenty-five. Mount Paum bears zero-four-five, range fifteen miles. Mr. Wilson has the deck and the conn, sir."

"Stable element?"

"Running like a Swiss watch, sir."

"Very well. Good night." Ingram rolled to his side.

"Captain?"

"Hmm?"

"Quartermaster has a wake-up call in for you at 0615. In the meantime, try to get some sleep, sir."

"Good night, Mr. Duquette."

"Yes, sir. Good night, sir." Duquette walked out and closed the door softly.

And what about Landa? It had taken a

lot of self-control for Ingram to shake the man's hand. Once done, it didn't seem so bad. And yet, something still lingered between them. Would they get over it? The uncertainty tugged at him.

He felt more than heard the door open and close. A flashlight clicked on. "Captain? Sir?"

The voice was unfamiliar. Ingram sat up and turned on the light. He rubbed his eyes, feeling ridiculous fully dressed. But he was damned if he was going to be blown over the side again without shoes. They had saved him on the *I-57*. He wondered if . . .

"Captain?"

"What time is it?"

"Nearly four-twenty, sir." It was Gibson, a third-class radioman of nineteen years. He had a full beard and in this lighting looked like Captain Hook. "Message, sir. Mr. Wilson told me to bring it in." He handed over a clipboard.

SECRET
DTG: 09290337L
TO: COMDESFORSOPAC
FM: COMTF 58.38
INFO: A) DESDIV 11
B) MAXWELL

1. CASUALTY STB HI PRESSURE

TURBINE. COMPLETE LOSS OF OIL PRESSURE.

2. ONLY 20 KTS AVAILABLE.
3. THOMAS DETACHED TF 58.38. AT 0323L.
4. CLUSTER ASSUMES COMTF 58.38.
5. ETA NOUMEA 09291930.
6. REQUEST AVAILABILITY DIXIE ASAP.

BT

Ingram signed the message and handed back the clipboard. Landa's ship had broken down and was headed back to Nouméa for repairs. Landa had turned over command of Destroyer Division Eleven to Al Peyton aboard the *Cluster*. Double duty. Ingram didn't envy Peyton, who would not only have to command his ship but also have to be the screen commander until Landa could somehow get back into the act. Talk about no sleep.

He yanked the phone from the bulkhead bracket and punched the button for CIC.

"Combat, Hanley speaking, sir."

"Mr. Hanley, have you read the message about the *Thomas*?"

"Captain? Yes, sir. Gibson just laid it on the DRT."

"I have a feeling we'll see the *Thomas* coming down our track on a reciprocal course. Let me know if you pick her up on radar."

"Aye, aye, Captain."

Ingram snapped off the light and closed his eyes. Two minutes later he was staring at the overhead, counting seconds between a full roll from starboard to port. Between six and ten seconds, depending on how the helmsman threaded the swell. Sometimes he could —

"Dammit." Ingram stood and snapped on the light. The bulkhead chronograph read: 0422. He was reaching for his life jacket when the phone buzzed. "Captain."

It was Hanley. "We have a radar contact, Captain, bearing three-four-seven, seventeen miles. Course appears to be one-two-zero, speed twenty."

"Very well. Please notify the bridge."

Ingram bracketed the phone, splashed water on his face, jammed on his garrison cap, and walked out.

It was a three-quarters moon, bright enough to see a half dozen figures on the bridge. But he hadn't taken more than three steps when the bosun's mate of the watch called, "Captain's on the bridge." He took his chair on the starboard bridgewing, grabbed binoculars, and stared at the spot where the *Thomas* should be.

"Evening, Captain." Jack Wilson stepped up and handed a cup of coffee to Ingram.

"Thanks Jack. How you feeling?"

"Arm's fine, sir." He pointed. "We have the *Thomas* out there on radar about ten miles."

"Visual?"

"Intermittent. She's in the shadow of the land." Wilson pointed off toward the Poum Peninsula, which was near the northern end of New Caledonia.

Ingram was taking his first sip when a signal light jumped at them.

Wilson barked to the signal bridge. "Santorini?"

"It's the *Thomas*, sir." Santorini peered through his bulwark-mounted high-powered binoculars. " '*To Maxwell. From Comdesdiv11. Proceed on duty assigned.*' "

It was Landa telling them to stick to their original orders and rendezvous with the *Franklin*. Ingram heaved a sigh of relief. He'd been worried that Landa would find a reason to order the *Maxwell* to reverse course and accompany the *Thomas* back to Nouméa.

"Okay, Jack," said Ingram.

Wilson spun and said, "Santorini, give 'em a roger."

"Yes, sir." The signal lantern clacked a reply.

Ingram took another sip, settled in his chair, and looked up. With the ship's easy rolls, the mast swept across the vastness of space, occasionally touching the three-quarters moon. But in spite of the moon's brilliance, the sky was still studded with thousands of stars. Often, he'd wondered about the heavens. They looked so cold, so stark, yet so dazzling. The stars gave him a great sense of order in spite of their randomness. In another sense, the skies were mocking him with their unfathomable distances, which were measured in light-years. In the end, he knew, it was an order arranged by God: beautiful, never fully understood, but there for him to look at and admire and to take comfort from. And he realized that the last time he had looked up to a sky like this was when he was alone in the water, with nobody but a monkey, adrift on a piece of flotsam. He'd survived. The Maker of the Heavens had watched over him and brought him through. Miraculous. He wondered if —

"Captain, excuse me."

"What?" Ingram checked his watch. 0431.

"Another signal from *Thomas*, sir," said Jack Wilson.

The *Thomas* was well aft, and Ingram had to peer around the stacks to see a small, blinking pinprick of light, nearly over the horizon. "What's he say?"

Wilson urged the signalman, "Come on, Santorini."

Santorini clacked his light a couple more

times. "It says, *'Follow me,'* sir."

"What?" Ingram stood, and with the rest of the men on the bridge watched the dim little light blinking on the horizon.

Santorini stood high on a pedestal and responded. "Here we go. *Repeat, follow me. Sonar contact, zero nine two, range four thousand yards, classified possible sierra sierra.*"

Ingram said, "Jack, do it! And sound general quarters, one ASW."

"Aye, aye, Captain." Wilson leaned into the pilothouse and called, "Right ten degrees rudder. Steady up on course one-two-zero. Boatswain mate of the watch, sound general quarters one ASW."

The boatswain's pipe blew, the 1MC gonged; men tumbled grousing from their bunks. Tugging on pants, shoes, shirts, and life jackets, they ran to their general quarters stations.

Lieutenant Eric Gunderson, the ship's operations officer, walked up and reported. "I've relieved Mr. Wilson as OOD, sir. All stations manned and ready, Captain."

Ingram checked his watch. Three minutes and ten seconds. "We're kind of rusty, aren't we, Mr. Gunderson?"

Gunderson, a tall, lanky Midwestern farm boy whistled, "I'll say, Captain. It's been awhile."

Just then, the 21MC went off. "Bridge, combat."

Ingram walked over and pressed the lever. "Bridge."

It was Kelly. "We have First Edition on the TBS." First Edition was the TBS (talk between ships) radio call sign for the *Thomas*.

"Well, patch it up here," said Ingram.

"Combat, aye," said Kelly.

The speaker squeaked: ". . . *goblin able now bearing zero-eight-four, range two-two-zero-zero. Classified submarine. We hear machinery noise, including a shaft wobble.*"

"All right!" Gunderson thumped a fist on the bulwark. "They got the bastard."

Ingram held the plotting desk in a death grip. *Impossible.*

"You okay, Captain?"

Ingram reached past Gunderson, yanked the phone from the bracket, and punched up Hank Kelly.

"Combat."

"Hank. Did First Edition say 'shaft wobble'?"

"I heard it that way, Captain."

Ingram muttered, "They don't know what they're fooling with."

"Captain?"

Ingram measured his words. "Mr. Kelly, please confirm that with First Edition. If they say yes, then I want you to advise extreme caution. Especially if the target turns back toward them with a positive up Doppler."

"Sir?" Kelly didn't sound like he was buying it.

"Do it, Mr. Kelly. And tell them to stand by to evade a torpedo if the Doppler goes up. I'll explain later."

"Aye, aye, Captain." Ingram knew Kelly was rolling his eyes as he hung up the phone.

Ingram turned to Gunderson. "Eric, tell main control I want turns for thirty-two knots as soon as possible."

"But, Captain, we don't have superheat on boilers two and three —"

"Do it! Now!"

"Yes, sir." Gunderson leaned into the pilothouse. "Tell main control we want thirty-two knots as soon as possible. Give us an estimated time."

There would be a lot of grumbling in the boiler rooms, Ingram knew. Number two and three boilers were on standby. It would take precious minutes to cut in the superheaters and generate the speed Ingram wanted.

The lee helmsman rogered into his sound-powered phones and announced, "Main control reports they'll be ready for thirty-two knots in fifteen minutes, sir."

Gunderson said, "Very w—"

"Tell main control," Ingram interrupted, "that I want full superheat in five minutes."

The bridge phone buzzed. It was Kelly. In a dry tone, he announced, "First Edition sends, '*One: Request Crackerjack join up as soon as possible. Two: In the meantime advise Crackerjack stick to fundamentals.*' "

"Fundamentals? Is that it?" Ingram demanded.

"Afraid so, sir. Ahhh, Skipper, if you don't mind me asking, what do you have in mind?"

Just then there was a great flash on the horizon from the *Thomas*'s direction.

"Jeepers," said an open-mouthed Gunderson.

Five seconds later, a great *boom* echoed across the water.

"Todd, what the hell is it? Captain? Captain?" Kelly demanded.

With Gunderson, Ingram gawked at the horizon, the phone held loosely at his side. "Shimada," he said.

FORTY-THREE

29 SEPTEMBER 1944
U.S.S. *MAXWELL* (DD 525)
20°17.5'S, 163°57.1'E
CORAL SEA

The engineers cut in superheat to boilers two and three, and seven minutes later all four of the *Maxwell*'s boilers delivered 60,000 horsepower to her screws, driving her at thirty-three knots through dead-calm seas. With the new dawn, Mount Poum, a cone-shaped peak of 1,500 feet, stood before them, contrasting starkly against the anthracite sky. But it brightened with each minute, details of Nouméa becoming more apparent in the new dawn. It seemed the fifteen men on the *Maxwell*'s bridge were rooted in place. Binoculars jammed to their eyes, they peered forward, searching, praying for a sign of the *Thomas*. The only sound was that of the *Maxwell*'s bow wave cascading higher and higher as the destroyer galloped toward the *Thomas*'s last known position.

Ingram grabbed the phone and punched CIC.

"Kelly."

"Hank. What was the time of the *Thomas*'s last message?"

"Ahh, let's see . . ." Papers rustled. "Four-fifty-six, Captain."

"Nothing since?"

"Not a peep."

Ingram drummed his fingers for a moment and looked up. The mountains stood out in greater detail. The dawn would be cloudless, brilliant. Once the sun rose over the peaks, they'd be a sitting duck if the submarine was still around. "Okay, what time is sunrise?"

"0544, sir."

"And how far to the barrier reef?"

"Ten miles. Recommend we slow soon. By the way, do you see Neba and Yande Islands off to port?"

Ingram looked into the gloom. "Yes, barely."

"Watch it. Chart says shallow water up there."

"Whatever we're looking for is well away from there." Ingram knew they'd soon be upon the debris of war. Bits of wood and cork and canvas would be strewn about. Human wreckage would be splayed over life rafts or bobbing in the water, life jackets keeping them afloat. Jerry Landa was out there along with Howard Endicott, her skipper, and 329 other men. He hoped they had had time to get off the *Thomas*, that none were maimed or burned. "Sonar conditions are good out here," Ingram continued. "I'll reduce speed in another six minutes. In the meantime, please advise Task Force 58.38 and COMDESFORSOPAC of our situation."

"Right away, Captain."

Ingram hung up and found Vincent, his talker. "Ask Mr. Wilson to step out here, please." During antisubmarine warfare operations, Wilson became the antisubmarine warfare officer and shifted his GQ station from gun control on the flying bridge to the sonar shack, which was just behind the director barbette room and pilothouse. With all the electrical equipment, a half dozen men, and just one vent blower, the five-by-eight sonar shack became very hot.

Moments later, a hatless Jack Wilson walked out, coffee cup in hand. His shirttail was out and sound-powered phones were jammed over his head, the cord trailing back into the sonar shack. He raised his head, the wind ruffling his dark brown hair, reminding Ingram of a dog's head out a car window, sniffing at the wind. "Sir?"

"I'm slowing in six minutes. Stand by to gain sonar contact."

"Any idea what we're looking for?"

"Jap I-class submarine."

Wilson scratched his head. "Can you tell me what a Jap submarine would be doing out here in the boonies, so close to the coast?"

"Wish I knew." Ingram had almost said, "A hunch." A larger question running through his mind was, What was Shimada doing so close to Nouméa's northwestern tip? Could it have something to do with Taubman? Are these two trying to meet? Maybe so. It would make sense.

Wilson turned to go back into the sonar shack.

"And Jack . . ."

"Sir?"

Ingram stepped close. "I wouldn't be surprised if you find this baby has a distinctive sound, a wobble, like a propellor shaft out of alignment."

Wilson looked at Ingram, wide-eyed.

Ingram forced a grin. "But then again, maybe not. Now go on in there." He slapped Wilson on the rump.

Five minutes later, Ingram told Gunderson to slow to fifteen knots. The new day had brightened to reveal a black spot on the water about three miles ahead. A dark, foreboding feeling in the pit of Ingram's stomach was validated when he laid his binoculars on it. Sure enough, heads and lifeboats bobbed among the wreckage. He turned to Gunderson.

"That's what we're looking for."

"The *Thomas*?" Gunderson gasped.

"Tell your lookouts to keep their eyes peeled on that. Also, they may see a sub periscope nearby."

"Jeepers."

"And we better get the deck apes ready to pick up survivors. Have them rig out the whaleboat."

"Yes, sir."

To Vincent he said, "Call down to the wardroom. Tell Monaghan we'll be bringing in survivors soon." At general quarters, the wardroom was converted to a battle dressing area complete with hospital equipment.

"Morning, Skipper." Kelly walked out on the starboard bridgewing. "Duquette has it under control in CIC. Thought I'd come up here to see if I could help out."

"Actually, Hank, I was going to call you," said Ingram. "Can you go down to the main deck to coordinate picking up survivors?"

"Aye, aye. Do you want to —"

"Sonar contact," blared the bridge speaker. "Bearing zero-five-two. Range forty-eight hundred yards."

Gunderson called to the helmsman, "Come left to zero-five-two."

"Watch for a torpedo," said Ingram. "Now's the time if he's going to nail us."

He walked over to the 21MC and punched sonar. "Sonar, bridge. What's his course and speed?"

Wilson's metallic reply was, "Zero, Captain. No Doppler. He's DIW." Dead in the water.

Gunderson raised his binoculars and pointed straight ahead. "Look at that."

Ingram trained his binoculars. "Bastards." The bearing and range to the submarine was the same as the bearing and range to the survivors.

Kelly asked, "Todd? What the hell is it?"

"Sonofabitch is lying right under our guys," Ingram growled.

Kelly's lips pressed tight when he realized the *Maxwell* couldn't fire depth charges lest they kill the *Thomas* survivors on the surface. Worse, they couldn't steam near the target with any speed. The wake would certainly create bedlam among the wounded. Possibly even kill them. He punched the 21MC. "Sonar, bridge. What's he doing now? Any Doppler yet?"

"Just sitting there, Captain. Still speed zero. Sitting duck. I have to say you are clairvoyant. We just had some machinery noises. Some of it definitely sounded like a shaft wobble. How did you know, Skipper?"

"Magic."

"Maybe some night after a few scotches

at the O-club, you'll share your secret?"

"Right."

"You ready to unload? We have a good firing solution."

"Can't. He's sitting right under the *Thomas* survivors."

"You're shitting me."

"Wish I was."

"Well, then, we'd better think about this. We're well within his firing range."

"Don't I know it. Let me know if anything changes." Ingram flipped the switch off.

Kelly's face grew red in the gathering sunrise. Or was it his temper, Ingram wondered. "We can't pick up our guys as long as that Jap is there," said Kelly.

"Okay, then. Why don't we move back a few thousand yards, and just let this whole thing cool down."

"Makes sense to me."

"Right. Mr. Gunderson," Ingram called. "Reverse course."

"Yes, sir," replied Gunderson. To the helmsman, he ordered, "Right full rudder. Steady up on course two-three-two."

Maxwell leaned into her turn. She was almost halfway around when Ingram said, "He can't stay there forever, Hank. He —"

"Torpedo!" blared the sonar loudspeaker. "Bearing zero-four-seven, range three thousand. Coming right at us."

Damn! Shimada had made his move sooner than Ingram expected. At the same time, Ingram couldn't help but admire Shimada's skill; his shot was very well aimed and timed. Ingram kicked himself, knowing he'd just done a very dumb thing, presenting himself broadside to Shimada. "Mr. Gunderson. Come left and steer a course to comb the wake."

"Yes, sir," replied Gunderson. He yelled into the pilothouse, "Shift your rudder. Steady up on course zero-four-seven."

The bow came around as officers and men alike rushed to the port side of the bridge to watch for the deadly missile. "Sound the collision alarm," shouted Ingram. "Set Condition Zebra throughout the ship." He dashed over to the port bridgewing.

Vincent was there first, pointing to a white wake streaking toward them. "Holy shit, that thing's fast! We ain't gonna make it."

"Sure aren't," yelled Ingram, intent on the torpedo's track. The ship wasn't turning quickly enough. "This is the captain. I have the conn. Starboard engine ahead full, port back one-third."

Smoke belched from the *Maxwell*'s stacks as her engineers spun their throttles, her uptakes squealing at a high-pitched whistle as they delivered air to her hungry boilers. Closer, closer, the torpedo streaked. The ship shuddered as the screws bit harder.

"Jeez," Kelly rasped through clenched teeth.

One more trick. "Hard left rudder," Ingram called.

With the rudder hard over, *Maxwell* turned faster, her bow sweeping past Nouméa's jagged peaks, just seven miles away.

In seconds, the white torpedo wake streaked down the starboard side.

"Wheeeooo," said Gunderson.

Kelly said dryly, "So solly, Tojo. Looks like your magnetic fuses are as screwed up as ours."

"Rudder amidships, steady up on zero-four-seven; all engines ahead two-thirds, make turns for fifteen knots," Ingram barked. To Gunderson he said, "Eric, you have the conn. Bring us to a full stop within three hundred yards of those men out there."

Gunderson said, "Yes, sir, but what's keeping him from shooting at us again?"

Ingram checked the bridge plot. "Range is down to fifteen hundred yards. We're too close, almost in the arming circle. Plus, he's not going to waste torpedoes. He only has four."

"Only four?" said Gunderson. He and Kelly looked at each other, Kelly rolling his eyes.

Ingram paced the bridge. *What to do? Men, fellow sailors, out there dying.* He pounded a fist on the bulwark. If he stopped to pick them up, he would be a sitting duck again. Just as bad, he couldn't go after Shimada with depth charges lest he blow up his own sailors. A Hobson's choice. *Have to do something.* "Mr. Gunderson, launch the motor whaleboat. The coxswain's orders are to first pick up the most seriously wounded."

"Yes, sir," said Gunderson.

Kelly drew Ingram off to the side. "Skipper?"

"What?"

"We have to kill that Jap."

"And in so doing, you want me to kill Jerry Landa and everybody else out there?"

"How 'bout dropping an ashcan right here. Maybe scare him?" Kelly asked.

"Waste of a good depth charge. No, we have to do something else," said Ingram.

"Well, shit. Pardon my French, Skipper, but it's only a matter of time before he opens out on the other side of those guys and takes another shot at us. He must have tons of torpedoes."

"No, he only has four."

"Well, let me ask again, how the hell do you know that?"

FORTY-FOUR

29 SEPTEMBER 1944
U.S.S. *MAXWELL* (DD 525)
20°17.9'S, 164°09.3'E
FIVE MILES OFF NOUMÉA COAST

The sun rose over Mount Poum, shining directly into their eyes. Crisp sunlight spilled onto Nouméa's coastal plain as if it were a blazing, verdant stage. Coconut palms were suddenly visible on the beach, and in the distance a gleaming waterfall cascaded down a steep cliff.

Gunderson ordered all back two-thirds; then all stop. Dead in the water, the *Maxwell* rolled in lazy gray-green swells three hundred yards from the survivors. Incredulous shouts and cries were barely discernable, some waving their arms over their heads.

Kelly searched Ingram's eyes.

But Ingram couldn't prove that the contact out there was Hajime Shimada. He would think him daft, crazy. And with what happened at the hotel the other night with Taubman, he worried over his officers' loss of confidence. "Hank, I have a feeling for this Jap. He's just like the one who —"

"Torpedo!" Wilson dashed out of sonar and pointed straight ahead. "Shit! Right there."

The track was headed right for the bow. Gunderson and Ingram exchanged glances. All way was off the ship. Dead in the water, the *Maxwell* couldn't get out of the torpedo's path.

"Bastard!" Kelly leaned out and shook his fist. The others joined in, shouting obscenities and anything else that came to mind.

Clang! At nearly forty-five knots, the torpedo smacked the ship just under Mount 52 and bounced away. Then it veered out about ten feet and passed under the keel of the whaleboat, now suspended just above the water. Her crew gripped the gunnels, watching white-faced as it streaked beneath. The torpedo paralleled the ship and was almost clear of the stern when suddenly it ducked under the starboard screwguard.

The lee helmsman leaned out of the pilothouse. "Captain. Main control reports that something hit the starboard screw."

Ingram asked, "What do they —"

A thunderous explosion threw them to the deck. The ship shuddered and vibrated as gray-white water cascaded high into the air and then spilled hissing back onto the stern.

Ingram was surprised to find himself on his knees. Many were down with him, some groaning, others holding their heads. "What?" Slowly, he pushed himself up. "Damage control, reports."

Vincent's Adam's apple bobbed. His lips moved, but no sound came out.

"You all right?"

"Sir!" Vincent wheezed.

"Then get on it."

Vincent punched his talk button and muttered a request. After a few moments, he said, "Explosion flooded after steering. One man injured. They're securing after steering, sir."

Ingram breathed a sigh of relief. "Is that it?"

"Yes, sir, I . . . Wait, it's the DCA." Vincent clamped his hands to his head. "Shit," he muttered.

"Come on," Ingram barked.

"Damage control assistant reports, sir, that the port screw is seriously damaged, maybe a blade gone."

"Dammit." Ingram called into the pilothouse, "Carlton, how's your rudder?"

With a look of disbelief, the helmsman spun his wheel. "Looks fine, Captain. A little sluggish on the port side, though."

"But is it working?"

"Best as I can tell, Captain."

Vincent said, "More damage control reports, Captain."

Ingram ran a hand over his face. "Go ahead."

"Repair party reports starboard shaft alley flooded. And there's a split seam near frame 166 in the aft engine room."

"Is the flooding under control?"

Vincent said, "Working on it, sir."

"Why am I not impressed with that answer?"

Vincent said, "That's what they're telling me, Captain."

"Any other casualties?"

"No, sir."

Ingram felt as if sand were chafing through his veins. And suddenly his stomach seemed to be jumping. He said to Kelly, "Hank. Get down and see what you can do about the aft engine room."

"Yes, sir." Kelly turned and dashed for the ladder.

Gunderson said, "Torpedo must have been sliced in half by the starboard screw and then decided to go off as it was falling away."

"Ummm." Ingram rubbed his chin.

"Dammit," said Gunderson. "It's only a matter of time before that Jap opens out and sticks one in our magazine. Maybe we should get out of here, Captain?"

"How much speed do we have available?"

Vincent said, "Engineers say four, five knots max on the port shaft. Starboard shaft is secured."

As if in confirmation, Wilson reported over the loudspeaker, "Screw noises, bearing zero-three-nine. Range four hundred. I hear your shaft wobble. Down Doppler, stern aspect. He's moving away. Man oh man, stand by for another torpedo."

The sun glinted on Ingram's face. "I'll be damned."

"Sir?" Gunderson asked.

"Torpedoes," said Ingram. He grabbed Gunderson's shoulder. "Eric. I want you to steer a course to go around the survivors and follow the contact. Stay as close to the sub as you can without going in there and injuring survivors. Do you understand me?"

"Yes, sir. But the way things are, he can probably go faster than us."

"What he doesn't know won't kill us. Now I'm going to the quarterdeck. Call down to Combat and have them send Mr. Duquette to me there."

Wilson walked out on deck, his sound-powered phone cord trailing, and stood beside Gunderson. The what-the-hell-are-we-doing expressions were evident on both their faces.

"Hello?" Ingram asked.

Wilson planted his hands on his hips and asked, "You mind letting us in on your secret? I don't need any more thousand-pound warheads for breakfast."

"He can't shoot accurately," said Ingram. "His warheads can't arm at this distance."

"He did alright with the last one."

"A fluke."

"Yes, sir. But what do you have in mind?"

"Jack. I want you to give Eric vectors to the submarine. Keep us right on top of him, got it?"

"Do my best. You mind telling us what for?"

"I'm going to stick a FIDO down his periscope."

"What?"

"Get in there, Jack. Duquette will buzz you from the quarterdeck and relay my instructions. We'll get this bastard yet."

"The odds say he fires first."

"Jack, I have news for you. We're about to change the odds." Ingram scrambled down the aft ladder to the 01 deck and then down the portside ladder to the main deck, running aft for the quarterdeck. Fifteen seconds later, he drew up before the crates. Stacked in a cluster of four, each crate was about eight feet long. Black letters on the top were stenciled TORPEDO, MARK 24.

Remington, a dark-haired torpedoman chief with beefy arms and chest, asked, "Help you, Captain?" During antisubmarine operations, Remington and his torpedo gang manned the six depth-charge launchers mounted port and starboard aft of the quarterdeck. Wearing headphones, Remington's job was to call out depth settings for the depth charges and relay firing orders from sonar or the bridge.

Ingram said, "You bet. Grab a crowbar, on the double."

"Sir." Remington stepped over to a compartment, the brass plate over the hatchway announcing TORPEDO SHACK. He spun a dogging handle, yanked open the hatch, and walked in. Soon he came out palming a crowbar. "Mind telling me what we need it for, Captain?"

Ingram grabbed the crowbar and went to work on one of the crates. "We're giving this to the Jap for breakfast."

Remington gave a dark grin. "Worth a try, sir. Here, let me." He grabbed the crowbar and, with knees bent, put his back into it. Soon the nails squeaked in protest as the boards lifted.

Duquette ran up. "Captain?"

Ingram said, "Get on the quarterdeck phone, buzz sonar, and get updates from

Jack on the submarine."

"Yes, sir." Duquette yanked the phone from its bracket.

Off to starboard, a group of men in the water waved frantically, their faces and arms blackened with fuel oil. A voice drifted, "Hey . . . you sonofabitch. Why ain't you stopping?"

"Jap submarine," Ingram yelled and pointed straight down. "We'll be back. Hold on." He stepped into the torpedo shack, found another crowbar, and joined Remington at the crate. Working furiously, the top was soon stripped off.

Ingram and Remington dug inside, throwing packing material over their shoulders. Finally, a stubby Mark 24 torpedo lay before them, its body a dull copper-gray, the warhead black. Thick, olive-drab paper was taped over the top of the nose. Ingram peeled it off, finding a deep round cavity about eight inches in diameter. "Fuse! Do you see one back there, Remington?"

Remington fussed at the other end of the crate. "Like this?" He lifted a square carton marked FUSE MARK 142, FOR MARK 24 TORPEDO ONLY.

"Ever mounted one before, Chief?"

"Not on one of these babies. But then there's always time for on-the-job training." He took it from the box and held it up.

"Well, do it. We have to launch this thing before the Jap finds out how screwed up we are."

"Sir." Remington dashed to the shack. He soon emerged with tools stuffed in his pocket. Gingerly, he eased the fuse into the cavity and then inserted the screws. "Seems pretty basic."

Duquette held the phone to his chest. "Skipper, Jack has screw noises. They're increasing. Looks like he's opening out."

"Dammit. You about done, Chief?"

"Couple of more turns, Captain."

"Put a nickel in it."

Remington bent over the torpedo. Sweat beaded on his forehead as he worked the last screw. "Done."

"Okay. Is that the arming lever?" Ingram pointed to a small stud near the warhead.

"Yes, sir. It's set on Safe."

"Okay. Push it to Arm. Now, that lanyard back there. Is that what starts the motor?"

Remington said, "Makes sense to me. And here's a motor on/off stud. Right now, it's in the off position."

"Okay. Switch it to on and then let's lift it out of here and toss it over the side to see if —"

Duquette yelped. "Geeez."

"What?" Ingram demanded.

"Sonar reports range to the submarine

has increased to five hundred yards, sir."

"Hurry!" Ingram shouted. "Chief, what does one of these things weigh?"

"Close to seven hundred pounds as near as I remember, Captain."

"Well, get some men over here."

"Dixon! Stallworthy. Gonzolez. Frick. Get over here, dammit," Remington yelled.

Together the six of them, three on each side, reached in the crate and worked their hands and forearms under the torpedo.

"One, two, three," Ingram called.

With a collective grunt, out it came, its dull finish gleaming menacingly in the dawn. Even with six men, the weight seemed like two thousand pounds to Ingram. It was all he could do to keep his feet.

Remington grunted, "Mr. Duquette, could you rip off them damned wooden shrouds?" Being an aerial torpedo, the Mark 24 was protected by wooden boxlike structures around the warhead and fins. They were designed to break off upon hitting the water.

Duquette stood, his mouth agape.

Ingram gasped, "Do it, quickly, Mr. Duquette. And then tie off that lanyard to a pad eye."

"Yes, sir." Duquette grabbed a crowbar and quickly ripped off the wood even as the six men staggered to the port side, the torpedo's nose facing aft.

Through clenched teeth, Ingram asked, "Tony, you tied down yet?"

"Another moment . . ."

"Dammit," Remington yelled, "the motor can't go unless —"

"Done!" shouted Duquette.

"Over the side!" Ingram yelled.

Together they tossed the torpedo in nose first. Just before hitting the water, the lanyard snapped taut. The counterrotating propellers spun; black smoke hissed out the back. Then it disappeared.

Ingram grabbed the phone. "Jack. Torpedo away."

"I hear it. Motor's running. Sounds like it's doing doughnuts."

"Acquisition phase."

Wilson voice went up an octave. "Shit!"

"What?"

"I think we forgot something."

A feeling of dread swept through Ingram. "What?"

"What if that fish doesn't have any limits to avoid surface craft? It could come after us."

"One way or the other, we're dead, Jack."

"Yeah, but — Whoa! This thing's taking off. Wow! You should see this. Beautiful. High-pitched screw noise zipping right down the Jap's bearing. Wait . . . The Jap's heard it, too. He's cranked up to full speed. Weeeo. Listen to that shaft wobble. Listen to his —"

After a moment, Ingram asked, "What?"

"Damn. One loud bang. There's another. Bubbles. Shit. Another bang. And . . ."

"Now what?"

"Air hissing. Must be trying to blow ballast. Another bang, big one that time. Breaking up noises . . . He's headed for the deep six."

"How deep is the deep six?"

"Um, fathometer says . . . 437 fathoms," said Wilson.

"Deep enough."

EPILOGUE

In the dark, men break into houses, but by day they shut themselves in; they want nothing to do with the light. For all of them, deep darkness is their morning; they make friends with the terrors of darkness.

— JOB 24:16–17

EPILOGUE

1 OCTOBER 1944
POUM, NOUMÉA
NEW CALEDONIA

Before the Second World War, Poum was a near-aboriginal fishing village on Nouméa's west coast close to the northern tip. The village was on a peninsula jutting down the island's southwestern side. An idyllic setting for a South Seas vacation, the beaches were graced with fine white sands; palm trees swayed gently in afternoon breezes under a backdrop of jagged dormant volcanoes topped with afternoon thunderheads. More recently, the airstrip at the bay's northeastern end was host to Navy and Marine fighters and long-range PBY reconnaissance planes. A Marine garrison was situated around the base and was responsible for the airstrip's integrity along with the integrity of Nouméa's entire north end.

But the war had moved on. Gone were the stubby F4F Wildcat fighters and their big brothers, the F6F Hellcats. The only planes remaining were a half dozen PBYs. Their task: patrolling a sedate Coral Sea, only twenty-eight months previously the stage for a vicious sea battle between United States and Japanese aircraft carriers. Left behind was the detritus of war: empty fifty-five-gallon drums, a rotting PT boat on the beach, its darkened ribs jutting into the air, vacated Quonset huts, a few wrecked airplanes, a truck turned on its side; everywhere, broken glass and rusted tin cans.

Twelve Marines played softball near the airstrip's western end, barely paying attention to a bug-smasher sideslipping beautifully in a crosswind, the pilot setting her down on the coral airstrip. The twin-engine Beech taxied to the ramshackle one-room operations hut; the pilot cut the mixture and the engines wound to a halt. The first to emerge was Captain Jeremiah T. Landa, followed by Commander Todd Ingram. Both wore pith helmets, working khaki shirt and trousers, and jungle boots. Last out was Lieutenant Commander Oliver Toliver III. Similarly dressed, Toliver carried his cane with his left hand, his right arm in a black silk sling. Waiting near the ops hut was a short, slender, dark-haired Marine captain in jungle fatigues, an M-1 carbine strapped over his shoulder. He had high cheekbones and a deeply tanned face and, to Ingram, looked like a pure-blooded

American Indian. Just behind him were two enlisted Marines with no rank showing, also in jungle fatigues. One carried a Thompson submachine gun, the other a sawed-off shotgun.

All three had been in combat, Ingram saw. He'd seen plenty of them on Corregidor and Guadalcanal. Their eyes searched everywhere, their heads cocked to every sound. They knew exactly what was going on in every direction. The captain saluted and said, "Good afternoon, gentlemen. My name's John Quicksilver. How was your flight?"

Landa rubbed his rear with both palms. "Two hours of bump and run, Captain. My ass is tired. Those things don't have any cushions. Especially when we have updrafts and downdrafts and side drafts and every which draft around those damned mountains."

Quicksilver's face was like concrete. A long bayonet was strapped to his boot, and Ingram decided he'd rather not meet him in a dark alley, his slight stature notwithstanding. Quicksilver narrowed his eyes. "Are you ready, sir?"

"You bet. How far is he?"

Quicksilver waved a hand inland. "About two thousand yards thataway. Has a house on a hill overlooking the harbor. Very nice, actually, with a view of the bay. But we've got it surrounded. He's not going anywhere."

"Does he know you're there?" asked Toliver.

"No, sir," said Quicksilver. "Sleeps in the day, goes out at night. He's on a short tether."

"Who's that?" Ingram nodded toward a civilian standing in the shade of the ops hut. He wore tan trousers and leather shoes. A white coat was drawn over a ruffled shirt. Tall and slim, he had a pockmarked face, a Vandyke beard, and black, slicked-back hair.

"That is Monsieur La Barrie, the local gendarme," said Quicksilver. "We're in luck. He speaks English." He reached out and waved the man over and made introductions, saying, "We're going in, Mr. La Barrie. Do you want to come along?"

La Barrie said in a quiet voice, "As I've said before, Monsieur Quicksilver, I protest. What you are doing is illegal."

"Sorry, sir," said Quicksilver. "But this gent is suspected of being . . ." He looked toward the three naval officers.

"A Nazi," said Ingram.

La Barrie shook his head slowly. "*Non. Non.* Monsieur Dufor is a French citizen. I have seen his papers."

Landa stepped before La Barrie. "Sir, we have a strong reason to suspect that he is a

German, a Nazi, a sailor of the Kriegsmarine. That he was trying to rendezvous with a Jap submarine right out there." Landa swept an arm toward the bay.

La Barrie rolled his eyes. "Japanese submarine? Be serious, sir. We haven't seen Japanese for over two years."

Landa stepped closer. "Oh, yeah? Well, guess what? We just —"

"Monsieur La Barrie," Toliver interrupted. "We've d/fed radio signals to his house. He's been observed paddling through the surf in the middle of the night. Now that's strictly against regulations."

La Barrie said, "May I remind you gentlemen that this is French soil. And that you have no jurisdiction. If this man is a criminal, than we will try, convict, and punish him."

"Where?" Ingram growled.

La Barrie shrugged. "Nouméa. In a French court, of course."

Ingram said, "Bullshit. Not of course." He spun and walked toward a pair of jeeps. "What are we waiting for?"

The hill was about two hundred feet above the bay and had an excellent view of the airstrip. They parked the jeeps at the base of the hill and walked a switchback road to the top. Finally, the roof and then a gazebo hove into view. Quicksilver held up a hand. There was a soft whistle. Quicksilver returned the whistle, and a blond, barrel-chested Marine slipped out of the bushes. After they conferred, Quicksilver turned and said, "Your man's asleep. You want to go on in?"

Ingram and Landa exchanged glances and nodded.

Quicksilver nodded to the blond Marine and pumped his hand in the air. Ingram was astonished to see Marines, in ones and twos, rise from the jungle like apparitions and walk toward the house.

Swearing in French, La Barrie walked around Quicksilver and headed toward the house.

"Get back here, Frog," Quicksilver ordered. When La Barrie didn't stop, Quicksilver whistled, then tapped a fist against his head. In two seconds, the blond Marine came up from behind, cupped a hand around La Barrie's mouth, and dragged him to the ground. They struggled for a moment, then La Barrie gave up the struggle, his eyes bulging.

Quicksilver rushed over and produced a leather thong. Landa stooped down and asked La Barrie, "We can do this the easy way or the hard way. Do you want to see this peacefully or do you want to be tied?"

"Ummmmff." La Barrie shook his head.

Landa looked at the Marine. "Okay, son. Let the little bastard up. But if he makes a peep, pop him over the head."

"Sir." The Marine released La Barrie.

The gendarme stood, brushing off his clothes with all the dignity he could muster.

Quicksilver and his two Marines stepped gingerly onto the front porch, their weapons unlimbered. At a signal from Quicksilver, they kicked open the door and rushed in. Ten seconds later, Quicksilver was on the front porch, waving Ingram, Landa, Toliver, and La Barrie inside.

Ingram walked in behind Landa. It was a big room with large windows with no glass in them. Reed curtains swayed gently in the wind. Martin Taubman lay on a couch. As Ingram walked in, Taubman rose and shuffled over to a desk, yawning and running his hands through his hair.

La Barrie said in English, "Forgive me, Mr. Dufor. These men forced their way in here. I will, of course, protest to the governor general. There will be serious repercussions. They will be sent back to America in chains. We will . . ."

Taubman spotted Ingram. His shoulders sagged. Then he saw Toliver. "My God . . ." he mouthed. He sat heavily at the desk.

"Surprised, Fritz?" Toliver asked.

"How . . . how did . . . you . . . ?"

Taubman stammered.

Toliver's eyes went dark. "My pistol was stuck in my belt. That's where your bullet hit, right on the butt. Pieces splattered into my arm. It'll be in a sling for another two weeks, thanks to you, Fritz." Toliver waved to a Telefunken transceiver on the desk. "Nice set, Fritz. Can you raise Berlin?"

La Barrie's hand went to his mouth.

Taubman said, "Don't mind him. He's just a little Vichy who sells people out."

"About what I figured," said Toliver.

"He was helping you?" asked Ingram.

"Of course. Food, antenna wire, everything. I paid him well."

Landa said, "Maybe you'd better have a talk with Monsieur La Barrie, Captain Quicksilver."

Quicksilver drew next to La Barrie. "Oh, I intend to, sir."

"Just don't kill him," said Landa. "We should deliver him in some sort of condition to the gendarme in Nouméa."

La Barrie squeaked, "No. No. I didn't realize."

Ingram walked over to Taubman. "No more chess games, Martin."

"No?"

"No. In fact, I have a little present for you." Ingram pulled a red and white checkered Scotch House scarf from his pocket and threw it on the table. "Captain

Shimada won't be needing this anymore. So I guess you can have it back."

Taubman's eyes grew wide, color draining from his face. "No! Impossible." He held the scarf up, then flipped it over and examined the label. "Where did you find this?"

Ingram said, "We got the *I-49* two nights ago, Martin. Nothing much left except this, a few boxes, and someone's sandal."

"Where?"

Ingram pointed toward the ocean.

"Impossible! What about the . . . the . . . I mean . . . ." Taubman lapsed into German.

"You mean the gold, Martin? Look straight down 437 fathoms, that's where you'll find it."

"How did you get out?" Taubman asked.

"It wasn't easy, Martin," said Ingram. "No thanks to you, I —"

An explosion. Two, three. Taubman's chest blossomed red, his mouth shaped into an O. His hands spasmed into space as he pitched back. Just as the chair fell over, a Luger fell from Taubman's hand and dropped to the floor with a clatter.

Toliver moved in, his .45 still firing. He stood over Taubman's body and fired two more rounds into the jerking, twitching corpse. He then stood, looking down, the smoking pistol dangling at his side.

It was silent. A thick blue cloud of cordite smoke hung in the room. All were open-mouthed, even the Marines.

"Jeez, Ollie," said Landa.

Toliver shoved the .45 back into his sling. "The kid wanted to be a lawyer."

Ingram asked, "What kid?"

"Back in . . . Nouméa." He waved his good arm southeast. "Benne, the SP."

Landa pointed to the corpse. "He could have been worth a lot for intelligence. I mean, you ought to know. What's your boss going to say?"

"Truth is, Todd would have been a dead duck in about two more seconds. Didn't you see where his hand was going? That's the same stunt he pulled on us in Nouméa. Besides, the bastard had it coming." He whirled and pointed to La Barrie. "Maybe you too, you Vichy sonofabitch!" he said through clenched teeth. "I hope they stand your dead little ass against the wall and chop you in half with a fifty-caliber."

A white-faced La Barrie inched toward the corner, finding cover behind Quicksilver.

"Damn. Never seen Ollie so worked up," said Landa.

"That's not all," muttered Toliver. He walked over to the bed and grabbed a valise off the bedside table. Turning it over, he savagely dumped the contents on the rumpled bedcovers. Toothpaste, cuff links, neckties, dirty underwear, tumbled out. Still muttering, he said, "Where the hell is it?" A bracelet, socks. Toliver swept his hand through it all. "Ah."

"What?" said Ingram.

Something glistened as Toliver tossed it over. "You forgot something," he said.

Ingram caught it and opened his hand. It was his Naval Academy ring. "I'll be damned."

The memories swept through him. Graduation. His first command, the minesweeper *Pelican*. Corregidor: just before they'd escaped Corregidor, he'd given the ring to Helen to wear on a leather thong around her neck, ostensibly because he'd lost so much weight it slipped off his finger. The real reason was that he loved her but was too preoccupied by the invading Japanese to realize it. There were other memories: their desperate trip through the Central Philippines, Mindanao, and on to Australia, and Helen's bravery during that horrible time when she had been captured and tortured by the Japanese. During their escape through the Philippines, Ollie had saved his life. And he'd just done it again.

They'd all been through a lot. After regaining weight, he'd slid the ring back on his finger and returned to shipboard duty aboard the U.S.S. *Howell*, married Helen, and more recently, skippered the *Maxwell*. He looked up, awestruck at the odyssey this ring must have taken, halfway around the world and back.

For the first time that day, Toliver smiled. “Okay?”

“Thanks, Ollie,” said Ingram. He slipped it on his finger and ran his hand over it. It felt good. “Thanks a lot.”

“Ringknocker,” muttered Landa. To Quicksilver he said, “Hey, Lieutenant, you guys have any beer around here?”